at Sheffield University, so sitting in pubs talking about life and love is something they've been doing for the last ten years. Now they're writing books together they just take their laptops and write it all down, but little else has changed. Jimmy still tells Laura off for always being late, and Laura can still drink Jimmy under the table.

Their friendship survives because Laura makes tea exactly how Jimmy likes it (he once took a picture of his perfect brew on Laura's phone so she can colour match it for strength) and because Jimmy noted Laura's weakness for custard creams and stocks up accordingly.

Follow them on Twitter at @LauraAndJimmy, Instagram @LauraandJimmyBook and at facebook.com/laurataitandjimmyrice.

Also by Laura Tait and Jimmy Rice

THE BEST THING THAT NEVER HAPPENED TO ME

and published by Corgi Books

THE NIGHT THAT CHANGED EVERYTHING

Laura Tait and Jimmy Rice

CORGI BOOKS

TRANSWORLD PUBLISHERS
61–63 Uxbridge Road, London W5 5SA
www.transworldbooks.co.uk

Transworld is part of the Penguin Random House group of companies
whose addresses can be found at global.penguinrandomhouse.com

Penguin
Random House
UK

First published in Great Britain in 2016 by Corgi
an imprint of Transworld Publishers

Copyright © Laura Tait and Jimmy Rice 2016

Laura Tait and Jimmy Rice have asserted their right under
the Copyright, Designs and Patents Act 1988 to be
identified as the authors of this work.

A CIP catalogue record for this book
is available from the British Library.

ISBN
9780552170826

Ty⌐   ⌐ Devon

Pe   future
for   is made

For Rosemary Cowan and
Archibald Carmichael Cowan

Prologue

REBECCA

Opening Night

Where's Jamie?

I have never nailed the art of arriving at a party by myself.

I should have come with Danielle. She was still trying to chivvy me into the shower as she was painting her lips coral and giving herself a *Go get 'em tiger* look in the mirror above the fireplace, but I was balls deep in *Art Deco: Design, Decoration and Detail* and told her I'd meet her here.

I hover awkwardly at the entrance to the bar. Being five foot ten makes it hard to be inconspicuous when you can't find your friends, but at least it makes it easier to scan a room, and I spot Danielle laughing with two men I don't recognize.

One chats incessantly with the look of someone who can't believe his luck and is scared that if he stops talking, she'll disappear. The other looks on shyly. Neither is in with a chance – she and Shane, her on-off boyfriend, are on again. Again.

He'll be here later.

I'm too nervous about my presentation for East House Pictures on Monday to do small talk with strangers. The old cinema in Hackney is in a state of disrepair after years of neglect, and there's a proposal to restore it next year. And if our pitch goes well, our company could be the one that gets to design and rebuild it.

I grew up dreaming about designing my first building the way other little girls dreamt about getting married. I'm only here tonight because Jamie deserves the support, and my shoulders relax as I spot him serving behind the bar. He planned to play host but I guess he underestimated how busy his opening night would be.

As I fight the crowds, I take in how different the room looks since the last time I saw it, when Jamie put his hands over my eyes as he led me into a disused railway arch, then took them away with a *Ta-da!* and explained he was opening his own bar.

I smile, chuffed he took my advice to restore the walls rather than plaster over them. They now have the names of cocktails in huge letters stained on top of the exposed brickwork in a haphazard fashion.

There's just enough room beyond the red, leather-covered booths for a makeshift dance floor before you reach the sleek back counter illuminated by low-hanging, oversized light bulbs.

Squeezing myself into a gap, I try to get Jamie's attention, but he's at the other end of the bar, chucking a bottle in the air and letting it spin, before catching it expertly in the other hand and pouring it into a Boston Shaker without missing a beat. The girl whose drink he's practically turned into a West End performance claps in appreciation. He winks. I roll my eyes.

I'm drumming my fingers impatiently on the granite surface when a barman returns with a load of empties. I'm hoping he's about to get back behind the bar, but he disappears off into the crowd.

'Hello there.' A smiling barmaid finally appears in front of me. 'What can I get you?'

'Can I have a single-malt Scotch, please? One ice cube.' I glance behind me to make sure Danielle is still in the same place. 'And a Cosmopolitan.'

Despite the fact that Jamie promised to only employ fit twenty-something models who want to sleep with him – and he wasn't short of offers from this particular brand of applicant – his new barmaid is about five foot three, round-cheeked and in her late thirties by the looks of things. I feel a rush of affection for Jamie. He's a big show-off, but a lovely one.

Something shoves me and I realize a guy has forced his way in and is holding out a twenty. I clock him look at me, double-take slightly and turn his body as much towards mine as the space will allow. The glare I give him is toxic.

'Cheer up, love,' he tells me with a nudge, 'it might never happen.'

'It already has,' I reply, eyes straight ahead. 'Earlier, a stranger invaded my personal space, called me love and offered me unsolicited advice.' I sip the whisky that has just been placed in front of me. 'So I killed him.'

Jamie catches the last of the exchange and I can tell he's trying to suppress laughter as he serves the guy.

'You really have to stop throwing yourself at my customers like that,' he says, pouring himself a small whisky as soon as the man is gone. 'You'll get a reputation.'

'Sorry, I just hate it when people say shit like that. Like anyone stands around grinning.'

'He was just trying to chat you up. You're not an easy person to—'

'Oh, don't start,' I warn him with narrowed eyes. 'Let's talk about Arch 13. This is all kind of aces, Jamie. Your own bar, finally!'

'You don't think I should have waited until the twelfth or fourteenth arch came up for rent, to be on the safe side?'

'Nah – you make your own luck.' I look around again in awe. 'I'm so bloody proud of you.'

His smile is humble and neither of us says what we're both thinking. It should be his parents standing here telling him how proud they are. Instead, they've stopped talking to him. They never liked him working in a bar after uni, but they tolerated it, presuming it was a stopgap before he finally used the chemistry degree they paid for to become the next Alfred Nobel. Now they've realized he'd rather be the next Tom Cruise in *Cocktail* they're not exactly cock-a-hoop.

But running a bar is perfect for Jamie. Our preference for premium booze was the first thing he and I bonded over at university. As everyone else lined up their pound-a-bottle luminous alcopops and sixty-pence-a-shot lighter-fluid vodka, I was ordering a Scotch off the top shelf while Jamie was refusing to drink his Tanqueray and tonic in a plastic cup.

'These are on me, Erica,' Jamie tells the barmaid when she brings Danielle's cocktail. Then he turns back to me with an apologetic smile. 'I need to serve for a bit but let's catch up later. Go mingle.'

'Yep, we all know how I love to mingle,' I drawl, but I take my drinks and do as I'm told.

'Better late than never,' is the first thing Danielle says. 'You really must do something about your punctuality, Becs. It's rather annoying.'

'Sorry,' I say with false sweetness to my best friend who has never once been on time for anything in her life. 'But I realized my toenail colour clashed with my dress, and even though I'm wearing closed-toe shoes, I couldn't possibly go out until I'd repainted them.'

'One day you're going to stop going on about that,' she huffs. Then, turning to the guys she's talking to: 'Russ, Tom, this is Rebecca.'

They say hello and I fear we're stuck with them.

My fear is realized and magnified when Danielle's mobile rings and she motions to us that she's going outside so she can hear better.

'Shane? Shane?' I hear her yelling into the mouthpiece as she retreats.

I check my own phone for messages and then when there are none, I check my work emails. Unsurprisingly, there are none at half nine on a Saturday night. When I eventually slide my phone back in my pocket, the two lads are deep in conversation between themselves. I wonder if this is what Jamie means when he says I'm unapproachable.

The barman who was collecting glasses appears with a tray laden with a beer, a coke and a big pink cocktail, garnished with about eight different fruits and a cocktail umbrella. He hands Russ the beer and Tom, the shy one, the coke, placing the cocktail on the shelf next to them.

'WHOA!' I leap back, my drink spilling down my front as someone barges into me. It's the same guy who squeezed in at the bar.

'Sorry,' he says, his mouth curving down in an almost comical *oopsy* expression. It's clear now that he's shit-faced. He reaches a hand out to dab my wet top so I hold out my own hand to block him. 'Leave it. It's fine.'

'Everything all right?' asks the barman, with the tray still in his hand.

'Accident,' the guy mumbles, holding up his palms before stumbling away.

'Twat,' I mutter, before turning to the barman. 'Thanks. You couldn't grab me some napkins, could you?'

'Sure.'

'And a large single-malt Scotch,' I yell at his retreating back.

While I wait, Russ and Tom take their drinks to the pool table, leaving me alone. Where the feck is Danielle?

'Here you go.' The barman places my drink on the side and hands me some napkins.

'Thanks.'

I dab myself self-consciously and he doesn't go away, then I realize I haven't paid for my drink. 'God, sorry,' I say, grabbing a tenner from my purse. 'Keep the change.'

He waves away my money, looking bewildered. 'Um, no, that's OK.'

Jamie must have known it was for me.

'OK, thanks.' I press the napkins back against my top.

He still doesn't move but suddenly laughs, scratching his head. 'Do you think I work here?'

As his words sink in I feel blood creep slowly into my cheeks. 'You don't?'

'Nope.'

'But the tray of drinks . . .'

'. . . were for my mates. I'd just got a round in.'

'And you were collecting glasses earlier!'

'It was rammed and there was a massive queue at the bar – I thought I'd help them out.'

'But why did you get me a drink?' I squeal.

He thinks for a moment then smiles. 'I honestly don't know.'

I cover my hot cheeks with my hands. 'Oh my God, I'm so sorry. I'm mortified.'

'Don't be,' he chuckles.

I make myself meet his eyes, pleasingly having to tilt my head back and look up – a gesture I don't get to make often. They're dark brown and long-lashed, and he holds my gaze for about two and a half seconds. Something weird happens. Like an electric shock – a chemical surge – though I'd never describe it that way out loud, because then I'd have to punch myself in the face. I blink and shift my gaze, taking in the rest of his face.

It's a nice face. You don't see many clean-shaven men these days, I realize. It makes him stand out. That and the slight kink in his nose, which suits him.

'I'm Ben,' he says.

'Rebecca,' I say, holding out the hand that's not full of wet napkins.

He grins. 'Strong handshake.'

'Thanks,' I say, though I don't know if it's a good thing or a bad thing. It's a good thing at work, but is it a sexually attractive trait? Christ, who am I?

He picks up the cocktail from the side and starts to sip it.

I look at it. Then look at him. 'Really?'

13

'I'm mates with the fella that runs the place.' He looks at his drink and sighs. 'He stitched me up.'

'You know Jamie? He's one of my best friends.'

'Mine too! We went to school together in Manchester. Then obviously he came to London for uni and I stayed up there.'

'Oh, you're *that* Ben,' I say. 'Jamie's mentioned you.'

'How do you know him?'

I explain how he, Danielle and I all lived together at university.

'Ah, you're *that* Rebecca. I've met Danielle, actually, at Jamie's old bar. That's her with Jamie now, isn't it?'

I look over and see her slipping her mobile back into her bag. Wonder what Shane wanted. Did he miss his flight from Ireland? Going to be late? A no-show?

'Yep, that's her.'

I should really close this conversation and go over as I can't stay too late tonight, and it's Jamie's big night. But . . .

'So you live in London yourself now, don't you?' I ask him, remembering what Jamie has told me.

'Since last year, yeah. Guess I needed a change of scenery. I went travelling, thinking I'd work out what to do with my life while I was away, but I've been back a few years and I'm none the wiser still.'

'What did you do at uni?'

'History. So, of course, my options were limitless.'

'They were?'

'Yeah. I could have been a comedian like Sacha Baron Cohen, or a novelist like Salman Rushdie. Or, actually, a Prime Minister – Gordon Brown did history.'

'So . . .'

'I temp in HR for London Transport.'

14

'Ah, that classic cliché.' I smile. 'Running away to the big smoke to fulfil a life-long ambition in personnel.'

Sarcasm comes as naturally to me as flirting does to Danielle, but as soon as it's out of my mouth I panic. What if he thinks I'm mocking him?

Thankfully he properly laughs, flashing straight white teeth, and if I was that sort of girl, I'd say his laugh is like sweet, sweet music, but I'm not, so I won't.

'That's why I'm temping,' he says, meeting my eyes again. 'I'm still trying to work out what my life-long ambition is. I want to leave my mark, you know?'

A girl pushes her way through the middle of us to get to the bar and the spell is broken.

'Where did you travel?' I ask, enjoying the way he moves his hands whenever he talks.

'All over Asia.'

I try to conceal a smile. 'Be honest, Ben . . . did you spend a year drinking Thai whisky from a bucket, playing drinking games at your hostel and making people take photos on a beach while you jumped really high in the air?'

'Not the whole year,' he says, laughing again, then looking thoughtful. 'My favourite was staying the night with Buddhist monks on a Japanese mountain.'

'Mount Koya?'

'Yeah! Have you been to Japan?'

'I lived there.'

'No way – how come?'

'We travelled a lot with my dad's job.' Someone else pushes through, then I notice Ben closes the gap ever so slightly so no one else can pass between us. I get a faint whiff of cigarette smoke and wonder if it's from him. 'So where do you live?'

15

'Here in Greenwich, with those two.' He nods towards the pool table where Russ and Tom are still playing. 'I work with them too.'

'Are they as passionate about HR as you?'

'Pretty much,' he says with a laugh. 'Tom's always wanted to be an artist and Russ has always wanted to be a superhero, so it's the logical career for everyone. What about you?' His eyes find mine again. 'What was your dream when you were a kid?'

'Becoming an architect, like my dad.'

'Nice. So what was your degree in?'

'Architecture.'

'That makes sense. What do you do now?'

'I'm an architect.'

'See? We're the same. Indecisive.'

We both laugh, then sip our drinks in tandem.

'So, what was Jamie like in school?' I ask.

'Same. Popular, confident. Good with girls. He was going out with Freckly Fiona for a while before he moved.'

'He did that alliterative nickname thing even back then?'

'Yeah. Talking of which . . .' He looks around. 'Any idea which one Tidy Tania is?'

'Who? Also, why have I never heard of this Freckly Fiona?'

'I guess he doesn't really like to talk about it. She didn't take it well when they broke up.'

I see him turn to Jamie again. 'Anything going on there, do you reckon?'

I look over too, seeing Danielle with her arm around Jamie's waist and Jamie with his arm slung around Danielle's shoulder.

'Nah, they're just the world's two biggest flirts. Jamie's probably the only man in here who doesn't fancy Danielle.'

He looks confused. 'I don't.'

We eye-lock again, the tension thick.

'Ben?'

'Yeah?'

'Your drink is dripping on your shirt.'

'Arggghhh. Crap.'

He straightens the straw to stop the flow.

'Want me to go get you a napkin? I owe you one.'

He laughs that lovely laugh again, then pauses and says: 'I do if it has your number on it?'

It's spoken as a question and his eyes are looking for mine again so I know I'm meant to answer, but I freeze. I can't reply how I'd usually reply to such a cheesy line, because my standard ripostes are designed to make the guy run away, and I don't want that to happen.

What would Danielle do?

She would calmly take a pen out of her bag and write her number on to a napkin, kissing it to leave a red imprint of her lips before handing it over and shimmying away.

I laugh inwardly. No way I'm pulling *that* off.

The silence is growing.

'You've finished your drink,' Ben says, nodding at my empty as if the last thing he said wasn't a question after all. He's making it easier for me not to answer, and I hate myself. 'Can I get you another?'

Out of the corner of my eye I see Danielle retreating towards the door with her coat on. Why is she leaving? 'Sorry,' I tell Ben. 'I just need to check in with Danielle quickly. I'll be back in two minutes.'

17

I rush towards the exit, bumping into Jamie on the way.

'Hey,' he says. 'I didn't realize you were still here. I've hardly had a chance to talk to you all night. How's work going? Are you all ready for Monday?'

'Getting there,' I say, mentally groaning when I remember how much I still have to do tomorrow. 'Where'd Danielle go?'

'Shane called earlier and said he was running late. He asked her to meet him outside when he gets here. Seemed he isn't in the mood for a party.'

I sigh. Danielle wouldn't leave a friend's party for anything usually, but Shane is her weakness. The kryptonite to her Superwoman.

Jamie is still talking but I'm only half listening. I position myself to face the room so I can look for Ben without Jamie realizing. Eventually I see him standing by a booth, chatting to his friends.

'Anyway,' Jamie is saying, 'I need to nip back behind the bar while Erica takes her break. Are you sticking around?'

'Er.' I glance at Ben again. He's deep in conversation – there's no way I can go over and interrupt. 'I should really head off.'

'What is it you keep looking at?' asks Jamie, twisting his neck. 'Ah ha. That's Ben,' he tells me, lowering his voice. 'He keeps looking over at you, I've noticed.'

'He does?' I try to keep the keenness out of my voice but fail, and I can see Jamie is taken aback.

'You like him!' Jamie says incredulously.

'Why? What's wrong with him?'

'Nothing, he's a legend. It's you – you never get doey-eyed over anyone.'

'I'm not doey-eyed, you knob.'

I go to slap him on the chest but he catches my arm and laughs.

I glance over at Ben one last time. He's whispering something to Russ. There really is no way I can butt in. And it's even more awkward now Jamie has cottoned on.

'I'm off,' I say, a cheery smile covering my disappointment. 'I'll see you later.'

'Will you be OK getting home? Shall I get you a cab?'

'Don't be silly, I'm only round the corner.'

'Fine,' he says, knowing there's no point arguing. 'Text me when you're home. And good luck on Monday.'

That's that then, I think as I turn on my heel and start making my way out. Who knows, I might even run into Ben again at some point. He's friends with Jamie, after all. Even though he's lived in London a year already and tonight's the first time I've met him. And maybe by the time I see him next he'll have a girlfriend in tow. Someone like him won't stay single for long.

I'm passing the pool table when I make up my mind, in a moment of madness that I can only blame on drinking whisky on an empty stomach, to turn back around, march up to the bar and grab one of the red napkins.

'Erica, do you have a pen I could borrow? Thanks.'

I scribble my number on it, wondering if Ben is watching me now but not daring to look because I know I'll bottle it if he is. It goes against every instinct I usually have, but I'm scared this will be my only chance to let him know that . . . I felt it too.

'Give that to Ben,' I say, returning to Jamie, who takes it with a smirk. 'And shut your face!'

'I didn't say a word.' He holds up his hands with a laugh after he's tucked it into his shirt pocket.

'Good, because if this goes tits up and he doesn't call, I'm going to need you to unfriend him so I never have to face seeing him again.'

I have a feeling, though, as I walk out the door and pull on my jacket, that it won't go tits up.

It feels like something has just begun.

Eleven Months Later

Chapter One

BEN

Tuesday, 23 September

'I'm so proud of you,' I say, as Rebecca lays knives and forks on the dining table.

'I still can't believe it,' she says. 'My first building to design.'

Her company is overseeing the rebuilding of a cinema in Hackney, thanks in no small part to her pitch eleven months ago. She found out yesterday they're making her the lead architect, so I've come round to her and Danielle's place to cook a celebratory meal.

'It was never in doubt,' I say.

How could they not give it to her? It was one of the most attractive things about her that night we met – her passion for what she did.

I kind of hoped it would rub off on me.

I still *am* hoping it'll rub off on me.

The intercom buzzes, but Danielle is in the shower and Rebecca is still setting the table, so I answer it myself, planting a kiss on Rebecca's temple as I go. I glance back from the door and see her smiling.

'All right, Nicholls,' Jamie says to me, once he's

conquered the two flights of stairs.

'All right, Hawley,' I say, stepping aside to let him in.

Jamie's eyes are immediately drawn to the bath-room.

'Jeez, what's that *noise*?'

The three of us stop and listen as Danielle adds an unscheduled key change to a Black Eyed Peas song. Rebecca and Jamie share a knowing look.

'Remember at uni when we ended up in that karaoke bar?' Rebecca says, shuddering at the very idea.

'You mean 2 Unlimited-gate?' Jamie puts down his gift bag and addresses me. 'She thought people were singing along but they weren't, they were saying, *No, no, no, no*.'

Danielle pads out of the bathroom in her dressing gown, a white towel Mr Whippied on her head.

'Rebecca was just saying how much she's going to miss your singing when you move out,' Jamie calls over.

Danielle's cousin has bought a place in Blackheath and offered her a room for bugger-all rent. Which I'm secretly pleased about.

'She'll get over it,' Danielle says. 'Just like I got over not being able to steal your facemasks after living with you at uni.'

She vanishes into her bedroom with a smirk while Jamie turns his attention to my shopping bags.

'What're we having?' he says.

'Cambodian beef curry.'

I learnt the recipe from a hostel owner in Phnom Penh.

Jamie nods. 'Nice, anything I can do?'

I pluck the red onions from their bag, kicking a basket

of wet washing out of the way to make space before handing him one of the knives from the set I bought on the way here.

'The box says this bad boy can cut through the sole of a shoe,' I say.

'That's an everyday problem solved.' He laughs. 'I thought you were skint, though?'

'Overdraft.'

Rebecca tuts, but I think she gets why I'm suddenly buying stuff for this place. We haven't talked yet, but with Danielle moving out, it makes sense for me to move in. That's why I was happy when I found out she was going. I mean, I like living with Russ and Tom, but I'll be twenty-eight in a couple of weeks, and I've had enough of wondering who stole my cheese.

I keep imagining cooking for Rebecca every night, always giving her the best portion, and I can't do that with the single, blunt kitchen knife that she and Danielle have been getting by with for years.

'Bastard onions,' says Jamie, burying his eyes in his elbow.

'It's weird,' says Rebecca, 'chopping onions never had any effect on me.'

'Shocker,' I say.

She gives me a curious look. 'What do you mean?'

Seriously? I turn to Jamie for help.

'To be fair, Becs,' he obliges, 'you're the only girl I know who didn't cry at the end of *Titanic*.' He cackles to himself. 'Actually, Ben is the only lad I know who did, so . . .'

'I wish you'd stop telling everyone I cried at the end of *Titanic*.'

Jamie and Rebecca are clearly amused.

'Hold your breath near the onion,' I say, ignoring them. 'Then it won't make you cry.'

I can tell he's sceptical but he does as he's told, and a minute later the onions are chopped and Jamie is tearless.

'Maybe you should have tried that trick in the cinema?' he says.

Jamie rejoins Rebecca at the dining table while I chop ingredients for the marinade in front of the kitchen window. I can see Natasha and Angus strolling around the perimeter of the green.

'Tash looks like she's about to pop,' I say.

'Who's Tash?'

'Natasha and Angus, your neighbours, from down-stairs,' I say, but Rebecca looks none the wiser. 'Have you never spoken to them?'

'What would I speak to them about?'

'The weather? The fact she's having a baby? European fishing quotas? It's a bit strange you've never—'

'Yes, but you're the guy who gets into random conversations on the Tube – *that's* strange.'

She's never got over the fact I did this on our first date. We'd been to Vertigo 42 in the City for champagne and panoramic views, and while Rebecca checked her work emails on the DLR back to Greenwich I got chatting to a fella wearing a Man City shirt with Kinkladze on the back. She has since told me that this cancelled out any points I'd earnt for being a gentleman and not trying any funny business.

'Only Danielle could be late for a dinner party at her own house,' says Jamie, peering towards her bedroom door.

Rebecca picks up one of the napkins she has transformed into swans. 'What's the rush?' the swan says.

It was our second date when I discovered her talent for origami. We'd gone for tapas, and before the first dishes arrived she made a rose from her napkin and handed it to me with a smirk. I told her I'd contemplated bringing flowers on the date and she laughed a worried laugh and said she was glad I hadn't.

When Danielle finally appears she is several inches taller and has the white towel scrunched in her hand.

'High heels for dinner in your own flat?' says Jamie.

Danielle chucks the towel at him.

'I'd be careful around Ben and his new toy in a nice pair of shoes like that,' he adds.

Danielle looks confused but no one tries to explain.

'You look stunning,' says Rebecca instead.

'Well, if I can't make the effort to celebrate my bessie mate getting her first big project, when can I?' She and Rebecca trade a smile. 'Though to be honest,' she adds, turning to me and Jamie, 'the real reason I'm wearing heels is because I feel like a dumpy little midget next to *her*.' She points to Rebecca, then clops back to her room. 'One second!'

When Danielle reappears she is carrying something in her right hand. 'I made something for you,' she says, handing whatever it is to Rebecca.

'This is brilliant!' says Rebecca.

It appears to be a crumpled crisp packet with a hole punched through to make a keyring. Rebecca sees that I'm not quite understanding *why* it's brilliant.

'Danielle once said the only thing she found annoying about me was discovering empty Frazzles packets around the house.'

'But if you put them in the microwave for five seconds

they shrink and turn hard,' adds Danielle.

Fair enough.

'I got you something too,' says Jamie, reaching for his gift bag.

Rebecca draws a wrapped bottle from the bag, her decisively green eyes broadening. She is wearing a dark blue dress that she knows always reminds me of the first time I came back, when I ripped it off. Not like the Incredible Hulk. More unbuttoned it really fast and threw it recklessly on the floor, where she seemed to keep all her other clothes.

Rebecca tears the paper, catching my gaze for a split second to communicate that she's hating the attention, but when she sees what it is . . .

'Jamie!' she gasps. 'This is, like, three-hundred-pound whisky.'

'Not at wholesale it's not.'

Danielle pouts. 'All right, Jamie – way to outdo me.'

'Wasn't difficult,' he replies, draping an arm around Danielle's shoulder. 'You literally gave her rubbish.'

With my ingredients chopped, I measure soy and oyster sauce on instinct and add the steak pieces to the marinade for about twenty minutes. I hope they like it.

'I couldn't care less about the sofa,' Rebecca is saying when I start listening again. 'But, man, I'm going to miss this dining table.'

I join them.

'Yeah, I've got happy memories of this table too,' I say, giving Rebecca a look to see if she'll play along.

'It's just so versatile,' she obliges, and the other two look puzzled, oblivious to the fact that under the table I'm sliding the tip of my foot down Rebecca's shin. The corners of her lips are starting to crack. 'I mean, it's great for spreading all my work sketches out,' she says, 'and eating, and—'

'Oh yeah, versatile,' I chip in. 'It's perfect for dinner parties, and reading the Sunday papers, and—'

Having mad sex while the Sunday papers are strewn across the room. It was a few weekends ago while Danielle was visiting her dad and stepmum. Rebecca was finally better after a stomach bug, and when I got out of bed to make us ham and cheese toasties, she followed me in here, hoisted her arms around my neck and, well, we never made it back to the bedroom.

'OK, we get it,' says Jamie, raising his palms to stop us. 'Jeez, anyone would think you'd had sex on it.'

Danielle laughs until she realizes that neither Rebecca nor I are saying anything, and that both of us are gazing around the room as if we hadn't even *heard* Jamie.

'Eww!' she moans, and I flee to the kitchen to fry the beef.

'Well, Nicholls,' says Jamie, laying his knife and fork on his empty plate, 'that was the best Cambodian beef curry I've had in ages.'

I laugh.

'Seriously, though, Becs,' says Danielle, 'you should keep hold of this one.'

'He's pretty hard to get rid of,' says Rebecca, before directing a private smile my way.

I have to stop myself from asking her here and now: *Shall we live together?* But I learnt that night at Arch 13 that Rebecca doesn't like being put on the spot. Sometimes it's better to be patient, and so with this, asking her to live with me, I've waited, because I want her to

29

know that I'm serious, and that it's not another one of my whims.

I'm going to do it on Friday, after I've *finally* met her dad, which is another thing I've had to be patient about, what with Rebecca working every hour God sends to bag the cinema project.

I'm not even worried living together will change things. We managed to spend a week together in Rome for her birthday without killing each other, and a holiday is the first of the relationship tests, isn't it? Come through that and you can probably live together; come through the living together test and the next step is marriage; then you get a dog to see if you'd be good parents.

Maybe I'm getting a bit ahead of myself.

'How's Markus?' Rebecca asks Danielle.

Sadly for Markus, the only test Danielle seems to set is: are you Shane? He dumped her on the night Rebecca and I met, but she still isn't over him.

'Why do guys always think I want a relationship?' she says.

'You sleep with them,' says Rebecca. 'You can see why they'd get confused.'

'It's just two people rubbing body parts together,' Danielle whines. 'How come Jamie can have mindless, meaningless sex and everyone understands what it is but when I do it men assume I'll want to date them?'

Danielle chucks her crumpled swan on to her empty plate and helps me clear the dishes. She checks her phone for the umpteenth time as I fill the sink with water.

'So how is Shane?' says Rebecca casually.

Danielle turns and puts her phone against her chest, blushing. 'No, I haven't . . . We haven't . . .'

'I know that look!'

Danielle makes a show of slapping her phone on the sideboard. We work wordlessly for a minute or two while Jamie wipes down the table and Rebecca puts away the condiments. We're a well-drilled team.

'When did he get back in touch?' Rebecca asks.

Danielle has been drying the same plate since Rebecca caught her out. The pots are starting to pile up.

'A few days ago,' she answers guiltily.

Rebecca doesn't say anything.

'We've been texting all day and then suddenly he's gone off the radar without warning.' Danielle scoops up her phone. 'I'm thinking my last text might not have got through.'

'Whoa, whoa, whoa.' Jamie stops what he's doing. 'You're not texting him again, are you?'

'How else am I going to know if he got my message?'

'What are you thinking happened to it?' asks Rebecca. 'Did aliens abduct it? Did it fly over the Bermuda Triangle?'

I dodge aside so Jamie can put the anti-bacterial spray back under the sink.

'The rules are quite clear,' he says. 'You can only double text if you're an actual thing.'

'Or during an argument,' I say, and then smiling at Rebecca: 'Not that I'd know about that, obviously.'

'*Not that I'd know about that, obviously,*' mimics Rebecca, then laughs when I whip her legs with the tea towel.

Danielle places her plate in the cupboard with a clack. 'I know the rules,' she says. 'But Shane is complicated. He doesn't reply to anyone the first time around, he's really busy. And also forgetful. He's always leaving his phone somewhere.'

31

The three of us eyeball her until her chin sinks towards her torso. 'OK, OK – I'll wait for him to text me. God!'

Once everything is cleared away Rebecca joins me at the window, wrapping her arms around me from behind. She nestles her chin into my shoulder so that her dark brown hair falls down the front of my shirt. We stare at the moon, its roundness pared only slightly at one side.

'Dinner was lovely,' she whispers. 'I'll thank you properly when we're alone.'

'Right, everyone,' I say, turning around with a clap of my hands, 'time to finish your drinks and go home.'

Rebecca laughs.

'This *is* my home,' says Danielle.

'Not for much longer,' I point out.

Danielle looks crestfallen.

'He's joking around,' says Rebecca, laughing.

She goes to sit on the couch with Danielle, but I stay where I am, contemplating the last eleven months.

'Remember that time you bought a telescope because you decided you wanted to be an astronomer?' says Jamie, following my eyes to the moon. 'How's that working out for you?'

I ignore him. 'I was just thinking how fast the last year has gone.'

'It'll be your anniversary soon,' says Jamie.

'Wow, a year!' calls Danielle. 'When was your first date?'

Rebecca asks Jamie the date of his opening night.

'October the twenty-sixth last year,' he says before I can point out that, actually, it was a couple of weeks before we went on a proper date.

Then Danielle changes the subject with a loud groan at her phone.

'Just delete his number!' Rebecca pleads.

I watch Jamie laugh at the spectacle of Rebecca and Danielle going back and forth, and I try to remember if I've ever properly thanked him for being the matchmaker when he had a million other things to think about: getting Arch 13 off the ground, trying to placate his parents. They still haven't visited the bar.

'I still owe you one,' I tell him now. 'For the napkin.'

He smiles. 'I just hope it doesn't all go to pot on Friday.'

'How do you mean?'

'Oh, you know. Rebecca being so close to her dad, and all that. She dumped a guy once cos her dad didn't approve.'

'Ta for that.'

He cracks up. 'Just thought I should warn you.'

'Leave him alone!' interrupts Rebecca. 'Although he's right,' she says to me. 'I did dump Nick McDermott cos Dad wasn't keen.'

I fold my arms, suddenly feeling quite anxious about the whole thing.

'Actually, that reminds me,' says Rebecca. 'I need to go into work on Friday morning before we get the train to Kent.'

'I thought you had the day off?'

'I did, but Jake wants to introduce me to the structural engineer I'll be working with on the cinema.'

'Talking of which . . .' says Jamie. 'We're supposed to be celebrating!' He picks up the thirty-year-old Glenfiddich he bought her. 'Let's have a toast.'

'Not that,' Rebecca bawls, scuttling over to take it

from him. 'I'm not wasting that.' She looks at me. 'Ben, let's open that prosecco your mum got us.'

'Life's too short to save good whisky,' Jamie protests, but I'm already fetching the bubbles from the fridge.

The cork proves stubborn, eventually releasing with a pop, and the three of them shove their glasses underneath the bottle to collect the spillage.

'To Rebecca!' says Danielle.

'To my awesome girlfriend!' I say, winking at her.

'To friends,' adds Rebecca.

We all clink glasses, and the last word is Jamie's.

'To life!'

Chapter Two

REBECCA

Friday, 26 September

Whizzing over Blackfriars Bridge with London's skyline in my periphery is one of my favourite parts of the day.

I love the English Baroque-style dome of St Paul's – the tallest building in London as recently as the sixties – and I love the eighty-seven-storey Shard. I love the twinkling windows of The Gherkin (though I hate that name).

I love the wind on my cheeks and the freedom of not being governed by timetables and specific routes – I can leave whenever I want and take any path, no matter how narrow. And I love the fact that for forty minutes I don't have to think about anything else. My mind is focused on the road ahead, and the traffic around me, and the judging of time and distance as I weave in and out of the gaps between cars, buses and pedestrians.

And most of all, if I'm totally honest, I love that it's not the Tube, because the temptation to punch slow walkers in the back of the head is just too overwhelming at 8 a.m.

As I'm finding out today. I had to leave my bike at

home because I'm getting the train straight to Dad's at lunchtime with Ben.

'Good morning!' A blonde girl I don't recognize greets me in a Scottish accent when I arrive at Goode Architecture Associates on a commuter-rage comedown. 'I'm Jemma.'

Shit, I forgot the new receptionist has her induction day today. Not everyone was a fan of Mandy, our last one, but I liked her. She mightn't have been the happiest soul, or indeed the most welcoming by nature, but she was organized and efficient, and that's really all I wanted from her.

This girl's round, pretty face is smiley and friendly. Double shit.

'Morning,' I reply, hoping she won't take offence if I don't stop and chat.

At the top of the stairs I keep my head down, not slowing my pace or giving anyone the chance to engage me in conversation – I want to get my shit together before my meeting. But right before I sit down, the boss's door swings open and I hear my name being called. I close my eyes and take a deep breath, trying to channel the me from yesterday. The me who hadn't done the maths yet. The me who was entirely focused on the job at hand, and not preoccupied with the realization that Ben and I might have accidentally made a tiny human.

'Rebecca, perfect timing,' Jake is saying. 'This is Adam Larsson from Bensons. You'll be working together on the cinema.'

Ah ha, the infamous Adam Larsson. I've never met him but I've heard Eddie's tales of their debaucherous nights out, which inevitably end up with Adam going home with someone. He's fit, but if his smug smile is anything to go by, my gosh doesn't he know it.

'And this,' Jake tells Adam, a little proudly I'm touched to note, 'is Rebecca Giamboni, head architect on the project.'

'Er, hi,' says Adam, his smile faltering as his eyes flick from me to Jake. 'I assumed I'd be working with Eddie.' Then, remembering himself, he holds out his hand. 'Good to meet you, Rebecca.'

'And you,' I say, gripping his hand firmly despite my risen heckles at his evident disappointment that I'm infiltrating his boys' club. And I always got the impression from Eddie that this guy was smooth.

'Rebecca's one of our rising stars,' Jake adds.

'Looking forward to working with you,' Adam tells me with smirk.

'Likewise,' I lie, looking forward to wiping the smirk off his face.

Not by punching him or anything – by designing a really frickin' impressive cinema.

I can't tell how on board Adam is with my initial ideas as he responds to everything I say in our meeting with a non-committal nod. So when it's his turn to talk, I do the same, even though his ideas are pretty good. Jake's enthusiasm makes up for it, though, and by the time we draw the meeting to a close, I'm feeling excited.

If I'm pregnant it really is the worst timing in the history of procreation, I note as I finally sink into my chair at my desk. I'll be furious with myself.

It's not that Ben and I aren't careful. I'd never leave this shit to chance. I'm on the pill, and that's why I wasn't too worried when my period didn't come. But this morning I was sitting eating my cereal at the kitchen table, and a memory popped into my head of what we'd done right where my bowl of Crunchy Nut Cornflakes sat. A memory that made me smile and blush at the same time, and then I remembered that I'd been sick for a few days before that, throwing up everything that passed through my mouth. Including my pill?

My desk phone rings, snapping me out of it. Christ, I think, blinking: I'm meant to be working on the most important project of my life – Jake has hinted that a promotion could be on the cards if it goes well – but I'll be lucky to keep the job I already have unless I start to focus.

'Sugar?' asks the new receptionist as soon as I pick up the phone.

'Pardon?'

'I've made you a tea,' she explains. 'Just wondered how you take it.'

'Oh, er . . . White, no sugar, please.'

Or better still, with a spoonful of coffee and no tea-bag.

'On its way.' She hangs up.

Bit weird.

I scrunch up the page I'm drawing on and lob it into the bin, then regret it. The blank page in front of me doesn't scream busy and, as I feared, when the new receptionist brings my tea up, she hovers by my desk.

'Thanks, Emma,' I tell her as she sets the mug down next to me.

'Jemma,' she corrects me.

'God, sorry – Jemma. I'm terrible with names.'

'With a J.'

'Um . . . right.'

'Just in case you look me up on Facebook. Ooh, by the way,' she squeals, 'have you ever noticed how much

Adam Larsson looks like Eric Northman? You know, from *True Blood*?'

'Nope – never seen it.'

'I recognized him from a copy of *Architecture Weekly* I was reading in reception before my interview. I was actually just looking at the pictures but I thought it might make a good impression. Anyway, it's basically vampire porn.'

'*Architecture Weekly*?'

'No, *True Blood*. You should watch it.'

I feel my shoulders tense as she plonks herself down in the chair opposite me. I don't want to be a dick, especially on her first day, but if she's looking for a gossip then she's come to the wrong desk. I should introduce her to Eddie.

'This your other half?' Jemma asks, picking up the framed photo next to my computer. It's a snap of St Basil's Cathedral in Moscow, the first building I ever fell in love with, taken with my old film camera on a holiday with my dad and brother when I was eleven.

I laugh. 'Just a building I like.'

'Do you have a boyfriend?'

'Yep.'

'How long have you been together?'

'Eleven months,' I tell her.

'So it's serious?' Is *she* serious?

'Yes, you could say that.'

'You dinnae seem happy about it.'

'I am, I am, it's just . . .' It's just I don't feel comfortable with the intrusive questioning. I can't say that, of course.

'He's meeting my dad for the first time later,' I say instead, hoping she'll leave it there. 'Just a bit nervous.'

I'm not lying, I realize. I've been desperate for Ben to

meet my dad, but have struggled to find a weekend all three of us could do. Now the day is finally here, I have butterflies. They're the two most important people in my life: what if they don't get on?

'I havenae had sex for months,' Jemma says.

'Oh,' I say. 'That's, um . . .'

'You're lucky to have someone,' she adds, swivelling herself in the chair so fast that eventually, when she lifts her legs off the ground, she carries on spinning.

She's lucky, I think. At least she knows she's not pregnant. *Oh, God, please don't let me be pregnant*, I pray for the hundredth time today. There's no room in my life for a baby right now. What if they take me off the project? And even if they don't, how likely are they to promote me if I'm off on maternity leave in nine months?

'Thanks,' I tell Jemma, trying to keep my voice even. 'And, um, thanks for the tea.'

'Any time,' she says, mid-spin.

I gulp down the last few mouthfuls then stand up and pull on my leather jacket. 'I should shoot off, actually. Train to catch.' Test to buy. Stick to pee on.

'Cool,' she says, slamming her feet on the ground to stop the motion. 'I'd better head down anyway. I've been told never to leave my phone unattended.'

From the queue at Boots I spot Ben, leaning against the wall of Paperchase, glancing around the station.

He's wearing navy jeans and a pale blue shirt with buttons on the pockets, sleeves rolled up to the elbows, looking ruggedly handsome. He's quite a catch. Lord knows why it's me he chooses to be with.

I notice a girl in jeans and a blazer glance his way when she walks past, as if trying to catch his eye, and

40

my heart beats a little faster. She's pretty, and curvy, and I can't help wondering what Ben will think if he realizes he could have someone like that.

But he doesn't even bat an eyelid – just glances at his watch.

I smile in relief.

When I count my blessings, I count Ben twice, and as I slip the Boots bag into my holdall, I pray I'm not about to mess it all up.

He looks up as I finally walk towards him, and breaks into a grin. 'Hello, gorgeous.'

'Hello, handsome.'

I kiss him hello, breaking my lips away after just a few seconds, even though I could kiss him for ever. Ben doesn't take it personally. Every time he's ever tried an alfresco cuddle I've wriggled out of it, and more than once he's clocked my involuntary looks of discomfort at a couple snogging in front of us in a supermarket queue or at a bus stop.

'You look hot,' I tell him, leaving him in no doubt that we'll finish that kiss once we're alone. 'That's a sexy shirt. Blue is a good colour on you.'

'Ta very much,' he says, appraising himself with a downward glance. 'Hot was exactly the look I was going for to meet your dad.'

I laugh. 'Is it new?'

'Yeah, I was early so bought this and the jeans.'

I step back and look him up and down. 'I can't believe you bought an entire new outfit just to go to my dad's.' He didn't need to do that – no wonder he's always skint at the end of the month – but I can't help my heart wanting to explode with love. 'Platform five,' I add, glancing at the departures board.

41

'What did you get from Boots?' asks Ben as we pass through the barrier.

Crap, I didn't realize he'd seen me come out.

'Nurofen,' I mumble. 'I've had a cracking headache all morning.'

'Buonasera,' Stefan greets me at the front door, dramatically kissing both my cheeks, before shoving me out the way so he can do the same to Ben.

My brother whole-heartedly embraces his Italian heritage, which is pretty funny because there's feck all outward evidence of his quarter-Italian genes. He inherited my mum's English-rose complexion: fair, freckly skin and a shocking intolerance to the sun.

He's also inherited her attraction to tall, dark, handsome men.

'I didn't know you were coming down,' I tell him, hanging up my coat while Stefan takes Ben's.

'A man who doesn't spend time with his family can never be a real man,' he tells me in an Italian accent.

Stefan is ginger, for crying out loud. He looks more like Prince Harry than Don Corleone.

'Dump your stuff then come meet big Marco,' he says to Ben, disappearing back into the kitchen.

'My brother likes you,' I whisper proudly to Ben.

'He *likes* me?' he whispers back, pretending to look panicked. 'Should I change out of the sexy shirt?'

'God, no – Stefan has always had much better taste than me.'

'Hey, Becky,' says Dad from the kitchen door, slinging a tea towel over his shoulder and opening his arms for a hug.

'And Ben, hello.' He releases me and shakes Ben's

hand. 'It's good to finally meet you.'

'And you, Mr Giamboni.'

Stefan is chopping herbs with his back to us but from the shake of his shoulders I can tell he's suppressing a laugh at Ben's formality.

'Just getting the dinner prep out the way,' says Dad. 'Spaghetti bolognese all right for you?'

'Smashing,' Ben says, his grin faltering as he peers into the saucepan and sees all the raw ingredients my dad has chucked into it at the same time.

Anyone watching us could be fooled into thinking mine's a culinary family – all slicing, chopping and mixing in Dad's huge open-plan kitchen, with its professional-looking eight-hob thingy and its central island with pots and pans dangling above it.

Truth is, Dad and Stefan are just as bad as me.

'You've a lovely home, Mr Giamboni,' Ben says, staring around the kitchen in awe, and I shoot Stefan a *Don't even think about it* look, though I'm struggling not to laugh myself. But I'm touched how much effort Ben is putting in to make sure my dad likes him.

'Thanks,' says Dad smoothly, not mentioning the fact he designed the renovation, extending my Granny's house on the edge of the quaint seaside town of Deal in Kent after she died. I love this place too – it's just the right mix of traditional and modern. Classy, but not flash.

'And, please, call me Marc.'

I give Ben a tour of the house while Dad makes a pot of coffee.

'Is this Stefan's?' asks Ben as we reach the room at the end of the upstairs corridor.

'It's mine,' I tell him with a laugh. 'Why?'

43

'The plain blue walls just don't scream teenage girl.'

'That's how you know it's not Stefan's,' I say, sliding my hands under his shirt and up his back. 'Anyway . . . blue is my very favourite colour.'

'Good to know,' he mumbles, planting soft kisses down my face, closer and closer to my mouth until his lips are on mine.

'Mmmm,' I mumble, smiling into his kiss. 'That really is a sexy outfit.'

'*You're* a sexy outfit,' he mumbles back.

I pull my face away from his and smirk.

'I don't know what that means either,' he says. 'Just don't stop kissing me.'

My lips find his again, then we fall sideways on to my bed, running our hands over each other.

'We should go back downstairs,' I tell him, making no attempt to move.

'Yeah, we should,' he agrees, sliding a finger across my jaw, down my neck and into the V of my dress.

'You know,' he tells me, 'your dad isn't nearly as scary as I thought he'd be.'

'You're talking about my dad while your hand is under my bra?'

'Sorry,' he says, laughing. 'I was just wondering why he didn't like that Nick guy.'

I tilt my head and sigh. 'I don't know, really. He just didn't trust him. He didn't like how much time we spent up in my room.'

'Right.' Ben springs up from the bed and smooths his shirt with his palms. 'Let's get back downstairs.'

Dad's living room is a cosy den; the only room that is pretty much unchanged since Granny lived here, but now her bookcases are filled with design books and

autobiographies rather than spy novels and old issues of
Reader's Digest.

'Who plays?' asks Ben, gesturing at the piano.

'Rebecca,' says Stefan.

Ben's eyes widen as he looks at me. 'Why don't I know
this?'

'Can't you tell she's got penis fingers?' says Stefan.

'Pianist fingers!' I yell.

'That's what I said.'

'Anyway,' I say to Ben, hitting Stefan with a cushion, 'I don't play. I took a few lessons when I was young,
when we were back staying with Granny. I gave up,
though.'

'Too impatient,' clarifies Stefan.

'Not true,' I lie.

Dad leans back in his chair and crosses his legs.
'She thought she'd come away from her first lesson
being able to give a full rendition of Beethoven's Fifth
Symphony.'

'Well, who wants to spend an hour doing scales?' I
complain.

'See?' says Stefan.

'A few weeks ago she asked me to show her how to do
a perfect boiled egg,' Ben says, leaning conspiratorially
towards the others. 'Then she tried it herself once, and it
was only half cooked when she opened it, so she bashed
it to death with her spoon and poured herself a bowl of
cereal. She hasn't tried it again since.'

Dad and Stefan burst out laughing and I glare at Ben
with faux hurt, though I'm happy to see the three of
them being so pally.

Ben's eyes lock with mine, and even after eleven
months, the intimacy of his look still has the same effect

it did on that night at Arch 13. It's an effort to tear my eyes away.

I don't know why I was worried earlier. Everyone loves Ben and everyone loves my dad. The two of them not getting on would be like Phillip Schofield and Dame Judi Dench meeting and deciding they're not really each other's cup of tea.

'Can you still play anything?' asks Ben.

I shake my head as Stefan grabs my hand and drags me up. 'Let's do a duet,' he says.

'We don't know any—'

'Yes, we do. We nailed it – don't pretend you've forgotten.'

Reluctantly I sit next to Stefan on the stool.

'It's that crap one everyone knows,' I announce over my shoulder to Ben. 'It was in the film *Big*.'

I start the lower notes and wait for Stefan to come in with the melody.

He gets it right for about five seconds before he starts hitting the wrong keys. He doesn't stop, though; he just carries on as if he's doing it right.

'Stop going off-piste,' I yell at him.

'I'm here and I'm perfectly sober,' he says.

'Knob.'

'Sshhh, and concentrate, before you ruin our recital.'

'The piano originally belonged to Alice, my wife,' Dad tells Ben as they both chuckle.

'Oh, Dad, I forgot to tell you.' I stop playing and spin around, before the conversation goes down that road. 'Danielle is moving out.'

I fill him in on the details.

'So what's next for you?' he asks.

My eyes find Ben and I see him look down into his

mug. It's painful to admit – and I won't out loud – but I was so sure Ben would instantly suggest moving in when I told him about Danielle. That's what he does, he jumps right in. It never occurred to me that he wouldn't ask.

Worried he'll think I'm trying to coerce him now, I inject some enthusiasm into my answer.

'It'd be weird living there with anyone else. I guess I'll just rent by myself until I can afford to buy somewhere. It'll be nice to have my own space.' There you go, Ben – off the hook. 'It might have to be a studio flat, or somewhere further afield where the rent isn't so high. Charlton, maybe.'

'You know,' says Dad, 'if you feel ready to buy somewhere now, I can help you.'

'What do you mean?'

'With a deposit. I've set something aside for you. So if you're ready to buy somewhere, then let's have a chat about it.'

'Wow.' I laugh, taking it in. 'Thanks, Dad.'

Ben looks as shocked as I do – but when our eyes meet he gives me a grin.

I look at Stefan, wondering if he knew about Dad's secret fund. 'He did the same for me when I bought my flat,' he says. 'So don't go thinking you're the favourite or anything.'

'I wouldn't be too sure about that, son,' says Dad, getting to his feet and patting Stefan's shoulder playfully. 'Now if you'll all excuse me, I need to set the table for our delicious Italian feast.'

As a family, we always eat at a table. Admittedly, we ate out half the time when I was growing up, but even at home, it was always at the table. No telly, no phones, no computer games. Music was OK as long as it was quiet enough to chat, because Dad always insisted meal times were family times.

It's a habit I never got out of until I met Ben. The first time he cooked me dinner at his he carried the shepherd's pie through, and I followed excitedly holding the crockery.

'For the love of God, what are you doing?' I asked, watching in horror as he placed the pie on top of a magazine on the coffee table.

'Thought we could sit on the couch and eat,' he said, looking perplexed as he watched me set two places at the dinner table. 'Watch a film or something?'

So we did. And after we finished eating, Ben pulled my legs on to his lap while we watched the rest of the film. We ended up falling asleep, me snuggled into his shoulder.

Then that became the norm, though I would never suggest it when coming to my dad's.

The feast, when we eventually sit down to eat it, is far from delicious. It is, at best, edible. We all know it. Dad doesn't pretend to be a good cook – he just isn't a believer in not doing something just because you're a bit crap at it.

'That was really nice,' says Ben, soaking up the final spot of tomato sauce on his plate with burnt garlic bread and swallowing it, before sitting back and patting his tummy.

'It was?' asks Dad.

I feel the corners of my mouth twitch.

'Absolutely.'

Stefan picks up his napkin and wipes his mouth, and I can tell once again he's trying not to laugh.

'Would you like more?' I ask Ben sweetly. I pick up the pot without waiting for an answer and serve a huge dollop on to his plate. 'There you go.'

'Lovely. Ta.'

He gives Dad a smile.

'You are welcome,' I say.

He manages to finish his second portion and I'm still struggling not to smile when Ben says: 'Oh my God – who's that?'

'That's Alice,' says Dad, following Ben's gaze to the photo on the fireplace as he tops up our wine, not seeming to notice I've barely touched mine. 'Their mum.'

'God, she looks like you, Rebecca.' Ben stands and goes to pick it up, looking perplexed. I avert my eyes, but the image in the frame is imprinted in my mind. My mum is gardening. Her fair hair is piled on top of her head in a messy bun, and even though she's crouching, you can see how petite she is. Her dungarees hang loosely from her shoulders, rolled up at the bottom above her tiny, bare feet. I take after my dad in every way, except . . . 'It's the eyes! Those are your eyes. That's incredible.'

I try to turn my attention away, and think about something else. I take a sip of my wine but all it does is make me realize how dry my mouth has become, and it hurts to swallow.

'I'm just nipping to the loo,' I announce, turning quickly but catching the confusion on Ben's face.

Picking up my handbag en route, I rush to the bathroom, locking the door behind me, leaning my head back against it and shutting my eyes. I feel like a terrible person. No wonder Ben's confused – I've never told him anything about my mum or exactly how she died. It's not that I want to keep it a secret or anything. I just find it hard to . . .

Once my breathing is back to normal I reach for my bag and pull out the pregnancy test I bought at the station. I thought I could put it out of my mind for the night – to pretend it's not happening. But suddenly I know I can't walk back downstairs without knowing.

I can't even begin to think how Ben will react if I tell him about this. If he isn't ready to live with me then *Have Babies* is way down on his To Do list.

My hand shakes so much I almost pee on it. Please, please be negative.

Chapter Three

BEN

The plates are cleared and *Marc* is loading them into the dishwasher when Rebecca finds us in the kitchen. I direct a smile her way but it's like her eyes are embroiled in a particularly competitive game of dodgeball.

'Why don't you two go for a stroll?' her dad says. 'Walk off your dinner and let Ben see a bit of Deal.'

Rebecca scratches the inside of her wrist, acting as though no one has said anything.

'Good idea,' I say, and her eyes jink to me at last, but only for a microsecond.

I can tell something's up, and she obviously doesn't want to go for a walk, but if I've done something wrong then I'd quite like to know, and I can't exactly ask her in front of her dad and brother.

'Fine,' says Rebecca. She fills her lungs and moves her hands from her hips so that they press into her belly. 'I could do with some fresh air, anyway.'

We stride down a cobbled street towards the town centre. I've had to adapt my natural walking pace over the last eleven months, because Rebecca walks everywhere like she's trying for a personal best. I normally find it amusing, but today she has no particular place to be, and it almost feels like she's trying to run away from something.

Within a few minutes we reach a quiet seaside strip that feels undiscovered, or like it never wanted to be discovered in the first place. There are no amusement arcades, and the fish and chip shop is closing up even though it's not yet eight o'clock.

We cross a deserted road and join a path of wooden planks that leads on to a pebble beach. For some reason I feel nervous.

'How's your headache?' I say, remembering the Nurofen.

For a second she looks at me like she hasn't a clue what I'm talking about. 'Oh, yes. Better, thanks.'

The only sound as we stray on to the shingle is the lingering whistle of a man walking his Labrador. The tide is coming in, and I waltz away from a line of frothy water that spills towards my feet, to see if she'll laugh, but her smile is dutiful.

'Has today been a total disaster?' I say. 'Is that why you've gone quiet?'

Rebecca stops.

'Oh, Ben,' she says, her thoughtful expression dissolving as she looks me in the eye. 'Today hasn't been a disaster at all.'

She gives me a reassuring smile and hooks her arm guiltily into mine as we start walking again. When I look at her I can see mischief in her expression.

'What?' I say.

'I was just thinking about today.' She pinches her lips in on themselves. 'I didn't realize how good a suck-up you were.'

'Suck-up?'

'Well . . .' She tilts her head momentarily. 'I've never seen you defer to anyone before. Except me, obviously.'

I laugh, though I'm not really following.

'It's one of the reasons I fell in love with you,' she explains. 'You're a bit Che Guevara about authority.' She puts Che Guevara in air quotes. 'Albeit a pale, less mysterious, far less cool Che Guevara.'

'I'm cool!'

'But today, with my dad, you were like—'

'And I'm mysterious.'

She stops, regarding me. 'OK, I'm a fair woman. I distinctly remember one occasion, when we first started dating, you left it ages before replying to one of my texts.'

'Well, there you go.'

'Forty-five minutes or something.'

'Oh, be quiet, penis fingers.'

'Don't *you* start!' she says, laughing. 'Really glad you liked Dad's spag bol, by the way. Did you enjoy your seconds?'

I eyeball her. 'I can't believe you did that.'

'It was too good an opportunity to miss. I knew you'd be too polite to say no.'

I bump her shoulder with mine, but our arms remain hooked and she boomerangs back into me.

'I just wanted to make a good impression, is all.'

Rebecca holds my gaze. 'It was sweet.'

Lads always ask whether you're a bum, legs or boobs man, and I'd always answer legs. But for the past eleven months, since meeting Rebecca, I reckon I've become an eyes man. Obviously I haven't said that out loud, because whichever lads I was with would have downed the rest of their pints, left the pub and never contacted me again.

'So you're not going to dump me like Nick McDermott?'

She laughs again. 'That was *never* gonna happen, Ben.'

I feel relieved, although I still don't know what was up back at the house.

'Can't believe Dad's giving me a deposit,' she says.

'I know, right?' I say. 'You should start looking at places, get a feel for what's out there – I'll come with you.'

My enthusiasm isn't one hundred per cent genuine, but I'll get over it. I guess I should be grateful the whole topic came up. I'd be popping the *Will you live with me?* question right now if she hadn't told her dad that she couldn't see herself living in the flat with someone new.

Yes, I'm disappointed, but as an ex-girlfriend once pointed out, I'm a bit of an emotional express train, and I know Rebecca is more like a cross-country service that stops at every town. It's another reason I fell in love with her. I've got bored of every girlfriend I ever had before Rebecca. I guess I like a challenge.

So I'll wait, and maybe in a couple of years we'll buy somewhere together. That's the reason I accepted a permanent job at London Transport – so I could start saving for a deposit. Which reminds me: I really should start saving for a deposit.

'You know I designed my very first building on this beach?' she says. 'Sometimes I'd spend my summer holidays here if Dad was on a particularly busy job. Granny would bring us to the beach but I hated it back then. You can't make sand castles out of pebbles.'

I grin, happy to be finding out something I don't know.

'One year we came here just before Christmas. I was seven or eight. Me and Stefan were going to spend a few days with Granny and then Dad would arrive on

Christmas Eve and we'd have Christmas together. So the day we arrived it started to snow. It just kept falling, and the next day Granny brought us here and I swear you couldn't see a single pebble. The beach was completely white. Stefan wanted to build a snowman but I made him build a snow house instead. I was like the foreman, telling him what needed to be done until we had a mini mansion with windows and everything. It even had a front garden.'

I widen my eyes to show that I'm suitably impressed.

'The next day we came back and it was still there, good as new. Same the day after, even though most of the snow had melted. The next day Dad was arriving and I couldn't wait to show him. He was knackered from his flight but it must have been obvious how excited I was so he came along to the beach. Except the house wasn't here. It had finally melted.'

I stop and draw her into me, overcome by affection.

'Dad still claims it was the only time he ever saw me inconsolable as a kid. I just wanted to make him proud.'

After a few moments I withdraw from the hug so that I can take her hands in mine, as though I'm about to say something sincere and comforting. 'And you call *me* a suck-up?'

She laughs, but it stumbles.

'What's up, Rebecca?'

She presses an index finger into the corner of each eye in turn, like she's trying to shove any tears back into their ducts.

'It's the sea breeze, it makes my eyes water.'

'There isn't a breeze, Becs.'

She digs her right foot into the pebbles, looks to the sky and sighs.

'I took a pregnancy test earlier.'

I feel like a puppet whose strings have been cut. My jaw just drops. And then it's like I'm on my deathbed, except the thing that's flashing before my eyes is not my life over the *last* twenty-seven years, but my life over the *next* twenty-seven, the life of an unborn child, which in my head is a boy, and I'm taking him to the park in his first-ever Man City top, and then I'm teasing him about the bum fluff on his chin, and then we're in the pub for his first legal pint.

'It was negative,' says Rebecca.

A heaviness swells inside my chest, and I realize it is disappointment. Neither of us says anything for what seems like minutes.

'I don't understand,' I say, confused. 'You're on the pill – how could it even be an issue?' I try to look into her eyes but they're playing dodgeball again. 'I mean, my boys are obviously good, but . . .'

I trail off. I guess the whys and wherefores aren't important right now.

'So this is why you've been so distant the last hour or two?'

'No.' She shakes her head but without conviction. 'I don't know.'

Rebecca starts walking again. I follow, intending to ask what she means, but she takes my hand and squeezes her fingers into my palm, and I know it is her way of acknowledging that she's not the easiest girlfriend.

'I reckon I'd be pretty good at all that dad stuff,' I eventually say.

'I reckon you would too,' she says. 'That's if . . .' She nods insinuatingly at my crotch.

'What?'

'Well, you've got to wonder after today's result whether your boys have got it in them.'

I stick out my foot to trip her but she sees it coming and mocks me with a *Ha*. We start to walk back, and as I hook my arm around her ribcage it dawns on me exactly why I'd wanted the pregnancy test to be positive. It would have given my life some kind of purpose, but I was being an idiot, because Rebecca already gave me that eleven months ago.

'I'd be lost without you, Becs.'

She glances up at me and smiles like she's prepared to tolerate my soppiness on this occasion. 'Aw.'

'No, seriously,' I say, looking around the town exaggeratedly. 'I've absolutely no idea where I am.'

She laughs, not even pretending to be scolded, and I think she knows that I wasn't joking first time around at all.

Chapter Four

REBECCA

Saturday, 4 October

The estate agent is late.

Ben and I sit on the steps outside a 'deceptively spacious and charming two-bed garden flat with original features' in East Greenwich, waiting for a woman called Liudvik. I drum the step with a baton made from three rolled-up property specs.

'What's the time?' I ask.

Ben looks at his watch. 'Two minutes since you last asked.'

I sigh. Twenty minutes late.

As far as steps go, they're not the best – crumbling so the edges are smooth rather than sharp, with cigarette butts jammed in the crevices. They're not enough to put me off, though. I'm realistic about what I can get. It won't be a showroom when I move in. But that's fine. Original features! That's far more my taste, and if it means I need to do it up a bit, so be it. That'll make it so much more my own.

'This takes the piss,' I groan, checking my phone for missed calls, and wondering how much of my annoyance is actually about the fact Ben never suggested we move in together.

I wonder if I'm the only one assuming we're long term. Maybe I've been assumptive. Ben's passion for things tends to be short lived.

'I know,' Ben admits. 'It is a bit . . . Oh look, this'll be her now.'

A red Mini screeches to a halt at a twenty-degree angle from the kerb.

'Sorry, sorry, sorry,' a lady cries in a heavy accent – Russian perhaps – as she jumps out of the car and hurries past us down to the front door. 'I'm Liudvik. Hope you veren't vaiting long?'

'Oh, don't worry about it,' Ben replies cheerily. 'I'm Ben, and this is Rebecca.'

'Hallo,' Liudvik replies, not looking our way as she tries one key after another.

'*Oh, don't worry about it,*' I mimic quietly in Ben's ear.

'I feel sorry for her,' Ben whispers back. 'She's a mess.' As he says it, our estate agent drops her folder on the floor, and papers fly everywhere.

'There,' she says with a smile as the door swings open, though her lip is trembling. 'This is lovely flat. You vill love.' Then she starts to pick up her notes, talking to herself.

Never believe an estate agent who tells you, *You vill love*. I should know this. I should also know 'charming' is just another word for 'little' and 'original features' means 'nothing has been updated since the building was built last century' – and not in an adorable, shabby-chic way, but in a can't-believe-this-hasn't-been-condemned-yet way.

And 'deceptively spacious'? Well, if you believe this is

spacious, you have indeed been deceived.

'It's kot charm, yes?' Liudvik says, stroking a wall, then examining her fingertips and wiping them on her trousers.

'If by charm you mean that you could have a shower and cook dinner at the same time, without missing the ten o'clock news, then yes, sure.'

I'm back to the front door eight seconds after starting my tour of the place.

'Sshhh,' Ben says with a titter. 'Hey, do you reckon I'd be a good estate agent?'

'But I thought you loved working in HR?'

'Maybe I could be a comedian, like you.'

Despite my teasing, I'm grateful he's here: his presence means it's becoming a funny story, as opposed to a tragic waste of my time, or indeed the tragic mystery of a Russian estate agent being found under the floorboards of a derelict flat in south-east London . . .

'Anyway,' she tells Ben while I inspect the bedroom again, 'I'd buy soon – it's popular area and this place has lots potential.'

'Potential' means 'currently shite', and it occurs to me I should probably drag Ben away from her before the impulsive spender in him says something li—

'I'll take it,' I hear him say.

'What the feck are you doing?' I cry, running through. 'I don't want to live in this hellhole.'

I arrive in time to see Liudvik handing Ben her pile of paperwork.

'She couldn't get that closet open with one hand,' Ben explains.

I sigh, relieved.

'I just don't understand how they can get away with

charging so much for this,' I tell him.

Liudvik tilts her head and looks at me like I'm an idiot.

The reason for this becomes clear once I've seen the other two places. Turns out the first one was pretty good for my budget. The second one, described as 'a blank canvas', is so blank it has no toilet, shower or sink. The last one isn't an actual home. Seriously, back when the whole building was someone's mansion, the section Liudvik is trying to flog me was probably used to house the dustpan and brush. Not even a Hoover – Henry would have refused the living conditions.

'What do you reckon?' asks Ben, though my face says it all.

'I need a drink. Let's say bye to the Russian and get the hell out of here.'

'She's Ukrainian.'

'How do you know?'

'I was chatting to her about it earlier.'

Course he was, friendly bastard.

'That was the most depressing experience of my life.' I throw myself dramatically into our booth at Arch 13 and slump over the table. 'Why does Danielle have to move out?' I sigh heavily. 'I don't want to live by myself.'

Ben looks at me as though he's confused.

'What?' I ask.

'Nothing,' he says, reviewing me for a second or two longer before his face returns to normal. 'So what are you going to do?'

I sigh. That's the two-hundred-thousand-pound question. 'Maybe I should widen my search. Try somewhere a bit more up and coming?'

'Estate-agent-speak for currently down and out?'

61

'Maybe I should ask for a bigger mortgage.'

'Maybe you should give yourself a bit more time. There's no rush to buy, is there?'

'Maybe I should sell a kidney.'

'Maybe we should live together.'

'Maybe I should—' I sit bolt upright. 'Hang on, what?'

'What?' he echoes.

'Did you just say . . . ?'

'Yeah, OK.' He adjusts himself in his seat like he's trying to get comfortable, though he ends up in the same position he started. 'I said it: we could live together. If you like. I thought you wanted to live by yourself, but if you don't, I'm just saying, I . . .' He shuffles in his seat again. 'Look, I don't want to push you into anything. But it's my last chance to say anything, so . . .'

I stare at him, baffled. 'Ben, do you want to move in together or not?'

He stares back. 'Yes, yes, yes, yes, yes.'

'You need to be clearer, Ben . . . Is that a yes?'

'YES.'

'Why haven't you asked before? I figured you were having doubts about us, or you weren't ready or something.'

'Doubts? I'm not having doubts, you wally – I wanted to ask but then at your dad's you said you couldn't imagine living at the flat with anyone else, and then you started to look for somewhere to live by yourself.'

'I didn't think I had a choice – you never asked. So, er . . .' I shrug, unable to stop a smile spreading across my face. 'Are we doing this?'

'I'm in if you are?'

'I'm in.' Relief washes over me – he *is* in this for the long haul.

He grabs my head and kisses my lips, laughing at my scrunched-up face.

'Put her down, Nicholls, and drink your beer,' interrupts Jamie, placing a pint in front of Ben, followed by a glass that clinks with ice as he slides it towards me. 'And a Scotch for the lady.'

'I can't see any ladies,' says Danielle, appearing in a puff of Chanel No. 5. 'Sorry I'm late.'

'Not like you,' says Jamie with a wink. 'Drink?'

'Mojito please.'

'Coming up.'

'Hang on a bit, mate,' says Ben. 'We have something to tell you.'

'We're moving in together,' I add quickly, in case they think we're about to announce an engagement or something ludicrous like that.

Is that ludicrous?

Yes, of course it is.

'No big deal,' I add, squeezing Ben's hand under the table and watching Danielle to see her reaction. I can't fool my best mate – she'll know it's a massive deal.

'Of course it's a big deal,' says Jamie, patting Ben's shoulder then mine. 'You can have those drinks on the house.'

'You were going to charge us for these?' asks Ben.

'Thank goodness for that,' Danielle says to no one in particular. 'When she texted saying the house hunt was horrendous, I was worried I'd be stuck with her for ever.' Then to me: 'Nice one, Becs. So will you stay in the flat?'

'We haven't really discussed it,' I admit, looking at Ben.

'Yeah,' he agrees. 'This is pretty much breaking news you walked into. Might make sense until I can save a bit more towards a deposit.'

'Will Russ and Tom mind?' I ask.

'Nah, it was just the two of them there before I moved in – they were doing me a favour, to be honest. I can move in as soon as Danielle can get out.'

'No need to sound so excited about it,' says Danielle, giving Ben a shove. 'But I can move any time. Next weekend if you want?'

'That'd be perfect,' I say, then seeing Danielle pout, add: 'I mean, that'll be really sad.'

'I want tears!'

'I'll be crying on the inside,' I promise.

'Let's do that, then,' says Ben, clapping his hands together. 'That's just before our anniversary.'

'He's taking me away on a surprise,' I tell the others, before turning to Ben, who's still grinning. I grin back.

'Do you have seven hundred pounds to give Danielle for her deposit?' I ask.

'Yeah.' He lowers his voice. 'We'll also need a new dining table.'

'Definitely.' I chuckle. 'And a new sofa, come to think of it – that's Danielle's too.'

'And a new bed.' He turns to the others, looking smug. 'The springs have gone on Rebecca's old one.'

'Yep, it never really recovered from my student days,' I say, trying not to smile.

Jamie pats Ben's back sympathetically. 'And on that note, I'll get back to work.'

There's a gaggle of giggling girls waiting for him at the bar. He's still chatting to one of them when Ben and I finish our drinks and Ben gets up to replenish them. 'Same again?'

'Please,' I reply.

'While you're there,' Danielle yells at Ben's retreating

back, 'tell Jamie to stop flirting with Tidy Tania and make my bloody Mojito.'

She moves up into the space Ben has just vacated to sit next to me.

'Has Tidy Tania still got a boyfriend?' I wonder aloud.

'Yep.'

'That's a shame.'

'It is, but anyway . . . I can't believe you're moving in with a boy.' Her tone is disapproving but her smile tells me she's teasing.

'We lived with Jamie for years,' I remind her.

'You know what I mean. A *boy* boy.' I do know what she means. 'Are you scared?'

'Nah, I'm excited. It's Ben. It'll be easy.'

'How do you know Ben's The One?'

It's not a question I was expecting, and I nearly shrug and say *I don't know*, or quip that I'm still deciding whether he is or not. But something about Danielle's tone and the sad way she keeps glancing at her mobile on the table makes me reconsider. She's opening up. We don't do it often – not because we don't trust each other, just because we don't feel the need to. But if she's showing me her vulnerable side, I'll show her mine.

'And don't be a prick and say, *You just know*,' she adds scornfully when I open my mouth to reply.

'I wasn't going to say that!' I protest. I was totally going to say that.

So I give it more thought, searching for an answer in the bottom of the empty glass I'm still holding. How do I know Ben's The One?

I don't know how to explain the way I feel when Ben looks at me. Like everything around me just disappears. And it doesn't sound enough to say it's because of how

65

much we laugh together, and how everything turns into an adventure, even if it's a game of Scrabble on a rainy day.

'Got it,' I say finally, with a decisive finger snap. 'They find your faults endearing.'

Danielle looks sceptical, so I continue . . .

'Like, you know how you always moan that I'm a bit messy?'

'A total slovenly slut.'

'Whatever. It annoys you I'm not as tidy as you, but Ben doesn't mind. He thinks it's cute.'

'Cute? Seriously?'

It's true. When I'm at Ben's, he laughs in bemusement at the discovery of my left shoe in the middle of the living room, when he's already picked up the right one from the hall floor. And after breakfast at Dad's last Sunday he walked into the kitchen while I was trying to force the door shut on the overflowing dishwasher. I was groaning in frustration, so he wrapped his arms around me and kissed my creased forehead, telling me I was adorable when I was angry. Then he emptied the clumsily loaded machine, smiling and shaking his head at the same time as he scraped the food off the plates, before systematically reloading it.

'Seriously. And I know I break his balls about him being such a softie, but it's one of the things I love most about him. Did he tell you about the donkey he's adopted in Ireland, by the way?'

'Is its name Shane?'

I snort. 'I wouldn't mind but he's already got an elephant in India, a tiger in Malaya and a child in Africa.'

'Soppy sod.'

'Totally. But you know what?' I lower my voice even though Ben is way out of earshot over at the bar. 'I think I knew he was The One that first night I met him in here.'

A cloud passes over Danielle's face and I mentally kick myself. That was the night that she and Shane broke up.

When she got in the next morning I'd started banging on about Ben and giving Jamie the napkin, but she barely said a word. I'd never seen her like that – it really hit her hard this time.

Danielle sighs and smiles. 'You guys are dead lucky, Rebecca – you know that?'

'Not as lucky as whoever you end up with,' I say. 'And that's not Shane. It'll be someone way more special than Shane.'

'You think?' she says, picking up her phone and glancing at the screen.

'Yes,' I insist. 'He'll have to be pretty special if he's going to find your singing endearing. And you'll only recognize him when he comes along if you get Shane out of your head.'

'He's not in my head. I'm, like, totally over him.'

'Then delete his number.'

'I can't,' she says, like I asked her to poke her own eye out.

'I can.' I grab her mobile.

'No!'

'Why?' I hold it in the air.

'Because I . . . I might . . . I should . . . Oh, fine! Do it.'

I press some buttons and a few seconds later, Shane is erased.

'That's fine,' she says. 'I don't care. Not. A. Bit.'

She drums her long fingernails on the table top in a show of indifference.

'I've never seen you look so devastated.'

'That's about not living with you after the weekend. Nothing to do with Shane.'

'Danielle?' I say, playing with a coaster and feeling my cheeks redden. Why am I so crap at this? I can't even have a sentimental moment with my best friend without feeling like a dick. 'You know I'll miss you, right? I love living with you. I know I sound excited about living with Ben but I'm really sad too, that we won't be living together any more.'

'Oh, Rebecca,' she cries, shifting right up next to me so she can wrap her arms around me and squeeze me so hard that I wouldn't be able to get my arms free to reciprocate the hug even if I wanted to.

'I know you're not enjoying this,' she mumbles into my shoulder. 'Neither am I. But this is what girls do, so get on board.'

Neither Danielle nor I are touchy-feelers; it's one of the reasons we work.

'For the love of God, pull yourself together,' I tell her, though I'm smiling.

'That's OK,' Ben says, appearing with a tray. 'I've got this. You two just have a cuddle.'

Danielle breaks away to pick up a food menu. She pulls a face. 'We eating?'

Ben and I pull the same face. If one thing lets this place down, it's the food, but we can feel ourselves settling in for the evening.

'Or,' I say slowly, 'when we start to get hungry we could just start ordering cocktails that have fruit on the side.'

'Yep, that's a better plan,' Danielle agrees, slamming the menu back down. 'Here comes Jamie.'

'I meant to ask you guys,' Jamie says, squeezing in my side of the horseshoe booth with a beer while Ben gets in the other end next to Danielle. 'How'd it go with Padre Giamboni?'

'Good,' Ben and I say slowly at the same time, our eyes meeting in an unspoken pact not to bring up the slightly wobbly bit of the weekend. It couldn't have gone better otherwise.

'Rebecca's dad is lovely,' Ben adds.

'Isn't he?' Danielle says dreamily.

'Don't do that,' I tell her.

'I'm just saying, he's a single, eligible man—'

'No, don't go there,' I warn.

'And you probably don't realize this because he's your dad but he's really rather—'

'No, no, no, no, no.' I put my fingers in my ears.

'And I probably would,' I still hear her say.

'My dad could do way better than you,' I tell her with a grin, then take a big gulp of whisky. 'He really liked Ben, though. So did Stefan.'

'I reckon Stefan fancied me a bit,' says Ben.

'Stefan fancies Jamie,' I tell him.

Jamie gives a nonchalant shrug. 'He's only human.'

Chapter Five

BEN

Sunday, 26 October

'Happy anniversary, Becs,' I say.

I kiss her as I put down the picnic basket, and together we approach the very edge of the cliff. I was scared of heights when I was little, but I was fine when I went up The Shard with Rebecca, and the London Eye with Russ and Tom, so the queasiness I feel when I peer down at the waves crashing into the foot of the cliff comes as a shock.

'Shouldn't there be a yellow line or something?' I say. 'Like at train stations, to stop you getting too close?'

'Why did you bring me to Beachy Head if you're scared of heights?'

I ignore her mocking eyes and open my arms for her to walk into.

'I'm not scared of heights,' I tell her. 'And I brought you here because I've seen the way you look at the painting in your bedroom.'

'*Our* bedroom,' she corrects, nuzzling herself into me. 'It looks exactly like the picture, doesn't it? The light-house, everything.'

Sensing that she's having a moment, I swallow my nausea and stand with her for several minutes.

'Come on,' she finally says.

I unfurl a blanket and start unloading the food while a cloud the size of Russia shoves itself in front of the sun.

'Do you want my coat?' I say, gesturing for her to sit.

'I'm fine.' She follows my instruction, crossing her legs. 'Thanks, though.'

'I know October isn't exactly perfect picnic weather.'

'Don't worry, I'm warm-blooded,' she says. 'And this *is* perfect. If it was sunnier we wouldn't have the place to ourselves.'

We make light work of the sandwiches I've prepared – half BLT, half cheese and pickle, the whole lot cut into quarter triangles – and wash them down with black coffee (Becs) and tea (me) from the flasks I bought especially.

'Had you been looking for someone?' Rebecca says, batting away strands of hair that the wind has swept across her face.

'What do you mean?'

'A year ago, before we got together – had you been looking for someone?'

I go to read her expression but it's illegible.

'I guess I was always looking for some*thing*,' I say.

She places her palms on the turf behind her and leans back in anticipation.

'I spent my life jumping from obsession to obsession,' I say, 'trying to work out what the point of everything was.'

She bites her bottom lip at one side, trying not to smirk, a mannerism I've become very familiar with over the past year.

'That's why I went travelling after uni,' I say, following the slow progress of the meteorological Russia with my eyes. 'I thought I'd find whatever it was, and I had the best time, but sometimes . . .'

A gust of wind causes me to shiver and now her smirk does come. 'Do you want *my* coat?' she says, raising her voice to compensate for the breeze.

'Oh, get stuffed.'

'Sorry, carry on . . .'

'I forgot where I was now.'

'I think you were looking for something.'

'Ta,' I say sarcastically. 'So, yeah, sometimes I found myself looking at some ancient ruins or a palace or whatever and it was like I was playing the *part* of an awestruck tourist. It didn't feel much different from looking at the photos on Google.' I laugh. 'I came back with even less idea what the point of everything was than when I left.'

'This feels like when you ask someone with limited English a question and they answer a completely different one.'

'Except instead of just smiling and nodding politely, you're taking the piss.'

Rebecca nods unashamedly.

'I am answering the question, though,' I say. 'Because I was still wondering what the point was when I turned up at Jamie's that night.'

Rebecca goes for some more coffee but it's all gone. I reach into my inside coat pocket and produce a hip flask full of her favourite whisky.

She thanks me with a squint.

'Continue,' she says after taking a swig.

I look out to the sea in an attempt to re-find my muse.

'That night was like the story of Christopher Columbus,' I say. 'He was actually on his way to Asia, trying to find a better route from Europe than the arduous journey across land, when he stumbled on an island in the Bahamas. That's how he discovered America.'

I did my dissertation on the birth of the United States. I think this might be the first time it's come in useful.

'What's your point?' she says.

'You're my America.'

Rebecca takes another reckless gulp of the whisky. 'Thanks. I think.'

She tightens the cap, slips the hip flask back into my inside pocket and kisses the tip of my nose before re-treating.

'Didn't you tell me Columbus died thinking he'd actually landed on Asia?' says Rebecca.

'That's not really the point.'

'I'm just saying: your analogy is kinda shit.'

'I was *kinda* working off the hoof.'

A year! It's mad, but I really have to try hard to re-call my life before Rebecca came along. It's like there was *Pre-Rebecca*, where I spent weekends on sticky dance floors wondering if I'd ever meet the right girl, and then *Rebecca*, where I spend weekends with the girl of my dreams, buying dining tables, couches and beds.

'Did you bring us dessert?' she asks.

I answer by pulling out a huge slab of her favourite salted caramel. Rebecca breaks it into several pieces with her knee and together we look out into the rainbow of blues, the dirty dishwater that crashes against the cliffs becoming a fish pond turquoise and eventually a deep sea blue. The further we stare, the deeper the colour, and even though it's been a year, I can still feel myself falling deeper and deeper.

'What went through your head when Jamie gave you the napkin the next morning?'

'I've told you that loads of times.'

It was a good while after I got her number that I realized what Rebecca does: she asks questions, bombards you with them, so she doesn't have to talk about herself. And that's normally fine, but for once I don't feel like indulging her.

'Tell me about the painting?' I say.

She doesn't answer straight away. Instead, she retrieves the hip flask, unscrews the cap and takes another swig, then she leans her back into my chest, so that I can smell her hair, the coconut of her shampoo. I fold my arms around her body.

'My mum came here and painted it a few months before I was born,' she eventually starts. 'Dad let me take it when I left for uni.' Rebecca adjusts her head towards the lighthouse momentarily. 'This, here, was her favourite spot in the world.'

We'd been going out about a month when I asked Rebecca why she never mentioned her mum, and she told me she'd died. She didn't go into details; just that it happened when she was really young. Whenever I've pressed her on it since she has told me it's a story for another time, and so here and now I say nothing for fear she'll become self-conscious and shut down.

'She died giving birth to me.'

Rebecca's voice is quivering and I feel a thick lump rise through my throat.

'Dad says she always dreamt of having a little girl, but as I arrived in the world, she left it.'

I sit there, stunned. I cannot even begin to imagine.

I realize now that Rebecca shuffled into me so that I couldn't see her face, nor she mine, as she told the story. I squeeze her tight and say nothing, knowing that comforting words would only make her feel uncomfortable.

'It's weird to think if she hadn't got pregnant with me, she'd still be here with Dad and Stefan.'

'You can't think like that, Becs.'

I hear her sniff, so I reach for a tissue, but when I twist around I see that she isn't crying. She just looks a bit dazed. I give her the tissue for her nose anyway.

'Thanks.'

I watch her examine it.

'How long has this been in your pocket?'

She laughs into the tissue, a snotty laugh that precedes blowing her nose.

'Whisky,' she instructs, and I oblige, watching her tilt her head back and forward again. She breathes into the burn.

'Do you and your dad speak about it much?' I ask. 'I mean, shit – you must have had so many questions when he told you.'

She shakes her head. 'There are questions but it's all in the past. I know he and Stefan never blamed me. We were a happy family but I always felt something was missing. That's why I ended up living in eight different countries in seven years – I think the only way my dad could move on was to throw himself into his work.'

The pieces start falling into place like Tetris. When she got upset at her dad's a few weeks ago – it wasn't just about the pregnancy test. We'd been speaking about her mum.

I want to tell her that talking to her dad might help, because no matter what she says, it is a little bit strange that we've been going out a year and this is the first time I'm hearing any of this. But the last thing I want is for her to regret opening up, so I decide it can wait for another time.

'I'm sure if your mum was here she'd think he did a pretty good job with you.'

Rebecca places a palm on to the back of my hand, a signal that the conversation is at an end. I become aware again of the sound of waves crashing into the bottom of the cliff, as though they'd been on pause while Rebecca was speaking.

'Come on, we're supposed to be celebrating.' She gets to her feet and holds out a hand for me to do the same. 'I think that last sip of whisky has gone to my head.'

Rebecca pulls my body into hers and we begin to move in tandem, a spontaneous slow dance with the sea and the wind providing the music, and as we sway together it's like I'm bursting with love, as though my body isn't big enough to hold it all in. Who gives a shit what the point is? This – *this* – is all that matters.

'The B and B we passed,' says Rebecca as we dance around the picnic blanket, laughing to ourselves. 'I think that's where Mum and Dad stayed the time she did the painting. I'd like to stay one time.'

'Let's do it tonight.'

She crooks her mouth dismissively. 'We have work tomorrow.'

'We can call in sick.'

'I can't call in sick. I can't even call in sick when I am sick.'

I feel like I've been told off, and it must show, because after a couple of seconds Rebecca gives me a soft smile.

'Come on,' she says. 'Let's find a pub.'

We pack away our stuff and set off.

'So, do you still want to go on the cable cars for your birthday?' she asks.

'Why wouldn't I?'

'Er, because you're scared of—'

'I'm not scared of heights!'

Rebecca laughs as we walk past a flock of sheep, the terrain rising towards the highest spot, 530 feet above the sea. We eventually come to a pub called The Beachy Head.

'How do you think they came up with the name?' jokes Rebecca, stopping to examine the stand-alone pub sign made wonky by the wind.

She steps closer, as if assessing the soundness of the steel frame with an architect's eye, but then her attention is drawn to something on the floor. When she picks it up I see that it is a ring with a chunky diamond cyst. She tries it on.

'Nice,' she says, examining her upturned hand. 'Not my cup of tea, but it's pretty.'

'Not your cup of tea?'

'I don't know,' she says eventually. 'It's nice, but kind of generic.'

'I'll make a note of that,' I say.

She rolls her eyes but her smile remains as we hand in the ring behind the bar, and right then the seed of an idea is planted in my mind.

Chapter Six

REBECCA

Saturday, 1 November

I pull the hood up on my parka to block out the wind as we all stand outside the Royal Victoria Dock waiting for Tom to arrive so we can get on the cable cars.

'Such a shame Jamie misses out on Saturday nights,' says Danielle.

'Tell me the last Saturday night we didn't end up in his bar anyway?' says Ben.

'True.'

'Brilliant,' mutters Russ under his breath, as Tom comes into view with a girl in tow. 'Avril's with him.'

'Sorry,' Ben says, shivering in another cold gust of wind. 'I couldn't not invite her.'

'Who?' asks Danielle, rubbing her leather-gloved hands together.

'Tom's girlfriend,' says Russ.

'Whatever you do, don't mention Avril Lavigne,' Ben tells Danielle and me.

Russ nods. 'I mentioned Avril Lavigne when I met her and it was like I'd pissed on her shins.'

'Thanks for the heads-up,' Danielle says with a laugh.

'Happy birthday, mate.' Tom moves a wrapped book-shaped present from his right hand to his left and greets Ben with a toothy grin and a handshake. I can't help but wonder if his over-enthusiasm is to balance out the fact that Avril looks like a hostage being led into a forest by a tribe of savages rather than to a cable car by a group of friends.

I squeeze Ben's arm as we board the glass carriage. By the looks of things, we've not got much daylight left.

'Don't look down,' I whisper to Ben as we make our slow ascent.

'Oh, eff off,' he says, shoving my shoulder with his.

'Hang on.' Russ cuts short whatever he's saying to Danielle to stare at Ben. 'Are you afraid of heights?'

'No, I used to—'

'Don't worry, Benji,' says Danielle, pulling two bottles of prosecco from her bag. 'This'll take the edge off.'

'Look, I'm not scared of heights.'

Russ cracks up. 'You are – you're scared of heights. What a girl.'

'What's that supposed to mean?' Avril says – her first full sentence since we met her.

Russ rolls his eyes as if to say, *Oh, here we go.*

'Are you implying that girls are in some way weaker in nature than men, and therefore more likely to be scared of heights?'

Like Tom, Avril is thin, though not as reedy as him. She's wearing a vest top and lacy cardigan, and a long pleated skirt that covers her shoes. Her dark wiry hair sprouts down to her shoulders underneath her beret. If I didn't already know she was a poet, I'd wonder if she was on her way to a fancy dress party dressed as a poet.

Not sure what Tom is supposed to be in his bowler

hat, but I'd bet money that accessory is Avril's doing.

'No, Avril,' says Russ wearily, 'I'm not implying that.'

'Where's Big Ben from here?' asks Tom, in an obvious attempt to diffuse tension.

'Wrong part of the Thames,' I say, eager to help him out.

'You know,' says Ben. 'George from the post room at work was telling me a flock of starlings once landed on the minute hand of Big Ben and set the time back five minutes.'

'That must be the moment you chose to set your watch,' I say to Danielle, making everyone laugh.

'Big Ben isn't actually the clock,' says Avril, looking around the group like we're all idiots. 'It's the—'

'Yes, we know,' says Danielle. 'It's the bell. Now, let's have a drink.' She passes round some plastic cups but Avril quickly grabs the one she's about to hand to Tom and gives it to Russ instead.

'We don't drink, do we, Tom?' she says.

Russ peers out through the glass wall and I can tell he's avoiding looking at anyone.

'Nope,' says Tom cheerily.

'I just don't feel like we need to drink in order to enjoy ourselves,' April adds condescendingly.

'What a fun sponge,' Danielle mutters to me, and I swear I see Avril's head twitch in our direction.

We toast Ben then float across the sky, sipping our drinks in silence for a minute, watching the sun sink behind the dome of the O2. A tension hangs in the air and I try to think of something to say to turn it around, desperate for Ben's day not to be spoiled.

'I've booked Gauchos for seven p.m.,' I share. 'Thought we could have a drink first.'

'I can't eat in Gauchos,' Avril barks at Tom, as if the rest of us aren't there. 'Vegetarians don't eat at steak restaurants.'

'There will be something on the menu for vegetarians,' I say with a confidence I don't feel. I'm already having to bite my tongue. If this were the other way around and a guy was controlling a girlfriend like this, everyone would go spare. How come it's acceptable the other way round?

Ben squeezes my hand, and I feel grateful how well matched we are. We might be different, but he still understands me. He's been great since I told him about my mum, seeming to sense that it's not something I want to talk about.

I attempt another change of topic. 'How's your love life, Russ?'

He answers with a pfft, then says: 'I've got a theory. I think the longer you're single, the longer you're likely to stay single. You become more desperate – and girls can smell it a mile off.' He laughs to himself. 'I fucking reek.'

Ben laughs. 'Like those forty-year-old cruise ship singers who audition on *X Factor* – you can see the desperation in their eyes.'

'And then there's all the bad habits you get stuck in. The only difference is their bad habits are singing out of their noses and waving their fists when they sing, mine are eating my dinner bang on six o'clock and taking a couple of comics with me to the bog.'

'Both would put me off,' says Ben.

'I fully understand, buddy,' he says. 'Rebecca, do you have any fit single mates that would go for me?'

'I don't know, Russ, I'll ask them. Danielle, would you go for Russ?'

Danielle laughs and looks ready to reply, but none of us will ever know what she was about to say. Because at that moment, Avril turns her lips to Tom's ear and says: 'If she does, you'll be the only one in your little trio she hasn't fucked.'

I don't get her joke, and look to the others, expecting them to share my confusion. But the others don't look confused. They look horror-stricken. I laugh into the silence, nervous for some reason, but no one joins me. And it dawns on me: it wasn't a joke.

Your little trio. That's how she refers to Russ, Tom and Ben.

The only one she hasn't fucked. What about Ben?

'What about Ben?' I say.

Tom chews his bottom lip, while the others stare at Avril in disbelief.

'What?' she says with a shrug. 'I didn't think anyone else could hear me.'

The pain is physical. My stomach clenches and my head spins. I feel dizzy, like I might throw up. Is this what Ben felt like when he was standing on the cliff edge at Beachy Head? I'm aware there's an argument unfolding but I'm still trying to process what I've just found out.

'You really have a way with words,' Danielle spits at one point. 'Tell me – has any of your poetry ever been fucking published?'

'Do you have a problem with me being a poet, Danielle?'

'No, I have a problem with you being a cunt, Avril.'

In my dumbfounded state, I almost laugh. Everyone's still talking over each other but I can't take any of it in. I'm vaguely aware of Ben and Danielle taking turns to repeat my name again and again, each time more urgent than the last, but I feel disconnected, like it's a TV in another room.

With my head pressed against the glass I watch the sun drop lower and lower, until the horizon burns bright orange. If I wasn't frozen to the spot, I'd take a picture – my camera is in my bag. Ben and I haven't got many pictures of just the two of us, we realized while rearranging the flat the day he moved in. I've bought him a frame for his birthday.

Ben slept with Danielle. That happened. Avril said so, and no one has denied it. That actually fucking happened.

I don't. That's what Ben said the night I met him when I implied everyone fancies Danielle.

I need to get out – why are we moving so slowly? I drop my face into my hands, as if by doing so no one can see me any more. I feel a hand on my back but I shrug it off violently. Finally I feel a jolt, and we're no longer moving.

'When?' I croak, and even though it was barely audible, everyone shuts up.

Please say never. Tell me I've got the wrong end of the stick.

Ben takes a deep breath. 'Ages ago. You and I weren't—'

I get up and leap towards the exit.

'Rebecca!' Ben says, as the glass door slides open. But I'm already halfway out.

Chapter Seven

BEN

I step off the cabin straight after Rebecca but already she is away, down the steps and through the barriers.

I check my pockets, panicking as Rebecca becomes smaller and smaller to my eyes. Where the fuck is my Oyster? I pat down my pockets one last time but there is nothing else for it.

Planting my arms on each side of the barrier, I vault it, clipping my left foot as I arch over but just managing to keep my balance.

A man shouts behind me as I accelerate into a jog. I glance back and see a ticket officer gesticulating at Danielle. The others watch me with concerned expressions, except for Avril, who is through the barriers herself and casually cupping her mouth to light a cigarette.

What the fuck was she thinking?

I notice heads turn as I break into a sprint. No one used to bat an eyelid when Jamie and I ran home from school. Is that how you know you're getting old? When you can't run without people staring? Why am I thinking about this now? I think it's because this whole situation seems surreal.

Let them stare. Rebecca is the only person that matters right now. I need to reach her, to explain.

I see that she's heading not towards the O2 but to North Greenwich station, so I zigzag round a parked car and twist left.

When I reach the station I stop momentarily to get my bearings. She'll be heading back to the flat or to Arch 13, which means she'll get the bus.

I start to run again, but there's no sign of her as I follow the line of bus stops that arcs around the station. At the final stop I turn, desperate and exhausted, and at last I see her, sitting on a bench in the shadow of a vending machine. I bathe in the relief for a second before stepping towards her.

She is pretending she never saw me sprint past, even though she must have. Her hands are tucked under her armpits, and her eyes are screwed up like she's concentrating hard on something. The frustration, and the fear of not knowing what she is thinking, is like a hand squeezing my heart.

I approach her gently, like a rare bird that has landed in the garden. She uses both hands to smooth her hair away from her face but still does not look at me.

When I sit on the other end of the bench she twists her position so I can no longer see her face, but within seconds she realizes the gesture is insufficient and stands.

'You're overreacting,' I tell her.

Silence.

This is what she's like in arguments: she locks the door and pulls down her shutters. That's why I never told her about sleeping with Danielle.

OK, that's not why I didn't tell her about sleeping with Danielle. I didn't tell her because what was the point? I would have been shooting myself in the foot. Soldiers actually did that during the First World War to get out of service. But I didn't want to get out of anything. I knew within a couple of dates that I was falling in love with Rebecca and I've never had a single doubt. What does it matter what happened before we started seeing each other?

'Can't we talk about it?' I say.

Rebecca bridles. 'Oh, suddenly you want to talk about it?' Her words are screams pretending to be whispers and doing a bad job. 'You're a year too late, Ben.'

The sun has disappeared, leaving smears of purples and dirty yellows like a bruised eye.

'It was before we . . .'

I see Rebecca glance self-consciously at a man who has approached the vending machine. He is reviewing the contents as though reading a book, left to right, top to bottom. Finally he puts in some coins.

'I want to spend the rest of my life with you, Becs. It's you I fell in love with.'

Vending machine man starts to bang his palm against the side of the machine, which obviously hasn't upheld its part of the contract. A few metres away a huddle is forming at the nearest bus stop.

'Tell me what I can do to make things right?' I try, but Rebecca's attention is elsewhere now, to a bus that is pulling in.

The man bangs harder, his fist clenched now, but nothing comes out.

'Don't come back to the flat tonight,' Rebecca says.

I go to say something but my brain is a fog. She stands up and moves away from me.

'Rebecca!'

'Don't follow me.'

The bus is one of the new ones that allows you to board at the front, middle or back, and I'm about to tell her that I'm going to need some stuff, but she has jumped the crowds and boarded at the back. I watch her disappear up the stairs.

I step forward to go after her but something holds me back. I know Rebecca, and if I cause a scene on the bus it will make things worse. Right now she just needs some space.

Vending machine man follows her on to the bus having given up on whatever he wanted. A few seconds later the bus is on its way, and I'm left alone on the concourse wishing that another flock of starlings would come along and turn back time.

I stand there, stunned, only vaguely conscious of a can clattering to the bottom of the vending machine.

If someone had told me when I woke up this is how my twenty-eighth birthday would end, I'd have laughed, but although it's fucked up, I know I should be grateful for one thing: that Rebecca doesn't know everything.

I just need to keep it that way.

Chapter Eight

REBECCA

Monday, 3 November

I can't believe it was just a month ago I sat there banging on to Danielle about how you know you've found The One when they find your faults endearing. What the hell did I know?

I pause at the door to review the living room before leaving for work. Two crusty cereal bowls decorate the coffee table; cushions hang off the sofa; the blanket I spent the whole of yesterday wrapped in is on the floor – partially covering the open pizza box and its one remaining slice of ham and mushroom; six half-drunk mugs of coffee sit on four different surfaces. *Six?* Christ, he's only been gone two days.

And then it hits me: there's no one here to find *this* endearing.

My phone vibrates once in my hand and I know without looking that it's a text from Ben. I unlock my keypad and let my thumb hover for a second. Any affectionate thoughts I feel for him and his ninja-like ability to clear up after me are short lived. The image of him and Danielle in bed together seeps back into my consciousness, followed by the image of his face as I boarded the bus and pulled out of North Greenwich station, and I feel wretched again.

This is what it's been like all weekend. I'd miss him and my phone would ring, and it would occur to me that all I would need to do to put an end to feeling like this was to answer it. But then the visions would come. Images so vivid I felt like I was there, watching Danielle kneeling on the bed dressed only in matchy-matchy underwear (I wish I didn't know that she religiously coordinates her knickers and bra), and undoing the buttons on Ben's shirt. Then running her hand down the dark cluster of hair on his abdomen and reaching for his belt.

At one point I had to run to the loo and throw up the pizza, my mobile ringing away in the background.

Still standing at the door, I ignore his text and punch the word *cleaner* into my phone, then email it to myself before shoving the door closed behind me.

My bike is leaning against Ben's in the downstairs hall, nestled under its handlebar, as though his bike has its arm around mine.

'For fuck's sake, Ben!' I complain as I try to wrestle it free. I mean, strictly speaking this isn't Ben's fault but blaming him for everything helps. I need to stay angry because feeling angry doesn't feel as bad as feeling betrayed and hurt and stupid.

'Everything OK?' the heavily pregnant woman from the flat downstairs asks passive-aggressively as she opens her door. What did Ben say her name was again?

'Fine,' I mumble as the bikes separate. 'Thanks.'

The ride does its job of clearing my head, and as I chain up my bike I feel relieved to be at work. I considered pulling a sickie for the first time ever this morning. I barely slept all weekend so when the alarm went off at six o'clock, I defiantly pulled the quilt over my head and thought, *Bugger that for a game of soldiers*. But after a few minutes I lost my resolve and dragged myself out of bed, determined not to let this throw me off course, and I'm glad I did. There's something comforting about being at work. From the imposing framed prints of buildings hanging in reception to the distinctive smell of freshly vacuumed carpets. It's just any old normal Monday, I tell myself.

Having to shower in the crappy cubicle is the only drawback of cycling to work, but I'm in and out in minutes. Then, after shaking my hair out of the shower cap, putting on a little make-up and slipping into a smart black shift dress, I'm back in reception.

'How did you do that?' Jemma asks, handing me a tea. 'It was like watching a contestant in *Stars in Their Eyes* walk through that screen and come out transformed. Except as a sexy architect instead of an eighties pop star.'

I blush and thank her for the tea, planning to sneak out to Pret for a coffee in an hour or so.

'Think I might divert my phone to reception,' I say before I head up. 'If I get any calls just tell them I'm busy.'

At my desk, I chuck my mobile back in my bag so I won't clock whether Ben and Danielle add to the barrage of texts they sent yesterday. I do feel bad for not answering Jamie's calls and messages, but right now I'm too scared to find out whether he knew about this all along. That would make him more Ben's friend than my friend and I've never wanted to think of him that way.

Opening Outlook with trepidation, I find emails from

Ben and Danielle. I leave them all unread.

I reply to my cleaner email with, ***Tidy up after yourself, you lazy cow.***

Then, focusing on the task at hand, I dig out the ground-floor plans I made last week and head into Jake's office for our catch-up.

I know where I am with my work. The lines aren't blurry on floor plans – they're solid and clean. Either they are there or they aren't, and whether or not anyone has crossed them isn't debatable. Why couldn't it have been the same with my relationship? Am I just crap at that side of things? I keep thinking back, looking for clues that it wasn't as perfect as I thought it was, but I can't find anything, which makes me feel like even more of an idiot.

My boss taps his sticky-outy bottom lip as he examines the pages, then looks me in the eye. He's about to ask something serious – I can tell.

'You'll be honest with me, won't you?'

I nod, wide-eyed. 'Course.'

'Do you think I should shave my head?'

I glance at my designs, then back at Jake.

'Sorry?'

'My hair is getting thinner and thinner. It's making me look old. But will I look even older if I'm bald?'

I'd never seen this anxious, vulnerable side to Jake until his wife left him last year, a week before he turned fifty, and he developed an obsession with his appearance. The first thing he did was put himself on a no-carb, high-protein diet that made him look puffy and aged – his face looked like an over-baked potato with two raisins stuck in it.

'Um, no.' I shake my head. 'Bald is good.' But not

wanting to add to his paranoia, I quickly add: 'Your hair doesn't look thin, though.'

He smiles. 'Beautiful.'

'Sorry?'

'Your designs,' he says, tapping the page. 'You're thinking like a senior architect.' I breathe a sigh of relief that we're back to talking about work.

The subtext is clear. Senior architect is the next step on the ladder for me. If I can stay on top of the cinema project, that's what Jake could promote me to.

I thank him, then manage to go the rest of the day without having a proper conversation with anyone. This is deliberate – I'm scared conversing will lead to me having to admit what happened at the weekend, and then inevitably whoever I'm talking to will want to offer me words of advice, and I just don't want it. No one here even knows Ben. There's nothing anyone has to say that can help me. And I don't want everyone knowing my private life.

At five o'clock my phone rings, making me jump. I wonder why it's not gone through to Jemma, then I realize it *is* Jemma.

'Hello?'

'Only me,' she says. 'I've got your boyfriend on the line. Says he cannae get through on your mobile so I thought you might want to take this one.'

'No, just take a message, please.'

I try to make my voice sound normal.

'It sounds like it might be urgent.'

'It's probably not.'

'But what if there's been an accident or something, and—'

'Look, there's not been an accident,' I snap. 'I don't

92

want to take the call. He's not my boyfriend any more.'

'Oh,' she says. 'Righteo.'

I feel bad when I hang up; I hope I didn't offend her.

But then she turns up at my desk five minutes later carrying two cups of tea in one hand and a packet of chocolate digestives in the other, and I sort of wish I had offended her because then this wouldn't be happening.

'So what happened?' she asks, wheeling over a chair to join me at my desk.

I pretend to be concentrating on something on my screen. I can't talk about this here.

She dips a biscuit in her mug. 'Are you OK?'

'Yep, I'm fine.' My throat feels dry so I sip my tea.

'But you've been together more than a year. You said it was serious.'

I shrug, feeling the blood pound in my head. 'I guess it wasn't.'

She looks into my eyes – presumably in search of red rims or puffiness. 'But aren't you upset?'

'I'm not much of a crier.'

I'm crying a frickin' river on the inside, if the truth be told, but the truth doesn't need to be told to someone I've known for a few weeks.

'Well, I guess you've loads of time to meet someone else,' Jemma figures, reaching for another biscuit.

'Sure, but that's not really what I'm—'

'I mean, how old are you? Thirty? Thirty-two?'

'I'm only twenty-seven,' I point out, aghast.

'You're *my* age? I thought you were way older.'

Well, this is cheering me up.

'Oh, you don't look old,' she says quickly when she sees dismay in my face. 'I figured you used some super-fancy moisturizer to keep you looking so young. I just mean that you seem old. Not in a bad way – just really together, and sorted. You have a proper career and you have this really mature, dignified aura about you.'

I force a smile. 'Thanks. And really, I'm OK.'

I'm only OK when I don't think about it. Maybe I'll stay late tonight and get ahead with my work. There's more to distract me here than there is at home.

'Ah, it was you that ended it?'

'What makes you say that?'

'That's why you're OK. You don't need time to get over it if you have all the power.'

'What power?'

'The relationship power. Whoever does the dumping has it all. That's why if you think you're about to get dumped you should get in there first and dump them. Then you have the power. They'll forget they were about to dump you and they'll want you back.'

'I don't think Ben was about to dump me,' I tell her, confused.

'Doesn't matter. Just know that because *you* dumped *him*, you're in control. You can still have him if you want him.'

Do I want him back? Yes. No? I don't know. The only power I want is the power to make Ben and Danielle sleeping together a thing that never happened, but that's impossible.

'It must work,' Jemma insists. 'It can't be a coincidence that I always get dumped, and they're always over me like *that*.' She clicks her fingers with a grin.

That makes me laugh – a real, proper laugh, for the first time since I stepped off the cable car on Saturday – and as I wipe the tears from under my eyes I pray she thinks they're all from the laughter.

I work until 8 p.m., then leave the office feeling shitty. As I cycle away, I try to clear my head and concentrate on the journey, but there's too much going on in there.

Like what am I going to have for dinner? Ben used to have it ready for me when I got home. I can't cook for toffee. And I still have to clean up. Then I remember the bins were meant to go out last night but before I can beat myself up too much about it a horn sounds loudly, and I realize I've just narrowly missed a collision with a white van. Thankfully he doesn't get out or wind down his window. Not that he needs to – the expletives he's mouthing are fairly unambiguous.

I pull over to the pavement while I wait for my heart rate to return to normal. That really was Ben's fault – my mind isn't on the road. And I know why.

There's something I've been avoiding that suddenly can't wait any longer. Someone I need to talk to. I jump down off my bike as I speed dial his number. It rings for ages and I'm just about to give up when I hear his voice.

'Rebecca! Thank God you called, how are—'

'Be honest, Jamie,' I interrupt. 'Did you know?'

Chapter Nine

BEN

Tuesday, 4 November

Benjamin Franklin once said that he who can have patience can have what they will. But then if Rebecca is my America, why the hell would I listen to someone who signed the Declaration of Independence?

Also, did Benjamin Franklin ever have to spend three nights concertinaed between the rigid arms of Jamie's leather couch? I don't think so. Did he ever have to wait three days for Mrs Franklin to reply to one of his telegrams?

Actually, they probably did take about that long, but even so, Benjamin Franklin can do one. I'm going round to the flat tonight. We can talk. That's what normal people do.

I've been waiting so long for any form of contact from Rebecca that I've started to develop survival techniques. That's what it's come to. For example, I put my phone out of reach at night. I slide it across the floor before switching off the light so I can't check it every two minutes.

I look at it now, strewn on the Formica, and if I hadn't

been staring at it relentlessly for days, I'd write to David Blaine and Paul Daniels and apologize for ever doubting them, and admit that magic really does exist, because it buzzes, right before my eyes. But I *have* been staring at it relentlessly for days, so David Blaine and Paul Daniels can do one too.

With most of my body still planted in a sleeping bag, I make a dive for it, keeping my feet on the couch so that I resemble a participant in a wheelbarrow race. Balancing on one hand and stretching with the other, I manage to snatch the phone without falling flat on my face.

My heart is thumping a techno beat.

Put the kettle on, Jamie has written.

'Tit,' I say out loud.

I allow myself to collapse on to the floor, where I sweep away the phone with my arm and watch it slide over the veneer towards the kitchen before ricocheting off the foosball table towards Jamie's bedroom, right at the moment his door opens. He stops and inspects the phone, which lands near his bare toes, and then me, a wounded Y on his floor, and he doesn't look as confused as you might expect.

'I'm not even going to ask.'

He heads to the kitchen and places a hand on the still-cold kettle.

'I think there may be something wrong with your phone, mate.'

I return to the couch. 'I thought it might be Rebecca.'

He stands by the kettle, not saying anything, as it starts to boil.

'I spoke to her last night,' he finally says. 'She said you texted her seven times yesterday.'

'You spoke to her? How is she?'

97

'On the verge of getting a restraining order, I expect.' He shakes his head. 'She wanted to know whether I'd known all along.'

'What did you say?'

'The truth – that I was as shocked as her. How could you and Danielle have *done it* without me finding out?' I sense him looking at me for an answer. 'How come neither of you told me?'

'We've been through this,' I say wearily, and then to change the subject: 'I'm going around there tonight.'

'I don't think she's ready yet, mate. Just give her a few more days.'

'For fuck's sake – I can't keep borrowing your clothes for ever.'

He pours the tea, adding half a sugar to mine, just how I like it.

'It wasn't seven.' I reach for my phone and go over to show him the messages, vindicated.

He takes the device from me. 'Mate, there are one, two, three . . . seven messages here without reply, and that's just yesterday.'

'Look at the times, though.' I point to the screen. 'Five of them were sent within three minutes of each other. Anything sent within a three-minute window only counts as one message, everyone knows that.' I return to the couch with my tea. 'Plus, rules go out the window in an argument – that's what we told Danielle when she was texting Shane.'

'I've got to get ready for a delivery at the bar,' he says, carrying his mug into his bedroom. 'Stop being a loon.'

Russ is scribbling on a notepad when I get to my desk, his tongue jabbed into the side of his cheek like a kid who's concentrating really hard on algebra.

'Morning,' I say to him and Tom.

Russ looks me up and down. 'Don't people usually let themselves go when they get dumped? How come you're dressing better?'

'I haven't been dumped,' I say. 'Yet.'

Tom bows his head guiltily so that his floppy hair resembles a lampshade. 'Avril really couldn't be sorrier,' he says.

Russ harrumphs, and I find that hard to believe myself, but I don't want to take it out on Tom. 'It's not your fault, mate.'

'You could have stayed in your old room, buddy,' says Russ.

I smile, grateful, but we both know it wasn't an option. Avril's always there, and I'd end up shoving the beret down her throat.

'I deliberately drank all her organic soy milk yesterday, if that makes you feel any better?' says Russ.

'That was my organic soy milk,' says Tom, but it's a quiet clarification rather than a protest.

Russ shakes his head as though he pities Tom. A few minutes later, once Russ is distracted by whatever he's writing on the notepad, Tom deposits a present on my desk.

'I didn't get a chance to give you it on your birthday.'

I open the present.

'Is this the book you were telling me about?' I say, examining the sleeve with a grin.

I couldn't stop raving about the Sistine Chapel when Rebecca and I got back from our trip to Rome, and Tom said he knew a great book on how it came to be. He nods now to confirm that's what it is.

'Ta, mate,' I say, touched.

Russ loops his eyes into their sockets. 'I'd have got you a present if it was a proper birthday, like twenty-one or thirty. Did I mention it was my thirtieth in a few weeks?'

I still can't believe Russ is almost thirty. He looks twelve.

'No, I don't think so,' I say.

'Er, yes, yes I did – end of Nov—'

'I'm pulling your leg, Russ. You've mentioned it about fifty-eight times.' I look at his notepad. 'What are you writing?'

'Diane from Match.com says she won't go on a date until we've spoken on the phone.' He tries balancing the Biro between his top lip and nose, but it falls into his lap. 'I'm making a list of things to talk about.'

'What've you got so far?' I ask, happy to be having my mind taken off things.

'OK, so . . . If she could be any animal what would she be?' He looks at me and I nod encouragingly. 'Top five superheroes? And why is she single?'

'Can I be there when you make the call?' I say.

Russ slaps his notepad shut with a grunt. 'At least my pathetic excuse for a life is good for something,' he says. 'That's the first time I've seen you smile all week.'

I switch on my PC, hoping there'll be an email from Rebecca waiting for me.

'I'm going to tell her my battery's low,' says Russ. 'Then if it gets awkward I can just hang up and pretend my battery died.'

I'm vaguely aware of Tom attempting a joke, and Russ calling Avril something rude in retaliation, but I've zoned out, because my dodgy monitor has finally stopped flickering and my screensaver has appeared. It's a photo of me and Rebecca outside the Colosseum, the day before our visit to the Sistine Chapel. Rebecca took it with an outstretched arm, sacrificing our chins for the iconic arches that she couldn't stop staring at. Suddenly I feel like a troop of Cub Scouts are practising knots in my stomach, and it's almost a relief when I feel a hand on the back of my chair.

'Can I have a word, please, Ben?' says our MD, using both hands to mime talking.

Nigel Richardson has a habit of illustrating everything he says in mime, as though everyone around him is deaf. When we get to his office and he tells me about a proposal to kill off all of London's ticket offices, he uses a pretend knife to slash his throat.

'What about all the staff?' I say, trying not to cough at the Brut fumes that follow Richardson everywhere.

'It's just a proposal from the directors at this stage. I wanted to bring in HR to bounce around,' he bounces his hand here, 'some ideas.'

People are always surprised I work in HR, but that's because they think it's all about disciplinaries and sacking people. Actually, most of the time it's about *giving* people jobs, or helping them get on in their careers, and when shit does go down, I see it as my role to make it as difficult as possible for the bosses to get rid of people.

'For a start you'd have to create a watertight business case,' I say, crossing my arms.

'Well, it's the twenty-first century.'

He points to the calendar and I frown, not following.

'If you want to know how to get from South Ealing

to Angel,' Richardson explains, 'you don't waste your time going to the ticket office – you look on your smart-phone.'

I pat my pocket and I realize I left *my* phone at my desk.

'Oyster cards, debit cards – the world is going contact-less.'

That's true enough: Rebecca has been completely con-tactless since Saturday night.

'But seriously, what happens to the staff?' I say. 'I mean, you have to look into whether they can be re-posted, and you'll need to go through consultation, possibly with Acas, and because the numbers of re-dundancies might be quite high we'll probably have to inform the relevant government departments, and obvi-ously there's industrial action to think about, and—'

'The directors are coming in on Friday – do you think you'd be able to come up with a document on all this for then?'

'Friday?'

It's doubtful I'll be able to get anything comprehen-sive down on paper by then, especially with my head as it is, but I badly want to get back to my phone, so I nod and tell him *Yeah, no problem*.

'One more thing,' says Richardson, standing to accom-pany me from his office. 'You're looking very smart again today, I like it.'

I always thought Jamie and I dressed pretty similarly but apparently not.

'Ta.'

There are no texts and no emails waiting for me when I go back to my desk. I check the time. One hour and forty-seven minutes of the working day without making contact. Benjamin Franklin would be proud, I think to myself as I walk towards the door, sensing Russ and Tom following me with concerned eyes.

Once outside, I press my thumb on Rebecca's name in my phone and smile politely at Michelle from Accounts, who is standing by the revolving doors smoking a cigarette. I walk down the street for privacy.

You've reached the voicemail of Rebecca Giamboni. Leave your name and number and I'll get back to you.

I close my eyes at the sound of her voice, remembering the conversation we had after the first time I heard her voicemail. I told her Voicemail Rebecca was a bit curt, and she joked that she couldn't speak right now and I should leave a message after the tone. Then when I started talking again she cut me off with a *beeeep*, just like the one I'm listening to now.

'Becs, it's me. I love you, I miss you. Call me back.'

I'm lolled on the couch, music drifting from my phone, which hasn't buzzed all afternoon, when I hear a key in the door.

'I thought you were working tonight?' I say.

'Thought you might appreciate the company.' Jamie puts down a plastic bag and starts leafing through his post. 'You heard from her yet?'

I shake my head. 'I feel like my life is on hold.'

'In which case . . .' He discards some junk mail into the bin and points an accusatory finger towards my phone. '. . . can we change the hold music? This is fucking depressing.'

'It's Damien Rice – one of the best—'

'It's wank, is what it is.'

Jamie comes over and snatches my phone.

'This from the fella who has a signed Chas 'n' Dave disc on his living-room wall,' I say.

He returns to the worktop, picks up the plastic bag and dangles it in the air. 'Thought we could have a beer by the river?'

I'd wanted to keep a clear head in case Rebecca calls back, and it's getting dark, but he has taken the night off, and got beers.

We take up a position on the concrete bank just outside his apartment, legs dangling half a metre above the water. Jamie pulls two cans from the plastic bag, tossing one into my waiting hands.

'Where'd you get to last night?' I ask.

It was past three a.m. when I heard the door.

'Lock-in.' He pulls the tab and takes a long first sip. 'With Tidy Tania.'

'While her boyfriend was . . . ?'

'They've split up,' he says neutrally. 'She wanted to come back here.'

'And you didn't because . . . ?'

He regards me, still in the trousers and shirt I borrowed for work, a triangle of shirt untucked at the side. 'With you on the couch?'

Jamie hunches his shoulders like he's not that bothered anyway.

'I was too tired,' he says. 'It's been a strange week.'

His smile is lopsided, but after a few seconds his lips even out into a full-on grin. 'I like to be on top of my game the first time I sleep with someone. I want to do everything I can to ensure they've got something to tell their mates about.'

'*I* try to do everything to ensure they've got *nothing* to tell their mates about.'

Jamie takes another glug. 'I'm not sure you need to worry about Rebecca and Danielle exchanging notes.'

'Too soon, Jamie.'

He laughs ruefully.

'So it's weird,' he says, straightening his legs so they're parallel with the water. 'You normally want to endlessly talk things through, but we haven't spoken properly since you got here.'

'What's the point?'

Jamie allows his legs to drop against the concrete and looks at me questioningly. 'It's just not like you, is all.'

I pause, contemplating what to say, how much to reveal. 'I've spent the past year with Rebecca pretending that Danielle and I never happened, and it's been easy, because it was just one night, it meant nothing, and I don't really see the point in dragging it all up now, especially when things have been going so well between me and Rebecca.'

Jamie nods into his can. 'I've never seen her happier.'

'Really?'

'Really. You're good for her. A couple of years ago it was just work, work, work with Rebecca.'

'And now it's just work, work?'

'Pretty much.' He laughs. 'Seriously, though – you're good for each other.'

If it was daytime the buildings opposite would be reflected blurrily in the Thames like Impressionist versions of themselves, but the sky has faded to an orangey black, and everyone has switched on their lights, so the reflections have been replaced by long streaks of light in the water, as though each building was a rocket taking off with a trail of fire. I never really noticed buildings before I got together with Rebecca, but her pointing out their features and explaining the idea behind their designs has apparently rubbed off.

'I was going to ask her to marry me.'

Jamie pulls his feet up and adjusts his position so he is facing me, legs crossed. 'What did you just say?'

'I bought a ring.'

'You did not buy a ring.'

I confirm my folly with a laboured nod.

'Why the fuck am I only finding out about this now?'

'I thought you'd think I was an idiot.'

'Well . . .'

I look down at the reflection of my shoes in the water. 'I applied for a loan the day after we got back from Beachy Head.'

Jamie locks his hands behind his neck and brings his elbows together.

'Jeez,' he says, still looking like he can't quite believe it. 'So when were you gonna do it – when *are* you going to do it?'

'I didn't know – *don't* know.' I shake my can to assess how much is left, then down the dregs and reach for another. 'I knew how, though.'

Jamie accepts the can I hold out, pulling the tab.

'She found a ring, when we went to Beachy Head, outside the pub. We handed it in at the bar. That's when it came to me. I'd take her back there. She'd said about staying at the B and B. Her mum stayed there. So we'd go and have another picnic and everything would be exactly the same, right down to the hip flask . . .' Jamie smiles. The hip flask was his idea. 'And again she'd find a ring by the wonky pub sign, except this time we wouldn't hand it in to the landlord.'

'How would you get it there?'

106

'I was gonna go there without Rebecca knowing, a couple of days before. I'd give the landlord the ring to plant before we got there. Then I was gonna lead Rebecca towards the pub, and when she found the ring she'd be like, *What the fuck?* And that's when I'd get down on one knee.'

Jamie lays a hand on his chest. 'I'm choking up here, Nicholls.'

'I'd obviously make sure no one else was around when I did it – you know what she's like.'

'Nah, fuck that – get a dance troupe to serenade her and film it for YouTube.'

I laugh. 'Can you imagine her face?'

'She'd never speak to you again.'

I sigh. 'She might never speak to me again anyway.'

I bury my head in my hands, and when I look up again Jamie has returned to his previous position, legs dangling. 'You know when you walk anywhere with Rebecca and you can't tell her to slow down – you just have to wait for her to wear herself out?'

I nod, unsure where he's heading.

'That's what this is. I get why she's pissed off. I would be. But the anger – she'll wear herself out with it.'

For some reason I find myself thinking about the Chas 'n' Dave disc on his living-room wall. He made me listen to one of their albums once after I dismissed them as a comedy act. And you know what? They're actually all right. Their songs are happy, uncomplicated, but when you listen to them, their lyrics are full of wisdom. And that's Jamie to a tee. But what if this time he's wrong?

'Thanks for taking the night off, mate.' I look at him. 'And ta for letting me kip on your couch, and the clothes.'

He bats away the sentiment with his hand.

'People at work keep saying how smart I look.'

'That's because your work clothes are scruffy.'

'Are they fuck!'

'They are. It's your way of rebelling against the system.' He points at the bit of untucked shirt. 'I bet that's been like that all day, hasn't it?'

I laugh until I feel his hand reach under the loose bit of shirt. He pinches the top of my boxers.

'Just checking you haven't been borrowing my pants,' he says.

I elbow him away.

'I mean, I love you, but—'

'I bought some new ones on my lunch break yesterday.'

All this talk of boxers reminds me that he could have pulled a girl he's fancied for ages last night.

'Sorry I stopped you bringing Tidy Tania back.'

Jamie chuckles drily. 'I wouldn't have brought her back anyway.' He downs the last of his second can and takes the keys from his pocket, spinning them around his index finger. 'She's only just split up with her boyfriend – she's too vulnerable.'

'Rebecca's right about you, Hawley.'

He demands an explanation with his eyes.

'She says you're all talk when it comes to women.'

Jamie smiles to himself as he isolates the key to his apartment and places a hand on my shoulder. 'You coming?'

'I'll follow you up in a minute.'

I watch him disappear into the building, waiting until I can no longer see his silhouette behind the darkened glass of the main doors before dialling her number. I wait again, for the line to connect, and finally it rings, once, twice, three times.

You've reached the voicemail of Rebecca Giamboni.

Maybe it's the beer, but I have to take the phone away from my ear. The sound of her voice has caused another knot to form in my stomach, and for the first time an unbearable thought starts to blossom in my mind.

What if Voicemail Rebecca is all I get now?

Chapter Ten

REBECCA

Thursday, 6 November

The buzzer goes. That'll be my curry.

'*Ciao*!' Stefan greets me as I pull open the door. 'What's happening?'

'What's happening,' I tell my brother, 'is that I've had a mental day at work and I'm starving and I thought you were my dinner and you're not, and now I hate you.' I cross my arms. 'Why are you here?'

'Meeting a mate in Greenwich for a drink so I thought I'd drop off your housewarming gift.' He holds out a WH Smith bag. 'And your warm welcome has confirmed it was definitely the right decision.'

'I've lived here for nearly five years, Stefan.'

'I know, but you've never lived with a boyfriend. It's a big deal.'

'Oh,' I mumble, taking the bag and pulling out the book inside, pursing my lips as I read the cover. '*Delia's How to Cheat at Cooking*?'

'I like Ben,' he says by way of an explanation. 'I don't want you to scare him off.'

I turn away and move towards the sofa but he must

catch the look on my face.

'Rebecca? What's wrong?'

'Nothing.' I move the case to *The Killing* DVD off the sofa so he can sit next to me. I'd actually been hovering dangerously on the verge of watching it. I know I'm mad at Ben but it still feels wrong to break the cardinal rule of not going ahead in a boxset we've started together.

Stefan sits and looks around. 'Where's Ben?'

'Oh, um, he's . . .' I get up and pour us both a whisky from the decanter on my bureau, just so I can keep my back to him. 'We're kind of on a break. Drink?'

'Why?' he cries. 'What did you do?'

'What makes you think I did anything?' I spin round, angry at the injustice. 'If you must know, I kicked him out when I found out he slept with Danielle.'

Stefan gasps then stands up and heads for the door. 'Where is he?'

'Stefan!'

'No one hurts my sister and gets away with it.'

'Oh, calm the feck down,' I tell him, dragging him back towards the sofa. I don't point out that Ben would wipe the floor with him in a fight.

'That *bastard*,' he mutters, grabbing one of the glasses I'd put down on the coffee table. 'He seemed such a lovely bloke. I never had him down for a cheat. And with your best mate!'

'Well, he didn't cheat exactly,' I admit. 'But yes! What a bastard!'

'What do you mean? I thought you said—'

'I did – I said he slept with Danielle,' I say, taking a casual sip of my whisky. 'It was before we started going out.'

He looks confused. 'So why have you kicked him out, exactly?'

'I only just found out.'

'Right. But still, why have you kicked him out exactly?'

'He never told me!'

'I get that. But, at the risk of repeating myself: why have you—'

'Oi, whose side are you on?' I hit him with a cushion. 'What happened to not letting anyone hurt your sister?'

Just then the buzzer goes. 'That'll be my curry.'

Stefan goes to the window and peers out. 'Nope, it's a guy but he's not holding a curry.'

'Shit.' I jump up. 'Is it Ben?' I've been ignoring all his calls and texts – of course he'd come over to try to talk.

'Nope, I don't think so. No, wait – it's that fit mate of yours who runs the bar.'

I run to the window and peer out to see the top of Jamie's perfectly styled messy bed-head. I buzz him in.

'Hi, Becs.' He greets me when he reaches the top of the stairs. 'You been avoiding me?'

'No,' I grumble. 'I've been avoiding your mates.'

'Our mates,' he says, making a beeline for the decanter and slapping Stefan's bicep on the way past. 'All right, mate? Long time no see.'

'Hi, Jamie.'

'Top-up, anyone?' Jamie holds out the decanter.

'Definitely,' I say, presenting my glass. No prizes for guessing what Jamie's here to talk about.

'Not for me, ta,' says Stefan, standing. 'I need to go meet my friend. But will you do something about *that*?' He waves a hand in my direction. 'It's all overreacty.'

Jamie nods. 'That's why I'm here.'

'I am not overreacting,' I protest.

'You are,' says Stefan. 'It doesn't sound like a big deal.'

'It's really not,' agrees Jamie.

'No offence, but you,' I point at Jamie, 'have slept with half the women in London, and you,' I point at Stefan, 'have slept with half the men. Of course you think it's no big deal.'

They both puff their chests out proudly.

'Why would she think that would offend us?' Stefan asks Jamie.

'I've no idea.'

Stefan says his farewells and I see him out, and when I get back Jamie is on the sofa, one arm sprawled along the back and his feet crossed on my coffee table, like he's modelling furniture.

'You here to get some clothes for Ben?' I ask.

'Nah, he looks much better in mine.' He leans forward and picks up my keys off the coffee table, twirling the tiny crisp bag in his hands with a thoughtful expression. I know he's thinking about when Danielle gave it to me, when we were all here together.

'Don't,' I warn him when he goes to speak.

'What?' he asks innocently. 'I was just going to ask if you knew exactly why it shrunk.'

'Danielle looked at it and it shrivelled up?'

Now it's his turn to say *Don't*.

'Go on then,' I say, dropping sideways on to the sofa.

'Well,' he says, twisting to face me. 'The plastic is made up of long molecules called polymers – a bit like strings of beads. In crisp bags these chains of molecules are stretched out almost straight.' He looks at me to make sure I'm following. 'Heating it in the microwave gives the molecules energy so they start to vibrate and

113

curl up. The bag shrinks and gets stiffer because all the polymer chains have curled over each other.' He chucks me the keyring, proud of himself.

'Amazing,' I tell him, studying the crisp bag then turning my gaze towards him. 'Tell me, have the movie rights been snapped up yet?'

He kicks my shin playfully then takes a sip of his drink.

'This is nice enough,' he tells me, 'but when are we opening the thirty-year-old Glenfiddich?'

'Told you, I'm saving it for a special occasion.'

'How about to celebrate the moment you let Ben come home?'

'That moment might never come.'

I get up to refill our drinks.

'Don't say that.' Jamie rubs the scar above his left eyebrow he got when he was run over as a kid. That small gesture is the only way you'll ever tell if Jamie's feeling distressed. 'I feel like my parents might be getting a divorce.' He laughs humourlessly. 'In fact, that would have far less of an impact on my life.'

'As long as you know, it's nothing that you did. We both still love you very much.'

'Seriously, though,' he continues, 'I get why you're upset. It must have come as a shock. But you and Ben hadn't even started seeing each other then. You can't be mad at something he did before you were together.'

'It's not about the fact they slept together,' I explain. It kind of is, but I realize that's irrational. 'It's about the lies.'

And I don't just mean about him lying by omission by not volunteering the information. On the night we met, he told me outright that he didn't fancy her. Yet he'd

114

already slept with her. He acted like I was the only girl in the room, but it was utter bollocks.

'What if he still likes her?' I ask weakly. 'You know Ben. He's not exactly a one-night-stand sort of guy. That's your forte. And Danielle's. He was obviously interested, and you can't just turn that off because the other person's not.'

Jamie laughs. 'This is Ben we're talking about – of course he can lose interest in an instant. Remember astronomy? Rock climbing? Cycling?' Jamie waves a hand in the general direction of the hall, where Ben's seldom-used bike still sits. 'Buddhism? Jeez, think about it, Becs – they're fleeting fixations. Learning Mandarin? Photography? Is he the new Chinese-speaking David Bailey? No – he lost interest as quickly as he took it up. You know what he's never lost interest in, though? You.'

'Yes, but what if liking Danielle didn't go away?' I demand, agitated that Jamie is sticking up for Ben. 'What if the only reason he gave up on it was because she wasn't interested. Jamie, HE FUCKED HER.'

'Stop shouting.'

'I'M NOT SHOUTING,' I shout. 'Look,' I continue with forced control, 'I know you thought you were certain about mine and Ben's future. I felt certain about it too. But I also felt certain about our past. That we met and we instantly connected and it was meant to be and blah blah blah.' I take a deep breath, trying to steady my voice. 'Ben can sit there and say that's all in the past, but he's the one that's always banging on about how important history is. This *changes* our history.'

'I'm just saying, cut him some slack,' Jamie says gently. 'Let's say you and I had slept with each other before you two got together . . .'

I cackle then see Jamie's mouth form into a pout.

'Sorry,' I say. 'Carry on.'

'Say we slept together, and it didn't mean anything, and then you and Ben got it on, and you knew that telling him about me would put him off, would you tell him?'

'Yes.'

'Really?'

'Well, maybe not right away, but I would eventually.'

'When? There's never a good time to drop into conversation something you think is going to hurt someone.'

'That doesn't excuse him keeping secrets from me.'

'Doesn't it?' he challenges. 'Look, whether or not keeping it from you was the right thing to do isn't for me to say. But you can't argue that the reasons behind it were good ones. Ben didn't want to hurt you. He didn't want to damage your relationship with Danielle. And most of all, he didn't want to give you a reason not to be with him. He's crazy about you.' He sighs. 'More than I think you realize.'

I think about what he's saying because it's Jamie, and he's rarely wrong about stuff. Would I have gone out with Ben if I'd known he'd already slept with Danielle? Hell, no. Has there ever been a time when he could have told me and I wouldn't have been upset? Probably not. My life was better when I didn't know that Ben has seen Danielle naked.

'You've always said he makes you feel special,' Jamie reminds me. 'Think about the things that happened since you got together, not the things that happened before it.'

I close my eyes and think of Beachy Head, and how perfect it was.

'OK, fine,' I mutter eventually.

'OK, fine, you'll let Ben come home?'

'OK, fine, I'll talk to him.'

'It's a start.' Jamie grins, patting my shoulder. 'By the way,' he adds, folding an arm behind his head and leaning back into the sofa, 'you would be lucky to sleep with me. I'm incredible.'

The buzzer goes. 'That *better* be my frigging curry,' I groan, running for the door.

Chapter Eleven

BEN

Friday, 7 November

The Tube brakes abruptly between Green Park and Hyde Park Corner, where I get off for work. I'm standing in the rush-hour crush, and the momentum sends the dotty-looking woman next to me chest-first into a man with bushy sideburns. She apologizes but Sideburns doesn't acknowledge it.

I figure we must be waiting for a signal to change or something but a couple of minutes later we still haven't moved. People start to look up from their phones and huff, and Dotty Woman is peering around the carriage through her oversized glasses as though looking for some kind of explanation.

When she turns my way I see she is chewing her lips and has gone white.

'You OK?' I ask her.

'Just a bit claustrophobic,' she says, eyes flicking to somewhere over my shoulder. 'I have this recurring dream where I'm trapped in one of these things, and when I ask people how we're going to get out they ignore me.'

'I'm sure we'll get going again in a minute.'

She looks around the carriage again, pulling at the ends of her plaited hair.

'There's a disused station just the other side of these walls,' I tell her. 'It's called Down Street. Churchill used it for secret meetings during the war. It'd take us about a minute to walk to, and we could go up to street level from there.'

The woman looks at me properly for the first time. 'If it's disused won't it be locked up?'

'Yeah, I guess so.'

'And dark?'

'I hadn't thought of that.'

'Perfect conditions for someone with claustrophobia, then.'

I go to apologize but she smiles to let me know she's only teasing. She introduces herself as Sandra just as the train starts moving again, and we're still chatting when we reach Hyde Park Corner. The whole exchange has me smiling up the escalators, and I make a mental note to tell Rebecca about it next time she moans about the—

Then I remember: the way things are going, I may never get to hear her whinge about the Tube, or anything, again. And the thought wipes the smile right off my face.

'How did your pre-date phone call go, by the way?' I ask Russ, because if anyone can make me feel better about my present situation, Russ can.

'I don't want to talk about it.'

There, easy.

I get on with my report on ticket office closures. I'm boring myself with the details of a required ninety-day consultation period when Russ pops up like a meerkat.

'Why is dating so difficult?'

'I thought you didn't want to talk about it?'

I stop what I'm doing and lean back in my chair.

'You reckon it's difficult these days?' I say. 'You're lucky you never lived in medieval times. Back then, if you fancied a girl you'd have to write her a poem.'

'Is that how you wooed Avril, Tom?' says Russ.

Tom tears off a piece of his chickpea sandwich with his spindly fingers and places it into his mouth.

'Actually, I drew a picture of her.'

I bloody love Tom.

'What did she think?' I ask.

I mean, here's me, always saying HR is a stopgap without really knowing what I might do next, but Tom is an artist, with actual talent, and I know he'll be out of here as soon as he catches a break.

'She said I got her nose wrong.'

Russ and I laugh, but then an email appears at the bottom right of my screen that steals my attention. Seeing the name, I lean into the desk, excited, but the small bit of movement causes my faulty screen to flicker.

'Bloody monitor!' I say, losing the cursor just as I was about to open the email.

'Language!' says Russ. 'There are ladies around.'

He gestures towards Tom while I stand on tiptoes, leaning over the screen to try to tighten the wires. Russ comes round.

'Let me,' he says, whacking the side of the monitor so that the flickering stops. '*Voilá*!'

I pull myself back towards the desk, gently this time,

even though the techno beat is going again inside my chest.

'Do you want to piss off now?' I tell Russ, who's just standing there.

He ignores me, squinting to try to read the email. I put my hand over the screen.

'You should be pleased,' he says, returning to his own desk. 'Sounds like she wants to meet.'

I read the email for myself.

Are you free for a chat tonight? 6 pm at the flat?

Finally! I hit reply.

I'll be there. I love you. Bx

Immediately my imagination starts to write a script of how the evening is going to play out, and it ends with me enveloping Rebecca in my arms, immersing myself in the scent of her, and whispering how sorry I am, and then, as she's just about to tell me that all is forgiven, I hear a forced cough behind me.

Richardson.

'I'm going to need you to stay late.' He taps his left wrist, even though he isn't wearing a watch. 'The directors can't get here until quarter past six so you'll have to give your presentation then.'

'Presentation? You never said anything about—'

Richardson's mobile bleeps, and he pauses me with a raised finger before walking off to answer the call.

'I'm not staying late,' I tell Russ and Tom.

Russ withdraws his tongue from the gap between his front teeth. 'Good luck with that.'

I return to Rebecca's email, knowing I'm going to have to reply again telling her I'll be late. For some reason I feel apprehensive.

'We really should form a union,' I say.

'Not this again,' says Russ.

'Do you seriously think they're going to stop at the ticket offices? Because they're not.'

'We're HR,' says Russ. 'It'd be like Radioactive Man joining The Avengers. Unions are our nemesis.'

My screen starts to flicker again. 'Do you use comic book analogies on your dates?'

'Nah, you don't reveal anything people can interpret as weird till at least date ten.'

Russ comes round again, and I presume he's going to give the monitor another slap, but instead he goes to open my top drawer.

'What do you want?'

'A stapler,' he says, looking perplexed. 'Who locks their top drawer?'

'I do.'

'Why?'

'Because people pinch my stapler.'

I take the key from my pocket and open the drawer only as far as is necessary to remove the stapler and give it to Russ.

'I never had you down as a stationery fascist, buddy,' he complains.

I wait for him to return to his desk before cautiously opening the rest of the drawer, pausing to check no one else is paying attention. Satisfied, I take the velvet box into my hand and open it. The ring is an antique with Rebecca's birthstone – Tanzanite. It's here because I haven't yet established any hiding places of my own at the flat, but I guess I can stash it at Jamie's now I've told him my plan.

I shove the ring in my pocket and slam the drawer

shut, intending to fire off another email to Rebecca, but it will have to wait because the movement causes my screensaver – the photo of me and Rebecca outside the Colosseum – to flicker once more.

And then the flickering stops, and the image is gone completely.

Chapter Twelve

REBECCA

'Rebecca!' hollers Jemma as I get back from my site visit.

'Hey, what's up?'

I stop at reception.

'Oh, the usual. Run off my feet doon here.' She dips the brush into her nail varnish and sweeps the maroon lacquer on to the tip of her thumbnail. 'Just wondered how things are with your man. Did you fix things?'

'Not yet.' I squirm. It feels weird talking to a near stranger about this. 'But he's coming over tonight.'

'Think you'll get back together?'

'I don't know.'

She looks up at me, fingers splayed. 'Do you still love him?'

'Yes.' I shock myself with how quickly I say it. No hesitation at all.

'Then what's the problem? Did he cheat on you?'

'No.'

'Steal your money?'

'Nope.'

She gasps. 'Listen to jungle music?'

I shake my head, laughing.

'Good.' She dips the brush in the bottle and starts

the second coat. 'I've been in all those situations and I wouldn't wish any of them on anyone.'

I sigh, propping my elbows on the reception desk, and rest my chin in my hands. 'He did something – not deliberately or anything – but I didn't think I could get over it. Now I'm thinking maybe I can but I don't know if I should.'

She looks up from her nails and scrutinizes me. 'You're a rather proud little soul, aren't you?'

I take a deep breath. 'A bit.'

'Would you rather—'

'I know, I know,' I mumble, biting my lip. 'Would I rather keep my pride and be lonely or swallow it and be happy?'

'Nope. I was going to ask if you'd rather have sex with a goat once and no one know about it or *not* have sex with a goat but everyone think you did.' She shakes her hands about in an attempt to speed up the drying process. 'Jesus, Rebecca, it's always aboot you and your problems.'

'Oh . . .'

'Argghh.' Jemma jumps up as her finger clips the bottle and it topples, spilling varnish over the oak desk. 'I need to get a cloth. Get back to me aboot the goat,' she calls over her shoulder.

'Will do,' I tell her, actually weighing it up as I walk to my desk. I acknowledge that it's an OK day, as far as Post-Revelation days go.

It's still early days but my initial plans for the cinema couldn't be going any better. I stood outside it earlier, just picturing what the final building will look like – the grand foyer, high ceilings and sweeping staircase re-stored to their former glory of the cinema's heyday, with state-of-the-art facilities to bring it up to date.

And maybe that's how I need to approach my relationship. Just because it started crumbling doesn't mean it can't be saved. The foundation can be restored and we can build on the rest – maybe even make it into something that's better and stronger than it was before.

Catching up on my emails, I find one from Danielle telling me she's got an early finish and asking – with almost deliberate casualness – if I fancy meeting for a glass of wine. She works in advertising sales for a men's magazine and gets to leave early if her team have beaten their target, and I finish early on Fridays anyway.

I realize that I don't feel angry at her any more, or even betrayed. I just feel . . . maybe Jemma's right. Proud. I tap out a reply telling her Ben is coming over. Should I add a kiss in case she thinks I'm just making excuses? I never do kisses so maybe it'll be weirder if I do.

Another email pops up while I'm deliberating: Ben, something has come up at work – he won't be at mine until 8 p.m.

I try not to feel exasperated at having to wait a couple more hours to see him. Now I've made up my mind what to do, I just want to put the shit storm behind me.

I drum my fingers on the surface of my keyboard while I think, then I scrap my email to Danielle and write a new reply.

What harm can one drink do?

It's barely gone six o'clock when we get to Arch 13, but it's already crammed with post-work revellers having thank-Crunchie-it's-Friday drinks, a notion I've never fully appreciated in the past, but after the week I've had I'm right on board.

Jamie saved us a booth, where Danielle sits now, biting her manicured nails. I've only ever seen her do that when she was waiting to hear from Shane. She doesn't notice me until I'm dropping my bag on the seat next to her.

'Hi, love,' she says, and I don't have time to respond before she launches into a speech that she has clearly prepared. 'Listen, Becs, I know you don't like to talk about things, and that's fine, but it's driving me mental that I don't know what you're thinking. I know you're upset about what happened between me and Ben, and I understand why.' She takes her first breath. 'But it really was just one meaningless, stupid incident and there's never been anything between us since . . .'

While she talks, I take the wine from the cooler and pour it into the glass Danielle had ready for me, topping hers up too. It's a New Zealand Sauvignon Blanc. That's what Danielle always orders because she knows it's my white wine of choice, even though she prefers Chardonnay. I've always been touched by that.

'So, look,' she's saying, somewhat fiercely, 'if you're mad at me, shout at me. Get it off your chest. Tell me I'm a slag and a bad friend if that's what you're think-ing, and then I can tell you how sorry I am and you can forgive me and then we can be OK again.' The fierceness dissolves. 'You're my best friend – one of the only people in the world I actually trust, and I need us to be OK.'

I sip my drink and pretend to think about it. 'You're not a slag,' I say eventually.

She glances my way. 'But I am a bad friend?'

'The worst.'

'I'm so, so sorry.'

'I forgive you.'

'We're OK?'

'We're OK. Just stop being soppy – it unnerves me.'

'Absolutely.' She salutes me.

Normality resumed, we catch up, and there are no more mentions of Ben until I realize he'll be getting back to the flat about now.

'You do know I don't like him like that, don't you?' Danielle asks as she divides the rest of the wine between us. 'I never have. I mean, he's great and everything, but there were never any feelings involved.'

I nod. I do know.

'I don't doubt it,' I reply, trying to keep it light. 'Just two people rubbing body parts together.'

'Exactly.' She sounds relieved. 'I wasn't thinking straight. Shane had just broken things off again and Ben had just been trying to comfort me, and it just . . .'

Even now she always looks the same when talking about Shane – a stoic smile that doesn't reach her eyes. Every time he broke it off and disappeared from her life she insisted it was fine, that she didn't care, and then she got hammered and slept with the first man she saw to try to make that true.

'Honestly, Becs,' she half-groans-half-laughs as she covers her face, 'this time was spectacularly humiliating.'

'Remind me.' They've broken up so many times they all blend into one.

'God, I'm cringing just thinking about it.' She peers at me through her fingers. 'He said something to me but there was a train going past right at that moment. I thought he said, *I can't live without you*. And I thought,

Finally! He's realized we're great together, and he doesn't want to mess about any more, and all that talk about taking me to Ireland to meet his family was actually going to happen. So I said, *You'll never have to live without me*, but he looked horrified, and went, *No, no, no, I'M LEAVING WITHOUT YOU*, really loudly, but by that time the train had passed and all the smokers standing outside turned to look at us.'

She laughs and I squeeze her arm, but something niggles me. Something I can't quite put my finger on. And also, I realize I haven't heard this story before, and I wonder why.

'Yet I still kept going back there until you made me delete his number. I mean, what was I thinking?' she continues. 'What did I ever find cool about some unemployed musician?'

'He was focusing on his *art*,' I quote Shane, though I'm distracted now. Whatever is bothering me feels just out of my grasp.

'Christ,' whines Danielle. 'He really is basically a lying, sponging, opportunistic twat, isn't he?'

'You miss him?'

'Sometimes.'

'Where were you exactly?'

Danielle stares at me. 'What?'

'I thought you and Ben met at the bar Jamie used to work at, but you said a train went past.'

Danielle picks up her wine glass and I notice her hand is shaking as she takes a sip.

'Um . . .' She shrugs, looking round the room like someone might save her.

Because that's what's been niggling me. The bar Jamie used to work in – where he worked when Ben

129

and Danielle met the first time – was in town. Nowhere near a train station.

'You're talking about here,' I say shakily. She's about to protest but I can see her mind working and I know she's realized she's caught herself out. It's in a railway arch – it's the only place I know where the trains are so loud you could mishear someone.

'But the night this place opened is the night Ben and I met,' I continue. 'And you and Shane split up that night. You didn't want to talk about it.'

I remember her reaction when I told her about Ben the next day, and now it's all coming together like a cruel jigsaw puzzle; the whole picture in front of me in gruesome Technicolor.

I stand up and grab my bag and coat.

'Rebecca, don't,' she says quickly, reaching out to touch my arm.

'Get off me,' I scream, shaking her away. She looks stunned, and I notice Jamie looking over from behind the bar. In fact, everyone is watching, I realize, but for once I don't care. I need air.

'Wait, please. I know you guys were chatting but it didn't even occur to me it was the start of something until you texted me the next morning.'

'Of course it didn't,' I practically spit. 'How could he possibly be interested in me when you were around?'

'Don't twist things,' she says firmly. 'I meant I didn't think you liked him. You never like anyone.'

'Why didn't you tell me any of this the next day? Why did you let me go on about the guy whose bed you'd just frickin' left?'

'You were excited. I felt bad. I'd never seen you like that about anyone so I wanted you to have him.'

130

'So you *let* me have him? Is that what you're saying?'

'No. Stop twisting my words.'

But I'm not twisting anything. It's all so very clear.

Feeling sick, I hurry away. I hear Danielle, then Jamie, call my name, but I need to get out.

I see a black cab with its light on so I flag it and jump in. I don't need it – I just don't want Danielle to catch me up.

'Where are we off to?' asks the driver.

I give him my address.

'Righteo.' He clicks on the meter and pulls away, and as I glance at his mirror, I see Danielle running after us.

'Hey, you,' Ben greets me as I open the door, but he only has to look at my face to realize this isn't the reunion he'd bargained on. 'Rebecca, what's up?'

'When did you sleep with Danielle?' I drop my keys on the coffee table and lean against the arm of the sofa, arms crossed.

He visibly pales. 'Ages ago. Before you and I—'

'Oh, change the friggin' record, Ben, and tell me the truth. When was it? I know, but I need to hear you say it.'

His breathing is jagged when he says: 'The night Arch 13 opened.'

'The night we now call our anniversary?'

'Rebecca, don't.'

'How could you?'

My voice is quiet but so full of anguish I barely recognize it as my own. Ben moves towards me but my stare stops him dead.

'Get out,' I tell him.

'Rebecca.' He looks at me pleadingly. 'I love you *so*

much. This has been the worst week of my life. Can't we just forget the whole thing?'

'No,' I whisper.

'Becs, we can get past this.'

'I'm not sure I can.' My voice is croaky from all the shouting.

'Don't say that.'

'It's true.'

'But—'

'You have to leave,' I say quietly. 'For good.'

'Rebecca, no.'

Ben's eyes have filled with tears, and he tries to reach out to me again, but I move away.

'Go, Ben. It's over.'

'No,' he says desperately. 'I'm not giving up on us just like that. I love you – I even went and—' He stops and takes a deep breath. 'Look, I'm not going anywhere until we've talked about this.'

'Oh, you want to talk about it? Fine.' I pull out a chair and plonk myself down at the table. 'Let's talk about when you told me you didn't fancy her?'

'What?'

'It could only have been, what? About three or four hours before you slept with her, you told me you had no interest in her? Then you waited until I'd left to make your move.'

'It wasn't like that.'

He rubs his eyes with the heels of his hands and then looks towards the ceiling. 'It just happened. I know that sounds like bullshit, but it did.'

'Sorry, Ben, not good enough.'

'She was upset – she'd broken up with Shane, and we got drunk. That's all.'

He's pacing the room frantically, gesticulating all over the shop.

'And then you started fancying her?'

'No!'

'So you *didn't* fancy her at all, but you slept with her because she was up for it? You want to be *that* guy, Ben? Really?'

'No,' he barks. '*I'm* the guy who met a girl he really liked, who didn't seem interested in me so I got drunk to cheer myself up, and when that didn't work I slept with someone to cheer myself up, and that didn't work either.'

'Oh, that's sad. Here,' I look around the room, 'I'm sure I have a tiny little violin lying around – let me play you something.'

'Look,' he pulls out the chair opposite me and sits down, burying his head in his hands, 'I'm not going anywhere until you understand what happened that night.'

A Year Earlier

Chapter Thirteen

BEN

Opening Night

'Anything going on there, do you reckon?'

My eyes are focused on Jamie and Danielle.

'Nah, they're just the world's two biggest flirts,' says Rebecca. 'Jamie's probably the only man in here who doesn't fancy Danielle.'

I can't tell whether she's giving me a chance to compliment her or just making chit-chat.

'I don't,' I say, hoping Rebecca will therefore infer that I fancy *her*, because right now it feels like she's the only girl in the world.

But she says nothing.

I normally find this kind of stuff easy. It's like Jamie says: check the mirror to make sure you're looking OK, look out for the girl giving you signals, make your manoeuvre. Mirror, signal, manoeuvre. And I did look OK when I left the house, and I definitely like her enough to make a manoeuvre, but, man, I have no idea whether this girl is giving me signals or not.

'Ben?'

'Yeah?'

'Your drink is dripping on your shirt.'

'Arggghhh. Crap.'

'Want me to go get you a napkin? I owe you one.'

I laugh, despite the situation. I can't remember laughing this much in ages. I reckon it's her delivery. Everything she says is kind of dry, and her eyes are ever so slightly squinty, like she's permanently questioning something, and basically I'm in love with her.

I think about what Jamie would do if an insanely hot girl asked him if he needed a napkin. He'd probably take a casual sip of his neat whisky and say something like . . .

'I do if it has your number on it?'

The words come out before my brain can inform my mouth that I'm drinking a pink cocktail, not a neat whisky, and that I can't take a casual sip because there are so many pieces of fruit that I'm having to use a straw.

Shit.

Rebecca looks awkward, like she's thinking of the best way to get out of here, and basically this is what happens when you manoeuvre without a signal – you crash.

It's as though the value of time starts to multiply, because the two or three seconds that follow feel like two or three weeks.

I attempt to save myself the embarrassment of a rejection by offering to get us another drink, but I can literally see the relief in her eyes when she spots Danielle heading towards the door.

'I'll be back in two minutes,' she says, and I'm content with that until I realize she's still dealing in multiplied time, and two minutes actually means, well, never.

I stand there, and even though I've only met the girl once, my crest is well and truly fallen. I can't take my eyes off her. She's so elegant, and together, and self-assured. In fact, I realize now, she has all the attributes of a woman who would have no problems giving me signals if she *was* interested.

So obviously she isn't.

I see Jamie glance my way. He's with Rebecca. Which means she wasn't going to find Danielle at all; she just lied to get away from me. And now she's probably telling Jamie all about me hitting on her, and he'll never tire of reminding me about it, but actually, this is partly his fault: he said he'd invent a cocktail especially in my honour if I cleared some glasses, and I ended up with . . .

. . . whatever this is. I look like a right tit.

I decide to stop looking, lest she think I'm some kind of stalker. I down the rest of the cocktail and go ask Russ and Tom if they want another drink. They don't.

'Same again?' says Jamie as I approach the bar.

I look around to see where Rebecca has gone and catch sight of her back as she walks out of the door.

'Very funny,' I say dejectedly. 'What on earth was that?'

'A cross between a margarita and a piña colada,' he says.

'And how was that in honour of me?'

'Because it can't decide what it wants to be.'

He trots off to serve someone else, clearly delighted with his joke, but I can't be annoyed with Jamie to-night. This place is awesome, and it's all his.

'I need to talk to you later,' he shouts over.

Oh, here we go – it starts.

'I'll look forward to that.'

I sit at the end of the bar feeling sorry for myself, glugging my pint in the hope it will make the image of Rebecca less vivid in my mind. I've just ordered another drink when I see Danielle pull up a stool just down the bar from me. She orders a Bramble and a Black Russian, which makes me wonder if Rebecca is coming back, but when they come she downs one and immediately picks up the other herself.

A group of people squeeze in beside her, all elbows and bags, and with a huff she shuffles up.

'Watcha, Ben.'

I watch her down the second drink.

'Are you OK?' I ask.

'Yes, I just . . . Me and Shane just broke up.'

'Oh.' I'm not really sure what to say. 'I'm sure it was just a misunderstanding.'

'Yup, I certainly misunderstood.'

She stretches her lips taut to reapply her lipstick and I try to remember if Rebecca was wearing any? I don't think she was.

'That's bad news,' I say.

'Blimey, Ben,' says Danielle. 'You're really cheering me up here!'

'Sorry,' I say, smiling as it dawns on me what a drag I'm being.

I open my mouth to explain but realize I can't tell her. She is Rebecca's friend, and anyway, who gets mopey about a girl they've met once?

'Girl troubles,' I say vaguely.

'Oh, well in that case,' she says, 'let's get shit-faced together.'

She waves Jamie over and doesn't seem to hear me say that I'm pretty pissed already.

'Two Jägerbombs, please, handsome!'

Jamie studies her for a second.

'Oh, don't look at me like that, Jamie,' she says. 'I could drink you under any table in here. Go on, pick one.'

Jamie laughs and starts on the Jägerbombs.

We polish off the shots and I've not even put my glass down when Danielle jumps to her feet as 'SexyBack' by Justin Timberlake comes on. 'I love this song!'

She throws both arms in the air and starts dancing on her own. A few blokes, including the one who knocked into Rebecca earlier, turn to watch, and she offers her audience a smile as she bounces her head from side to side. She attempts to coax me over to her with an outstretched finger but I stay put.

At the end of the song Danielle returns to her stool. She reaches for her latest cocktail, but takes just a sip this time.

'Rebecca always says I turn into someone else when it comes to Shane,' she says, looking sad. 'Have you met Rebecca?'

'Briefly,' I say, struggling to focus. The booze is really starting to go to my head. 'We got talking earlier.'

'I love Rebecca.'

'Me too.'

Danielle looks up at me and I realize what I just said. 'You love Rebecca?'

'No, I meant a different Rebecca – an old friend.'

'Well, I hope you never lost her because I can tell you that whoever said that thing about it being better to have lost and loved than never having been lost at all was talking shit.'

I decide against correcting her.

'Tennyson,' I say instead.

'Eh?'

'Tennyson was the one who said it. Married for forty-two years, died before his wife.'

'Then who the fuck is he to tell us it's better to have lost and loved?'

She looks up at me, smiling into her drink as she takes a sip.

'Are you laughing at me, Ben?'

Rebecca is right, Danielle probably could have any bloke in here. And even if she is the biggest flirt in the world, I feel flattered that she's flirting with me. It's at least taking my mind off things, though I still wish it was Rebecca sitting here beside me.

I look for Jamie so I can ask what he wants to talk to me about, but he must be changing a barrel or something.

'Where is Rebecca?' says Danielle, inspecting the room.

'I guess she went home.'

'Of course,' says Danielle. 'Maybe I should take a leaf out of her book. One more cocktail and I think I'll be dancing on the bar top, and I'm not even gonna tell you what happened last time I did that.'

I laugh tiredly.

'One more lager and I reckon I might fall asleep on the bar top.'

'Do you want to share a taxi?'

'OK.'

Danielle gets up.

'Shouldn't we wait for Jamie to get back?'

'I'll text him,' she says. 'I've had enough goodbyes for one night.'

We wait under the neon red Arch 13 sign for a black

cab, but we don't have to stand there long.

'Where are you going?' asks the driver as we climb inside.

'I don't know.' Danielle looks at me. 'Where are we going, Ben?'

I wake up feeling like my head might just break into tiny pieces if I were to move it so much as a millimetre.

Without opening my eyes I try to work out how I got so steaming drunk that I feel like this, but the night is a blur. I start from the beginning, and slowly things come back to me. Talking to Rebecca, finding out that she lived in Japan, laughing lots. I'm up to the point where my cocktail is dribbling down my shirt when the reconstruction is interrupted by an unfamiliar text tone.

I open my eyes, just long enough to see the blonde hair on the pillow next to me, and then I squeeze them shut.

Fuck.

I sense Danielle reach down the side of my bed for her phone. Daring to open my eyes again, I see that she is staring intently at her screen. I presume it is Shane. She looks ever so slightly confused.

After several minutes she returns the phone to her handbag and finally looks at me. I offer her a neutral smile, because I don't want to be horrible about the fact that, well, this isn't going anywhere. Who knows, maybe we might even end up being friends if she doesn't take it too badly.

'Let's just pretend this never happened, shall we?' she says.

Danielle sits up and twists on to her feet in one clean movement, then puts on her dress as smoothly as it slipped off. I get the feeling this whole thing isn't new territory for her, and quite frankly if I did have feelings for Danielle, I'd be thinking this little performance was quite mean. Thankfully, the only feelings involved – from both sides, it seems – were the ones we were trying to forget.

I offer to see her to the door but she thanks me and says there's no need, and she's literally out of the house within two minutes of putting down her phone.

I lie there, not quite sure what just happened. I can hear Avril in the room next door. She is clearly moaning at Tom, but I can't hear his replies even though the walls are paper thin.

When I was eighteen I'd wear a hangover with pride, but in my mid-twenties I'm at the point where I just want to hide away from the world for a day, possibly two, and that's what I fully intend to do until a text message of my own reminds me I'm supposed to be meeting Jamie for breakfast. He adds that he's got something for me.

Ibuprofen, hopefully.

Frank's is nothing special to look at. In fact, there is paint peeling off the window sill and most of the mugs are chipped, but the full English is up there with my Mum's, and Frank himself always greets you like family.

'You look rough today, Ben,' he says, ushering me to a table with some napkins wedged underneath one of the legs. 'Still, nothing one of my specials won't fix.'

Frank is Greek. The bottom half of his face is darkened by a shadow of stubble, while the top is permanently tanned, so that he resembles a *Crimewatch* photofit.

'Make that two, please, Frank – Jamie's on his way.'

144

A few minutes later Jamie bounds in looking ready for a heptathlon.

'When I said you needed to work out what to do with your life,' he says, sitting down opposite me, 'I didn't mean that you should *do* one of my best mates.'

'How did you—'

'Rebecca told me.'

I bury my face in my hands. 'It was just one night, mate.'

'That's not what Rebecca seems to think.'

What the fuck?

'What did she say exactly?'

'That she liked you. Well, she never said it in so many words, but—'

'Who likes me?'

'Rebecca.' Jamie shakes his head. 'Jeez, who do you think I was talking about?' Luckily his question seems to be rhetorical. 'She gave me this.'

He holds out a napkin, and for a few seconds I look at it in his hand, puzzled.

'Well, this isn't the reaction I was expecting,' he says. 'I thought you'd be made up?'

'I am, I just . . .'

I really thought she had blown me out. I would never have done anything with Danielle if I'd thought there was even a tiny chance . . . But I didn't, and so I did, and I know that means I can't . . . But then again, if we really are pretending like it never happened, then maybe . . .

I go to take the napkin, a strange guilt coming over me, but Jamie pulls it back.

'Not until you make me a promise,' he says.

'What do you mean?'

'I'm only giving you this if you like her.'

I think about the question for a good eighth of a second.

'I do, mate – I do.'

'Really like her, I mean. You're not getting this unless you promise me you'll treat her right, and won't get carried away until you're sure it's not another flight of fancy.'

He is looking right into my eyes.

'I promise, mate,' I say, locking everything that happened after I left the bar last night into a mental vault. 'You've got nothing to worry about.'

Chapter Fourteen

REBECCA

Monday, 10 November

It's only when I'm cycling over the bridge that it hits me: I didn't leave the house this entire weekend. I didn't even get dressed. No exercise, no fresh air, no human contact. That's not healthy.

Still, these are the things I've managed not to do:

- Talk to Ben. The only words I've uttered to him since he sat at our dining table, ripping up our How We Met story into teeny tiny pieces and sellotaping it back together again into something flawed, sticky and way less poetic, were to tell him to leave and never come back.
- Talk *about* Ben. Come to think of it, I haven't talked at all since Friday. Telling Ben to go was the last time I used my voice. That's a weird thought.
- Sit in bed sobbing while simultaneously eating ice cream and looking through old photos of the 'good times'.

- Throw away Ben's left shoes, smash his framed Manchester City shirt or wee in his shower gel.
- Talk to Ben.

Anyway, contrary to post-break-up protocol, I'm doing all right.

Mostly.

Actually, if I'm being really honest, I should also add these to the list of things I've not done:

- Cooked. At all. Meals this weekend consisted of an Indian takeaway, a Chinese and a pizza.
- Tidied the flat. It's already starting to smell like the bin section at an international street food market. In fact, the only semi-productive thing I achieved this weekend was relenting and booking a weekly cleaner. She starts today.
- Slept. I feel shattered – my limbs are bags of sand and my eyelids feel like they've got pound coins taped to them, yet my mind won't quit. Plus the newborn baby downstairs pipes up every time I come close to dozing off.

Which is why the first thing on my agenda as soon as I've chained up my bike is coffee.

'Coo-ee! Rebecca!'

Jemma is at the front of the huge queue that greets me when I open the door of Starbucks. I slope forwards, painfully aware how much everyone – me included – hates a pusher-inner. Any other day, this would be enough to hold me back. But today . . .

'Get a black coffee and whatever you're having,' I whisper, sneaking a tenner into her hand and then loitering by the condiment table.

'Anything to eat with that?' Jemma yells over, while others glare. I shake my head. They're so on to me.

'My diet starts tomorrow,' Jemma says once we're outside, holding up her latte with a double shot, hazelnut syrup and extra cream. 'Then I'll be on the skinny flat whites.'

'You don't need to lose weight, Jemma.'

She has a great figure. It's curvy and feminine, unlike my own tall, boyish frame. Hers isn't dissimilar to Danielle's. A size bigger, maybe, but no less sexy. The difference is that Jemma doesn't seem to know she's sexy. Danielle does. She'd never say it, but it's there in the little actions, like dancing rather than walking towards the loo in a bar, or eye-fucking the camera when posing for photos.

The thought takes me to a dark place.

'How was your weekend?' Jemma asks, slurping her drink as we cross the road.

It was lonely and depressing. Even worse than the weekend I found out about Ben and Danielle. Because now it was about me. It didn't happen before we met. I could have got over *that*, I realize now. That hurt, but at least it wasn't personal. Knowing it happened on the night we met changes everything. For ever.

'Good, thanks,' I tell Jemma.

It's just gone eight o'clock when I get to my desk – less than an hour to devise a more detailed proposal for East House Pictures. I need to be on top of my game.

'Keeping you up, are we, Rebecca?' Eddie Riley yells across the office.

I had nearly nodded off, my eyes fluttering shut and my head dropping towards my chest.

Shit. 'If anyone's keeping me up, Riley, it sure ain't you,' I yell back without looking, and the other guys snigger, which shuts Eddie up.

I grind my fists into my eye sockets, grateful I forwent mascara this morning.

Nine o'clock rolls around, yet when I peer down to reception, there's no sign of Adam. I sit upstairs, but the wall facing Jemma downstairs is Perspex, so I can see the entrance from my desk.

At five past, there's still no sign. Same at ten past. At just before a quarter past he finally strolls in, and Jemma sends him up before calling my extension.

'Sexy vampire has entered the building,' she squeals.

'Yep, seen him – thanks, Jem. Fifteen bloody minutes late – he might have called.'

Silence.

'Jemma?'

'Um, while I've got you on the phone, I have a message for you. Adam Larsson called and said he'd be fifteen minutes late.'

'OK, no sweat.' At least I found out before I made a dig at Adam. 'He's here now.'

'Giamboni.' He grins as he strides towards me. 'Good to see you.'

'Good to see you too,' I lie, taking the hand he's offering and shaking it firmly. I lead him to a meeting room, spread out my plans on a table and start talking.

'We just need to bear in mind it has a grade-two listed interior,' I say finally. 'So we need to maintain what we can of its art deco features, but the exterior is pretty run down and not structurally sound.'

He isn't saying much, just the odd grunt, but when I'm done he picks up the page. While he studies the

150

drawing, I study him. I'd be lying if I said he wasn't handsome – not that I'd admit it to Jemma. Lean, blond and blue eyed with a mass of stubble to make him look devilishly handsome rather than angelically cute. Yet, he leaves me cold.

It occurs to me that I can't imagine ever having sex with anyone other than Ben. But Ben and I will probably never have sex again. Sadness washes over me as I picture him on top of me, his hair messy as he closes his eyes and bites his lip. Then suddenly, in my head, it's Danielle underneath him instead of me, on the night we met, while I'm climbing into my own bed with a stupid grin on my face, wondering if Ben is thinking about me too. I despise myself as much as I despise them.

'It looks great,' Adam says, letting the page fall back on to the table.

'Thank you. What I'll do next is play around with—'

'As I said, it looks great,' he interrupts. 'But what am I doing in a fire?'

'Getting out and calling the fire brigade?' I quip, but even as I say it, I realize my mistake.

'Right. It's the getting-out part I'm worried about. What if I'm upstairs and the stairs are on fire? How am I getting out? Toilet window or . . . ?'

I grab back the page and study it, trying to see if I can invent a way out of this. Did I really forget the frickin' fire escape?

'Don't beat yourself up about it,' he smirks.

I'm not. I'm beating Ben up about it. For taking up my headspace and leaving me off my game.

'Well done,' I say, tossing the page back on the table. 'That was a test, and you passed. You can stay on my team.'

He chuckles, sliding the plan back over to his side of the table with his fingertips, while I pray to God I'm not blushing.

I gaze out of the window, watching a dark black cloud change the colour of the sky as Adam takes his pencil and decorates my drawing with some suggestions to make the concept more structurally sound. Is that what was wrong with mine and Ben's relationship? It looked pretty good on the surface, but was it structurally flawed? Instead of changing gradually over time, its strength keeping it standing, becoming even more beautiful with age, it just crumbles with the weight of his secret, because it was never made of strong-enough bricks. Still, at least it happened now. We might share a bed, a sofa and a dining table but what would have been the next step? Getting engaged? Probably, I realize. Christ, if he'd asked, I would have said yes. Then this would be even harder.

'Sorry, am I boring you?' snaps Adam, as I yawn.

'A little,' I say, intending it as a joke but worrying instantly that I sounded vindictive.

Just then my phone starts buzzing and Ben's name pops up with his stupid smiley face – a selfie he once took when I was in another room and added to his contact details to surprise me.

'Boyfriend?' Adam mutters.

'Not any more,' I mutter back, rejecting the call. I regret the words as soon as they leave my mouth, and I wait for Adam to whack me with the stick I've just handed him, but when I raise my eyes he looks embarrassed.

'Sorry, I didn't—'

'Don't be. It's fine. Anyway, are we finished here?

Clearly I've got work to do on these sketches.'

'Sure. Um, see you soon.' He gets up to leave, turning back when he's in the doorway – a safe distance so I can't cry on his shoulder, I expect – then adds, 'Hope you're all right.'

I stay rooted to my seat in the meeting room as he leaves. I don't know what's worse – the sexist structural engineer thinking I'm not on my game because I'm having man troubles, proving women are too emotional to be in charge, or him thinking I'm always that sloppy, proving women are too incompetent to do a good job.

I let my head drop into my hands. You twat, Giamboni.

Chapter Fifteen

BEN

I watch an apocalyptic cloud drift in front of the mid-morning sun, casting London into grey, and from my position at the window it suddenly feels like the entire city, the Thames and all the buildings across the water, and even me standing here, were drawn from a blunt pencil.

'What are you still doing here?' asks Jamie, fastening his dressing gown as he strides from his room.

'I called in sick.'

I was supposed to have a meeting with Richardson this morning but I feel as though I can barely move. People think heartache is an emotional pain and it is, but it's a physical pain too. It's an omnipresent ache in my stomach, a tightness in my throat, a numbness in my head and a tiredness in every limb.

Maybe it'd be different if I had a job I loved, that I could throw myself into as a distraction, but I don't, and the prospect of a round of *How was your weekend?* made me feel sick.

'I wish I had cigarettes.'

'Want me to go buy you some?'

I return to the couch, tucking myself back into the

sleeping bag. 'I thought you said every cigarette takes seven minutes off your life?'

'They do,' he says, depositing bread into the toaster. 'Want me to go buy you some?'

I can tell from his strangled tone he's only half joking. He's been pretty cheesed off all weekend, but what was I supposed to do? Once I lied to Rebecca about the timing I couldn't exactly tell him, because he's *her* friend as much as he is mine. It would have put him in an impossible position. But now he keeps saying stuff like, *That's why you acted weird when I handed you the napkin* and, *I wouldn't have given you it if I'd known*.

I switch on my laptop while he makes breakfast, neither of us speaking, and I must be in a world of my own because I jump out of my skin when he plonks himself down next to me on the couch.

'Want some toast?' he says, holding the plate out to me.

'No, ta,' I say.

'You need to eat.'

I wonder if there is a sentence more commonly spoken to the brokenhearted. Actually, I know that there is, because something else people keep saying is, *Try to keep busy*. Which helps until you stop keeping busy and the misery returns, redoubled as if angry that you attempted to leave its grip. Any respite hardly seems worth it.

Jamie crunches into his toast then nods towards the laptop. 'Are you looking at Rebecca's page?'

I turn the screen away from him. 'No.'

'It's adrenalin,' he says smugly. 'When you're embarrassed your body releases loads of it, and adrenalin causes the blood vessels in your face to dilate, which in turn lets in more blood, and basically that's why you've gone all red.'

I slap the laptop shut with a huff. 'She won't accept my calls, she isn't replying to my texts. I'm going mental.'

Jamie stands up, tsking. He approaches the chalkboard that hangs next to his fridge and uses his fist to erase a number belonging to an Anna.

'What are you doing?' I say as he pinches a piece of chalk between finger and thumb.

'Seeing as you're going to be here a bit longer than we originally thought, I think we need some rules.' He starts writing. 'Rule one, no Damien Rice. Rule two, no double texting.'

I go to argue but he silences me with a raised brow. 'And rule three, no Facebook stalking.'

'I knew I should have gone back to Russ and Tom's.'

Jamie sweeps an arm towards the door, all *be-my-guest*, and I get about as close to laughter as I possibly could right now.

Which isn't very close, but still.

In an attempt to *keep busy* I decide to leave the house. I wasn't planning on coming here. It just happened, because sometimes life is like that, you do stuff for no real reason at all. Like me and Danielle.

I step off the bus near the gift shop and zip up my coat as I start to navigate the chalky path that snakes through the olive landscape.

I take the packet of cigarettes that I bought at Waterloo from my coat pocket and stop momentarily to light up. Seven minutes less of feeling like this seems appealing right now.

I only ever smoked when I was stressed but I quit altogether when Rebecca and I started dating. She never said anything, but her disapproval was there in the slightest kink on her forehead. And anyway, I was the happiest I'd ever been, I didn't care about my job; what the fuck did I have to be stressed about?

Sometimes if we'd had an argument I'd go outside and light up – a small act of rebellion – but it's been months since I felt the coarseness of the smoke in my windpipe.

I follow the circumference of the bed and breakfast and approach the naked edge of the cliff. A lone seagull calls out like a weeping dog in the sky, its wings perfectly still as it surfs the wind.

You have to leave . . .

. . . for good.

Of all the words Rebecca said on Friday, it's the final two that I can't shake. I start to cry, and the holding-your-breath trick doesn't work when it's mistakes and not onions causing the tears.

I stand here, looking out at the sea through blurry eyes. There are no fences at Beachy Head to prevent you falling should a heavy gust of wind grip your body, and some instinct born of fright kicks in, stopping me getting too close to the edge. It is almost a relief to feel something other than heartache.

I inch forward towards the verge, imagining my body smashing to the foot of the cliff but knowing I could never do it, and not because life doesn't seem totally unliveable right now. I'd just never have the—

I'm startled by a heavy hand on my shoulder. Instinctively I bolt, twisting my body 180 degrees and finding myself closer than before to a fatal drop.

'It's OK,' says the complete stranger, displaying his hands submissively and retreating a couple of paces. 'I just saw you up here and thought I'd see if you wanted a chat?'

The man is dressed in a fluorescent yellow jacket, a red T-shirt that only just covers his belly, and jeans. The wind has blown chaos into his greying but thickset hair. He introduces himself as Brian.

'I'm from the Beachy Head chaplaincy service,' he says, almost jollily.

'Oh, right,' I say, not entirely sure what he wants.

'You know this is the second most popular spot for . . .'

He looks over the edge, and another burst of adrenalin colours my cheeks as I realize he's come to talk me down.

'I was pretty sure you weren't a jumper, but thought I'd better check just in case.'

Curiosity gets the better of me. 'Why couldn't I be a jumper?'

He shrugs. 'You don't seem too comfortable up here. You doubled back as soon as you got within three foot of the edge.'

He chuckles and I join in, this whole journey suddenly seeming a bit silly.

'Anyway, young ones like you are usually on their phones if they're thinking of jumping.'

'How come?'

Another shrug. 'Saying goodbye, maybe.'

Who would I say goodbye to? Rebecca is rejecting all contact, Jamie will probably never forgive me, and Danielle? How can we stay friends after this?

'We get about four hundred potentials here every year and of those about thirty . . .' Brian jabs his finger towards the sea. 'You get a feel for who might actually go through with it. Sometimes they do it in front of us, there's nothing we can do.'

I begin to apologize for wasting his time.

'We've got a little hut just up the road,' he interrupts. 'Fancy a cuppa?'

There isn't much inside Brian's hut. Just a couple of chairs, a large cardboard box full of blankets and a trestle table with a kettle. On the wall is a pin board with a contacts sheet, takeaway menus and a rota.

'Where're you from originally?' asks Brian, gesturing for me to sit on the Paisley chair next to the table while he makes a brew.

'Manchester,' I tell him.

'City or United? And bear in mind that if you say United there's still time for me to give you a little push off those cliffs.'

I smile and tell him City, and he hands me a paper cup. I go to take a sip but scald my top lip.

'What are you doing here, then?' he says, drawing a stool from under the table.

'Well . . .' I feel stupid, but I tell him everything.

'I was going to bring her here to propose,' I conclude.

Brian allows my words to linger for some time before responding.

'I'd never say this to my wife but I always think relationships are like a long journey. Sometimes the scenery will take your breath away, and then sometimes it's one long stretch of boring motorway.' He produces a wistful smile at something unsaid, a memory. 'And then sometimes you can't see what's ahead because the rain is coming down so hard, and that's when you need to slow down, not do anything rash, because the rain

159

always stops eventually, and then you'll be able to see clearly again.'

He sees that I'm not quite following.

'Give her time,' he adds. 'If it's meant to be she'll see that eventually.'

'I hope you're right.'

I stare into my tea before taking a sip. It's cooler now.

'Rebecca is an architect,' I say, and Brian encourages me to continue with a nod. 'She once told me that when you create a building, if you make a mistake it's there for ever. You can't change it.' I bite my knuckles, pressing my teeth into the skin. 'I hadn't realized she applied the same principle to us.'

Brian gets a text but he ignores it.

'I should go,' I say, rising.

'Already?'

'It's OK. It's been really great to meet you, but I reckon there are people far more in need of your time than me. My problems are all self-inflicted.'

He stands too, holding out a hand for me to shake.

'Did you ever hear about the Austrian army in 1788?' I say. 'They accidentally attacked themselves and lost ten thousand men.'

He chuckles.

'That's me – I'm the Austrian army.'

Chapter Sixteen

REBECCA

Friday, 28 November

I can't decide if it feels like a million years or fifteen minutes since Avril let slip that Ben slept with Danielle, and I walked out of the cable car and out of my relationship. It's actually a month. A month since I had a boyfriend. A month since I had an entire happy day. A month since I had a proper night's sleep.

Which is why I've spent half the morning trying to fill out this order for materials for the cinema. Working out how much I need is basic maths but you'd think I was trying to crack a previously unsolved quadratic equation.

I finally fill in some numbers when my phone rings.

'Word up, Becca G,' is Jemma's greeting.

'Never call me that again.'

'Understood.'

But it makes me smile. 'What's up?'

'What are you doing tomorrow night?'

'Got loads of life admin to do.' I'll probably have cheese on toast for dinner and watch an old movie but I have a feeling Jemma's going to invite me to the drinks I overheard her arranging with Eddie earlier, so my plans need to sound more essential. I make a point of not socializing with work.

'I'm going out with a few of the work guys. Don't make me be the only lassie with a load of men.' She titters. 'Actually, I love being the only lassie with a load of men, but it'll be fun if you come.'

'Sorry, Jem. No can do.'

'OK.' She sighs. 'That's not why I called, by the way – there's someone in reception to see you.'

I'm not prepared for who I find hovering in the lobby when I step out of the lift.

My throat restricts so my voice comes out as barely a whisper. 'Danielle.'

'Hey.' The artist formerly known as my best friend greets me with a careful smile. 'How are you?'

'Fine,' I reply impatiently, aware of how many people are milling in and out of the office, with it being lunchtime. I need to get rid of her without causing a scene.

'Can we talk?'

'Not now.'

I can't even bear to look at her – the betrayal hits me afresh every time.

'When, then? You haven't been answering my calls. You pretend to be out every time I call at the flat.'

Actually, I've been working late every night so I had no idea she'd been dropping by, but I don't bother correcting her.

'Just give me a chance to explain,' she pleads loudly.

'Sshhh,' I whisper. 'Just go.'

'No.' She crosses her arms. 'Not unless you have lunch with me.'

I stare at her coldly but she meets my gaze and stares right back.

162

'I can't,' I say.

'Why not?'

'I have plans.'

'What plans?'

'Lunch with a friend.'

'Who?' Danielle isn't an idiot.

'You ready, Becs?'

Danielle and I both turn to look at Jemma, who's buttoning up her duffel coat.

'Wha—' I start, but then I cotton on. 'I mean, yes! Ready.'

'Oh,' I hear Danielle mumble. 'Well, soon then?'

When I don't respond, she smiles at me sadly then turns and walks away.

'Thanks,' I tell Jemma as the clicking of Danielle's stilettos fades into the distance.

'No worries. It's windy out – you'll probably need a jacket.'

'Er . . .'

'We're going for lunch.'

'Oh, I didn't realize you actually meant let's go.'

'Oh, come on. There's a new Vietnamese place just opened round the corner,' she coaxes. 'All this week when you buy a main meal you get a free glass of wine.'

I need something to perk me up and suddenly the thought of a drink sounds immensely appealing.

'Oh, OK,' I agree. 'You had me at free glass of wine.'

'It was literally the last thing I said,' she calls after me as I head up to get my coat.

I close my eyes as I take my first sip of wine, feeling at least a little of the tension dissolve.

'So, I had a date last night,' Jemma blurts out as soon as we've ordered our food.

'How was it?' I ask to be polite, but I'm starting to regret this. I need a loved-up lunch companion about as much as I need a kick in the tit.

'It was shite.'

Jemma explains how he asked her during the starter whether she is for or against Scottish independence, then spent the rest of the meal laying into her for not having an opinion.

I snort, realizing I haven't genuinely laughed for weeks and this is actually cheering me up.

'So how're you finding single life?' asks Jemma.

'It's all right.'

'Liar. It's pants.'

'Being single isn't pants.' I sip my wine. 'Realizing that the person you thought was your soulmate took your best friend home and slept with her on the night you met him – now that's pants.'

She's the first person I've actually told and saying it out loud gives me the same dizzy sensation I got when I first found out.

Jemma's eyes nearly pop out of her face. 'The lassie in reception?'

'That's the one.'

I'd never planned to go into detail. Aside from the fact it's painful to talk about, it's really rather embarrassing. What does it say about me if my boyfriend slept with someone else the night we met?

I don't know why I tell Jemma. Maybe there's something in her self-deprecation regarding her own love life that makes me feel at ease. Or maybe it's the way she

164

rescued me from Danielle earlier that makes me feel like she's on my side.

'Ah, shit. You got blindsided.'

'I got what?'

'There's a theory that the length of time you take to get over a break-up depends on why you broke up.'

'Go on.'

'So with the Mutual Break-up, you get over it quickly because you both want it so you're just relieved rather than heartbroken or feeling guilty. But if it's the Got Dumped Break-up, it will take longer.'

'It wasn't either of those things.'

'I know – there's a few more, like the Circumstantial Break-up and the First Love Break-up. Then, right at the end of the scale, there's the Blindside Break-up. The one you never saw coming.'

'That's depressing,' I tell her. 'It's not a real thing, though, is it?'

'Yes, I read it in a real magazine.'

'But hang on, I ended it so I did kind of see it coming. And what if he was also my first love? And it was also—'

'I don't know, I didn't write the bloody thing.'

'And will Ben take even longer to get over it because he Got Dumped?'

'It's different for men – they're too self-involved.'

'That's the thing, though,' I protest. 'Ben isn't self-involved. He really isn't. He stayed in Malaysia for months as a volunteer building orphanages for children, for crying out loud.'

Jemma smiles sympathetically and nods. 'Maybe he's a paedophile.'

I spit the wine I've just sipped all over the table, so Jemma chucks me my napkin.

'Thoughtless, then?' she suggests.

I shake my head. 'Ben's the most thoughtful man I've ever met.' That's one of the things I'm struggling with, because you don't see this sort of shit coming from guys who take you on surprise picnics to Beachy Head for your anniversary because you have a painting of it on your wall, or to Rome for your birthday because you've said you always wanted to see the Colosseum.

'What the hell are you doing to that napkin?' asks Jemma.

'Turning it into a chicken. Learnt it in Japan.'

'Right.' She looks at it sceptically. 'Anyway, don't be scared to fall apart a bit. I have this friend, Holly, who totally fell apart after this thing she had with her boss blew up big time.' She stabs a chunk of real chicken with her fork and scoops it into her mouth. 'But she got over it. In fact, I'm off to her wedding next month.'

'Good for Holly.' I smile. 'But the last thing on my mind is meeting someone else.'

'Can't hurt to have a dabble, though – take your mind off Ben.'

'I don't even know where I'd meet someone,' I admit.

Maybe I'm not the sort of girl guys gravitate towards. Maybe they go for someone like Danielle, with her fluttering eyelashes and her pouty lips. I always thought it was only a certain type of guy who was drawn to that. Turns out it's every guy.

'I think I just need some time, Jem,' I add. 'I'm still trying to come to terms with me and Ben breaking up.'

'Fair enough. And don't worry, I'm sure he'll get his comeuppance. They always do.'

'I'm not interested in revenge,' I say. 'I didn't break up with him to make him sorry. I just can't be with him any more. Knowing what he did and how he's lied about it, it's just . . .' I push food around with my fork, wondering why I'm attempting to articulate something I haven't got straight in my own head yet. 'It's just changed something between us, and I don't know if I can ever change it back.'

'You're a bigger person than me,' she says. 'I'm all about the revenge. Once, a guy I was sleeping with got a call while we were having sex, and he stopped to answer it. Then he admitted he had a girlfriend and that was her, wondering where he was.'

'No way. What did you do?'

'Well, the idiot left in such a rush that he left his phone at mine, so I—'

'Smashed it?'

'No, I—'

'Called his girlfriend and told her what he'd done?'

'No, but these are great ideas – I wish I'd thought of them. I turned the language on his phone to Finnish before I couriered it to his office.'

'That'll teach him.' I laugh again, and it feels good. Maybe it's the wine.

Jemma takes my napkin from me, her forehead creased. 'Is this a vagina?'

'No, I told you – it's a chicken.'

'It looks like a vagina. Look, there's the—'

'Why would I make my napkin into a vagina?'

'Why would you make your napkin into a chicken?'

I go to grab it back but she holds it out of my reach.

'Teach me to do it.'

'Next time. You ready to head back?'

167

'If we have to,' moans Jemma. She's about to say something else but then suddenly grins and sits up straight, her eyes focused over my shoulder.

'Totally hot dude checking you out at two o'clock,' she stage whispers.

'Eh?' I ask, looking at my watch again. 'I don't—'

Jemma stares at me like I'm an idiot until I catch on.

'He's a hunk,' she says urgently. 'Take a look!'

'No, I don't—'

'Look,' she insists.

I follow the direction of her eyes and inadvertently make eye contact with the suited, bearded man on the table behind me.

'Stop staring,' Jemma hisses.

'But you said—'

'I know what I said but you could have been more subtle. What do you think?'

'About what?' I say, matching her hushed tones.

'About the hairy dude.'

I shrug. 'He's all right.'

'Talk to him.'

'Don't be ridiculous,' I tell her, standing up to put my coat on. 'Come on, let's get back.'

As bad luck would have it, beardy man and his companion – a thin, bald man also in a suit – are standing up to leave too. I'm careful not to look his way but he reaches the door at the same time as me.

'After you,' he says and smiles, holding it open.

'No, that's OK, you go,' I reply.

'No, go on.' He waves me through.

'No, honestly – you go,' I insist with a similar gesture.

He hesitates, then goes through, rubbing his hands together outside.

'Looks like it might rain,' he says, while we wait for Jemma, who has stopped just before the door. She is rummaging in her bag to check she has everything, and beardy man's friend is hovering patiently behind her.

'Yep, it's pretty dismal,' I reply, pushing the door that's swung shut back open. 'Come on, Jemma!'

Beardy man and his friend head in one direction and us in the other. Jemma waits until we're a few metres away before she asks me: 'What the hell was that? He was totally flirting with you and you totally blew him out.'

'I did not. He was making small talk while I was waiting for you.'

'That wasn't small talk. That was the flirtation equivalent of him wondering if you come here often and trying to get your phone number.'

'Rubbish. Anyway, I was perfectly polite to him.'

'Polite? That was the flirtation equivalent of telling him to go forth and multiply.' I stare at her blankly. 'You basically just told him to fuck off,' she explains.

Really? Bloody hell, how do people know this? I'm glad I'm not . . . Oh. Yes, I am.

Single.

Beardy guy was right – it's pouring by the time I head off to the cinema so I leave my bike and take the Underground; a decision I live to regret twenty minutes later when we sit at the platform for ten minutes while the doors open and shut repeatedly and the driver tells us wearingly over the loudspeaker that we're not going anywhere until whoever is blocking the doorway moves.

When I arrive on site, Adam Larsson is already there chatting to Ravi and Bobby, the building contractors.

I hurry towards them, shaking my damp hair out of its high ponytail so I can fit my hard hat on. Adam says something I can't hear and the three of them laugh.

'Hi there,' he says louder, glancing at his watch.

'I know, I'm late. Sorry – Tube problems.' I hope this doesn't get back to Jake – I already blamed Tube problems after I slept in last week.

'No worries, girl,' says Bobby. 'Better late than never. White, two sugars for me, please.'

Adam and Ravi both laugh.

'I'm truly sorry to have missed out on all this bantz,' I tell them with thinly veiled sarcasm, making Bobby and Ravi frown, and Adam smile.

'Let's make a start, shall we?' I mutter, stomping off.

'Careful,' Adam calls, laughter still in his voice. 'The floors are wet.'

I ignore him. I'm wearing boots with a good grip – I'm not an idiot.

'I was just joshing,' Bobby says, catching up with me. 'I didn't mean anything by it.'

'Oh, I know.' I make myself smile at him warmly. I've worked with Bobby before – he's a good guy. 'Public transport just tends to make me want to kill someone, and you're the first people I've seen. Let's talk shop. How's it all going?'

Bobby talks us through everything. It's all on schedule, despite the place looking like a bombsite.

That's what happens, though. It gets worse before it gets better. You have to pull things down and rip things out before you can start fixing them. You can't just pave over the cracks.

'It'll be gorgeous when it's done,' Ravi concludes, snapping his folder closed. 'Such beautiful designs.' He's sucking up to me in case he offended me earlier.

'Beautiful,' Adam agrees. 'If slightly impractical.'

Bobby and Ravi glance at each other, some silent agreement taking place between them to start a conversation about cement trowels and wander off.

'Wouldn't it be better to pull down the old staircase? It feels like it takes up a lot of room,' he continues, seemingly oblivious to my narrowed eyes. 'You can add a stairwell here.' He runs his finger along the back section of my floor plan. 'That way you can make efficient use of all the open space.'

I study the plan. Frustratingly, he has a point. But when I first walked into the building, imagining what the central staircase looked like in its heyday took my breath away.

'I'll take your opinions on board,' I say non-committally, stomping off again.

'Hey, stop – that's really weak.'

'How dare you,' I begin in disbelief, but by the time I realize he's not talking about my designs but the boards I have just stomped into, I'm already hurtling through the floor.

Chapter Seventeen

BEN

I never really understood the concept of daydreaming until four weeks ago. To me you were either present or not present, but these past few weeks I've discovered that place in between, when your body is there but your mind isn't.

Right now my body is in Arch 13 on a wet Friday night, but my mind is—

'Ow,' I bawl, clutching my arm. 'Pack it in, will you?'

Jamie strolls back to the bar as if nothing just happened.

'It's his latest rule,' I explain to Tom and Russ, who look concerned, and to Avril, who looks like she'd rather be embalming herself than sitting here with us. 'He reckons he's allowed to give me a dead arm every time my face looks like one of those miserable fish you see on David Attenborough shows.' I turn to ask Jamie what they're called but he's serving a customer.

'Trout?' offers Russ, who's had his hair cut short at the sides like a Premier League footballer.

'No, it begins with B.'

Russ looks diagonally to think. 'I can't think of any fish beginning with B,' he says. 'But I like the rule. We need to do something to stop my thirtieth turning into a damp squid.'

'Damp squib,' Avril jumps in.

Russ loops his eyes. 'I know, Avril – it was a joke because Jamie said Ben's face looks like a . . .'

He gives up.

'Your birthday isn't until Sunday, anyway,' says Avril.

Russ and I share a look over the rim of our pint glasses.

I've always seen Avril as proof that love is blind, but over the past few weeks I've realized that, actually, love has 20/20 vision compared with *unrequited* love. Because, although I vaguely recall there were things about Rebecca that annoyed me, I couldn't tell you what they were. The Rebecca in my mind now is a flawless example of what God intended woman to be.

'Bream?' says Russ.

'No.'

Russ twists his lips, his face a picture of concentration until he spots the present leaning against Tom's stool. 'Is that for me?'

An expression of gormless joy decorates his face as he tears the paper. He is confused at first, scrutinizing the comic-book version of his own face alongside that of a busty superheroine.

'Tom drew it,' I say.

'And Ben got it framed,' Tom adds.

Russ is overwhelmed.

'You're not one of those comic nerds who has crushes on the female characters, are you?' Avril says.

Russ puts his elbow on the table and raises a finger as if he's about to make a serious point. 'I'm glad you brought this up, Avril – and you two . . .' He admonishes me and Tom with a look. '. . . should have known better.'

Avril leans in to listen, though her expression remains tepid.

'It has always irked me,' continues Russ, 'right from when I was old enough to know about Emmeline Pankhurst and the feminist struggle, that the creators of comic books somehow believe that a female superhero can't be heroic without exposing cleavage and gusset.'

Avril angles her chin and nods, pleasantly surprised.

'At least that's what I tell girls when I'm trying to get their numbers.'

I'm mid-sip, and the bubbles rise into my nose as I laugh. By the time I've composed myself Jamie has hung up his apron and joined us.

'That's the first time I've seen him smile all week,' he says to the other three.

'I told him earlier,' says Russ. 'If the wind changes his face is going to stay like that.'

'I think the wind changed a few weeks ago,' says Jamie. 'My dead arms are starting to feel like domestic abuse.'

'I used to say that to Rebecca,' I say. 'About the wind changing – not domestic abuse.'

Jamie looks at me like I'm dog shit on his shoe. 'Right, from now on you have to put your hand up before speaking.'

Russ and Tom's laughter is interrupted by Avril grabbing her coat. 'As stimulating as this is, I've got a recital to attend.'

Russ slings his hands to his chest like he's devastated. 'You're leaving?'

Avril acts like she hasn't heard him and leans her

cheek into Tom so he can kiss it. Once she's gone Russ tells us about his latest date.

'The first thing she said was, *I hoped you'd be taller.*'

Jamie cracks up. 'Had you not met her before?'

'He meets them online,' I answer for him.

Russ puffs his lips. 'It's an expensive game.'

'Avril was very particular about splitting everything when we starting dating,' says Tom, and the rest of us indulge in more surreptitious glances.

'It's nice when they at least reach for their purse,' says Russ. 'But I want my future wife to look back on our first date and think, *He was a gent.*'

I suppose I should be listening, taking notes now that I'm apparently single too, but contemplating life without Rebecca is like trying to imagine a new colour.

'Beaked salmon?' says Russ.

I shake my head, and Tom explains to a confused-looking Jamie that Russ is trying to guess the name of the fish I apparently look like.

'Don't tell me,' says Russ, as Jamie's mobile starts to ring. 'I'll get it in a minute.'

Jamie steps away to answer his phone and Russ watches him with an admiring glint in his eye.

'Maybe I should have drawn a picture of him and Jamie instead,' Tom whispers to me.

'I heard that,' says Russ, glaring at us, but then his expression melts. 'Actually, I think I'd like that. Maybe note it down for Christmas?'

The three of us laugh together but then no one says anything for a few seconds, and that's all I need to fall into another daydream.

I think what makes all this worse is that I didn't see any of it coming. Rebecca and I weren't slowly chugging to an end like a Walkman low on battery. Things were good, more than good, and then in an instant they weren't. More like an uncharged iPod cutting out abruptly midsong. I just wish she'd answer my calls, or reply to one of my messages, so we could at least see if we could recharge.

'Blobfish!' says Russ excitedly.

'Yes, that's it.'

'I looked at your face just then and it came to me.'

I'm about to apologize, because it's his birthday and I know I'm being a drag, but Jamie interrupts.

'That was Rebecca on the phone,' he says. 'She's had an accident.'

'What?' I put down my drink. 'What kind of accident? Is she OK?'

I reach for my own phone but Jamie puts his hand on mine. 'She's fine, mate. Just a sprained wrist and a bit shaken up, that's all.'

'What did she say?' I ask, irked by his lack of urgency. 'What happened?'

'She had a fall during a site visit but, really, she's fine. I just thought you'd want to know.'

I hear him sigh and shout after me as I dart outside to call her, but it's all muffled, like I'm underwater, drowning in all the words I want to say to her.

'FOR FUCK'S SAKE,' I scream when her phone goes to voicemail after one ring.

Only then do I realize I'm standing in a huge great puddle, surrounded by my own blurred reflection. And it hits me: I used to envy Rebecca's unsentimentality; wished I could be more like that, even. But now it's the very thing that's preventing us from sorting all this shit out.

176

'Come on, Nicholls,' I hear Jamie say. He must have followed me out. 'You're scaring off the customers.'

I let him usher me back inside, my shoes squishing against the floor, and I want to thank him, but I know that if I said even a single word the tears would start to fall.

'My round,' declares Russ, zigzagging through a herd of bouncers and into the club.

I thought about going home, but there's nothing to distract me from the daydreams there, and when Russ argued that I needed to drown my sorrows, I figured it was worth a shot.

'Three lagers and three sambuca chasers,' Russ tells a barman who is wearing a shiny gold shirt and a black afro wig. 'Oh, and a coke for my friend whose girlfriend doesn't let him drink.'

'It was my decision,' says Tom, but I reckon even he knows it's not a credible line of argument.

Jamie downs his chaser in one, so of course Russ follows suit. I think about tactically ditching mine but all eyes are on me, and there are sorrows to be drowned, so I close my eyes, swallow and slap the empty glass on to the bar top.

'Nice hairdo, by the way,' says Jamie.

'Thanks, buddy,' says Russ. 'I've been doing a lot of thinking lately about why I'm single, and I decided it was my barber's fault.' He picks up his lager but doesn't drink any. 'So I went somewhere new.'

Across the room the DJ adjusts his fake moustache as he jigs to Chic's 'Le Freak'.

'What *is* this place?' I ask.

I look to Russ for an answer but he's busy sniffing his

armpits. Apparently content, he gestures to the dance floor. 'Let's do this.'

He leads us to a spot that seems to be a thoroughfare for people needing the bog, and the bottoms of my trousers are wet from the puddle, and the speakers are so loud that I can't hear anyone speak, so I have to gauge from their expression whether to nod or laugh.

Russ dances like no one is watching, which has the effect of making everyone watch, or perhaps it's just the girls checking out Jamie. Tom, meanwhile, manages to dance without moving either his feet or his arms, like a tree swaying in the wind.

And me? I try to get into the spirit, I really do, but this drowning sorrows thing is total bollocks. You think you can drown them but it isn't long before they get wise to what you're doing, before they learn to swim. Right now my sorrows are Michael fucking Phelps.

I'm not sure how long I zone out for but the next thing I'm aware of is Tom stumbling forwards, barely managing to keep hold of his drink, and when I focus I see a fella about my height with a huge, open collar elbowing his way through the crowd. I feel a firm hand on my back, his hand, but he doesn't make eye contact or say excuse me before using his weight to try to bulldoze me out of the way.

I stand firm, and now his elbow connects with the middle of my spine, and in this moment all rational thought is overcome by this frustration inside me. I turn and position both hands on his chest, pushing him away with more force than I intended. A section of the dance floor clears as he stumbles backwards, but soon he's coming back at me.

'Easy,' shouts Jamie, wrapping one arm around my

chest and raising the other to halt the fella with the collar.

Through the glaze of alcohol I watch them eyeball one another until eventually the fella withdraws with a baleful stare.

'Come on, mate. Let's have a break,' says Jamie, leading us from the dance floor.

We squeeze into a pew opposite the bar.

'You were like fucking Batman down there,' I hear Russ say.

Jamie wafts his hand as if it was nothing. 'Though if you do insist on comparing me to a superhero,' he says, 'I think Spiderman is generally accepted as the best.'

'I'm with Jamie,' says Tom. 'I mean, even if you take all of Spiderman's superpowers away, he'd still be a genius.'

Russ nods like Tom has made a perfectly valid point, as he always does when Tom dares to proffer an opinion on anything relating to superheroes or comics, but in a second or two he'll embark on a diatribe that contradicts everything Tom has just said.

But then Jamie nods to agree with Tom, so of course Russ folds his arms and looks thoughtful for a few seconds. 'And actually,' he concedes, 'Spiderman was a hit with the ladies – Mary Jane, Gwen Stacy, Kitty Pryde.'

Next, Russ wants to take a group selfie.

'Could you smile, please?' he cries when I don't display the requisite enthusiasm. 'It's like being on a night out with Morrissey.'

Russ examines his retaken photo while Jamie tells Tom about a contact he's got at a gallery in Covent Garden. I'm wondering if any of them would notice if I tried to make a French exit when I feel a body insert itself into the tiny column of free space beside me.

'Sorry,' says a woman in a green dress, glancing at our touching thighs with a smile. 'I'm Natalie.'

Her accent brings to mind haystacks and tractors, and is the kind you instinctively want to impersonate.

'Ben,' I say.

I smile politely before turning back to Russ, but he's walking off towards the toilets, and Jamie and Tom are still deep in conversation, and I don't really know where to look as the DJ lowers the music to say something, so I study the rim of my glass.

'You know a club is rubbish when the DJ talks on his microphone in between songs,' I hear Natalie say.

I laugh, then check the time on my phone.

'Am I keeping you up?' says Natalie, her lips twitching mirthfully.

'No, God, sorry,' I say.

Natalie picks up her something and coke, pinching the straw between her forefinger and thumb and bringing it to her frosty pink lips. I watch the liquid rise up into her mouth. Even though my heart isn't in it I feel obliged to say something. 'Where is your accent from?'

'Weymouth,' she says, placing a finger behind her right lobe. 'Is this Boney M.?'

'That's where the Black Death started – Weymouth.'

Natalie looks vaguely startled. 'Well, I never knew that.'

I watch her finish her drink, noting that the flush in her cheeks is the product of make-up. It occurs to me that she would look prettier without, but that's one of those comments that is never taken the way it's intended.

'To be fair,' she says, knocking my shin with her foot while crossing her legs, 'I think I might prefer the Black Death to a night in here.'

'Good point, well made.'

When I turn to the others Russ is back, and he's pointing to his phone and smirking at me, but I've got no idea what he's on about.

'We're going to dance again,' says Jamie. 'You coming?'

I lean into him. 'I might head home in a bit.'

I don't hear his reply so I try to read his expression and decide to answer with *Cool*. He gives me a quizzical look before following Russ and Tom to the dance floor.

'I don't know about you,' says Natalie, standing up, 'but I need another drink if I'm going to stick around.'

I go to tell her what I told Jamie, about heading home, but she is presenting her hand so that I have little choice but to accept it and follow her to the bar.

Our eyes meet as we clink our fresh drinks, and I'm not sure how, but suddenly it's like we're competing in a game of stare, and somehow, for the first time in weeks, I'm present, in the moment.

I cling to the feeling, the release from thinking about Rebecca, and it takes me all the way back to Natalie's place, and although she doesn't know it, I'm still playing the game of stare, because I can just about do this, stay in the moment, enjoy it even, as long as I don't close my eyes . . .

. . . I snap them open, expelling Rebecca's image from my mind, pulling away momentarily and then directing my lips across Natalie's jaw and down to her neck, keeping my eyes wide as she twists from underneath me. She shuffles out of her tight jeans and pants and hooks her legs over my hips.

181

I try to swallow down a queasiness ascending my throat. I've always thought that sleeping with a woman is like getting the Tube. The first time you've got absolutely no idea where you're going, and the map bears no resemblance to what London actually looks like. It is only when you've made a few journeys that it becomes second nature. Like with Rebecca, I know which lines to take, the quickest routes, the nicest spots to end up. But this, here in Natalie's bedroom, feels unfamiliar, and there is an excitement in that, in having this unfamiliar body saddled on my lap, but I need to stop closing my eyes . . .

A seed of guilt sprouts inside of me. What if Rebecca and I make up and she asks if I've been with anyone else?

Natalie's hands proceed towards the top button of my trousers, which she unfastens with a single, adroit flick, and now it is *her* lips kissing *my* neck, and I'm having to concentrate really hard on keeping my eyes open. I'm aware of a pool of sweat forming on my forehead, and her right hand is flat against my chest, and her left is—

'Are you OK?' she says.

When I don't answer she drops into the open space beside me, our journey halted by unplanned engineering works.

'It must be the sambucas,' I finally say.

'Perhaps.'

Her *perhaps* isn't followed by a full stop; it's a *perhaps* with an ellipsis, a *perhaps* that I'm supposed to wonder the meaning of.

'Perhaps?' I say, accidentally impersonating her West Country accent.

Natalie folds her knees into her chest and wraps her

arms around them. 'I think I've worked it out.'

'Worked what out?'

'You've got a girlfriend, right?'

I sit up. 'I told you, it's the drink.'

'Oh, it's not just *that*,' she says, directing a finger at my groin. 'That happens more than you think.'

'What then?'

'Well, for starters it feels like you're in a parallel universe.' She starts to count points on her fingers. 'Like, you don't shut your eyes when we kiss, which is a bit strange.'

'I just—'

'Then at one point I thought you might be about to cry.' I go to argue but Natalie talks over me. 'And then you keep checking your phone.'

'I could have been waiting for an important call.'

'At five past midnight on a Friday?'

I pull the covers over my chest, cold. 'Go on, Miss Marple . . .'

'The first thing that made me think was how your mate looked at us as we walked out of the club – like he was concerned or something.'

'Which friend?'

'The hot one.'

She returns my stare, not flinching.

'I haven't got a girlfriend.'

Now she cocks her head and reviews me through squinted eyes.

'I've just split up with someone, a couple of weeks ago. It's all a bit messy. I still—'

'So I'm your rebound?' I sense Natalie smiling. 'Except you couldn't get the ball over the net.'

'Ouch.'

She curls her lips into an empathetic smile.

'Shall we just go to sleep?' she says, collapsing on to her back again.

'I thought I could do this but . . .'

It dawns on me that being in the present sucks, because the present is exactly where Rebecca isn't.

I finally allow my eyes to rest, submitting to another daydream, and there she is, and I ache for her so badly that I'm lying in another girl's bed and I know that this time, whether any words leave my mouth or not, I'm going to cry.

'I reckon it might be best if I go home.'

Chapter Eighteen

REBECCA

Saturday, 29 November

I don't know if it's the rain on my window or the buzz of my phone that wakes me.

U ok hun? says the text from Danielle. It is a piss-take of the type of Facebook comment that irritates us both, and for a split second it makes me smile against my will. Jamie must have told her about my accident.

I hold up my bandaged arm, wiggle my fingers and sigh.

I suppose I was lucky to get away with a sprained wrist, a bruised left buttock and a dislocated pride.

TALK TO ME, says Danielle's next text.

PLEASE, says another.

Delete, delete, delete.

If I had any doubts about keeping Danielle at arm's length, they were demolished when I saw her standing in reception yesterday. The only way to keep the hurt at bay is to not see her. I guess I'm still rejecting Ben's calls for the same reason.

Wide awake now, I get up and make an instant coffee before settling on the sofa with my laptop. I check the news, then – for want of anything better to do – open Facebook.

Poor sleep combined with the mundane nature of friends' statuses mean I'm yawning as I scroll, but then something catches my eye.

Ben tagged at Arch 13 by Russell MacDougall. There's nothing surprising in that, and I'm really not expecting to find anything when I click through to Russ's page. So when I see the photo at the top it jumps out at me like a clothes line in the face.

Ben, with a girl. And that's not Arch 13 they're in.

My coffee turns to acid in my throat as my eyes take in every detail of the picture, posted last night. Like how close they're sitting and how intimate their conversation looks.

I look at Ben's handsome, smiling face, and the girl resting her hand on his exposed forearm. She's pretty. Pale and innocent-looking, with flushed cheeks and a feminine green dress. She looks petite, like a dancer. I can picture Ben gathering her in his arms, picking her up and spinning her round – something he'd have looked ridiculous doing to me.

Did they just meet last night, or were they out together? Did he go home with her? Is she still with him now?

Another photo shows him, Tom, Russ and Jamie, all grinning to the camera. I push down the feelings of betrayal that rise through me, and scroll to the next picture – Ben, about to neck a shot.

He's having the time of his life. He must think this break-up is the best thing that could have happened. From nights on the sofa watching boxsets to clubbing with the lads, drinking shots and pulling girls.

Maybe I didn't know him as well as I thought.

There are no more pictures of the girl so I click back to Ben's page to see if they're Facebook friends. I'm less than halfway down his mile-long friend list, over-friendly bastard that he is, when I give up. This is ridiculous.

I'm ridiculous.

Even if I do find her, what exactly am I hoping to discover from her page? No good can come of Facebook stalking her.

Or him.

It only takes a second to make the decision, and I act on it before I change my mind. One click, and Ben and I are no longer friends.

Realizing I'm shaking, I look at the clock to make sure it's gone midday – it has, just – and pour myself a whisky from the decanter. Then I sit on the chair nearest the window and press my forehead against the glass. The pavements are shiny with puddles but devoid of people.

It's the kind of day when you don't leave the house unless you have to, and I peer at the buildings around and wonder what's going on inside them.

It dawns on me I don't know anything about anyone that lives on my street. I know the couple downstairs with the new baby are the Kilgannons, but only from dividing up the post in the hall. Ben has told me their first names, but I always forget them. In fact, there's not one door I could knock on right now, just to see if they fancy some company. Tears prick the back of my eyes but I refuse to let them fall, sipping my whisky to distract myself. The lump in my throat makes it hard to swallow.

Then it's like I float out of my body and see myself.

Sitting here, on a Saturday, face pressed up against the window, staring at the rain, glassy-eyed and drinking whisky.

Could I be any more pathetic?

Why did I pretend to Jemma I had stuff to do tonight? Retrieving my phone from my bed, I tap out a text message and send it before I change my mind.

The pub in Soho is heaving when I arrive but I can't spot anyone from work. I do a quick scan, then queue for a drink.

I'm just getting served when I feel someone pinch my bum.

'Did you think you'd pulled?' asks Jemma when I spin around.

'You're lucky I didn't knee you in the groin,' I tell her. 'Drink?'

While I get the round in, Jemma hovers by a table where a group are putting on their coats, then throws herself into a seat as soon as one of them stands up.

'What did you do to your wrist?' she asks as I lay the drinks down and shrug out of my wet coat.

It takes her about five minutes to stop laughing when I tell her, then when I pull down the back of my jeans a couple of inches to show her my bruise, she's off again.

'Thanks for your concern,' I tell her as she snorts.

'What are we laughing at?'

'Nothing,' I tell Eddie, who's just appeared in front of us.

He checks we're OK for drinks then heads to the bar, joined shortly after by two of the quantity surveyors, and one more guy in blue jeans and a white T-shirt, who I don't identify until Eddie leans forward to talk to the barmaid.

'Oh, great,' I mutter to Jemma. 'I didn't know Adam would be here.'

'Didn't you?'

She eyeballs me.

'Course not.' It never even occurred to me, though I wonder why it didn't – I know he's friends with Eddie.

To be fair, Adam was great after my fall. He made sure I was OK, put me in a taxi to the hospital when I insisted there was no need for an ambulance and managed not to gloat once. I would almost have preferred it if he did – then I could have been irritated rather than embarrassed.

'Don't tell me you wouldnae bone him,' Jemma says.

I stare at her, aghast. 'I would not bone him.'

'I had sex last night.'

'Thanks for sharing. With who?'

'A guy I met at my local. He's the barman, actually. So I can never drink in my local again, but still, it was worth it.'

I'm not sure why she's telling me this, and my face must give it away because she adds: 'I thought you might like to live vicariously through me given that you aren't getting any.'

'Thanks,' I tell her. 'I'm good, though.'

'It's your own fault you're not getting any,' she continues. 'You could get it all the time if you wanted to, but you refuse to go on dates and you scare anyone who chats you up with your ice-queen act.'

'We've been through this. Online dating isn't for me.'

'You'll never find a man with that defeatist attitude.'

'I don't need a man,' I insist. 'I'm working on the

189

biggest project I've ever had – it's good that I can focus all my energy into it.'

'Tell that to your vagina,' she says in disgust.

Before I can reply, the boys have joined us and are saying hello. They seem happy but surprised to see me here. Adam takes the seat opposite me.

One of the lads announces that he can't get too drunk as his girlfriend drags him to church on Sundays, and she'll throttle him if he's hungover. Jemma responds by asking if he'd rather have a bell ringing every time he's sexually aroused or a stabbing sensation in his side whenever anyone says his name.

Adam leans towards me while they all chat, and I expect him to ask me how I'm feeling.

'I think we need to up our game a bit with the cinema,' he says instead. 'We're way behind and there're still a few issues we need to . . .' He notices that my jaw has literally fallen. 'What's wrong?'

'You just told me I need to up my game!'

'I said *we*.'

'You meant me.' I fold my arms, the bandaged one on top. 'And I'm feeling fine, thanks for asking.'

He leans back in his seat, regarding me thoughtfully. 'You don't like me much, do you?'

I look at the others to see if they're listening.

'Exactly how loud would this bell be?' Eddie is asking. Jemma starts donging loudly.

'You don't like me first,' I accuse, turning my attention back to Adam. Christ, that doesn't even make sense. He laughs slightly and rubs the dark blond stubble on his chin, but when his eyes meet mine, they're serious.

'What makes you think that?'

'You always give me a hard time.' I shrug, feeling uncomfortable. 'You bark orders at me, you call me by my surname, you don't even attempt to be tactful when you question my work. You just have no respect for me. You don't treat the other girls like that.'

He sips his beer thoughtfully. 'And why do you think that is?'

'Because you don't think I'm up to the job.' The booze has made me brave enough to look Adam in the eye and say vindictively: 'I guess you're just more of a man's man.'

He nearly spits out his drink. 'So I don't like you because I'm sexist? Rebecca, you just totally contradicted yourself. You think I don't like you because I treat you the same as I treat guys, but you also think I treat you like that because you're a woman?'

He sounds a little angry now, but keeps his voice down.

'It's because I respect you that I don't treat you any differently from how I'd treat a bloke. I didn't have you down for the sensitive type. If you must know, that's *why* I like you.'

I open my mouth to say something cutting, but realize I have nothing. He's right. I'm looking for things he does to be annoyed at. And did he just tell me he likes me?

Not that I care, but does he mean likes me, or *likes* me?

Adam's stare is challenging me but just then Jemma stands up. 'My round,' she announces. 'Give me a hand, would you, Rebecca?'

'What was all that about?' she asks when we get to the bar.

'Just Adam being a dick,' I tell her, though I'm not entirely sure now that he was. Did I go over the top?

'When I looked over you were both sitting there with your arms folded, staring at each other, like you were about to have a really aggressive game of chess.'

She orders the drinks then looks at me meaningfully. 'Apparently mimicking someone's body language is a sign of attraction.'

'Drop it, Jem.'

'Consider it dropped. Now let's do a shot while we're at the bar.'

Adam doesn't mention the cinema again after we get back to the table and I feel my mood improve. Everyone is a little drunk, apart from Adam, who seems to be one of those people who manages to stay in control no matter how much he knocks back. People say that about me, but I'm not feeling very in control right now.

'What's on the agenda for the rest of the weekend?' I ask Adam, determined to make an effort.

'Rock-climbing in the morning.'

'That's random.' But explains the muscly forearms.

He smiles. 'Then I'll probably do some work in the afternoon.'

'You work too hard,' I tell him, and instantly regret it. Ben used to say that to me and it made me pity him that he didn't have a job he cared about enough to want to work too hard. I don't want Adam to think I don't care.

'You should come out more often,' Eddie tells me when Jemma and I get up to leave at the end of the night.

I don't realize quite how drunk I am until the cold air hits me.

And Jemma's just as bad. 'Crap, I can't find my door key,' she moans, rummaging in her bag for a moment then just emptying all its contents into a doorway. 'Crap, crap, crap, crap, crap.'

She stands up and pats her jeans pockets. 'Maybe it fell out in the pub.'

'Go check,' I tell her. 'I'll get this.'

I start putting her stuff back in her bag when I see a pair of black Lacoste trainers in front of me.

'You OK?' says the voice attached to them.

'Adam.' I stand up. 'Jemma's lost her key – she's just—'

'Yes, I saw her on my way out.'

We look at each other for a moment, then both look away.

'You off home?' I ask.

'Yep. Got to be up early.'

'Course. Those rocks won't climb themselves.'

'It was nice to hang out with you tonight.'

'You too,' I tell him, and I think I mean it.

I don't see what happens next coming, though. Him leaning forward, bringing his face to mine. I can smell his aftershave, and the warmth of his body, despite the chill in the air and the fact we're not even touching. Yet.

But in the split second before we're about to connect, Ben pops into my head. He's leaning down, his lips closing in on the lips of the girl in the green dress.

'I'm sorry.' I pull away, shaking my head. 'I can't do this.'

'It's OK,' says Adam, taking a step back and running a hand through his hair.

Jemma bursts out of the pub. 'I can't find it and my sodding flatmate is on a sodding hen weekend until tomorrow.'

In that moment, fat, black clouds explode, drenching us all instantly.

'Fuck my life,' yells Jemma into the rain.

'You can stay at mine,' I tell her, trying not to look at Adam.

As soon as a taxi with its light on appears, Adam holds out his arm.

'Here you go, girls,' he says when it pulls over.

'Are you sure?' I ask.

He nods, opening the door. 'See you Monday.'

'See you Monday,' I repeat, grateful for Jemma's presence so we don't need to talk about what just happened.

Back at mine, I get out of my wet clothes and into my bathrobe, handing Jemma the one that Ben left behind.

'You all right?' Jemma asks as she puts down the kebabs we made the taxi stop for so she can get changed. 'You were quiet in the cab.'

I force a smile. 'I'm fine. Drink?'

'Aye, go on.' She pulls the robe around her and sits on the sofa, feet on the coffee table and kebab on her lap. 'So, how're you coping without Ben?'

'Fine,' I tell her, handing her a glass of red wine and a fork. It's the first time she's mentioned him this evening.

'Fine?'

'Yep.'

'Yep?'

'Sure.'

'You really don't like talking about it, do you?'

'I just don't think it helps to dwell on it.' I unwrap my lamb shish.

'Too right!' Jemma sets her food aside and grabs my laptop from the coffee table, turning it on.

'What're you doing?'

'Signing you up for internet dating.'

'No, you're not.'

'What have you got to lose?'

'I just don't see the appeal of dedicating precious time to hanging out with strangers.'

'And what about Ben?' Jemma asks. 'Do you really think he's sitting around crying into his whisky?' She nods towards the glass I left on the coffee table earlier.

'Nope, I don't suppose he is,' I tell her through gritted teeth, thinking about the girl in the green dress.

'Just take a look,' Jemma coaxes, tapping a few keys while I top up our drinks. 'Here!' When I get back she swivels the screen towards me triumphantly. 'Tell me you wouldn't?'

'Pilot underscore Dan,' I read aloud, looking at the picture of a guy in sunglasses, sitting in what looks like a cockpit. 'He's good-looking,' I admit.

'Yes.' She bounces back down next to me excitedly. 'So we're setting up your profile?'

'Maybe another time,' I tell her, snapping the computer shut. I'm not ready to date Pilot underscore Dan, or snog Adam, or do anything with anyone else.

And I can't believe Ben is.

Chapter Nineteen

BEN

Monday, 1 December

I stand up at my desk.

'I'm gonna shoot off,' I tell Russ and Tom.

I hook my arms into my jacket, conscious of Russ checking the clock on his screen.

'It's not even three o'clock,' he says.

'Richardson's in meetings for the rest of the day,' I say.

I'm cooking a roast for Jamie tonight – my way of thanking him for everything he's done for me this past month – so these few hours will give me a chance to get everything I need from the supermarket and prep the dinner.

'But you still haven't told us what happened with Natalie on Friday. It's the code.'

'What code?'

'The man code.' Russ opens his arms like it's self-explanatory. 'The same code that says you can sack off your friends, even if it's someone's birthday . . .' He clears his throat for emphasis here. '. . . if there's a chance of sex. The code absolves you, Ben, but it also – and this is crucial – it also requires you to tell us *everything*.'

'I don't kiss and tell.'

Russ recoils, disgusted, but I'm out of there before he can protest further, wondering as I go whether the person who first said they don't kiss and tell also cried in a stranger's bed.

Jamie is on the phone when I get in so I unpack my ingredients, cursing when I realize I forgot dessert. When he finally hangs up I'm manoeuvring a hot lemon up a chicken's backside.

He watches me, perplexed.

'You pierce the lemon and the juices help cook the chicken from the inside,' I explain. 'That way it needs less time and stays moist.'

Jamie rubs his hands in anticipation.

'Who was on the phone?' I ask.

'Danielle.'

Her name hangs in the air.

'How's she doing?'

Jamie pockets his hands as I shove the bird into the oven.

'She can understand why Rebecca isn't talking to her, but *you* . . .'

'It'd wreck Rebecca's head if she thought Danielle and I were hanging out after everything. I'm just trying to do the right thing.'

Jamie presses his fingers into his temples. 'You're probably right; I just wish . . .' His sentence tapers out. 'So have you heard from Natalie?'

I watch him trying to stifle his amusement.

'Oh, get stuffed.'

'I mean, I've had girls cry tears of *joy* in my bed before, but . . .'

I groan. 'Talking of crying: do you remember my onion trick?'

'Yep, you hold your breath.'

'Good.' I pull out a chopping board. 'You're making the gravy.'

'I can't make gravy.'

'It's got booze in – it's practically a cocktail.'

I talk him through softening the onions and adding the carrot and celery to let them sweat, suddenly enjoying myself. He's about to pour in the red wine when he stops and attends the chalkboard.

'What now?' I say.

'Your Facebook statuses. I've been meaning to mention it.'

'I haven't been on it since last week – I don't want to break *the rules*.'

'What was it now?' He rests a finger on the corner of his lips while he thinks. 'Something like: *It's Thursday night and I'm bored*.'

'What's wrong with that?'

'Because what you write isn't the same as what people read. You write, *It's Thursday night and I'm bored* but what your friends read is: *I'm so lonely without Rebecca, I wish she'd take me back*.'

'Bullshit.'

He ignores me and pinches a piece of chalk. 'OK, so the following are prohibited: Facebook stalking, double texting, Damien Fucking Rice,' he wraps an invisible noose around his neck, 'and cry-for-help statuses.'

'And you're allowed to give me dead arms?'

'But only when you look like a blobfish.'

'You're going to miss me when I'm gone, I reckon.'

He smiles. 'I think you might be right.'

It's weird to say it, because going back to the flat is what I want more than anything in the world, but I'd be sad not living with Jamie any more. It can put a strain on a relationship, can't it? Living together. You're in each other's hair, you discover all the other person's annoying habits. But if anything it's made us even stronger.

Probably best to keep this to myself.

'How's work?' he says.

I open the oven to baste the chicken, then hoick myself on to the worktop and answer his question with a fed-up shrug.

'Maybe I should just shut up and get on with it?' I say. 'I mean, most people don't like their jobs, do they? And it's not like I ever have to take my work home. Unless you count the time Russ hid Tom's mouse mat in my bag.'

'You should definitely shut up,' he says, slumping into the couch. 'But just get on with it? No way. Look at all the shit I went through to do something I love. My parents still aren't over the fact their only son runs a bar.'

'But what's wrong with running a bar?'

'It's not something they can show off about at . . .' He strangulates his vowels. '. . . Cheshire Law Society get-togethers.' His chest jerks for a single, silent laugh. 'The irony being, it was their careers that persuaded me I wanted the opposite.'

Jamie never really talks about his parents, and I feel honoured he's opening up now to help me sort *my* life out.

'For them it's all about how much you earn, your status. They both hated being lawyers – hated it. And

199

yet they worked long hours, didn't take holidays.' He stands up and takes in the view of the Thames from his window.

'You remember my eleventh birthday?' he says. 'I came round with my new mountain bike?'

'Yeah.'

'I didn't tell you at the time because I was embarrassed, but I never saw them the whole day. I just woke up to find it wrapped up in silver paper in the living room, and they weren't back from work when I got home from school, so I came to yours.'

I remember it. We hadn't been expecting him, and when Mum discovered it was his birthday she rushed out to buy a cake before Kwik Save closed. I never got a whiff of him being upset, but clearly it stuck with him all these years.

'Basically, they put up with being miserable so they could retire comfortably at fifty.' His tone is matter-of-fact, not bitter. 'But guess what? They're still miserable now. What's the point in making yourself miserable for a day that might never come?' His chest inflates as he takes a deep breath, and he holds it for a second before letting go. 'That chicken smells fit, by the way.'

He comes over to examine the tray that I remove from the oven.

'Rebecca is going to struggle to find another wife like you,' he says, and when I laugh he gives me a look I can't quite read.

'What?' I say.

'This is the first time I've been in your company for more than half an hour and haven't had to give you a dead arm. In fact,' he approaches the chalkboard again, 'rule six: cook for Jamie.'

After dinner Jamie pops out to buy dessert.

While he's gone I attempt to recreate the finale to the 2011–12 season, the ultimate happy ending, at the foosball table. It's 2–2 at the Etihad, and we're into the dying seconds when an off-balance Balotelli somehow manages to poke the ball into QPR's penalty box. I'm just about to scream AGUERRRRRO, and declare Manchester City the champions, when the little plastic ball gets stuck under the striker's foot, and history has suddenly been rewritten.

I sit on the couch, staring at the framed posters of old liquor adverts that hang above the table. Rebecca gave them to Jamie for his birthday a couple of years ago, before our own history was rewritten.

Disregarding Jamie's rules, I switch on my laptop and go to her page, except . . .

Her picture has vanished, replaced by a white silhouette.

What the fuck?

I didn't know where else to go. The only thing I know is this isn't how it's going down, Rebecca deleting me from her life, not answering my calls or texts, acting like she doesn't have a choice in all of this. So I grabbed the small velvet box and came to the flat.

I'd planned to ask her to marry me at Beachy Head, but sometimes in life you have to adapt, like when the English quelled the Spanish Armada by altering their formation during battle. That's what I need to do now, change formation, adapt, because she'd have to listen to me, wouldn't she, if I went down on one knee?

My hand is trembling as I slot the key in the lock, ready to talk over her protests, but before the door is fully open I sense the flat is empty, and that I'm going to have to wait.

I wander around, reacquainting myself with the things we bought together just a couple of months ago. I sit on the bed, I run my fingertips across the walnut surface of the dining table, I stand in front of the couch. It feels like my life is on pause and I'm walking through it, everything static except me.

It took the delivery men an hour and a half to hoist the couch up the two flights of stairs, and my muscles ached from helping, but as soon as the men had gone Rebecca slammed the door shut and drew me on to the canvas upholstery. The motion of our bodies caused the couch to shift across the wooden floors so that by the time we collapsed, breathless and hazy, it was almost in the kitchen.

When I set off from Jamie's tonight I was expecting to find the dishwasher overflowing and to be tripped up by Rebecca shrapnel, but the place is spotless and it's a blow to my ego. The boxset we'd been watching before she kicked me out is folded neatly on the shelf, as though she's finished it without me.

I slump to the floor, back pressed against the cold radiator, and it's like someone is blowing up a balloon inside of me, filling me with emptiness. I check the time. Just gone eight. There is a text from Jamie asking where I am but I ignore it. I wonder where she is, how long she'll be. I don't know when exactly I become aware of a blue light flashing against the wall.

Eventually I stand and walk over to the source. It's coming from Rebecca's laptop. I pick it up with both hands as though to test its weight, and I'm conscious now of my heart working beneath my ribcage, pumping blood into my arteries, delivering oxygen around my body.

I've never so much as looked at the screen of her mobile when it beeped, and I wouldn't be contemplating what I'm contemplating now if Rebecca would talk to me, but what if I find something that helps me understand what's going on in her head? An email to a friend or something?

I freeze.

It was the sound of a door closing somewhere in the building. I listen for four, five, six seconds. It's a Victorian house, and though the staircase would have been added when the place was converted into flats, it's still old enough for every third stair to creak. But I can't hear anything now. It must have been Angus or Tasha from the flat below, or Carl on the ground floor.

I examine the laptop again while a hundred different thoughts ricochet around my head. Almost all of them warn me not to do it.

I hold a lungful of air for as long as I can take, starving my brain of the things it needs to think, and finally I let go.

I flick open the screen, and what I see is so unexpected that I laugh.

A dating website?

It's open on some fella's profile but I'm too stunned to look properly.

Rebecca wouldn't do that, would she? It's not her, and Jesus, I've only been gone a month. I know she's not the type to hole herself up with a box of tissues listening to Adele songs on repeat, but surely she hasn't moved on this quickly?

I close the laptop and breathe, trying to think of some

other explanation, but my imagination is overwriting everything, and it seems to have upgraded to HD, because it's like they're here with me in the room, Rebecca and this Pilot_Dan twat. He's pouring her a whisky from the decanter but for once she doesn't want whisky. She grabs him by his tie and yanks him on to the couch – our couch – and afterwards they watch an episode of *The Killing*.

With my fists bunched I survey the couch to see if it has moved across the wooden floor since I was last here. The idea of her falling for someone new, that I won't be important to her any more, makes me want to throw up.

I sling my right foot against the wall, but the release doesn't help, it just makes my big toe – one of the few parts of me that wasn't hurting like hell – hurt like hell.

I need to get out of here.

I unhook the signed Man City shirt from the wall in the spare room and shove as much of my stuff as I can into bin bags. I don't have a lot, clothes mainly, but I want her to see that it's gone; I want her to feel how I'm feeling.

Yes, I went home with Natalie, but I was pissed, and I couldn't do anything because all I could think about was Rebecca, but this, this is premeditated shit, and it makes me wonder whether the whole thing with Danielle played into her hands. Whether this was what she wanted all along, for us to be over?

I can't face going back to Jamie's yet, and I'll have to call a taxi with all this stuff anyway, so I rest my bike against a bench on the green behind the flat. I sit with my head in my hands, and the frustration and disbelief and longing of the last few weeks is turning into something new.

Anger. It bubbles inside of me, causing my legs to shake.

My phone starts to ring, and my first thought is that Rebecca has arrived home; she's seen the empty spaces where my belongings were, and now she is calling, distraught.

I look up to the flat but the lights are still off.

Dejected, I pull the phone from my pocket, and if it was anyone else's name on the screen I wouldn't answer, but some primal instinct takes over, an instinct that says this could be the one person who might be able to make me feel better.

'Hello, darling,' says Mum. 'Is now a good time?'

I was stupid thinking it might be anyone else. Mum calls at the same time every week. That's what thirty-five years working in a school does for you. Her time is divided and punctuated by the rings of a bell.

'Well, I wasn't expecting you, but . . .'

'Very funny, darling,'

It's the same joke I make every week, and there is something calming now about the routine of our conversation, her telling me about some new hobby of Dad's (car boot sales is the latest), me asking about work. She's saying something about her role changing, from secretary to administrator, or something, but I'm finding it difficult to focus.

'How's your work?' she asks.

'Same old.'

'Oh, well . . .'

One thing about Mum is that her words quite often don't correspond to her intended meaning. Over the years I've developed my own version of Google Translate in my head, so I can copy and paste anything she says, press return and find out what she's really getting at. In this case *Oh, well . . .* means, *Do you really think I've enjoyed being a school secretary all these years?* Which is funny really, because I know for a fact she *has* enjoyed it, as she loves nothing more than organizing and telling people what to do.

'And how's Rebecca?' says Mum.

I knew it was coming, and I'd planned to answer in the same way I have for the past few weeks. Rebecca is fine, I've told her, because honestly, I thought we'd sort this out.

'Do you know yet if she's coming with you for Christmas?'

I rest my eyes for a few seconds, then look again at the kitchen window, and that's the moment when I finally realize what this is: the third phase I wasn't prepared for.

Post-Rebecca.

'Actually, Mum, I'll be coming on my own.'

There is a short pause. 'Are you OK, darling?'

'Yes, it's just . . .' I try to swallow but my throat feels like it's been vacuum packed. 'Rebecca and I have split up.'

Chapter Twenty

REBECCA

Christmas Day

'*Buongiorno!*' Stefan bowls into the kitchen, takes my face in his hands and kisses both cheeks. 'Merry Christmas. What's going on?'

'What's going on,' I explain, mixing the stuffing while Dad wraps pigs in blankets, 'is we got so fed up waiting for you to turn up, we started prepping dinner. The turkey is in the oven.'

'What's that?' He points at my bowl.

'It's, um . . . a delicious combination of ciabatta crumbs, Italian sausage, turkey liver and herbs.' I try to pretend I'm not reading straight from the packet, which I chuck at his head when I see him smirk. 'Cock off and chop the carrots.'

'Discs or batons?'

'Couldn't care less.'

'On it.'

'Good to see you, son,' Dad says, patting Stefan on the back.

'You too, Marco.' Stefan double-kisses Dad. 'Shall we

just shove all this in the oven with the turkey and crack on with presents?'

So shove it in we do.

We're not one of those families who take it in turns to open our presents – we rip the paper off simultaneously, so the process starts at 12.03 p.m. and ends at ten past.

'Last one,' sings Stefan, throwing me a red envelope. Inside is a card with a picture of a snowman with coal for his eyes and mouth and a carrot for his genitalia; and inside that are two tickets to see Erasure.

'Amazing!' I grin. We both love Erasure – my brother had a battered old tape that stayed with us in every car in every country we lived in growing up. One of my earliest memories is us both singing along to it as we drove back from France to visit Granny for Christmas.

'They're at The Roundhouse in April.'

'Can't wait. Want me to leave your ticket here or should I keep them together?'

'Oh, they're both for you. I got us two each as I'm taking someone and thought you could bring . . . someone.'

Ben. He was going to say Ben.

'OK, cool.' I force a smile. 'Thanks.'

Stefan and Dad exchange a look. My family have stopped asking how I'm feeling about Ben. Probably because my answer was always the same: *I'm fine*. Thing is, I'm not entirely sure any more that I am fine. It's nearly two months since we broke up. Isn't time supposed to be a healer? It feels more like a paper cut that has grown into a knife wound.

'You hit the wine early today.' I can tell Dad is trying to sound casual as he glances at the glass I've just lifted. 'You usually have your first with dinner.'

'Neither of you interested in who I'm taking to the gig?' Stefan interrupts. Dad and I both look at him. 'My boyfriend, Jonny.'

I swallow my wine and then, inexplicably, burst into tears.

The confusion on Dad's face is understandable – Stefan never has boyfriends and I never have tears. Even as a kid, if my brother was picking on me or I was upset that we had to move again, I'd either go off on my own and sulk or go into an angry rage. Stefan cried more than I did.

'I'm just . . . so . . . happy for Stefan,' I manage to blurt out between sobs.

'That's a bit weird, sis,' says Stefan, his eyebrows knotting.

Dad puts a hand on my shoulder. 'What's wrong, love?'

'Nothing,' I insist. 'Tell us about Jonny, Stefan.'

'Well, he works with me,' my brother begins, sounding uncharacteristically soppy.

I honestly don't know what's wrong with me. I am happy for Stefan, but this isn't about that. I guess it's about Ben, and him seeing other people, and not even calling me on Christmas Day. He hasn't contacted me for weeks.

And it's about having a spare ticket to Erasure and not having anyone to invite, as Jamie is all I have left and he'll be at work.

I never really had close friends before I met Danielle and Jamie. It took me too long to open up to people and then we'd move somewhere else and the connection would be lost.

'People have been saying for ages, *We should really set*

209

you up with Jonny, you'll get on really well,' Stefan is saying. 'And I thought, *Why? Because we're both gay? That automatically means we'll fancy each other?* But it turns out we do fancy each other.'

I was set up once. Sally – the one girl from sixth form I stayed in touch with, because she went to the same university as me – set me up with her friend Tommy. It never went anywhere and then Sally and I stopped hanging out much. I think she felt stuck in the middle.

We still occasionally meet for a catch-up, though. I wonder if she likes Erasure?

This is so much easier for Ben, I think angrily, wiping away another stray tear. He's so natural at meeting people. Plus, he's already bagsied the bar for New Year's Eve, so he's the one that will get to see Jamie.

What am I meant to do for New Year? I want to stay in, get a takeaway and have an early night, but I can't bear that pity in people's faces when you reveal you've no plans.

'Anyone smell burning?' asks Stefan, who has been throwing balled-up wrapping paper at the wicker bin in the corner the whole time he's been talking.

'The turkey!' we all cry in unison, jumping up and running through.

The potatoes are as burnt as the turkey, the sprouts are soggy and the carrots and parsnips are still crunchy, but we congratulate each other on our efforts and eat every last mouthful, washing it down with lashings of red wine and finishing with shop-bought tiramisu, which Stefan brought. I'm grateful Dad and Stefan don't mention me getting upset earlier.

'Let's play Trivial Pursuit,' Stefan says.

'Or Cluedo?' I suggest.

'Or cards?' he says.

'Actually, I'm feeling a little stuffed.' Dad leans back and rubs his belly. 'Think I'll go for a walk first. Anyone want to join me?'

'Nah,' replies Stefan. 'I'm wearing Converse – they're not waterproof.'

'It's not raining,' Dad points out. 'It's been dry all day.'

'Really? Damn it. That was an excuse – I just don't want to go for a walk.'

Dad laughs. 'Rebecca?'

'Sure,' I say. I don't feel like it much either but the fresh air might help clear my head. 'Stefan can load the dishwasher when we're gone.'

'If you're at the beach, do check in on your snow house, won't you?' he tells me.

'Bite me.'

He's still whistling 'Walking in the Air' as Dad shuts the front door behind us.

'Are you OK?' Dad asks gently, as we start our walk up the lane.

'Yeah, Stefan and I were just kidding around.'

'I know. I wasn't talking about Stefan.'

'I'm fine.' I sigh, knowing my dad is the one person besides Jamie I can't fool. 'Ben moved out.' He came and got his things one evening before I got home from work, just a couple of days after I saw him on Facebook with that girl. 'I just feel a bit empty, you know?'

'I know.' He nods. 'But if you and Ben weren't right, then you did the right thing. A break-up is part of the painful process you have to go through to end up in a better and happier place.'

I never told Dad the actual reason we broke up. Close

211

as we are, the details just seem a bit too personal to share with him.

'But what if we were right for each other?'

At least when we first broke up, I was in control. If I'd have changed my mind, all I would have needed to do was say so.

But now? I've no idea if he's seeing the girl in his Facebook photos – I'm too scared to ask Jamie. Apart from being too scared to hear him confirm anything, I don't want to put Jamie in the middle. It'd be like Sally and Tommy all over again.

'Only you can answer that,' Dad says, and we carry on walking in silence for a while.

'It's not just about Ben,' I confess, as we take the path down to the beach. 'I haven't been sleeping. Like, at all. So I'm tired all day.'

We stop at the foot of the pier and stare out into the sea, crashing loudly in the wind. I pull my coat tighter.

'And I'm starting to feel overwhelmed with this work assignment,' I continue. 'It's like I can feel everything start to slip from my control and I can see it happening but I can't do anything to stop it.'

'Then take back control,' he says, like it's that easy.

I carry on staring out to sea. Maybe it is that easy. I link my arm through Dad's as we resume our walk. 'Tell me about what you've been working on.'

I always feel inspired when Dad talks about buildings, thinking that one day I could be as good and as self-assured as he is, but for the first time I get the fear that I haven't got it in me. I keep smiling encouragingly as he talks so he doesn't pick up on it.

The dishes are gone when we get back and Stefan is sitting at the dinner table with three glasses of Scotch and a box of After Eights, shuffling a pack of cards.

'Shall we start with rummy?' he asks.

I feel like I need to be by myself for a bit so I rub my tummy.

'I've got a bit of indigestion,' I lie, lifting my glass and heading for the living room. 'I'm just going to lie down for ten minutes.'

I love this room. It's best when it's pouring with rain outside, and I get all snug on the sofa, wrapped in one of the blankets Granny knitted. Today is the first day in ages it hasn't rained, of course, which pretty much sums up my luck at the moment.

Plonking myself down on the sofa, whisky on the floor beside me, I flick on the TV. The national anthem blares out, marking the start of the Queen's Speech.

'In the ruins of the old Coventry Cathedral is a sculpture of a man and a woman reaching out to embrace each other,' she begins. 'It is simply called *Reconciliation*.'

I almost laugh into my whisky when she talks about how, one hundred years after the start of the First World War, Christmas is the time to celebrate forgiveness.

I should have brought the bottle through with me.

Last Christmas I was happy. Ben and I weren't at war, and I didn't leave work each day feeling defeated. Who would have thought it would all go so monumentally tits up?

'This carol is still much-loved today, a legacy of the Christmas truce, and a reminder to us all that even in the unlikeliest of places hope can still be found,' concludes the Queen.

Tears blur my vision as I look at my phone and the choir starts to sing 'Silent Night'.

I empty my glass then put it on the floor, picking up my phone instead.

Take back control, Dad said.

I find Ben's number and hover my thumb over the call button. I don't know what I'm going to say but I know that I need to hear his voice, just to feel reassured he's thinking about me too.

I press call.

Chapter Twenty-one

BEN

Dad looks at his watch.

'It's ten past three,' he says. 'The old witch will be done now.'

He raises his pint glass for me to clink.

'To the Queen!' I oblige.

It was my idea to give the speech a miss this year and come to the pub instead. All that reflecting on the year that's past – I just couldn't stomach it.

Getting the idea past Mum was the hardest part. She adores the Queen. It must be her upbringing because Uncle Pete and Auntie Helen are the same. The mere sight of Her Majesty on Christmas Day can be enough to make Uncle Pete teary. Though this could also have something to do with the 'Christmas brandy'. Which is the same brandy he drinks every day of the year, but adding 'Christmas' makes him feel better about being drunk by half ten in the morning.

In the end, Dad suggested we use Rebecca as an excuse. He told Mum I needed to get everything off my chest, father to son.

'I feel bad,' I tell him now.

'I don't,' he says. 'She's bought me a bloody rake for Christmas.'

'How do you know?'

We don't open our presents until after dinner, which Mum refuses to start cooking until the speech is over.

'You ever tried wrapping a rake so the other person can't tell what it is?'

I laugh, enjoying the distraction. After looking at Rebecca's laptop I made a decision: the only way I could move forward was to cut off contact, and yet every day there is still a part of me that hopes this will be the day she wonders why I haven't been in touch, the day she realizes this has all been a stupid mistake. But I'm kidding myself, and every glance at my blank screen is a reminder that Rebecca is doing just fine without me, thank you very much. I left my phone back at the house when Dad and I made our escape, because today I don't want to feel angry.

'We should head back,' says Dad, downing the remains of his pint.

The pavements are a shade lighter today, the rain that seems to have been pouring for months having finally ceased. Dad points at a sparrow as it lands on the handle of a climbing frame in the beer garden.

'Happy Christmas, birdie,' he says.

We watch the sparrow peek one way and the other, as if checking its flight path is clear, before fluttering away.

'Do you reckon it even knows it's Christmas?' I say.

'Like that Bob Geldof song, you mean?'

I laugh again, rejecting his offer of a cigarette.

'Do you remember the time you caught me smoking in the shed?' I lean against Dad's black cab while he puffs away. 'You asked me to hand the packet over and my heart was beating so fast – I was shitting myself.'

I watch the memory return to him.

'Then I realized you only wanted them so you could light up yourself,' I say.

'I was out there for the same reason as you,' he says. 'To get away from your mother.'

We snuck out there regularly after that. Our little act of rebellion.

Dad bends down to stub out his cigarette on a drainage gate and we're off. Because there are no other cars on the road the chug of his diesel engine seems even louder than normal, each gear shift eliciting a noisy jerk.

I notice a chip in his windscreen and recall an advert from a few years ago: all chips turn into cracks eventually. Is that what my Danielle secret was? A chip in a windscreen?

It's as though Dad has read my mind because he asks if I've heard from Rebecca. I gesture *No* and leave it at that. I've always been able to share things with Mum and Dad, but this afternoon, for the first time in months, I've felt like *me* again, and I want it to last just a little bit longer. And anyway, I haven't even told Jamie about cutting off contact. How would I explain why?

'Your mother and I almost split up once, you know?' says Dad when we pull up at some lights. 'Before you were even thought of.'

I turn to him, shocked. I've always thought they were unbreakable. Even the way they met was special. Dad had been homeless as a teenager. His parents booted him out when he was fifteen after he got expelled from a fourth school for shoving a teacher to the ground. He spent two years on the streets before someone agreed to give him a job washing taxis. He learnt to drive by moving cabs around the company's yard and one day they were desperate for a driver, so they gave him a chance. That was how he met Mum: driving her home early from a Christmas party. She asked who he was spending Christmas with and he said no one, and when she said there must be places for people who don't have anyone to spend it with, he said he didn't think so. So Mum set one up at her school and Dad went along. That was more than thirty years ago. I never realized it almost turned out differently.

'I saw some fella in a bar with his hand on her arm,' explains Dad, drumming his fingers against the steering wheel. 'So I floored him.'

I'm always surprised when Dad tells me stories like this. It's not the man I know.

'Turned out to be her boss.'

I wince.

'She didn't talk to me for a month,' he says, glancing at the lights. 'I dropped two trouser sizes.'

'How come?'

'I was so miserable I couldn't eat.'

I reach over to pat his belly as the lights change and the car struggles into motion once more. 'Maybe Mum should stop talking to you again for a few months?'

Mum was the only person here when we left, but most of her side of the family have turned up now. Uncle Pete is stationed on an armchair, clutching a hanky in one hand. He never married or had children, but two of my other cousins from Auntie Helen's side are here. Felicity, who recently turned seventeen, offers me and Dad a dutiful smile while Conor, who's a couple of years younger, grunts some form of greeting but doesn't look up from *my* iPhone.

'Oi.' I swipe it from him and click off the game he's been playing.

'You missed a wonderful speech,' says a voice from behind us.

I turn around to see Auntie Helen wearing a red tissue hat like a crown. I make a show of looking disappointed at missing out.

'Don't worry,' she says, her face becoming gleeful. 'We recorded it so you can watch it later.'

Auntie Helen opens her arms. I go to kiss her cheek, noticing the smell of hairspray mixed with peppermint as she whispers into my ear: 'Probably best waiting until Uncle Pete has gone, mind – it was all a bit too much for him again.'

'Thanks, Auntie Helen.'

She seizes both of my hands and squeezes them. 'Now, let me look at you.' She examines my face as though peering through a magnifying glass. Finally she says: 'Good.'

Without elaborating Auntie Helen releases my hands. 'Conor and Felicity are here,' she says, just in case I'd missed them sitting a few feet away. I humour her by waving at them and this time they completely ignore me. 'Sadly your cousin Matthew couldn't make it,' adds Auntie Helen. 'He's gone to Switzerland with a friend.'

I know Matthew is in Switzerland with his fiancée – her parents own a chalet there – but Auntie Helen is obviously concerned about the effect such knowledge would have on the newly single me. In fact, as we catch up she goes out of her way to avoid mentioning Rebecca, which is quite amusing, really.

219

I go to see Mum in the kitchen, where she is tunnel-boning the lamb ready to stuff it with her special Christmas stuffing: dates, cranberries, nuts and breadcrumbs. She taught me everything I know.

I fetch the mix from the fridge, which is crammed with quiches and *Finest* pizzas and buffet selections. Mum prides herself on always having just-in-case food, but at Christmas it goes from 'just in case we have visitors' to 'just in case there's an earthquake and our house is designated as an emergency shelter'.

'How's work?' I ask her.

Mum shakes her head as though there's nothing to report.

'They're taking the piss out of her, that's how work is,' Dad interjects.

I remember Mum mentioning a few weeks ago about her role changing, but I've been so preoccupied with my own problems that I never bothered to follow up on it.

'Why, what's going on?' I say, feeling guilty.

'Let's not talk about work at Christmas, darling.'

'They've changed her role without consulting her,' says Dad. 'Now she dreads going into work every day.'

'Oh, don't exaggerate, Trevor.'

'This wouldn't have happened if you'd stayed in your union,' he says.

'So your old role doesn't exist any more?' I ask.

Mum nods.

'And this new role is not something you wanted or would ever have applied for?'

She shakes her head, more decisively this time.

'You know you're entitled to redundancy?' I say. 'I can help you get what you're entitled to – I can do all the work for you.'

Mum looks at me, and then at Dad, then scrunches her face up like I've suggested she joins a cheerleading team or something. 'I'm too old to do anything else. What would I do with myself?'

She stuffs and rolls the lamb, and I hear her mumble *redundancy* and titter as I wait with the string.

'Why aren't we having turkey like normal people?' drawls Conor, skulking into the kitchen as Mum ties the meat.

'Where are your manners, Conor?' Auntie Helen shouts through.

'They just texted to let me know they can't make it.'

I hear Auntie Helen sniff her disapproval from the living room but she lets it go.

'Lamb is a better choice when there's loads of people,' I tell Conor. 'There's lots of fat so it stays moist.'

He nods interestedly, then says: 'Are you gay?'

Auntie Helen comes into the kitchen and whacks him round the head. 'By the way,' she says to him, 'your presents just texted – they can't make it either.'

'A Kindle!' whoops Felicity. 'Thanks, Ben!'

Seeing what I got Felicity, Conor quickly rips off the wrapping on *his* present.

'These are, like, proper Beats!' He puts on the head-phones. 'Cheers, Benny Boy – these are the balls!'

'Language, Conor!' says Auntie Helen.

'What? I said balls, not bollocks.'

Auntie Helen turns her attention to me. 'You really shouldn't have spent all that money, Ben.'

She's right, I *really* shouldn't have. But I wanted this to be a Christmas to remember.

'A rake!' Dad is saying. 'Just what I wanted, dear.'

'No need for sarcasm, dear.'

Having opened all his presents, Conor nurtures an expression of complete disinterest until I unwrap my gift from Mum and Dad, at which point he snorts into his elbow.

'Get it on,' he bawls.

Uncle Pete looks confused. 'What is it?'

'It's a onesie,' says Dad.

'A bear onesie,' adds Mum.

Uncle Pete is none the wiser. 'What the hell is a bear onesie?'

'It's a onesie that looks like a bear,' says Conor, barely able to contain his excitement. 'Now put it on, Ben*der*.'

Uncle Pete has given up trying to understand what is happening but Felicity has put down her phone and even Auntie Helen seems amused.

'We want to see what it looks like on, Ben,' she cajoles.

'Fine, fine,' I say, sulking for effect. 'But just remember that I'm cooking brunch tomorrow and it would be a shame if all your Christmases were spoilt by a bout of food poisoning.'

When I return in the onesie Auntie Helen claps her hands in delight and orders Felicity to take a photo.

'It's all right,' says Conor, pointing his new iPad at me, 'I'll email you mine after I've put it on Instagram.'

I feign a punch to his arm, but it doesn't shut him up. Everyone is in hysterics now, even Uncle Pete.

'Oh, I'm sorry I've embarrassed you, Ben,' says Mum, grabbing my tail, which I grab back with an *Oi*, pretending to be precious.

'Yeah, he just can't *bear* the embarrassment,' shouts Conor, and the laughter redoubles, and I'm laughing too, feeling relaxed and happy for the first time in months.

'I just thought it'd be nice for you to have something to snuggle up in,' says Mum.

'Since you can't snuggle up to Rebecca any more,' chips in Conor, silencing the room.

'Conor!' says Auntie Helen, slapping him with force on the back of his skull.

'Soz, I was doing such a good job not mentioning Rebecca too.'

He receives another whack.

'What was that for?' he protests, but Auntie Helen is back laughing at me now.

I inspect myself.

'I'm going to pop to the shop,' I joke, breaking the tension. 'Anyone want anything?' Everyone laughs again and normality resumes.

I decide to keep the onesie on as we settle down in front of the *EastEnders* Christmas special, but I'm not really watching.

Out of habit I check my phone but of course there is nothing, and for some reason I find myself thinking about the chip in the windscreen, and how Rebecca is so stubborn that her eyes will always be drawn to it. I've just got to accept that it's over.

'Sorry about what I said earlier,' confides Conor as everyone else sits glued to whatever is happening in the Queen Vic. 'Like, about Rebecca.'

'It's OK, mate,' I say, and as the dum dum dums sound over the closing shot and the credits begin to roll, I realize that it is OK. *I'm* OK.

Not good and certainly not great, but OK, and that at least is progress.

223

Chapter Twenty-two

REBECCA

New Year's Eve

You can't start a new chapter if you keep re-reading the last one.

I groan loudly, shove my phone under my pillow and try to go back to sleep. That's the third inspirational quote my friend Sally has sent me since I told her about me and Ben.

I never even gave her the details – I just casually slipped it in when I replied to her *Merry Christmas* round-robin text message on Christmas Day.

It was shortly after Ben rejected my call after one ring, so when my phone beeped I thought it might be him to say sorry, he was in the middle of dinner, but would call back. She must have sensed something in the tone of my reply, because now she's under the impression I need talking down from a ledge.

Unfortunately, by the time she began her touchy-feely assault, I'd already accepted her invitation to bring in the New Year at a pub in Waterloo with her and her friends.

She means well, I know. And I should be grateful – I guess I do need to get out of the house. When you're in a couple, the few days between Christmas and New Year are an excuse to sit around watching boxsets and eating cheese.

When you're single they're about feeling alone and eating cereal straight from the box.

Maybe that's just me.

Feeling too hot, I roll on to my back and kick off my quilt, sighing heavily. I might be feeling more positive about tonight if Sally hadn't also revealed that Tommy, the friend she set me up with at university, is coming. I was only seeing him for a few weeks but he was more interested in being a lad than being in a relationship, and would stand me up in favour of getting wasted in the student union. He was obviously capable of changing his ways for the right person, though: he recently got married.

Not that I care – it's just that the last thing I need right now is a reminder of another relationship I couldn't make work.

Christ almighty, maybe Sally is right. I do need an attitude transplant. She's a good person, and she's trying to cheer me up. It was lovely of her to include me in her plans. And something does need to change. Maybe I should write some New Year's resolutions.

I try to open the drawer on my bedside table but it's jammed with the crap I sweep in there every time I remember the cleaner is coming. Maybe I'll just make the list in my head.

My resolutions:

- Sleep better. Listen to whale music?
- Stop dropping the ball at work. Will be easier once sleeping better.

- Stop wondering whether Ben will get in touch today. It's been two months since we broke up. Get over it.
- Learn to cook. Something. Anything.
- Expand my social circle.

That'll do for now.

I jump out of bed with a new determination, but pause on the landing, aware that I've a good nine hours before I'm meeting Sally.

I attempt a bath. Trying to emulate the women in adverts who look like they haven't a care in the world as soon as they lean back in the tub, I light candles and switch my radio to Magic FM.

I haven't had a bath since the time Ben convinced me it would be romantic if we had one together, I realize as I sit on the edge of the tub waiting for the water to fill.

'She's Always a Woman to Me' by Billy Joel is playing when I finally slide my body into the hot water, and as I feel my muscles relax, I think about that bath with Ben. After gallantly offering to take the tap end, he couldn't find a comfortable way to position his neck. He ended up lying diagonally, and I had to turn on my side and hold his ankles so I didn't go under. We ended up in hysterics as we tried to manoeuvre ourselves into a comfortable position, eventually settling with our heads at the same end, spooning, with his face squashed into the back of my head.

'Told you this would be romantic,' Ben said after a few moments, which set us off again.

Yep, this is much easier. Comfortable, relaxing, and . . . kind of boring.

The last straw is when Céline Dion comes on.

Shrugging my arms into my bathrobe, I head through to make coffee, which I'm spitting into the sink ten minutes later. How can anyone mess up coffee?

I've watched Ben do it a thousand times. Three scoops into the cafetière, fill it with hot water, plunge, pour, enjoy a delicious smooth brew.

So how come it tastes like dirty bathwater when I do it? I pour the rest of the murky brown liquid down the drain then drop the mug with a clang. The handle breaks off. Bollocks.

I pour myself a whisky instead – it's a special occasion after all – and scour the kitchen for food.

Zero, zilch, zip, nada, nothing . . . feck it. I'll get dressed and go and eat at Arch 13. It'll be quiet now ahead of tonight's party so I can catch up with Jamie, and Ben won't be there until later.

The bar is virtually empty when I arrive but Jamie doesn't hear me approach. I climb on to a stool as he stands with his back to me, chopping a pineapple.

'What's a girl got to do to get a drink around here?' I yell with my elbows on the bar and my chin in my hands, as if I've been there for ages.

Jamie turns around, his face breaking into a grin. 'What are you doing here?'

'I was really bored.'

'Jeez, thanks,' he bites, pouring whisky into two glasses, glancing up at me as he does. 'You look fed up.'

I answer with a shrug.

'Cheers,' he says, sliding my drink down the bar so that I have to push my hand out to block it before it flies off the edge.

'That was risky,' I tell him, taking a sip.

'I trust you,' he says. 'Now talk to me.'

'Honestly, I'm fine. I'm just not a fan of New Year.'

'You had a great time here last year.'

'Yep, and I'm sure you and Ben will have a great time again tonight.' I don't mean it to come out as snarky as it does, and when Jamie looks hurt I wish I could take it back. It's not his fault.

'That's not fair, Becs – I want you both here, and I won't pick sides.' He puts down his drink then brings his chopping board over and carries on slicing. 'Not my fault if you want to stay in and be a martyr,' he adds, smirking playfully.

'Oh, feck off,' I tell him, leaning over to steal a chunk of pineapple. 'I'm not staying in, anyway – I'm going to a pub in Waterloo.'

'With who?'

'Remember Sally from uni?'

'Self-help Sally?'

'That's the one.' My stomach rumbles and I remember why I came.

Jamie goes to get some bottles to stock up so I order food from Erica, who brings it out to me worryingly quickly.

'Enjoy,' she sings as she lays it in front of me in a manner I can only describe as apologetic.

'For the love of God, Jamie – what is this?' I ask when he gets back.

'Well, what did you order?' He peers at my plate.

'The Oriental platter. But what is this specifically?' I show him the beige pastry I've bitten into, which now has brown gunk oozing from its core.

'What does it taste like?'

'Shit.'

'Well then . . .'

'Seriously – I don't even know if it's meat or something else.' I submerge it in soy sauce and toss it in my mouth, grimacing. 'Man, I miss Ben's cooking.'

Jamie doesn't respond so I dunk another unidentifiable triangle into my sauce and meet his eyes. 'How is Ben?'

'Ben's good.'

Good?

'Good?' I repeat, waiting for Jamie to give away more, without me having to ask for it. I wonder what he's been up to the past few days. Maybe he's been seeing his new girlfriend. Maybe they had a bath together. I bet it was really romantic.

'Yep, good,' he repeats back. 'You know Ben. Bit frustrated with work so I'm just trying to help him figure out what he should be doing.'

'Good luck with that.' I laugh drily. That's one thing I don't miss about Ben – him coming home from work and moaning about his job every day, but doing nothing about it.

I shove my platter away, unsure whether my loss of appetite is due to the conversation or the food itself.

'Why don't you come tonight?' Jamie pleads.

'Ben is coming.'

'So? I'm not saying you need to mouth-kiss him at midnight or anything. You need to find a way to be in the same room as each other, though.'

'Why?'

Jamie looks hurt. 'For my sake.'

I feel terrible. I haven't given nearly enough thought to how this must be affecting him. His friends are everything to him.

'Sorry,' I say. 'We will. Just not tonight.'

'Do you want another drink,' he says. 'Or are you heading off?'

I peer reluctantly out at the windy forecourt then hold out my glass. 'What time is it?'

He glances at the clock. 'Five o'clock.'

'Plenty of time. Make it a large.'

Sally and her friends are already at the bar in Waterloo. They're sitting in a window seat, so I sneak up and press my face against the glass grotesquely, knocking. Sally jumps a little, then laughs.

'Tenner, please,' the doorman barks.

'Holy moly!' I exclaim, reaching in my bag for my purse. It's a less-than-average pub, and usually free to get in.

He grunts. 'New Year's.'

'Helloooooooooooooo,' I greet Sally's gang loudly as I walk in. The smiles freeze on all their faces. 'Sorry I'm so late.'

'Hi,' says Sally, getting up to hug me. Good old Sally. A big advocate of the healing power of the hug. 'Um, are you OK?'

'Great. Super-duper, in fact. Lovely day, isn't it?' I point outside. 'Excuse my hair, by the way – it's a little wind-swept.' And come to think of it, I don't remember brushing it when I nipped back to get changed. I remember pouring myself a whisky, though. And another.

'All right, Rebecca?' Tommy says unsurely as he stands to kiss my cheek. 'How are you?'

'More to the point,' Sally interrupts, 'how drunk are you?'

'I'm not drunk.'

I'm shit-faced. But though I may not have brushed my

hair, I'm no longer wondering whether Ben will get in touch today, so, you know, swings and roundabouts.

'I'll get you some water,' says Sally. 'Wait here.'

'Where would I go?' I call after her, then turn to Tommy. 'You got married,' I say, holding Sally's white wine in the air. Tommy hasn't changed – he's a rugby boy, and looks it, but with a soft, cuddly quality about him.

'I'm aware.' He clinks his beer bottle against the side of the glass I've tilted towards him, and I can tell he's trying not to laugh.

'Contratolshions.'

'You mean congratulations?'

'What I said.'

'Drink this.' Sally is back with a pint glass.

'Only if it's gin,' I joke. Neither of them laughs. 'I don't need water,' I insist, but as I say it, the room revolves and suddenly I'm thirsty as hell, like I possibly might die if I don't drink the water.

'Fine,' I say, taking the glass nobly. 'If it'll make you happy.'

I down it, and for a horrible moment I think I'm going to throw it back up, but I just hiccup.

We're all silent for a minute or two – even their friends who have been chatting amongst themselves up until this point – until Sally says, *Hold your breath*, and I realize I'm still hiccupping.

'Everything OK?' shouts the barmaid collecting glasses from the next table. It's loud in here, but with talking and clinking rather than music or fun.

'Fine, thanks,' Tommy says. 'Could I order some chips, please?'

The barmaid nods and walks away.

'Rebecca?' Sally takes my hands in hers, stroking my palms with her thumbs. 'Is this why Ben left you? Because of your drinking?'

'*What?* No,' I say. 'And he didn't leave me. I threw him out.'

'Why?' Sally asks, while Tommy raises his eyebrows.

'He slept with Danielle.'

They both gasp.

'Your best mate Danielle?' says Tommy quietly. 'Christ. Let me get you that pint of gin.'

'I can't believe it,' Sally insists. 'I know I only met him once, but he didn't seem the type.'

'He had us all fooled,' I say.

'How did it happen?'

'She was upset, he was comforting her.'

'Man, that's bad.' Tommy shakes his head.

'I know. He's a bad man.'

'That was his excuse?' asks Sally in disgust.

'Yep, and us not being together yet, blah, blah, blah.'

'Hang on . . . What do you mean?' Sally says, hands pausing mid-stroke. 'You weren't together yet?'

'No, we were. Kind of.'

Tommy pushes the chips that the barmaid has just brought towards me. 'Here, eat these. So, how long had you been going out?'

'Well, we weren't going out per se,' I say, devouring the chips. 'But we had met. That night.'

'Had anything happened? Did you kiss?'

'No, but we talked. Anyway,' I add as I watch them exchange another look, 'it's not about the fact he slept with her. He's been lying to me about it ever since.'

'Has he?' asks Tommy. 'You asked him if he'd slept with her and he said he hadn't?'

'That's not the point,' Sally steps in. 'He's not been honest, and shouldn't get away with it on a technicality.'

'Exactly.' I love Sally.

'Look,' she says to me, 'things will get better. You know what they say: an arrow can only be shot by pulling it backward. So when life is dragging you back with difficulties, it means it's going to launch you into something great.'

'Who says that?' I ask, while Tommy rolls his eyes.

'Make fun all you want. All I'm saying is you have your whole future ahead of you.'

'Everyone has their future ahead of them,' Tommy points out.

'Rebecca,' says Sally, ignoring Tommy, 'you will get over this.'

'Or,' Tommy says after a moment, 'crazy idea . . .' He waves his hands around his head to illustrate the crazy. '. . . you could forgive him.'

'Are you kidding me?' I ask.

'Why not?'

'Did you miss the part about him sleeping with my best mate and not telling me?'

'No, I doubt anyone missed it. You speak rather loudly when you're drunk.'

'Yep,' agrees the barmaid, taking the empty chip bowl. 'We all caught it.'

'Surely you understand why he didn't tell you?' Tommy continues. 'Why does it have to be one strike and you're out with you?'

'What's that supposed to mean?'

'Do you remember why we broke up?'

'Because you weren't ready for a relationship. At least

not with me. You were more interested in boozing with your roommates.'

'That happened once,' Tommy says, raising his own voice. 'I really liked you, and I thought things were great, then there was one night the lads were trying to get me to stay out, taking the piss out of me for wanting to leave to be with you, so I stayed out. I was nineteen and at university, but you made out like I'd proved I couldn't be trusted, and dumped me.' He lowers his voice again. 'Not that I care or anything – I'm married now.'

I try to think about what he's saying but my head feels fuzzy. I think my hangover is kicking in. Is he right? Was it just one time?

'Tommy's right,' says Sally gently, though she's looking at him funny. 'Not about Ben – what he did was wrong, and I can see why you'd find it hard to trust him again. But you don't make many allowances for people. It's like you're so scared of needing anyone that as soon as they let you down once, you bail. Has Ben ever done anything to hurt you before?'

I think back to our year together. There was bickering, but nothing like this.

'I don't think so,' I admit.

'Don't be afraid to let people in. That's all I'm saying.'

I'm about to say more when I realize that all of Sally and Tommy's friends have paused their conversation. Even the ones that aren't looking my way have shut up so they can eavesdrop subtly, some looking amused while others look bewildered. I feel myself blush. What am I doing here? I don't know these people. This is far lonelier than being by myself at home.

'You know what, Sally?' I stand up shakily. 'I might go. I'm not feeling great.' She doesn't try to stop me.

'Let's arrange another catch-up soon, though,' I add to be polite.

'Deffo,' she says brightly. 'Maybe we could do lunch? Or grab a coffee?'

'Sure.' She really must think I have a drinking problem.

The fresh air is a relief. I move far enough away from the bar not to be seen then stop and sit on a wall. How did I end up here? The streets are busy, full of groups of friends, laughing as they rush to their next party, and couples holding hands as they head towards the bridge to get a good spot for the fireworks.

This time last year I had all those things: friends, stuff to laugh about, someone to kiss at midnight. Maybe Jamie was right. Maybe I should have been at his party.

A taxi crawls past and although I'd planned to get the train, I find myself waving it over.

'Where are you off to, love?'

I go to say my address but stop. I look at his clock. 11.27 p.m.

'Arch 13,' I tell him, leaning forward. 'Head towards Greenwich station and I'll direct you from there.'

Chapter Twenty-three

BEN

'I'm OK,' I tell Jamie. 'Not good, not great, but OK, you know?'

'That's progress,' he says, standing up from his stool to applaud the band he booked for the New Year party.

They've finished the first half of their set and Erica is turning up the background music for the interval. Jamie gives the singer a thumbs-up as he and his bandmates head outside for a smoke.

'Christmas was a turning point,' I say. 'I kind of accepted that it's over.'

He smiles to show he's heard me, but still doesn't offer an opinion, almost like he's sceptical. A few seconds pass.

'So what are Danielle and Rebecca up to tonight?'

I frame it like a casual enquiry to show that, really, I'm in a good place, a place where I can chat about my ex in passing without it being a big deal.

'Danielle said it'd be too hard to spend it in Green-wich without Rebecca, so she's going to a house party in Shoreditch with her cousin.' Jamie sighs, and I know he's thinking that *last* year we spent it all together. 'And Rebecca's seeing friends.'

I want to ask him which friends, but that would transform my casual enquiry into an enquiry dressed in a tuxedo and bow tie, so I change the subject.

'I've been reading that book Tom got me for my birthday,' I tell him. 'You know Michelangelo didn't actually want to paint the Sistine Chapel? He wanted to sculpt, but when the Pope asks you to do something you do it, right? So he spent years doing something he never enjoyed, but then he had the Sistine Chapel to show for it, whereas all I've got to show for my years at London Transport are a set of Acceptable Internet Usage guidelines, and it didn't matter when I was with Rebecca, because the rest of my life was perfect, I had direction, but . . . Are you even listening to me?'

'It's not that I'm not listening, it's just that some of the things you say go straight to my Junk folder.'

His answer takes me aback, and I sulkily ignore the sarcastic grin he offers me. After a few silent moments I wonder if being hungry is making me oversensitive.

'I dread to think what the Chef's Special Sauce consists of,' I say, examining the menu.

I order a cheeseburger and when Jamie goes to help Erica serve, something he said earlier comes back to me. *Rebecca's seeing friends.* 'Friends' is what I'd tell a mate if his ex was with a new fella. A mental JPEG opens without me double clicking on it: Rebecca flirting with Pilot_Dan via a sideways glance.

'Has Rebecca got a new bloke?' I ask Jamie when he retakes his stool.

'What?' He turns to me. 'No, not as far as I know.'

I study the dregs of my lager, trying to work out if he's telling the truth as the band resumes with Marvin Gaye.

'I know she's online dating,' I say.

He looks at me wearily. 'Rebecca?'

'It's true.'

'How do you know?'

I finish my drink and pick up the new one Jamie just dispatched on the bar. 'Heard it through the grapevine.'

He scrunches his face dismissively.

'Seriously, what makes you think Rebecca – Rebecca! – is meeting guys online?'

He stares at me, waiting for an answer, and I understand now that I've driven down a road with no room for a U-turn.

'I saw it on her laptop.'

'What are you talking about?'

Now it's me sighing. I explain everything.

'So, just so we're straight,' he says. 'She deleted you from Facebook so you went round there to propose?'

'Yes.'

'And because she wasn't there, you did the obvious thing: you snooped on her laptop,' he folds his brow, 'and saw she'd been on a dating website?'

I was expecting Jamie to be indignant on my behalf, but if anything he looks pissed off at *me*.

I'm vaguely aware of the singer thanking his audience but neither Jamie nor I are paying attention now. It's a relief when my cheeseburger arrives because it means I don't have to look at his accusing eyes, but I can sense him watching me, so that I become conscious of the way I'm eating.

'You masticate too much,' he finally says.

I stop chewing. 'Pardon?'

'I've always thought it about you. I don't know why I've never mentioned it before.'

I take another bite of my burger and in a deliberate act of rebellion swallow after two chews. I instantly regret it.

'To be fair,' I tell him, 'this burger is so overcooked that if I didn't chew it thirty times I'd need a chimney-sweep to remove it from my throat.'

He doesn't take offence.

'I'm not just talking about food,' he says.

'So what, I'm supposed to be happy she's dating other people?'

'I'm not saying that, but sometimes in life you just need to swallow.'

We smirk like teenage boys, levity returning, then turn to watch the band. I see that one of the girls dancing at the front is Tidy Tania. She steals a glance our way, and I realize Jamie is sacrificing another chance to get with her to spend the night with me.

'So anyway,' he says, 'how's that turning point working out for you?'

'Piss off, Hawley.'

It's annoying, but he's right. I came back from Manchester thinking I was getting there but now I'm not so sure. It's being here, this place, where we met, and where this time last year we were so happy. And even though Jamie says he doesn't believe it, I know what I saw on her laptop.

I shove my plate away, feeling the anger bubbling again.

'Maybe you should think about getting your own place,' Jamie says.

I see his eyes venture my way but I don't react, waiting instead for him to play his full hand. 'I love having you at the flat, and I've never eaten so well, but if you really are going to reach a turning point . . .'

239

I concentrate on wiping a column of condensation from my pint glass.

'Is this because my bike's in the way?'

'It's not about the bike.'

The place erupts for the band once again and Tidy Tania looks at Jamie with an *Oh my God, they're so good* face.

'So what, you just want me out of the flat to stop cramping your style?'

'You know it's not like—'

'What then?'

'You want me to be honest?'

'Be my guest.'

The singer asks the bassist what the time is, but it's all part of the act. With beads of sweat making tracks down his temples he tells the room there's time for one more song before the countdown to midnight.

'No one wants you and Rebecca to get back together more than me, but it's not looking likely, is it?'

'I know, and I told you earlier I'd accepted that.'

'Yes, and then you've spent half the night asking about her.'

I tighten my grip on my glass. I'm on the defensive now. 'Exaggerating much?'

'I know you were hurting but looking at her laptop, that's not good, mate.'

Why is he saying this? I know he's frustrated that Rebecca and Danielle aren't here, and I know this whole thing has affected him too, but he's supposed to be my oldest mate, to have my back, and yet it feels like he thinks it's totally fine that Rebecca is going on dates already.

'I'm speaking as a friend,' he says. 'I don't like what it's doing to you.'

'What's that supposed to mean?'

I'm morphing into a petulant teenager but I can't stop myself.

'Look, when sad stuff happens you can either let it eat at you or create something positive from it. You're letting it eat at you and life's—'

'Don't tell me, *Life's too short*.'

Jamie pinches the top of his nose between finger and thumb, as though trying to explain something to an idiot.

'You know how many heartbeats most people get?'

'Enlighten me.'

'Three billion, if they're lucky. You can't waste them moping around feeling sorry for yourself. You need to make as many of them as possible count for something.'

'So I'm not allowed to be upset that the girl I loved more than anything in the world doesn't want me any more?'

He rubs the scar above his eyebrow. 'You've just wasted seven heartbeats asking me that.'

He tries to act all jokey but he's pissing me off.

'It's not just the Rebecca thing,' he says when he clocks that I'm not smiling. 'It's your work situation. I've heard it for years, and you're right, it wasn't so bad when you were with Rebecca, but if splitting up with her has made you remember how much you hate it, see it as an opportunity; do something instead of just talking about it.'

The singer thanks the audience again, and then the countdown begins. Ten, nine, eight . . .

'I knew you weren't interested earlier.' It's my wounded pride talking now. 'All that masticate bollocks was just your way of telling me to shut the fuck up, wasn't it?'

Jamie raises his palms, a placatory gesture. 'Calm down, mate. I'm just—'

'Don't tell me to calm down.' I stand up. 'You know fuck all about how hard these past few months have been for me. How could you? You haven't been in a serious relationship since sixth form.'

Three . . . two . . .

'You're incapable of taking anything seriously, that's why you decided to run a bar rather than get a proper job.'

The trumpet player launches into 'In the Midnight Hour' and Jamie looks stunned.

I stand there, regretting everything I've said but not knowing how to take it back. Instead I leave, away from the kissing revellers and the overcooked burger, away from Jamie. I walk out, into the street as fireworks light up the London sky.

I feel relief as fresh air fills my lungs, but it doesn't last long. I realize that I can run away from all of those things, but I can't run away from the one thing that hurts the most – the truth.

Chapter Twenty-four

REBECCA

Friday, 2 January

New Year 1–0 Rebecca.

First day back at work and I was supposed to come in and kick ass, but not only am I still not sleeping, now I have a whole new layer of angst to contend with.

Arrghhhh, I groan internally, rubbing my eyes. Why oh why did I go back to the bar on New Year? Or at least, why didn't I leave again when I realized Ben wasn't there after all? If I hadn't been so gutted about missing him, this never would have happened.

As soon as I woke up this morning the memory of Jamie being there in my bedroom came flooding back. No matter how hard I try to pretend it never happened, my mind won't let me block it.

Having to avoid Ben and Danielle was bad enough – I don't want to have to avoid Jamie too. But how can I face him?

'Rebecca?' The voice makes me jump out of my seat.

'Sorry, Jake. Yes?'

'Can we have a quick catch-up?'

'Sure,' I say, wondering if he's going to ask me if he's

carrying any holiday weight or whether he's too old for his new goatee.

'I'll get straight to the point,' Jake says, waving me into the seat opposite him in the meeting room. 'We're in bad shape. The pre-planning stage is way behind schedule. Some of this is down to workforce problems, so we've signed off an increased headcount, but there're a couple of things I need your help to get to the bottom of.'

He opens his notepad.

'According to the schedule, the piping was meant to be delivered to the site before Christmas. It hasn't turned up yet, and it's holding up the groundwork.' He looks up at me. 'Do you know what date you sent the order?'

'Definitely three weeks ago.' Is when I shoved it in my top drawer with the intention of sending it as soon as I got back from lunch, but forgot. Fuckity-fuck. 'I'll chase it.'

'Please do, as a matter of urgency. Also, I can't find a signed copy of permission from the Local Planning Authority. Do you have a copy of it?'

My palms sweat. I haven't sent anything to be signed. Schoolboy.

'Have they contested anything?'

Please say no. We won't be able to go ahead without the signed agreement, and will have wasted shitloads of money. I'll get sacked. And then I'll be single and un-employed, and I'll probably have to move back in with Dad, and—

'No,' Jake says. 'But it's vital we have it.'

'I'll dig it out,' I promise.

Jake pushes his glasses up on his head and rubs his eyes. 'Can I say something, Rebecca?'

'Sure,' I reply, digging my fingernails into my palms. No one ever asks for permission to say something if the thing they're going to say is good.

'And please take this in the spirit it's intended.'

Balls.

'This is an important project for the firm.' He brings his hands together, as if in prayer, and taps his chin with them, as though deciding how to word this. 'And the reason we put you on it was because you're one of the most thoughtful architects we have. Your natural instincts about what is worth restoring and what needs modernizing are exactly what the cinema needs. And I know you can do it. This is your chance to really shine, and make a name for yourself.'

'Thank you,' I say slowly, aware that he hasn't finished.

'But the bottom line is we need to know that you're up to it.'

My heart hammers in my chest. Jake doesn't know if I'm up to it?

I know I've made a few oversights recently, but I had no idea my boss was questioning my ability.

'I am,' I try to assure him. I consider telling him I've had a few personal problems but I don't want to sound like I'm making excuses.

He smiles and nods, getting up to walk me to the door and I shuffle back to my desk, stinging from his words.

My desk phone rings and Jemma's name pops up on the screen.

'Do you know how many calories are in a Terry's Chocolate Orange segment?' she asks without waiting for me to speak. 'Forty-six. Imagine what the whole orange is. I hate myself. You OK?'

I make a noise that indicates things could be better.

245

'Bad day?'

'Kind of.'

'Want to talk about it? The Lion has just had a refurb, we could check it out after work?' Jemma continues. 'Have a cheeky glass of wine as it's Friday?'

'Sounds good.' I'll just go for one glass, I think as I hang up. Take the edge off.

'Rise and shine!'

'What the hell . . . ? Hang on, who's that?' I glance at the silhouette that just pulled back the curtains. 'Jem? Is that you?'

'It is. I didn't like to stick you in a taxi alone in the state you were in so I came back with you and stayed over.'

'Was I drunk?'

'Steaming.'

'Ouch!' Untying the wrap dress I still appear to be wearing, I discover a big, purple bruise on my right hip. 'Oh my god!'

'That'll be when you fell off the table,' says Jemma.

'Ha, seriously, though . . .'

Jemma isn't listening. She's on her phone, which she thrusts in my face. There's a grainy video of someone dancing on a table to 'I Don't Feel Like Dancing'. No sooner has it sunk in that it's me then there's a crash and I disappear off the screen.

'If I ever do that again, rather than film me could you perhaps make me get down instead?'

'I can't promise that. But don't worry, this is just between you, me and, so far, a hundred and four YouTube users.'

'You didn't!'

'Course I didn't. You hungover?'

'Nope.' I sit up, then immediately lie back down again. 'Yep. A little. Must be because I didn't eat anything.'

'Except the chicken.' She sees my blank expression. 'Remember? Lucky Fried Chicken? He asked how many pieces you wanted and you challenged him to see how many pieces he could fit in a box?'

'Classy.' I groan. 'How'd we end up so drunk?'

'Think we were doing shots at that place after The Lion.'

We went somewhere else after The Lion?

'Why were we doing shots?'

'Because my New Year's resolution is to lose two stone and I figured that mixers have unnecessary calories.'

'You don't have two stone to lose, Jem,' I tell her, closing my eyes again to stop the throbbing in my head.

'I don't just want to be thin, I want to be emaciated. Like, so people wonder if I'm a smack head. You made any resolutions?'

'Generally to be less of a fuck-up.'

'Well, you're nailing it so far.'

I start to laugh but it makes my head worse.

'Sorry I woke you, by the way,' says Jemma. 'My data has run out on my phone so my maps won't work. I just need directions to the station.'

'Give me five minutes and I'll walk you there.' I should probably get out of yesterday's work clothes.

'I'm so far from home,' Jemma whines as we take the river path down towards the train station. 'My friend Holly lives in Blackheath and it always takes me years to get home.'

'I'm not surprised when you walk at that pace,' I half-joke.

'You don't need to march at a million miles an hour when you have access to the Tube. You should all move to north London, it's so much bet . . .' She slows – practically to a halt – to focus on something across the road. 'OK, fine. I'll move here instead.'

Jamie is on the other side, waving at us.

I feel my cheeks redden as we leave the path and cross the street towards him, visions of him in my bedroom invading my head. I banish them and wave back.

'Hey.'

'Hi,' he says with an easy confidence I envy. He kisses my cheek then holds his hand out to Jemma. 'I'm Jamie.'

'Oh my God. . . and I'm Jemma! Our names are practically the same,' she gushes as she shakes his hand. 'Rebecca's told me all about you.'

Jamie tries to catch my eye and I hope he doesn't assume she means I've told her all about the other night.

'I'm just about to open up if you girls fancy coming in for a coffee?'

'Jemma has a train to catch,' I tell him, avoiding his gaze.

'Och, I'll get the next one,' says Jemma. 'A coffee would be ace.'

'Or maybe a hair of the dog?' I suggest. I might need a drink to get through this.

'So, how's 2015 treating you?' Jamie enquires as I help pull down chairs from tables. Jemma wanders off to give herself a tour.

'All right,' I mumble. 'And you?'

'Not bad.'

'Good.' I wonder if he's said anything to Ben about what happened on New Year's Eve but I can't bring myself to mention it, so I just ask: 'How's Ben?'

'Haven't seen him since the party,' says Jamie.

'How come?'

'I think he's gone back to Manchester.'

Now it's Jamie avoiding eye contact, and I'm about to ask why Ben has gone back so soon after he was there for Christmas, when Jamie says: 'I think I have a plan for him work-wise.'

He stops and leans on the back of the chair he's just placed on the floor, and I think he's going to say more about his plan for Ben, but what he says is: 'Look, about the other night . . .'

'We really don't need to talk about it, Jamie,' I whisper, finally meeting his eye. 'Let's forget it. We're good.'

'This place is wicked,' calls Jemma from one of the red horseshoe booths.

Jamie turns from me to smile at her. 'I'll get the coffee machine on.'

'Make mine Irish,' I call after him, sliding in next to Jemma, just as she's clambering out the other side.

'I'll give him a hand,' she tells me.

I watch her climb on to a stool and lean across the bar to chat to Jamie. I have to hand it to her: when it comes to men, she's not scared to do the chasing. No matter how many setbacks she has, she'll keep taking risks.

A few minutes later Jamie disappears out back and returns with a piece of paper and a pen, handing it to her. Oh my God – is she giving him her number?

'I know exactly what you're up to, you know,' I remark when she returns a few minutes later.

'You do?'

She looks slightly embarrassed.

'Jem, it's so obvious,' I say. 'Why would you go up to

the counter unless you wanted to speak to Jamie without me hearing?'

'Right, here you go, ladies.' Jamie carries over the
drinks on a tray, then pulls a chair over and sits on it
backwards. He and Jemma exchange a look.

What's going on?

'She knows,' reports Jemma.

'She heard?' asks Jamie.

'Hey, it's no big deal,' I say quickly. I don't want either
of them to think I have a problem with them swapping
numbers. I especially wouldn't want Jamie to let what
happened the other night stop him.

Jemma sighs and pulls a sheet of paper from her
pocket, holding it up for me to read the messy letters
written across it in Biro.

'Uoitu . . . hang on, I can't really—'

'Sorry,' she yelps, turning it round. 'It was upside
down.'

Intervention.

'Um . . . ?'

Jemma takes a deep breath. 'Jamie is worried about
your drinking, and I agree. So this is an intervention.'

'Seriously?' I smirk. 'You're hosting an intervention
on my drinking . . . in a bar?'

They glance at one another, and Jemma shrugs. 'It
was a spontaneous intervention. A spintervention, if you
will.'

'Well, if I'm going to have to sit through this, I'll need
a proper drink. Mine's a large Scotch.'

They don't crack a smile.

'I don't have a drinking problem,' I insist, laughing.

'That's exactly what someone with a drinking problem
would say,' Jemma tells Jamie sadly.

'I heard that.'

'You were meant to – otherwise I'd have said it when you werenae here.'

'Rebecca,' Jamie laughs, folding Jemma's sign in two, 'you do drink a lot these days.'

'I've always drunk a lot. We all drink a lot.'

'It's different now. You used to know when to stop. You didn't drink alone. You didn't have memory blanks. You never missed a work meeting because you were hungover.' He gives me a gentle smile. 'You weren't careless or clumsy, or in no state to look after yourself. I'm worried that you'll get hurt if you're not careful.'

'She fell off a table last night,' Jemma reports. 'Show him your bruise!'

'I'm not going to show him my bruise.'

'Oh, I have a video. Here, Jamie.' She starts to play it like we're in court and it's exhibit A.

Jamie tries to crease his forehead in a look of concern, but his eyes are laughing.

'Turn it off.' I grab the phone. 'And stop being such a tell-tale, Jemma.'

'Don't blame her,' Jamie argues. 'I brought it up. I was worried and Jemma agrees.' I shoot Jemma a look and she just stares back at me with wide-eyed innocence. 'We're not saying you're an alcoholic. But if drink starts to affect your job or your relationships, or makes you do things you regret after, it is a problem.'

I can only assume his last point refers to New Year's Eve. My cheeks burn.

I need to be an adult and get over that. I've already lost Ben and Danielle – I can't lose Jamie too.

Or Jemma, for that matter. I'm not sure how I would have coped without her. My friendship with her is probably the best thing to have come from my break-up with Ben. It's like the antidote when the pain of Danielle's deceit creeps into my head.

'No one is saying you should become teetotal,' Jamie continues.

'Christ, no,' shrieks Jemma. 'That would be even worse. I mean, *we* could no longer be friends.'

'But you've not been yourself lately. We just want you to be happy, so we want you to know we're here for you if you want to talk or anything.'

'Exactly,' chips in Jemma. 'Turn to us. Not the bottle.'

The humiliated part of me wants to tell Jamie to go feck himself and storm out.

But there's a sensible part of me that acknowledges that everything he just said is true. And that this must have been a hard thing for him to say to me.

The humiliated part means I can't quite bring myself to thank him, though.

He winks at me. 'I need to finish setting up. Holler if you need anything.'

'Thanks for that,' I hiss at Jemma, when he's gone.

'For what?' she asks, like butter wouldn't melt.

'Agreeing with Jamie.'

'He's fit.' She shrugs. 'He could have asked me to help him bury a body and I'd have gone along with it.'

I shake my head but can't help laughing. 'Let's go.'

I walk her to the station and give her a quick, awkward hug. 'Thanks, Jem.' She looks pleased.

'Nae worries.' She starts walking up the steps then stops and turns round. 'Hey, what did you mean when you said you knew what I was playing at? You seemed surprised when I told you.'

'I thought you were giving Jamie your number.'

'Ha ha, as if.'

'I thought you fancied him?'

'Course I do. But you've told me how girls in there throw themselves at him every night. I'm way too insecure to go out with someone like that.'

Then the train pulls in, so I've no time to tell her she shouldn't be.

Chapter Twenty-five

BEN

Monday, 5 January

I head straight to the office from Euston, having boarded the first train down from Manchester. I've been dreading going back to work, though it'll at least be nice to catch up with Russ and Tom.

'George Riley is leaving,' is the first thing Russ says to me.

George works in the post room. We started on the same day, and even though there is more than thirty years between us, he's one of the people I get on with most in this place.

People wondered how long he'd stay on after Dorothy from reception retired last month. It's like when one half of an old couple dies, and everyone speculates that the other half mightn't survive without them. They die of a broken heart. Unless they're like Rebecca, in which case they forget the other one ever existed and carry on as normal.

'When did he hand in his resignation?' I ask, wondering why I don't already know about all this.

'He didn't. Richardson has asked *me* to hand it to *him*.

He says the new receptionist can sort the post now.'

'They're binning him?' I say, stunned. 'This place!'

Russ nods solemnly, then spots my bag and asks where I've been.

'Up north for a few days,' I tell him. 'See the family.'

I had to get out of London. I was so angry with myself. I don't know where all those words came from. I admire Jamie more than anyone else I know, and to say what I said . . . I've been cringing ever since. And the stupid thing is everything he said was right. I *should* be trying to turn breaking up with Rebecca into something positive, because it *has* made me realize how much I hate my job.

I just needed to get away for a bit for all of this to sink in, and now that it has I know exactly what I need to do. I'm going to spend the next three months looking into new careers and saving as much of my wages as possible, then I'm quitting.

'I got back from my sister's yesterday,' says Russ. 'I had the best New Year ever.'

'How come?'

'Babysat my nephews.'

I look sceptical.

'Seriously,' he says. 'There were no twatty bouncers on the door, no one looking repulsed when I tried to kiss them at midnight.' He rips a piece of paper from his notepad, screws it up and throws it on to Tom's desk for no apparent reason. 'I didn't have to dodge any vomit on the street. Although, actually, Jackson was sick on his bedroom floor after the second pack of wine gums.' He goes all smiley at the memory. 'They were supposed to be in bed at nine but I woke them up to watch the fireworks from their bedroom window.'

'That actually does sound like the best New Year,'

I tell him, slightly moved. 'How about you, Tom? What did you get up to?'

'Avril and I walked up to Primrose Hill with a blanket and a flask of peppermint tea.'

'Also sounds awesome,' I say. 'The fireworks must have looked incredible from up there?'

He hunches his shoulders.

'He never saw them,' says Russ. 'Avril got annoyed at all the people so they went home and listened to the countdown on Radio 4.'

'Radio 4?'

'Avril doesn't have a telly,' Tom says. 'She says it pollutes the mind.'

'Of course she does,' I say.

Once my monitor finally stops flickering I catch up on my emails, the most recent of which is from Delilah, the office manager, complaining about the food that was left to go mouldy in the fridge over the break, and saying that from now on any food left in the fridge at close of play on Fridays WILL BE DISPOSED OF. The email subject line is: *The Year of Clean.*

'Some people need to have a word with themselves,' I say to no one in particular.

'The year of clean?' says Tom.

'Yeah.' I delete the email. 'I'm going to make this the year of getting out of this place.'

'I'm going to make this the year of leaving stuff in the fridge on Fridays,' says Russ, leaning back in his swivel chair. 'That and meeting my future wife.'

I contemplate a joke but decide against it. 'How about you, Tom?'

Tom sucks his teeth like he hadn't seen the question coming at all.

'Sack off Avril?' suggests Russ.

Tom objects with a tut and then, as though he doesn't want Russ's words to linger in the air, immediately provides an answer. 'I hope this year I have an exhibition, for my sketches.'

Russ raises the mug he keeps his pens in. 'Here's to me and my future wife visiting Tom's exhibition for his sketches.'

Tom and I raise our stationery mugs. As we're clinking I catch a whiff of Brut. Richardson is standing beside us with an impatient smile.

'We were just asking Ben what he's going to make this the year of,' says Russ.

Richardson puts a hand on my shoulder. 'Closing down the ticket offices, I expect?'

He mimes pulling down the shutter at a ticket office and chuckles to himself, because hundreds of people losing their jobs *is* amusing. For some reason I find myself thinking about George Riley. He was the one who told me about the starlings turning back the time on Big Ben.

'No, actually,' I say.

I see Richardson glance at Russ, whose face goes rigid with the effort of not cracking up, and then at Tom, whose head now hangs over his keyboard like he's got something really important to type.

'What do you mean, *no*?' says Richardson, hooking his thumbs into his trouser pockets like a chubby butcher.

'Precisely what I said: no.'

I sense disbelieving eyes homing in on me from across the office.

'Well, thankfully you don't have much say in the

matter,' says Richardson, circulating a self-satisfied grin around the increasing number of onlookers, and for a few seconds I hesitate.

I think again about all the things Jamie said on New Year's Eve.

'Actually, I do.' I stand up, adrenalin streaming around my body. 'I quit.'

Richardson guffaws. 'Well, as you know, if you want to quit you need to write a formal letter of resignation.'

His tone is priggish and his smile smug.

'I'll tell you what,' I say, holding out my palm as if it was a piece of paper. 'How about I mime you one instead?'

Jamie and I haven't seen each other since I stormed out of the bar, and he looks slightly puzzled when I walk through the door.

He is standing alone at the foosball table. On any other day I'd go over and try to guess from the trajectory of the ball which City goal he was recreating, but there are things that need to be said first.

I drop my bag and I'm about to launch into it when I hear the toilet flush. I notice a pair of stilettos by the door.

'Have you got a girl here?' I say.

'No.' He's still got the look of someone who wasn't expecting me. 'Well, yes, but—'

The bathroom door opens.

'Oh.' Danielle stops momentarily before walking awkwardly towards the foosball table. 'Hi, Ben.'

It's the first time I've seen her since the break-up, and it takes a second or two for the words to come out. 'Hi, Danielle.'

I stand there, not quite sure what to say. Jamie glances at me, then at Danielle, then back at me, and his second glance compels me to speak.

'What's the score?' I oblige.

Jamie doesn't answer, so that Danielle has to.

'I don't know,' she says. 'What *is* the score, Jamie?'

'I'm really not sure myself,' he says.

Danielle cackles and turns to me. 'He's losing eight–two.'

'Eight–two?' I walk over to observe. 'Jesus, Jamie.'

'To be fair,' he says, 'my guys keep getting distracted by *that*.' He uses the hand controlling his goalkeeper to gesture towards Danielle's cleavage, which is exposed by her low V-neck jumper. I avert my eyes before awkwardness descends on us again.

'And she keeps singing,' says Jamie.

'That's what people do at football,' she says. 'They sing.'

'Which is why I'm never taking you to a football match.'

Danielle explains that she's working from home until her meeting in Greenwich a bit later on. She points towards her laptop. 'I have to keep moving the mouse so it looks like I'm online.'

'Shouldn't *you* be at work?' Jamie asks me.

I hesitate so that by the time I answer they're both staring at me. 'I just quit.'

They let go of the handles.

'Jeez, Ben, surely this should have been the first thing you said when you walked in?' says Jamie.

'Actually, the first thing I was going to say when I walked in was sorry, but then . . .'

I look at Danielle and when she smiles it occurs to

me how much I've missed this. Hanging out as a group. I've been so busy missing Rebecca that I hadn't really thought about it, but Jamie obviously has, and it didn't take me long to understand that that's why everything came out at New Year, because he's frustrated at the situation.

'You know I don't mean those things I said. You're my frigging hero when it comes to work. It was just my bruised pride talking, but I know that everything you said was spot on. I do masticate too much.'

Danielle releases a dirty laugh, but tries to disguise it as a cough when she realizes neither Jamie nor I are amused.

'Long story,' Jamie tells her, picking up the tiny ball from the pitch.

'Basically,' I say to them both, 'I was a total dick, and I'm sorry.'

'You don't need to apologize at *all*,' says Jamie, studying the ball instead of looking at me. 'I was a total dick too, so let's forget the whole evening ever happened.'

He holds out his hand and I shake it, and now we do laugh.

'So what the fuck happened at work?' says Jamie, and the two of them lean against the foosball table while I sit on the couch and go over what happened.

'I hadn't planned to do it *today*. I was going to give it a month or two to save up a bit, but then Richardson came over and said what he said and I just thought, *Fuck it*. I mean, nothing's going to concentrate my mind like being unemployed, right?'

'Follow your gut,' says Danielle.

Jamie looks at her. 'Normally I'd be with you on that,'

he says. 'But not with Ben. His gut has a very poor sense of direction. His gut is pre-satnav.'

'He's right,' I agree. 'But one thing I do know for sure is I need to get my own place.'

'You don't have to do that, mate,' says Jamie.

'On the subject of apologies,' I say, ignoring him and turning to Danielle. 'I'm sorry I haven't been a very good mate lately. I know this whole thing has been—'

'It's OK,' she cuts me off. 'I know you had to put Rebecca first.'

Her name almost feels tangible, as though she is here in the room, which only serves to remind us all that she's not. The silence is eventually broken by a beeping inside Danielle's patent handbag. She delves inside and spends at least a minute reading the text message.

Jamie looks knowingly at Danielle so that I feel like I'm witnessing some kind of private joke.

'It's Shane,' she eventually explains.

'I thought Rebecca made you delete his number?'

'*He* texted me.'

'Yes,' says Jamie. 'To see if he could borrow money.'

'And you presumably told him to F off?' I say.

'Of course,' she says. 'Though I paraphrased a bit.'

'To what?' I ask.

'*How much?*' answers Jamie.

I can't help but laugh.

'This is all Rebecca's fault,' says Danielle, folding her arms huffily. 'I wouldn't be replying if she was here to stop me.'

Danielle scrutinizes the message again.

'What's he put?' asks Jamie.

Danielle sighs. 'It doesn't matter.'

'Danielle?'

She sighs. '*Haha.*'

'*Haha*?' says Jamie. 'That's what you spent three months reading?'

'I was trying to work out what to text back.'

Jamie and I share a disbelieving look, then he snatches the phone.

'Oi,' moans Danielle.

'You can't reply to *Haha.*'

'Why not?'

'Do you want to tell her?' he says to me.

'Jamie's right,' I say. '*Haha* is text speak for *Go away now.*'

Danielle's bottom lip protrudes at the injustice.

'On the subject of dating,' I say to Jamie, 'did anything happen with Tidy Tania after I left on New Year?'

Jamie nibbles at the nail of his thumb, then gets up to fill the kettle.

'No.'

Without asking if anyone wants a drink he pulls three mugs from the cupboard.

'Why not?' I ask.

He rolls his shoulders, adding teabags and sugar to the three mugs.

'Why are you avoiding the question?'

'It was New Year's Eve, I was too busy,' he says to shut me up.

We watch him make the tea and bring it over but he ignores our eyes, and then deflects the attention back on to me.

'Ben is worried that Rebecca is online dating.'

Danielle's laugh sounds like a handbrake being yanked. 'Er, no,' she says.

'That's what I said,' says Jamie.

262

'But . . .' I start, but I censor myself, because I don't want Danielle to know *why* I'm suspicious.

'Listen,' says Jamie, 'I know Rebecca isn't exactly open about this stuff, but I talk to her a lot, and she hasn't given me any hint at all that she's ready for anything new, and even if she is online dating, which I maintain she definitely isn't, she's hardly going to end up with any of them, is she?'

'How do you know?'

'Because . . .' A few seconds pass. 'Because unexpected break-ups are like house fires. You can't just buy a load of new stuff and move back in. You need to give the house time to air, otherwise you're just going to stink of ash and fire.'

I smile. 'You're saying Rebecca stinks?'

'That's exactly what I'm saying.'

'Good. I like that.'

Our eyes meet and we exchange a grin, and if the world was different and these kinds of things were acceptable I'd go over and give him a hug.

'You're a good mate,' I tell him instead.

'The best,' agrees Danielle.

Jamie sips his tea. 'I'm not going to argue.' He slurps the drink. 'And actually, there's a way you can repay me.'

'How?' I say.

'You can come and cook at the bar a few nights a week.'

'What are you talking about?'

'I was going to ask you anyway, but now you've quit your job you don't really have an excuse.'

I'm totally confused. 'But you've got a chef?'

'He walked out on Saturday after all the complaints.'

'He just walked out without giving you any notice?'

'Isn't that exactly what you've just done?'

I lift the mug to my mouth. I've already drunk the tea; I'm just stalling to think.

It's not as if I couldn't do with the money but . . .

. . . I don't know.

'Burgers and nachos aren't exactly my thing, mate.'

'Then change the menu.'

He says it flippantly, as though placing his professional kitchen in the hands of a complete novice isn't a big deal at all. Cooking for him here is one thing, but I'm not sure I'd know where to start in a proper kitchen.

'And do I need to remind you of rule six,' he says, wagging his finger towards the chalkboard. 'Cook for Jamie.'

I look at them both, a nervous grin cracking my lips.

'You'd be doing me a huge favour,' he adds.

'OK, I'll do it.'

Jamie slaps his hands together in delight and Danielle looks just as pleased as she stands up.

'What time is it?' she asks.

Jamie checks on her phone before returning it to her. 'Ten past eleven.'

'Shit, I'd better go if I'm going to make this client meeting.'

'What time's it start?' I ask.

'Half ten.'

Chapter Twenty-six

REBECCA

Friday, 13 February

'I didn't know you were left-handed.'

'Holy crap,' yelps Jemma with a jump. 'You shouldn't sneak up on people like that.'

'I didn't,' I protest, glancing back at the lift. 'I just came out and walked right up to you. It's lunchtime.' I notice her placing an arm over what she was writing so I can't see it. 'What you doing?'

'Nothing.'

'Then why do you look guilty?' I spot a red envelope next to her and grin. 'Aw, you're writing a Valentine's card.'

'What of it?'

'Who's it for?'

'No one.' She piles both hands over the top half of the card so all I can see is the sign-off. *Love, your secret admirer.*

'I didn't realize people still sent anonymous Valentine's cards.'

'Well, they do. It takes me aboot three days to open all mine. And my flat always ends up looking like a cyclist got killed there because of all the flowers.' She keeps laughing until she starts to sound demented, then peters out. 'So, what are you wearing to the company do tonight?'

'Dunno. I'm going to grab something now.'

'You haven't got a dress yet?' She opens her mouth and covers both cheeks with her hands dramatically, leaving the card uncovered so I can't help but notice the name.

'Dear Rebecca,' I read aloud. 'Um . . . Jemma?'

'Twat!' she scolds herself, slapping her own forehead. 'OK, fine – it's for you. I'm in love with you.'

What?

Jemma cracks up. 'You should see your face. I'm not really. I just thought a card might boost your confidence a bit after the shite few months you've had. You get all weird when guys chat you up, even though you're pretty and stuff.'

She was sending me a Valentine's card so I'd feel loved? I'm so touched I can't speak for a moment.

'Just to reiterate, though,' she adds, 'I don't want to rub fannies with you.'

'Understood.' I pick up the card and study it. 'Did you want me to think that my secret admirer has only just learnt to write?'

'Piss off,' she cries, grabbing it back. 'I was writing with my left hand so you wouldn't know it was from me. Ballsed that right up, didn't I?'

Then she grins. 'You never know, though, you might get a real one from you-know-who.'

'Nah, I haven't heard from Ben since before Christmas.' I try to keep my voice light. 'I hardly think he'll be at home right now writing poetry. Not for me, anyway.'

'Ben? Why would your ex send you a card? You split up months ago.'

'Three and a half months.'

'Exactly. I was talking about the hot vampire – I don't care what you say, there's definitely pent-up sexual chemistry between you and he's—'

'Coming through the door right now,' I interrupt. 'Sshhh.' I nod at Adam as he approaches reception. 'Hi.'

'Afternoon,' he says, his eyes flitting unsurely from Jemma to me and back again. Did he hear us? 'Just dropping off this for Jake.' He holds up some paperwork.

'Nae bother – I'll call him.'

While Jemma's on the phone I rummage through my handbag, even though I'm not looking for anything, then pull out my mobile as if to demonstrate I've found it. It's weird: since the night we almost kissed, Adam and I have been working well together, and I'm fine when we're talking about the project, but I can't talk to him about anything else without feeling awkward.

'You going to the grand party tonight?' he asks.

'Yep. You?'

'Yep.'

'Head on up.' Jemma hangs up and waits until Adam's out of earshot to squeal: 'See?'

'See what?'

'The sexual tension was so thick I could have actually had sex with it.'

'Bollocks was it.' Sometimes I wish I thought like Jemma, seeing every single bloke as a potential mate. 'Anyway, I'd better go get a dress.'

'Oh yeah, I forgot that's where we were.' She opens her mouth and covers both cheeks with her hands dramatically again. 'You haven't got a dress yet?'

'It'll be fine,' I tell her, but my nonchalance is fake. I've been putting off finding a dress ever since I got the bloody invitation to the Goode Grand Party, because I hate shopping, I really do. I hate the queues, I hate trying on clothes in busy changing rooms. I hate the pushy sales assistants asking if there's anything they can help with when you're just looking, and I hate the lazy sales assistants who are nowhere to be seen when you need something in another size.

'I'll come help you,' says Jemma, jumping down from her seat.

'You don't have to do that.' If there's one thing I hate more than shopping, it's shopping with other girls.

'I insist.'

'Oh. Great.'

I feel like a dick as we trawl round House of Fraser and I have to admit – as much as I hate to – I miss Danielle.

I wouldn't have been running around trying to find a dress at the eleventh hour on her watch.

She'd have found me something – and come over to do my hair and make-up too.

As a kid, I was always unsure and awkward when it came to dressing up. Maybe it was the lack of females in my life. No mum, no sister – and because I was shy and we moved around a lot, I never had close girlfriends until I went to uni. It felt easier kicking about with my brother and his mates – girlfriends were much harder work until I met Danielle.

Then again, maybe I got it right as a kid.

This is all right, I think, holding a silky, navy Coast dress against my front. The sort of thing Danielle would have suggested.

Not the sort of thing she'd choose for herself, though. Her outfits scream party girl.

The thought annoys me for some reason.

Maybe that's why she always made sure I was dressed a little more conservatively than her: so it would be obvious who the fun one was.

I hang up the dress and carry on wandering through the store, and find myself stopping at a dress that's far more up Danielle's street.

'*Show* me,' yells Jemma through the changing-room curtain five minutes later. This is why I hate shopping with other people.

'What do you think?' I say, pulling back the curtain.

The dress is blood red, with a short, A-line skirt. Maybe it's time for me to be the party girl, I figured. The stilettos are a little higher than I tend to go for, but it's time I try something new.

'It's perfect.'

'Really?' I bite my lip. It is short.

'Definitely. I mean, tonight is the night you wanted to introduce your colleagues to your flaps, right?'

Oh.

'Look at the back in the mirror and lean over a little,' she continues.

Oh dear God, what was I thinking?

'And don't take this the wrong way, pal,' she adds, 'but those shoes make you look like a tranny.'

'There's no right or wrong way to take that.' I sigh, sinking down on the bench and feeling the cold wood making direct contact with my buttocks. 'You know, I think I might just give tonight a miss.'

'What the bloody hell is wrong with you?'

'I miss Danielle,' I tell her with a sigh.

'Um, thanks very much.'

'Don't be silly.' I give her a small smile. 'It's just . . . not having anything to wear tonight reminds me that it's pretty much down to her that I actually own clothes. She gave up trying to drag me shopping. She used to make notes whenever she saw something she thought would suit me. Then she'd send me a link to it online, so all I had to do was enter my card details if I liked it.'

'Sounds like a good friend,' she says, and then more gently: 'Maybe you should make up with her?'

I always did like the outfits she suggested for me. I have to give her that – she always got my style spot on, despite us having totally different tastes.

Then again, maybe she was just pretending to have different tastes, because she'd secretly already worn all my clothes the night I met them.

'You seem in a really good place at the moment,' adds Jemma. 'Think you could forgive and forget? Bet she misses you too.'

'Nope, I'll get by.'

'OK then, I'll help find you something. But we're going to have to take a half day – I can't turn this around in fifteen minutes. I can only work with what I've got.'

I cave, and after we've phoned the office to clear the time off, Jemma drags me to a boutique in Old Street, where she collects dresses off the rails like it's *Supermarket Sweep* before pushing me inside the changing room.

'Oi, Cinders!' bellows Jemma, as I try them on. 'Hurry up. I just phoned that salon across the road and booked me a blow-dry and you an updo.'

I sigh loudly.

'You're welcome,' she adds.

Nothing suits me and I'm close to giving up when I pull on an ankle-length satin gown in a shade of green so dark, it's almost black. The front falls into a low V, but not dramatically so. The back is so low it ends just above my bum.

'Rebecca!' Jemma squeals, when I pull back the curtain. 'You look like a movie star!'

'A transvestite movie star?' I joke, but when I look in the mirror properly, I have to admit, this dress works for me.

'Not at all.' Jemma shakes her head. 'And it's floor-length so it'll hide your big boat feet.'

I buy it, and as we leave the salon after getting our hair done – me walking, and Jemma jogging next to me, trying to keep up – I reluctantly admit to her I'm glad she made me do this.

'Fun, isn't it?' She beams. 'We're like the *Sex in the City* girls.'

'Don't push it.'

'Let's get our make-up done in Selfridges, then go get ready in the pub.'

'Ta-da.' Jemma emerges from the pub loos a couple of minutes after me and gives me a twirl.

'Jem, you look lovely.'

'Oh, fuck off.'

'You do.' She does. The sleeveless, gold, lacey top of her dress clings in all the right places, while the layered skirt puffs out flatteringly.

'Be honest,' she says, 'do I look like a hippo in a tutu?'

'God, no. That's perfect on you.'

'You sure I don't look like a fat Christmas fairy?'

'Not at all. You look gorgeous.'

'All right, calm down. I'm still not going to have sex with you.' Jemma hands me her bags. 'Prosecco?'

'Lovely.'

I've barely touched a drop of drink since Jamie and Jemma's Spintervention six weeks ago. I have to admit (though not to them) that I'm feeling miles better. I'm sleeping well, I'm finding it easier to concentrate and I've not had any more morning-after angst to deal with. I still blush when I remember New Year's Eve, though thankfully Jamie seems as happy as me to pretend it never happened.

'The guy that was standing next to me at the bar,' Jemma says as she puts my glass down. 'I recognize him.'

'Me too,' I agree. 'Maybe he's famous.'

I regret saying that because Jemma then lists every television show, film and band she knows, trying to work out which one he's in.

'Drop it, Jem.'

'I can't. *Hollyoaks*? Everyone is in *Hollyoaks*.'

'I don't watch it.'

'Oh, for fuck's sake,' she says, sounding disappointed. 'I know who he is.'

'Who?'

'That dude in the Vietnamese place that tried to chat you up on the way out of the door.'

'Eh?'

'Months ago. Had a beard at the time. Having lunch with a bald guy.'

'How the hell do you remember that?'

'I've got a frighteningly good memory.'

'Then how come I'm the only architect in the world without a pencil, because you keep forgetting to order stationery?'

She's right, though. I recognize his quiff and his rectangular, black-rimmed glasses.

'There's something a little Clark Kentish about him, don't you think?' I ask Jemma, cocking my head.

Before she has a chance to answer, something kicks off next to our booth, between a guy carrying three pints and a guy who isn't watching where he's going. The first guy ends up wearing his beers.

There's a bit of pushing and shoving, then Clark Kent rushes over, places his hands unthreateningly on each of the guys' chests and says something quietly to them, before they both scuttle off to their own friends.

'Superman!' says Jemma, winking at me. 'Hey,' she calls after him before he heads back to his friends. He turns around. 'Do you work in Farringdon? And sometimes go for lunch in that Vietnamese cafe on the corner?'

'I do,' he confirms, obviously confused.

'You were right,' she tells me. Then to him: 'Rebecca said she recognized you from when we had lunch there, but I was all, *Nah, that was months ago, how could you possibly remember him?*' She ignores my glare. 'Hey, are you and your pals standing? Come join us, there's plenty of room in our booth.'

Jemma's lucky she's already scored so many points with me today, otherwise I might very well kill her.

After he's hollered his mates over, the man introduces himself as Michael. Jemma holds court trying to establish whether the group would rather have their genitals on the back of their necks or the palm of their hands, and I pretend not to notice how Michael keeps looking at me.

I start to wonder if my hair is falling out of my huge

bun, but when I excuse myself and nip to the loo I find every strand in place.

Could Michael have been flirting with me? He was being very nice. But he seems like a very nice man.

The door swings open. 'Cab's here,' shouts Jemma.

Oh well. I'll never know.

The converted Ironmongers' Hall where the party is being held is already heaving when we arrive – folk are less inclined to be fashionably late when it's an open bar.

The hall is vast, with high ceilings, wood-panelled walls and huge chandeliers. White-clad servers work stealth-like around the room, topping up champagne flutes.

'Tell me we don't have to mingle with clients,' Jemma whispers to me, scanning the room.

'Well, we should . . . But, given the choice, I'd rather shoot myself in the face.'

'Great, then let's go stand by that entrance. It's where the canapés are coming in.'

No sooner have we claimed our spot than a tray of mini pulled-pork rolls appears in front of us.

'So, Michael was nice,' Jem says as she pops one in her mouth.

'Yep.' I shrug, sipping my champagne.

'And he liked you.'

'I don't know about that.'

'I do.'

'He was just being friendly. It's not like he asked for my number or anything when we said goodbye.'

'Would you have given it to him?'

'Probably not.'

'Oh.'

'Oh what?'

'Nothing.' Jemma looks around the room. 'Oh, look, a chandelier.'

'Jemma?'

'OK, fine. I gave him your mobile number . . .'

I groan. It's fine, I tell myself. I can just ignore any numbers I don't recognize.

'. . . and your landline.'

'What?'

'Oh, and your direct line at work. Plus my number in case he cannae reach you on any of the above. I said I'd put him through.'

'What's the matter with you?'

'What's the matter with *you*? He's handsome, brave and available. What single woman wouldn't give him their number?'

I go to answer her but realize I have nothing. Maybe she's right. What am I scared of?

'I'm just crap in those situations,' I tell her lamely.

'Really? I hadn't noticed.'

I spot Jake and wave hello, then notice Adam next to him leaning cockily against a beam.

'Ladies,' Jake calls, waving us over. 'Aren't you two a sight for sore eyes?'

'You both look great,' Adam agrees, meeting my eye. I instinctively look away.

'Oh, stop it,' says Jemma, clearly chuffed.

'You know what else is a sight for sore eyes?' Jake continues. 'The cinema. I went to see it yesterday, Rebecca. It's coming along splendidly. I'm impressed.'

I brush off his compliments, though inside I'm doing

the Riverdance. I've been putting in all the hours under the sun to turn things round since his diplomatic warning.

'Let's not talk shop, though,' he adds. 'You girls should let your hair down.'

'You know what this calls for, don't you?' says Jemma, after they've gone. 'Shots.'

Reluctantly, I get on board and let Jemma direct me to the bar.

'Do you do Jägerbombs?' Jemma asks the barman.

'I'm afraid not.'

I review the bottle shelf. 'Two Patrón XO Cafes, please,' I tell him. Then to a baffled-looking Jemma: 'It's coffee-infused tequila.'

'Yuk, gross. Change one of those to normal tequila!' she yells down the bar. 'Coffee tastes like bum rubbish. That's why I'm a tea lassie.'

'But you drank coffee at Arch 13 that time – I saw you.'

'Jamie is fit.' She shrugs. 'He could have given me a tumbler of his own pish and I'd have drunk it.'

'You should come to his for a drink soon,' I tell her.

'His house?'

'No, the bar, you knob. Maybe not on a night Ben's working, though.'

Jemma makes a face. 'You still OK with that?'

'Sure.' I shrug. 'Guess I'm a bit jealous they're getting to hang out together so much.' At least Ben's looking for his own place now so they won't be working *and* living together.

'Maybe you're not really over Ben,' says Jemma as she pours salt on her hand.

'It's not that.' I wave a dismissive hand. 'I just don't really feel part of the gang any more.' She looks like she's going to say something else so I pick up my shot. 'C'mon, let's do this.'

Jemma wants to dance but I make her wait until the dance floor is half full before I let her drag me on to it. She moves to every song like there's a routine and she knows it, and she ends up in a dance-off with Eddie to 'Moves Like Jagger'. Everyone steps back and gives them the floor, clapping and cheering.

That's what I'm doing when I feel someone standing close beside me.

'Hello, Adam.' I flash him a smile. I feel the good kind of drunk – oiled enough to feel confident and relaxed, but in control.

'Hello, yourself.'

Just as I'm trying to work out where to take the conversation from there, everyone starts joining in with the dancing and Adam takes my hand and spins me round. He's a good dancer. Maybe he learnt to dance at Lothario Night School.

I smile to myself and close my eyes, and allow myself to get lost in the moment. Things are good. Jake's impressed. Jemma's become a real mate. A decent guy wanted my phone number.

A few weeks ago it felt as if my life was snowballing out of control, but it finally seems like I'm getting myself on track again. Ben is no longer always the first thing on my mind when I wake up and the last thing on my mind when I fall asleep, although I'd be lying if I said he wasn't regularly on it between those two things.

I become aware of my own body as it moves with Adam's, and the feel of his hands on the bare skin of my back. It sends tingling sensations over my entire body.

It's been a really long time since I had sex.

For a moment the drink blurs my mind and it's Ben whose arms I'm in, but when I open my eyes it's Adam's blue eyes I see, not Ben's brown ones, and I'm OK with that.

'You look stunning, by the way,' he says softly into my ear.

'Thanks,' I reply, grateful he can't see my cheeks from that angle. 'You don't scrub up too badly yourself.'

'Careful,' he gasps. 'That was almost a compliment.'

'Almost.'

He smiles but his eyebrows knit together slightly. 'Remember that night we went out in Soho?'

'Uh huh.'

'Well, we never really talked about what—'

'Sshhh,' I tell him, making myself meet his eyes. 'I know what you're going to say, and you don't have to. I know we'd had a lot to drink. I don't want to complicate our working relationship either.'

He looks exasperated and starts to say something, but just then the lights get brighter, and I realize the music has stopped. The party is over.

'Um, I should say goodbye to Jemma,' I tell him, half of me wanting to run away but the other half curious about what he was going to say. 'Have a good weekend.'

'You too,' he says, releasing me.

I find Jemma and we head outside to look for cabs.

'You get this one,' I insist when I see an orange light.

'OK, doll. Text me when you're home.'

'Will do. And thanks for today,' I add, feeling a rush of affection for her. 'Thanks for everything, in fact. You were right what you said earlier – it has been a shit few months, but you've been a good mate.'

'You know what, Rebecca?' she says seriously, taking my hands and meeting my eyes through her false lashes. 'I really think things are about to turn a corner for you.'

'Really?' I ask, touched.

'How the fuck should I know?' she asks, dropping my hands. 'But it felt like the right thing to say.' Then she plants a kiss on my forehead and clambers into her taxi.

Chapter Twenty-seven

BEN

Saturday, 14 February

I try to open the door but the postman seems to have deposited his entire sack through the letterbox, and it won't budge.

'My door was the same this morning,' Russ quips.

'Sorry,' says the landlord, squeezing past Tom, Russ and me, then shoulder-barging the door so he can show us around. 'It's been a while since anyone lived here.'

The reason for this soon becomes clear. It's a converted basement in an Edwardian house. The website had pictures of a bathroom, a bedroom, a kitchen and a living room, but it turns out they're all part of the same room.

'And this is the en suite,' says the landlord, pointing to the toilet without a hint of irony.

His accent is reminiscent of the Kray twins but he looks more like a Chuckle brother.

'The advert said there was central heating?' I ask when I notice there are no radiators.

The landlord waves a finger in the air like, yes, he's just remembered the advert *did* say that.

'I'll just go and get it,' he says, disappearing without another word.

Russ and Tom are wearing the forced smiles of people who can't think of anything positive to say.

'I could paint you something to hide some of the damp,' says Tom eventually. 'That could be my moving-in present.'

'Fucking hell, Tom,' says Russ, 'are you gonna rob the paint aisle at B&Q?'

The two of them have offered me my old room, but the whole point of this is to move forward, not backwards. Though admittedly *this* doesn't feel like much of a step forwards.

'You should see his latest doodles, though, Ben.' Russ clocks Tom giving him an evil. 'All right, all right: sketches.' He pulls a pear from his pockets and starts eating it like a chicken wing. 'Actually, they're shit hot. Like, you know sometimes you have to lie and be enthusiastic because it's your mate—'

'That's what I have to do with Avril's poems,' says Tom.

We turn to him, shell shocked. Tom has never said anything remotely unflattering about Avril before.

'Well, well, well,' says Russ, lodging an arm around Tom's shoulder. 'This *is* a devilish development.'

'Oh, leave him alone,' I say, as Tom starts to blush.

'No, no, no. Come on, buddy – what are they like? Can you give us a bit of one?'

Tom shakes his head and hides under his fringe.

'How's work?' I ask to help him out.

'You were the talk of the office for two days,' says Russ. 'That's the most epic resignation anyone has ever seen.'

'What happened after two days?'

'We got a toaster in the kitchen,' says Tom.

Russ approaches the two-seater couch. He scrutinizes it and then slaps the cushion, producing a plume of dust.

'So what have you been up to, buddy?' he asks, putting down the toilet seat and sitting there instead.

'Well, obviously I've been working four nights a week at the bar.'

They nod, wordless, as though expecting me to continue.

'Jamie has let me give the menu a revamp.'

'That's great,' says Russ, but I can tell from his tone that he's doing that false enthusiasm thing on *me* now.

'We really respect what you did,' says Tom. 'Giving up a steady job to go follow your dream.'

'What is your dream, by the way?' says Russ.

They're starting to sound like Mum. She's so worried she asked if I wanted the careers advisor at her school to call. And I don't have a comeback, because I'm no closer to knowing what I want to do with my life than I was when I quit six weeks ago – and now I'm having to extend my overdraft. I reckon I'm going to have to do some freelancing in HR to tide me over.

Which reminds me: I still need to get my deposit back from Rebecca, and we probably need to discuss the furniture we bought together at some point. I haven't wanted to push it, what with her having to cover the rent on her own, and I know she's good for it.

'Why don't you try to get a full-time job as a chef somewhere?' asks Russ.

The thought hadn't even occurred to me. It would be pretty cool, but then . . .

'I can't afford to retrain. You'd need qualifications

unless you want to peel potatoes for a year – and I wouldn't even be able to pay the rent on *this* place on those wages.'

I approach the window to see if I can spot the landlord but it's thick with dirt on both sides.

'I've got a second date tonight,' says Russ.

'What's supposed to happen on the second date?' I enquire. 'Kissing, sex?'

'You're asking the wrong person.' He stands up and then pulls the chain for effect. 'I can never tell whether they're up for anything physical, so I've developed a test.'

I cross my arms, intrigued.

'I'll initiate some kind of physical contact. I might pretend I can read palms so I can take their hand. Or I'll challenge them to a thumb war, and if they're reluctant, you know it's not going to happen, but if they're, like, ONE, TWO, THREE, FOUR, I DECLARE A THUMB WAR before you've even stuck your hand out, you know you're in.'

Finally the landlord returns with an electric heater, which he places in the centre of the room.

'There you go, central heating.' He laughs, but his face straightens when he realizes no one else is. 'So, what do you think?'

'What are the neighbours like?'

'Upstairs you've got David and Debs,' he says. 'Professional couple, very quiet.'

I give the place a final once-over. 'OK, then – I'll take it.'

I clock Russ and Tom making eye contact.

'This is the first place you've looked at,' says Tom.

He's right, but it's also the only place on the website

in my budget, and it's on the border of Greenwich and Blackheath so I could just about walk or cycle to Arch 13.

'I'll need references,' says the landlord.

'I can sort that,' Russ says. 'We used to live with him.' He emulates the landlord's hands-on-hips stance. 'He's a great cook, he's clean, he's, you know, a bit flaky, so you're best tying him down to a long tenancy but—'

'I can get references,' I interject.

'OK, then,' says the landlord, clapping his hands together. 'When can you move in?'

Jamie plonks two half-full plates on the stainless-steel worktop. He looks flummoxed.

'What's wrong?' I say, inspecting the remains of the Vietnamese rolls with nam jim sauce, one of my new dishes. 'Has there been a complaint?'

He starts searching the kitchen.

'No complaints,' he says. 'They want a to-go box.'

'Have we got any to-go boxes?'

'I don't know, no one's ever liked the food enough to ask for one.'

The orders keep flying in. Mediterranean platters, ceviche, rare beef sandwiches on pumpernickel bread.

'Two halloumi kebabs,' calls Erica, pinning the order slip to my board.

I prepare everything from scratch, deseeding and chopping the peppers for the kebabs, ribboning the courgettes and squeezing lemon over the cheese. What I love most is the instant feedback. An empty plate is my version of the crowd going wild when Agüero scores a goal.

I lose track of time, and before I know it I'm wiping

down the kitchen and joining Jamie at the bar, enjoying the tired satisfaction of a job well done.

There aren't many people left now. A couple sitting at the window cup hands across the table, silent but entirely at ease. Another pair share a margarita, their eyes chained as they lean into their respective straws.

Before I started going out with Rebecca I was never one of those single people who hated Valentine's Day, but today, if I'm honest, it has bothered me. But it's not about Rebecca any more. It's about me, my life. When we were together it was as though I was climbing nicely up a Snakes and Ladders board – but then I landed on the longest snake, and now I'm having to start again. And most days I just get on with it. The problem with Valentine's is that you have no option but to think about it, because everywhere you look there are happy people who are ninety spaces ahead of you on the board.

I watch Jamie place a metal stirrer into a cocktail shaker to create a makeshift bell. He uses it to call time.

'I don't get why you're always single,' I say, nodding at the bundle of cards stashed down the side of the till.

Jamie was with Freckly Fiona for the four years before uni, but since then his longest relationship has been a couple of months.

'You get tons of girls coming in here to see you.'

Jamie draws his phone from his pocket for no apparent reason and places it on the bar. The final couple say goodbye as they leave.

'I just don't want to risk messing anyone around after what happened with Fiona.'

I remember getting regular updates on her reaction after Jamie told her he didn't want to do long-distance at uni. She wrote to him every day for four months, then turned up at his halls with a collage she'd made with photos of them together. That's why everyone knew him at uni, apparently, because after that he was famous: the lad with the stalker ex.

I used to find all this quite amusing, but for the first time I can understand how Fiona must have felt hearing that the person she loved didn't want her any more. And who am I to laugh? I'm the fella who went round to my ex's house with an engagement ring.

'I know we dated for ages,' he says, 'but I never thought it was for *life*.'

Jamie goes to lock the door.

'So now you only want to get into something if you know it's for real?' I say.

'Exactly. I promised myself I'd always be straight up with people.'

'And you haven't met anyone you felt like that with? Not even Tidy Tania?'

When Jamie retakes his seat he twirls the ice in his tumbler for a few seconds. 'Not even Tidy Tania.'

I should have known this route of conversation would lead my mind to Rebecca. Jamie would never break any of her confidences, but he is adamant she'd never do the online dating thing, and he's probably right, but it's still hard not knowing what she *is* doing.

Whenever something happens my first instinct, even after all these months, is to call her, because she was my first tell, and I was hers, and you take that kind of thing for granted until it's gone.

Sometimes I find myself wondering how the cinema is coming along, or how she is getting on in the flat on her own.

Jamie downs the dregs of his whisky and tells Erica he'll finish clearing up.

'Listen to us,' says Jamie. 'Talking about relationships on Valentine's Day. All we need are some pyjamas and we could have a sleepover.'

He starts to remove glasses from the washer. Martini, flutes and hurricane glasses hang from a beam above the optics, while each tumbler has its own shelf around the tills. The faceted beverage glasses are stacked upside down on the bar itself. Everything has a place.

'Mate, with your new menu and my natural charisma,' he says, and I loop my eyes, 'business has never been so good.'

'We should celebrate with a cocktail,' I say.

'OK, but I've made enough tonight. You're up.'

'I wouldn't know where to start.'

'It's got booze in it – it's practically gravy.'

'Touché.'

He collects three bottles from the back of the bar and signals for me to come round.

'We'll have Rob Roys,' he says. 'It's pretty much a Manhattan but with Scotch instead of rye or Bourbon.'

'What am I doing?'

He fetches a measure. 'Four ounces of Scotch, two ounces of sweet vermouth and five or six dashes of bitters. But first you need some ice.'

I get to work.

'Shaken, not stirred,' says Jamie, in the voice of Sean Connery.

'Eh?'

'You know the reason we shake instead of stir?'

'No.'

Having measured everything out, he points me to

the shaker, which I place over the glass.

'Shaking with ice makes the drink go colder quicker. It takes twice as long to get the drink to minus seven Celsius – that's the lowest it will go – if you stir. Twenty shakes, forty stirs. But if you shake for too long, the ice will dilute the drink. Try it.'

I do as he says.

'What now?' I say.

'Use the strainer to pour it into the Martini glasses, then garnish with a little bit of lemon zest.'

When I'm done he lifts his Rob Roy, takes a sip and pouts. 'This is almost as good as one of mine.'

We cheers to that, then Jamie starts wiping the tables.

I find another cloth and join in. 'We make a good team, don't we?'

'I wish I could offer you something full time,' he says. 'The lease only allows food four nights a week, and even then it's supposed to be bar snacks.' He picks up a discarded menu. 'We're already pushing it with your Brazilian jim jams.'

I laugh. 'It's fine, I get it.'

'I'm loving working with you, though,' he adds.

'Me too, mate.'

We trade a grin.

'This is all getting a bit homo-erotic,' he says. 'Let's talk about tits or something.'

We pause to sip our Rob Roys, which do taste pretty good even if I say so myself.

'Hey, did I tell you I've got a place at a mixology competition?' says Jamie. 'The London heats are at the end of the month. The winner goes through to the national finals.'

I pause mid-wipe, impressed. 'I reckon your parents

would be pretty proud if they took the time to come and see what you're doing here.'

Jamie twists his lips to one side but doesn't reply. He clears the bar top and circles his cloth, round and round.

'The lease is up for renewal in October,' he says casually.

'Is it?' I say.

He stops and looks at me intently. 'The lease that says we can only serve food four nights a week – the terms are up for renewal in October.'

What is he saying?

'What are you saying?'

'I'm saying, maybe we should go into business together?'

I stand there, dumb having struck me right on the chin, and it takes me a moment to come round.

'But I haven't got any money – I've even had to disown my Malayan tiger.'

'I've got a good relationship with the bank.'

I let his offer sink in. Money aside, it does feel kind of . . .

. . . right.

It's like the glasses: everything has a place, and maybe mine is here, with my best mate, doing something I love.

'I mean, we'd have to get a proper business plan together,' says Jamie. 'And it wouldn't be something you could just back out of after a couple of months if you got bored.'

I'm still taking it in. 'No, course not.'

My eyes settle on stencilled letters that spell out BLOODY MARY on the wall. The ultimate cocktail, Jamie once told me, because it covers almost every taste sensation – sweet, salty, sour and savoury. The only one that is missing is bitter. It feels symbolic somehow but it's too late in the day for me to work out why.

'So what do you think?' I hear Jamie say. 'Shall we sit down next week and talk it through?'

I look at him. 'Mate, let's fucking do this.'

We shake on it, and then Jamie returns to his side of the bar.

'One for the road, Nicholls?' he says.

'One for the road, Hawley.'

Chapter Twenty-eight

REBECCA

Saturday, 28 February

It doesn't take long to locate the source of the wolf whistle.

'All right, darlin'!' a ruddy-cheeked workman hollers, leaning against the scaffolding, mug in hand. He looks a little surprised when I cross the road, and full-blown horrified when I stop in front of him at the entrance to East House Pictures.

'How can I help you?' I ask.

'Um . . .'

'I thought you were trying to get my attention?'

I know I'm being mean, but I've just had to commute into town on a Saturday morning, plus I'm nervous about later, and I really have always wondered what builders who catcall girls on the street are actually hoping to achieve.

'Was just paying you a compliment, wasn't I?' He shrugs. 'Everyone loves a compliment.'

The workman turns away, revealing an arse crack attempting to escape low-slung jeans.

'Are we playing builder cliché bingo?' I ask him.

'Eh? Look, feel free to carry on walking, love.'

'Feel free to put down your tea, pull up your pants and stop harassing girls in the street.'

'Stop breaking Si's balls and come and check this place out,' says Bobby, appearing from inside and chucking me a hard hat. The builder looks even more horrified as he registers who I am.

'He's making it so easy, though.'

I follow Bobby inside.

'Wow.'

The internal structure is all in place now, including my central staircase that leads up to where the second screening room and jazz cafe will be housed.

I stare up at the high ceiling, which now has decorative moulding around its edges and a huge groove in the centre, where the chandelier will be hung.

'Bobby, it looks stunning.'

'Does, doesn't it?' someone who isn't Bobby says.

I spin around. 'Oh, Adam! Hi.'

'Hey.'

I haven't seen Adam since the Goode Grand Party – just exchanged the odd abrupt email, but I'm starting to realize that's just his style. I'm less sensitive to his criticism these days so as he scrutinizes the staircase, I'm more than ready for whatever he's about to hit me with.

'You were right to insist on restoring the balustrade. The way you've positioned each section around it is genius.'

'Careful, Larsson.' I turn away to hide my blushes. 'That was *almost* a compliment.'

'Almost.' He smiles. 'I still think the ornate brass fittings are a huge waste of the budget.' I'm about to bite but I catch him winking at Bobby. 'I mean, where do you get such garish inspiration?'

'Your mum's bedroom,' I tell him, which is childish but satisfying, and makes them both laugh.

Bobby finishes the tour and I'm on a high by the time we're back at the entrance. If I've ever worked longer and more arduous hours in my career than I have the past few weeks, I can't recall it. In fact, I think if I'd discovered any on-site catastrophes this morning, I'd be throwing myself off the top of the scaffolding.

'Are you guys sticking around?' Bobby asks, discarding his hat and high-vis jacket. 'Me and the boys are heading to the cafe for a bacon sarnie if you fancy it?'

'Sounds good,' Adam says. 'Giamboni?'

'Sorry, I can't,' I tell them. And I truly am sorry because seeing the cinema's progress has put me in a camaraderie kind of mood. And I'm hardly doing cartwheels of excitement about my plans for today.

'What you up to?' asks Bobby.

'Just meeting someone.'

'Someone? It's a man, isn't it? I thought you were a bit dressed up for a trip to a building site at ten in the morning.'

'I'm not dressed up,' I snap, looking down at my khaki green dress and leather jacket like it's made of bin liners soaked in kebab meat. It's not that dressy. Maybe it's the boots – I rarely wear heels at all. Not that they're high, and I thought I could get away with it as Adam and Bobby are both so tall.

I glance at Adam but he's looking at his phone.

'Come on,' Bobby says, ignoring my discomfort. 'Spill. Who is he?'

'Just a guy.' Urgh, why can't I talk about this without

293

sounding like a fourteen-year-old? I take a deep breath. 'He's called Michael. Now do you think I should bring forward the order for the brass fittings as we're ahead of schedule?'

'Where'd you meet him?' interrupts Bobby.

Sigh. 'At the pub.'

'Isn't it a bit early for a date?'

'We're going for lunch,' I say defensively, even though I thought the same thing.

Michael said that it's easier to get to know someone on a daytime date. Which is all very well except I could do with a bit of Dutch courage, but if I start drinking Scotch in the morning it won't be long before Jemma and Jamie are calling another intervention.

'Well, you look lovely,' Bobby is saying. 'Doesn't she look lovely, Adam?'

'Lovely,' Adam agrees, without taking his eyes off his phone as he punches in a text.

'That your missus?' Bobby asks him.

'There's a missus?' I ask, enjoying the deflection.

Adam looks confused.

'The one that gave you sex vouchers for Valentine's,' Bobby clarifies.

'Oh, that never worked out.'

I snort, glad I'm not the only one getting ribbed. 'Shame – she sounds . . .'

'Like your mum,' Adam says drily.

'My mum's dead,' I tell him, deadpan, though I'm well aware I asked for that.

'Shit, Rebecca, sorry.' He looks mortified. 'I didn't—'

'That's all right,' I tell him, with a small smile. 'I'm out of here – enjoy your brekkie, lads.'

Jemma calls me just as I'm leaving the site. I'd tried to

phone her this morning but there was no answer.

'Hey, Rebecca,' she greets me with a yawn. 'It's me. There's an emergency. I need you. You have to leave whatever you're doing immediately and come over, otherwise you're a terrible friend. Et cetera, et cetera.'

'Jemma? What are you talking about?'

'I told you to give me a missed call if you need me to rescue you. That's not why you called?'

'No, I thought you were joking. And I haven't even met him yet. But you've missed your calling in life – you should totally be an actress.'

'Fuck that – the camera adds ten pounds. What's up?'

'I just want your advice,' I explain, crossing the road towards the station. 'If I decide pretty quickly I'm not interested, how long do I have to stay before I'm allowed to leave?'

'Oh, you've asked the right person – this exact thing happened to me the other week. Knew as soon as I saw him I didnae fancy him. I met him online, and at first I thought he'd used fake photos on his profile, but I think what he might have done is Photoshop his face on someone else's body. Not even like a body builder or anything – just someone with a normal body as this guy had really skinny arms and legs then a huge belly. Kind of looked pregnant, and you should have seen his—'

'Anyway,' I interrupt.

'Anyway,' she continues, 'I thought, *I can't just turn around and walk straight out again – that would be rude. Besides, he might have a great personality*. He didn't, though. He was really arrogant, and a wee bit racist. Particularly hates the Scottish, it would seem.'

'So what time did you leave?'

'Met him at eight and left about nine-ish, I think. Maybe just after.'

'Oh, that's good to know. An hour is enough, then?'

'No, I mean nine the next morning.'

'You're kidding?'

'Nope, I find it really hard to get out of those situations,' she explains sadly. 'God, I feel sick just thinking about it.'

'Um . . . OK, then. Thanks for your help.'

'That's what I'm here for. Want to meet in Arch 13 tomorrow for a debrief?' It's her new favourite bar since I took her there last month, and Jamie adores her.

'I'll think about it.'

When I hang up and head down into the Underground, I feel more nervous than ever.

Chapter Twenty-nine

BEN

I'm wrenched from a deep, Saturday-morning slumber by my ringtone. Groaning, I reach down to the bit of floor where a bedside table will be when I've got some cash to buy one.

'I bought a cat,' opens Russ.

'A cat?'

'You know – meow, meow.'

'I know what a cat is, I just didn't see you as a cat man.'

'CAT MAN,' he declares like the Hollywood voiceover fella. 'Seriously, though, neither did I, but Sarah Ward loves them, doesn't she? So I told her I was thinking of getting one, which was obviously a lie, and she said she'd come pick one with me.'

I hear the postman descend the steps to my flat, then I watch whatever he puts through the letterbox drop to the floor.

'Hang on,' I say to Russ. 'Who's Sarah Ward?'

'She's the new you, but fitter. I'd been trying to pluck up the courage to ask her out and then, boom, we're at the rescue centre.'

'Dear God.'

I hear him call the cat, repeating the name 'Mildred' four times. 'She's still getting used to her new name,' he explains.

'So what happened with Sarah?' I ask.

'Well,' he says, 'we got the cat to the flat and I'm giving Sarah the tour. We've got as far as my bedroom when little Mildred . . .'

He inhales, as though preparing himself.

'Go on . . .'

'Mildred starts pissing all over my bed.'

I crease up.

'It wasn't exactly the kind of damp patch I'd hoped for.'

After a few seconds Russ's laughter deflates into a sigh.

'I realize I'm a ridiculous human being,' he says. 'I'm just ready to settle down. Kids and that; holidays in Gran Canaria, if we can get a cat sitter.' I hear him click his tongue for Mildred before tutting in frustration. 'I'm starting to think it's never going to happen.'

'Why don't you just ask her out?' I say.

He scoffs. 'Because for me to ask someone out face to face I need to build myself up into a complete state of self-loathing. I'm calling myself a worthless coward; telling myself I'm going to die alone; basically, that I might as well jump off a cliff because I can't even tell a girl I like her. The little man in my head is becoming so abusive that I'm at the point of applying for a restraining order, and only then, because I can't take any more, can I do it. It takes months, years sometimes.'

He always provides these insights with the air of someone who thinks there's a victory around the corner, but now he sounds like someone who has accepted defeat.

'You could try writing her a note?' I encourage. 'That way you don't put her on the spot.'

'Or see the look of disgust on her face when she realizes I'm asking her out.' He laughs. 'But, anyway – I think I blew it with the damp-patch line.'

'You didn't use that on her?'

''Fraid so.' He laughs at his own ridiculousness. 'Do you think there are girls out there who find that kind of shit funny?'

'A girl who has the sense of humour of a lad, you mean?'

'Exactly! That's what I'm after.'

I become distracted by a rhythmic creaking of floor-boards in the flat upstairs.

'For God's sake!'

'What?' says Russ.

'They're at it again.'

'Who are?'

'David and Debs. The quiet, professional couple up-stairs.'

I hold the phone up so Russ can hear what I mean just as Debs moans like she's having a tattoo.

'I need some of that, buddy,' he says. 'If I don't get some action soon I'm worried I'm going to forget what to do.'

There's no danger of David and Debs forgetting what to do. I hear them every single morning. After she gets her tattoo it's as though she's eating in a Michelin-star restaurant where the chocolate fondant is to die for, and then she's on the scariest rollercoaster in the world. The first time I heard it I thought she might be crossing items off her bucket list.

'You won't forget what to do,' I tell Russ. 'It's like riding a bike.'

'I'm getting a bit too good on my unicycle, if you catch my drift.'

'Too much information, Russ.'

I get out of bed, swapping ears as I wriggle into my dressing gown. I go to pick up my post but, seeing that it's a bank statement, leave it on the floor.

'Have you ever been on a tricycle?' asks Russ.

'Can't say I have.'

I still haven't got round to buying a kettle, so I fill a saucepan and rest it over the hob before navigating the empty boxes and returning to bed while the water boils. I finally finished my unpacking when I got in from Arch 13 last night. Only one thing remains in a box, a velvet one, and even that won't be cluttering up the place for much longer if this afternoon goes to plan.

'Actually, I could have done with your help yesterday, mate,' I say to Russ.

'How so?'

'I need to know whether the Transfer of Undertakings and Protection of Employment Regulations apply to—'

He interrupts: 'I thought you'd left HR?'

'I have. I'm just doing a bit of freelance to tide me over.'

'Fair enough,' he says, and I can't help think the silence that follows is the sound of his disappointment.

I keep having to remind myself that it's only temporary. Jamie and I have drawn up a business plan for transforming Arch 13 into a gastro bar and we've got an appointment with his bank on Monday.

I've been on a total high since he came up with the idea, and can't wait to get started, though we've still got to convince the owner to change the terms of the lease.

Debs upstairs reaches the summit of The Big Dipper as my eyes settle again on the velvet box. Not wanting to delay it any longer, I pinch the sleep from my eyes and tell Russ that there is something I need to do.

Chapter Thirty

REBECCA

By the time I step off the train in Blackheath, I'm looking forward to the distraction a date will bring – despite my earlier nerves.

I spent the whole journey thinking about work – all the things that could still go wrong running through my head.

I'm also starving when I reach the tiny Argentinean steak house I picked out, where Michael spots me from his window seat and waves zealously.

'Hey, you.' He stands and pulls out my chair. 'How's your day been so far?'

'Well, I had to get up at the crack of dawn to go to work, check that everything is back on track,' I share, as my tummy rumbles loudly. Sexy. 'What about you?'

'I did sunrise yoga this morning.'

'Oh, lovely,' I say. What kind of madman gets up in the dark to do yoga? 'Then you really were up at the crack of dawn.'

I open my menu, deciding on a fillet steak with a side of creamed spinach, then snap the menu shut, trying not to feel irritated that Michael hasn't even opened his yet.

'So when you say it's back on track,' he says, 'when was it off track?'

'We just got a bit behind.' I don't tell him why. 'And there were a few differences of opinion on things.' He's still looking at me, waiting for more, so I explain about the staircase I was torn over, and how even Adam now concedes it was right to keep it.

As I'm saying it, I recall what Adam said today about the brass furnishings being a waste of the budget. Was he joking? I know he winked but that could have been one of those times someone jokes about something because they want to make a point. It wouldn't be the first time he'd disagreed with me.

Why am I thinking about work again? I used to go the entire weekend not switching off from it until I met Ben, who had a knack for taking me out of my head and into the moment.

I decide to change the subject. 'Thanks for sorting out the booking,' I say, looking around. 'The food is meant to be great.'

'No problem.'

The chalkboard sign outside blows over and one of the waiters runs out to rescue it.

'Look at that wind,' notes Michael, still not touching his menu as he peers out on to the heath.

'Do you know what you're having?' I ask hopefully.

'Let's have a little looky . . .' He flips open the menu and reads slowly.

I take the chance to study him. He has a nice but non-descript face, the only distinct features being his square jaw and his thick-framed glasses, which suit him. Do I fancy him?

Finally he gives a little nod and closes his menu, and

I shift my attention to the waiter.

'Ready?' he asks, catching my eye.

I order my fillet medium rare and Michael chooses a goat's cheese salad.

'Not fancy a steak?' I ask him, as the waiter retreats.

'I'm a vegetarian.'

'Why didn't you say?' I ask in horror.

This place was my suggestion – I feel terrible.

'Don't be silly,' he says, touching my hand. 'You said you wanted to try this place.'

That's incredibly sweet but all I can focus on right now is trying not to flinch, because his hand hasn't left mine. He's literally holding my hand across the table. That's weird, isn't it? On a first date? Have I just had so few first dates that I don't realize this is OK? Maybe I should roll with it.

'So, tell me more about you,' he's saying now. 'What do you do when you're not at work?'

I try to answer his question but my mind goes blank. What do I do? I rack my brains for something remotely interesting or impressive to tell him but my brain gives me nothing. It's too preoccupied with the hand thing.

'Um, I like to watch films and read, and I like seeing friends.' I sound like I'm reading out a shit CV. 'What about you?' What do you do when you're not holding strangers' hands?

Apart from yoga, he also likes cycling. I interrupt to tell him that I too like cycling but it turns out he goes on an annual cycling holiday where they spend a week touring whole countries, rather than just cycling to work to avoid the Tube.

Two nights a week he volunteers for the Samaritans helpline, and he also plays the trumpet.

'I play a little piano,' I tell him, feeling shallow and dull in comparison.

'Ooh, we should jam together sometime,' he cries.

Jam?

And that's why you shouldn't lie on dates: if it works out between us I'm going to have to learn to play the piano.

The thought of it working out with him feels like a surreal concept. He's done nothing wrong, but what would we do? Ride our bikes in tandem and jam on our instruments?

What am I meant to feel at this point in the date? All I feel now is slightly self-conscious, not very interesting and really, really hungry.

The waiter appears from the kitchen carrying two plates. 'Ooh, hopefully this is ours,' I say, using the excuse to rescue my hand from under his. The waiter walks past us to a couple in the corner. 'God damn it!' I say, half-jokingly.

'Be patient,' he teases. 'We only ordered five minutes ago.'

'I'm not impatient,' I lie. 'I'm starving.'

'How do you know you're hungry?'

'Um . . . I feel hungry.'

'Describe the feeling.'

'It's in my stomach. It's sort of . . . empty.'

'Painful?'

'No.'

'Uncomfortable?'

'Not as such. I'm just aware of it.'

'Then just be aware of it. There's no need to panic about it – it's not like you don't know where your next meal will come from. Once you achieve a mindfulness

305

about how you're feeling, it doesn't need to be a negative . . . Oh, look – here comes our food.'

Thank goodness for that – I was about to eat *him*.

'So how come you're a vegetarian?' I ask, my mouth watering as I cut a piece of my steak. 'Health or moral?'

'Bit of both, I guess.' He smiles at me as he pokes his fork into a piece of cheese. 'I feel like I can get everything I need from natural sources, without having to eat animals.'

'Oh. I feel bad.' I stare at the food on my fork. It looks so delicious, I'm salivating.

'Don't be silly.' He smiles. 'It's a personal choice.'

I attempt to move on by asking about his work. He's just taken a mouthful of food and he waits until he's chewed it thoroughly and swallowed before answering.

'I sell outdoor advertising space,' he explains. 'Billboards, posters on the Underground, that kind of thing.'

'I had a friend in ad sales, but for a men's magazine,' I tell him.

'What does she do now?'

'What do you mean?'

'You said you had a friend in ad sales. She changed jobs?'

'Oh, no – I meant we're not friends any more.' I don't know much about dating but I do know you're not meant to talk about your ex on a first date, so I wave dismissively. 'Long story.'

'You look sad,' he says.

'It's a sad, sad situation,' I quip, but it falls flat. I still tell myself that I was right to stop talking to Danielle, but whenever I talk about her I feel strangely blue. This isn't the time to go into it.

'It's all right when a friendship comes to an end,' he

says lightly. 'When you create the space for relationships that are not working to fall away, you make way for new people who are more in line with what your soul needs.'

I think about Danielle and Jemma, and Ben and . . . Michael's hand is back on mine.

I feel uncomfortable and weirdly depressed all of a sudden. And I don't know where it comes from, but I suddenly wish it was Ben sitting opposite me. I've not felt that for a while but he always knew how to distract me.

If I came home after a stressful day, it wouldn't be until Ben started talking and filling my head that I'd totally switch off.

'What are you thinking?' asks Michael.

'Nothing,' I say, trying to focus. 'It's been a stressful time at work – I just need to relax a bit.'

'Close your eyes,' he commands, putting down his fork and releasing my hand.

'Sorry?'

'Trust me.'

I look around to make sure no one is looking. 'Um, OK.'

'Breathe,' he orders. I'm already breathing, but it seems churlish to point it out, so I do it in a slower, more exaggerated fashion. I ease one eye open to see if he's laughing at me. He's not.

'Michael,' I whisper.

'Hmm?'

'What are we doing?'

'A breathing technique they taught us in yoga. It will calm you. Now sshhh.'

'OK.'

307

'Right, start with your feet and toes. Tense them. Are you tensing?'

I nod.

'Good. Breathe in . . . And out . . . And in . . . And out . . . And in . . . And relax. Good. Now tense your knees.'

I'm torn between mortification and amusement – how do you tense your knees? – and can't wait to tell Jemma about this. After my knees we do my thighs, my bum (which he refers to as my rear), my chest, my arms, my hands, my neck, my jaw and my eyes.

'Feel better?' he asks finally, after he's told me I can open my eyes again.

'A little.' I mean, it's definitely distracted me from other thoughts.

'You should start coming to yoga with me,' he suggests, picking up his fork again.

With me? Whoa, mister.

'I tried it once,' I tell him. 'It wasn't for me.'

Danielle dragged me along with her when we lived together. I'd had a stressful week and she suggested it might help me unwind, but all I could think about while I was trying to touch my toes was what I could have achieved if I'd spent that extra hour at my desk instead.

And don't get me started on the fifteen minutes we spent meditating.

'I disagree. Yoga can benefit anyone.'

'I'm just better with exercises that have a point.'

'You think yoga is pointless?' He raises his brows, but there's laughter in his eyes.

'You know what I mean. Like cycling to get somewhere. Or games where you're trying to win.'

Ben bought us tennis rackets last summer and we'd

spend hours on the courts in Greenwich Park. Our scores were always so close that whoever was losing would insist on one more game.

'Besides,' I add, 'I was rubbish at yoga. You won't be seeing me with my legs behind my head any time soon.'

He sighs. 'There go my plans for after lunch.'

We both laugh, and I realize I like Michael. I just don't *like* like him. People say you don't know what chemistry is until you have it, but I think it's the other way around. You don't know what chemistry is until you *don't* have it.

When Michael gets up to go to the loo I check my phone to find a text from Jemma.

How goes it?

I tap my reply out quickly before my date returns.

Chapter Thirty-one

BEN

After getting off the phone to Russ I shower and then set off towards Blackheath.

I walk purposefully as a strong wind frogmarches clouds across the sky, temporarily obscuring a sun that promises much but is delivering little. On the heath, a father and teenage daughter in windbreakers struggle together to contain an Asda-green kite.

I caress my fingers over the fabric of the box inside my pocket, trying not to attribute any kind of symbolism to this whole thing. It's all in the past now, I'm over it, and pawning the ring isn't symbolic of anything. I just need the cash.

I cross paths with a girl, the gusts doing their worst with her hair. She smiles, and though it could be a smile of camaraderie amid the gales, as opposed to a *smile* smile, I reason that if someone could bottle this feeling, the feeling you get after a second glance from a pretty girl, they'd be rich enough by far to never have to consider pawning anything.

I walk past the pond, where a pair of swans are reflected in the mucky grey water. A mother positions a pushchair so her child can see, then kneels down to explain something. I feel a pang of something but disregard it. Hands still pocketed, I curve my fingers around the velvet box as my feet hit the pavement. I'm walking past the shops and restaurants that border the heath when I see them.

It takes a second or two for the information to transmit from my eyes to my brain. I have to stop myself from staring. Instead I carry on walking as if nothing happened, my focus straight ahead.

It was Rebecca. With a man.

They were sitting at a table near the window eating lunch. A steak place I haven't been to but is supposed to be nice. My eyes fell not on Rebecca but her companion. It wasn't the guy from her laptop but someone new. He wore trendy glasses and had one hand on Rebecca's across the table.

I feel like my lungs are shrivelling, and as the wind buffets my face I struggle to breathe. I walk faster, changing course to walk not into town but back on to the heath.

I pat down my coat pockets for cigarettes but find none. I haven't smoked since polishing off an entire packet on New Year's Day. Instead I inspect the sky, where the clouds are still being frogmarched, and on the heath the kite fliers are still struggling to control their kite, and in the pond the shadowy reflection of the swans can still be seen. Everything is the same as it was a few minutes ago, except for the realization that I really have lost her, that *I'm* becoming history.

I squeeze the box tighter as I pass the parish church, with its witch's-hat spire, and the frustration that she can still do this to me, still make me feel this way when I thought I was fine . . .

I draw the box from my pocket and swing my arm, launching it with as much force as I can muster towards the pond, and turning immediately so that I don't see where it lands.

Erica comes into the kitchen carrying the same plate she left with just a few minutes earlier.

'I'm so sorry, Ben,' she says. 'The chap is saying he ordered the steak in his baguette well done, but I can't tell.'

On inspection I can see that Erica is being kind, because the steak is basically still grazing around a field somewhere in Somerset. Though I could have sworn the order said . . .

. . . the order said well done.

I'm struggling to concentrate. It's not only Rebecca with her new fella, it's Jamie. Did he know? Was all that stuff about house fires just made-up bollocks to make me feel better? I can't ask him because he's at his frigging mixology competition.

I re-do the steak baguette and when I'm done in the kitchen I take my place at the end of the bar, where I try to get everything straight in my head.

The thing is, all that stuff Jamie said, it worked. I thought I was OK, and it takes me three double brandies to work out why I was so upset when I walked past the restaurant.

It's because we were in a contest. Four months ago it was like our lives had been dismantled, and we had to put them back together, and it's not like flat-pack furniture, there aren't any instructions for this shit, and until one of us finished there was always a tiny, minuscule chance that we could have said *Fuck it,* and reassembled everything together.

But now Rebecca has finished, she's won the contest, and it doesn't feel fair.

None of this feels fair, I think to myself over another double measure. Kicking me out, not giving me a chance to explain. And now this hand-holding twat is probably eating at our dining table, watching TV on our couch, sleeping in our bed, and there is nothing I can do about it.

Or maybe, I think, grabbing my coat, there is.

Chapter Thirty-two

REBECCA

Do not answer it. That's my initial instinct when the doorbell rings at midnight. Because when someone is at your door, unexpected, at midnight, it can never be for anything good.

It rings again, making me bolt up in bed this time.

A drunk who has the wrong house?

The local pervert who's clocked I live here alone?

Maybe it's Michael? Maybe he didn't take it as well as I thought he did when I told him I didn't want to see him again. Maybe that calm, spiritual persona is just a front for the fact he's a madman who takes revenge on women who reject him by visiting them at home in the middle of the night wielding a machete.

The doorbell goes again but this time whoever it is doesn't take their finger off the button because it rings again and again and again and again, and I swear to God, I'll snap whoever it is's finger right off, machete-wielding madman or not.

I've been working all hours lately and all I wanted was a Saturday night in, to finally watch the last couple of episodes of *Broadchurch*, eat a greasy takeaway and fall asleep without setting an alarm. And I was just on the verge of scoring my hat-trick when the doorbell went.

Jumping out of bed, I move through the dark to peer through the blinds in the living room and see a tall figure loitering under the window. My heart skips a beat as I realize who it is.

'Jesus, Ben,' I groan into the intercom. 'You frightened the life out of me.'

'Can I come up?'

The clipped way he says it tells me I should have trusted my initial instinct about not answering it, but I'm too curious not to buzz him in.

Plus, there's something else. A weird, unexpected jolt of excitement about seeing him. It's been months.

I peer into the hall mirror and then, on a whim, run through to the bedroom, pulling my tatty old polo shirt off over my head as I go. I rake in a drawer until I find a black cotton strappy nightdress I can't have worn since Ben left, because it sure as hell wasn't me who ironed it.

Then I pull my hair out of its messy bun, running my fingers through it. I'm not planning to seduce him or anything, I just don't want him to think that single life has turned me into a slob.

I get back to the top of the stairs at the same time he does.

'We need to talk,' he barks, looking me up and down in disgust then peering over my shoulder. 'You alone?'

My heart wrenches but I try not to let the hurt register on my face. 'Yes. Why?'

I smell smoke on him as he walks past me and shoves the door closed behind him.

'Um, Ben? What are you doing here?'

'In the flat where all my furniture is? Am I not allowed to be?'

315

That's when I realize he isn't entirely sober.

'You don't live here, Ben.' I cross my arms. 'I think I'm allowed to ask why you're here, unannounced, at,' I check the clock, pointedly, 'five past twelve.'

'Well, that's what I want to talk to you about. You living here with all the stuff that I bankrupted myself buying while I'm in some shithole.'

'What's your point?' I ask, though it's pretty obvious what his point is. But he's pissed me off by turning up in the middle of the night to make it. He's had ample chance if that's how he sees it.

'My point,' he says, 'is that half of that is mine,' he points at the sofa, 'and half of that,' he points at the dining table, then stands at the bedroom door pointing at the bed, 'and half of that.'

He turns to face me. 'And I don't particularly like the idea of you and your new fella being all *versatile* on them.'

I pretend not to get the reference.

'My fella? What in the name of Jesus are you talking about?' Suddenly it occurs to me I'm not wearing any underwear – funny the things that pop into your head – and I pull the back of the nightdress down, though it's easily long enough to cover my modesty.

'That fella,' he waves a finger around his eyes, 'with the glasses.'

'Who?'

'Don't play dumb.' He staggers to the sofa, gives it a dirty look and then sits on the coffee table. 'You were having a romantic steak lunch with him just a few hours ago.'

'Michael?' He saw us? 'Shit, Ben, are you stalking me?' His eyes look like they're going to pop out of his head.

'Am I stalking you? Oh, get over yourself. I was walking past.'

'And it made you so mad you had to rock up in the middle of the night and have it out with me?'

'This isn't about that,' he snaps. 'It's about me wanting what's mine. Which is half this furniture. It's bad enough I'm living in some shithole the size of your bathroom, but it would be nice to have something to sit on.'

'This is about furniture?' I ask incredulously, fury simmering at the pit of my stomach. 'Fine – take what you want. Have you got a van parked outside? Or are you planning on carrying it to your *shithole* on top of your head?'

'Don't be ridiculous. It's not just about the furniture. You just have it so easy now, like . . .' He looks around. 'That knife!' He points at one of the knives he bought me, lying on a crumb-covered plate. 'I mean, do you need a fucking cook's knife to butter toast?'

'No. You said you bought those knives for me at the time but by all means, take them.'

He glares at me. 'It's not about the knives.'

I can't win.

'You keep telling me what this isn't about. What *is* it about?'

'Me getting what I'm owed. I need to get some cash together so me and Jamie can start our own business.'

'You're still talking about that, are you?' I laugh cruelly as I pick up my handbag from the hall floor and yank my purse out. 'Here, how much do you want? A hundred? Five hundred? A grand? How much does it cost to adopt an Adélie penguin? Because let's face it, that's what you'll really do with the cash when you get bored of your latest big dream.'

'Don't patronize me,' he says, waving my purse away. Thank God he didn't call my bluff – I have less than a tenner on me and I doubt he takes Visa.

'So what do you want?' I chuck my purse back down and cross my arms. 'To cut everything in half? Maybe we could use your special knives.'

Ben treats me to his dirtiest look.

'We could sell it and you could use your half to buy stuff with your boyfriend.'

I take a deep breath, and try to see this from his point of view. He's seen me and Michael, jumped to conclusions and thinks I'm with someone else, and he's transferring his anger. Which must mean he still cares. I feel myself start to soften.

'Listen,' I say gently, 'it's not what you—'

'And good luck to him.' He smirks. 'Because you're a real treat to live with.'

'What's that supposed to mean?' I demand, feeling defensive again.

'Well, is he a mind reader? Because Christ, Rebecca – I sure as hell never knew what you were thinking. I used to think you were just closed but I'm starting to realize you're actually emotionally stunted.'

My temples throb, and for the first time I feel proper anger. This has nothing to do with the furniture, or even Michael. It's the argument we never had when we broke up. It's been brewing for months.

'Look, Ben, if you weren't so shit with money then you might be able to afford to buy some furniture rather than coming round here in the middle of the night and shouting at me.' His mouth opens but I don't give him time to reply. 'And it's not that I'm emotionally stunted,' I insist, through gritted teeth, 'it's that when I've had a bad day I don't want to bring everyone else down by whining about it. Because I know what a bloody drag that is from living with you.' He goes to say something but I'm on a roll. 'You hated your job – I GET IT – but rather than actually attempt to find something you did want to do, you just brought all your negativity home with you every night so that I'd be depressed too.'

'Oh, I'm sorry, I thought you were supposed to be able to turn to your girlfriend for support. I didn't realize what you wanted was a relationship where we sit there and don't say anything, just holding hands across the table. Mealtimes look like a riot with your new bloke.'

'He's not my new bloke, you stupid idiot.'

'Pull the other one.'

I laugh in frustration. 'You've got it wrong, Ben.'

I watch the tension seep out of Ben's body and I know I should leave it there and send him home, but I can't. 'You know what, though? Living with someone who actually eats their meals at the dinner table rather than on their lap in front of the TV doesn't sound that bad to me.'

'Ouch.' He clutches his fist to his chest. 'Hit me where it really hurts.'

'Oh, grow up, Ben. Go home and sober up, and let me know when you're ready to talk about this like adults.'

'Oh my God.' He jumps up. 'I can't believe you have the audacity to stand there and tell me to grow up.' He points at me using both pointing fingers in case there's any confusion about who he's referring to here. 'You, who dumped me because of one stupidly small thing I did before we were even a couple. You, who hasn't spoken to your best friend for months for the same mistake.'

His words hit a nerve. A little spark of doubt that I was right to completely banish Danielle from my life is constantly there at the back of my mind, but I always extinguish it before it has a chance to get momentum. I do the same now.

'Well, at least you've got each other's shoulders to cry on. And you know, when she's really upset, you can always just shag her. But then I don't need to tell you that.'

'Oh, leave off.'

'No, I mean it – it must be very comforting for you both.'

'I've barely spoken to Danielle since you and I split up. I've seen her once, when she was with Jamie.'

'Yeah, right,' I mumble, turning my back on Ben as my worst fears are confirmed: the three of them hanging out together without me.

Thinking about Ben and Danielle still feels as raw as when I first found out. I thought I was over it but clearly I'm not – I've just been avoiding thinking about it.

Don't cry, I warn myself. If it's anger or sadness, choose anger.

'I haven't! We slept together once, Rebecca. Once. You and I weren't even going out yet. And I can see why you were upset when you found out but we can't undo it. We had sex. GET. OVER. IT.'

'It was never about those two minutes you shared,' I cry. It's a low blow, I know, and there's no anecdotal basis to back it up. 'It's about all that time you lied to me.' My voice gets louder. 'It's about the fact I can't trust you.' And louder. 'And me not wanting to be with you any more? That doesn't make me childish, Ben.' And the crescendo . . . 'It makes me NOT A FUCKING MUG.'

There's a bang on the door, making us both jump.

'Who's that?' I whisper.

'How the hell should I know?' he whispers back. 'Michael?'

'Why are you making speech marks with your fingers? That's his real name. And I told you – he's not my boyfriend. He doesn't even know where I live.' I hope.

'Rebecca?' a man's voice calls. 'Is that you? It's Angus from downstairs.'

Oh, shit.

I take a deep breath and answer the door.

'Sorry to knock,' says my bathrobe-clad neighbour. 'It's just the baby is sleeping, and we can . . . Oh, hey, Ben.' He seems happily surprised. 'I didn't realize you were back.'

'Sorry,' Ben and I say in unison, but while I'm about to assure Angus we'll be quiet and let him leave, Ben is stepping round me to shake his hand. 'How are you, mate?'

'Not bad thanks, pal,' Angus replies. 'So have you moved back in?'

'Er, no – not exactly. How's the family?'

Oh, give me strength.

I go and collapse on to the sofa to wait for them to finish catching up and just as I do, Ben's mobile starts to vibrate. I look at him chatting away. He hasn't noticed. I glance at the screen and I swear, as I do, my blood runs completely cold.

It's Danielle.

Barely spoken to her since we broke up? The absolute lying bastard.

The room spins. I need to say something but I don't

want to lose it while Angus is here. I didn't really think he was sleeping with her – I was just making a point – but the thought of them carrying on as normal tears me apart.

The phone stops but a few seconds later it buzzes again with a text, which shows up on the screen.

Where are you?

That's not a message you send to someone you only see through Jamie.

'Good to see you too,' Ben is saying. 'And sorry again about the shouting. We're done now.'

It takes every ounce of my being to keep my voice quiet as I hand Ben his phone and say: 'I think you'd better leave now.'

His eyebrows furrow as he checks his alerts.

'Least you have someone to go and cry to about your furniture,' I say as his face registers.

'I have no idea why she called me.'

I laugh humourlessly. 'Sure.'

'I mean it,' he insists. 'Isn't she with Jamie at the competition? Maybe she called to say he won or something?'

'Oh, quit with the lying. Even after everything that's happened, I still can't trust you. Be friends with Danielle. Fuck her again, for all I care.' I open the door and stand next to it, my back against the wall. 'Just leave. NOW.'

'No,' cries Ben, sliding his phone in his back pocket and pushing the door shut. 'You do not get to have the last word. Not when you're accusing me of something I haven't done.' He places his palms on the wall behind me, tensing his body so I can't wriggle free. 'I've seen Danielle once. At Jamie's. And I can't believe you'd think for a second anything else might have happened between us. There's been nothing between me and *anyone* since we split up.'

I stop wriggling and look at his face.

'Well, there's been nothing between *me* and anyone else either.'

'Really?' he croaks.

'Really.'

We stare at each other, just inches between his face and mine. I don't know which one of us it is that moves – maybe we both do – but the gap between our lips gets smaller, until suddenly it's barely there at all.

Then a loud insistent buzz breaks the spell and the gap widens again. Ben takes his phone out of his pocket and we both stare at it.

'It's not mine,' he says as the buzzing continues. 'That must be yours.'

I locate my phone on the dining table.

'It's Danielle,' I tell him in disbelief. 'Does she know you're here?'

'What? No – just answer it.'

'Hello?'

'Rebecca, thank God. It's me – I—' Her voice breaks into a sob, and fear grips me, melting the ice from my voice.

'Danielle, what's wrong? Has something happened? Are you hurt? Danielle, talk to me.'

'It's Jamie,' she croaks.

'What's wrong with Jamie?'

Ben rushes to my side and I hold the phone away from my ear a little so he can hear.

Her words don't seem to make sense. She's with him in an ambulance. A seizure at the competition. They're on their way to hospital.

'I can't get hold of Ben,' she adds.

'I'm here,' Ben says into the mouthpiece.

'Oh. Hi.' A few seconds pass. 'You should both come if you can.'

'We'll meet you there.'

I hang up.

'Call a cab,' I order a pale-faced Ben. 'I'll get dressed.'

Chapter Thirty-three

BEN

It is gone 1 a.m. when we arrive at the hospital. Rebecca scurries out of the taxi, and I find her waiting at the back of a queue at reception, already on tiptoes to peer over the shoulder of the person in front.

A drunk disregards the queue and sways towards the desk. Rebecca clicks her tongue when the receptionist starts to tend to him.

'Our friend is here,' she says, jumping the queue and positioning her body in front of the drunk. 'Jamie Hawley – could you tell us where he is, please?'

The woman elevates her string glasses to examine her monitor.

'He's in the neurosurgical unit,' she says, offering directions before resuming her dialogue with the drunk.

'Why is he in the neurosurgical unit?' I interrupt, but the receptionist either doesn't hear or pretends not to, and Rebecca is away.

Danielle is already there, listening to a doctor in puce overalls. The doctor seems to recognize that we too are Jamie's friends without needing to be told. He carries on talking, and immediately I understand that Jamie is about to have surgery, but I'm finding it hard to get my head around exactly what's happened. Something about a blood clot, and something else I've never heard of.

'As I've outlined, there are dangers,' the doctor continues. 'Stroke, brain swelling, epilepsy, and so on.'

I gasp, but when I look at Rebecca and Danielle they're still listening intently.

'But from what we've established from the head CT, removing both the clot and the complex arteriovenous malformation that caused it in one go would give Jamie the best chance of being able to move on with his life in a normal fashion.'

'What do you mean, *normal fashion*?' says Rebecca.

Dr Paul Stevens is a consultant neurosurgeon, according to his name badge. His thick dark hair is almost wiggish, and I find the jowls that buffer his face reassuring, for some reason.

'Let's just see how it pans out,' he says, inspecting the watch hanging from his breast pocket.

He tells us the surgery could take several hours, and that we should go home and get some sleep.

'Go home?' asks Rebecca.

Dr Stevens smiles understandingly. 'There are some blankets in the quiet room if you do want to stay. Someone will come and see you when there's news.'

As he departs my eyes are drawn to the white trainers on his feet. How odd they look, how out of place on a man who is about to cut a hole in my best mate's skull.

The quiet room is sky blue, which I guess is supposed to be calming, but I can't keep still. Rebecca and Danielle station themselves in a corner on the plastic chairs while I pace up and down the room.

'He was one of the last to be called,' explains Danielle. 'Everyone was given six minutes to make their cocktail

– something original – but before their go they had five minutes to prepare the bar. I was bursting because of the free cocktails, so I whizzed off to the loo while Jamie did his prep work. I looked right at him, to gesture that I'd be back in a sec, but he didn't see me.' Danielle pauses as though making an effort to recall the particular moment. 'I swear he looked totally normal. It was just like watching him behind the bar at Arch 13, but then when I got back everyone was around him and—'

It's as though there is a hairline fracture in Danielle's voice and she stops before it breaks completely. Rebecca leans forward to place a hand on her knee, but it's just for a few seconds, and her retreat is followed by a silence that stretches like an elastic band.

Rebecca and Danielle can't do small talk at the best of times, but all that leaves right now is big talk, fucking ginormous talk about everything that has happened these past four months, and this isn't the time or the place.

'His parents are driving down now,' says Danielle. 'They wanted to know how serious it was before setting off.'

'For fuck's sake.' Rebecca folds one arm across her chest, gripping the opposite shoulder. 'Their only son has collapsed.'

Rebecca might not be one for tears but I can see she is struggling right now, and I want so badly to wrap my arms around her, but I can't, because being here doesn't change what's happened, and it doesn't unsay all the things we said tonight. This is just an armistice, and no one is quite clear yet what the terms are or where it is leading.

I sit down next to her and close my eyes, trying to clear my head of all the shit, and when that doesn't work I pass the time by absorbing each and every poster on the wall, the ones featuring germs and hygiene outnumbered only by those offering spiritual guidance. I guess hospitals are a good place for them to reel you in, because everyone here is desperate. I don't think I knew what that word meant until tonight.

As we sit there time seems to slow. Not even in an abstract way. The tick of a plastic clock mounted on the wall sounds laboured, the night having become a form of purgatory with two possible outcomes.

Every so often someone passes by the blinded window to the corridor, and in each of these moments the norms of time resume, our pulses accelerating, but nobody comes into the room with news.

I think about Jamie, my best mate in the whole world, and maybe it's the hour, or the alcohol running through my veins, but I feel like I'm in some kind of daydream, and I'm going to wake up any moment with a dead arm.

I don't know what I'd have done without him through all of this. It's only when I notice Rebecca holding a tissue for me that I realize my eyes are teary.

'This is Jamie, remember,' she tries to comfort. 'The little boy who got hit by a van and didn't break a single bone in his body. He's indestructible.'

I laugh, genuine and snotty, into the tissue, and I'm grateful when Rebecca smiles, apparently satisfied that she's made me feel better.

I've heard him tell the story so many times over the years, about how he'd just been standing there playing when this van came flying out of nowhere. It was a woman, and she never stopped to make sure he was OK. It's how he got the scar on his forehead.

That's how Jamie tells the story, but I was there. We were six, and the van *was* flying, and the woman really didn't stop to make sure he was OK, but what he doesn't mention is that it was a toy van, and the woman in question was another six year old, Jessica Parris, also known as Pigtail Parris. She threw it after Jamie refused to kiss her on the lips.

This isn't the time to break Rebecca's illusion about Jamie being indestructible, though. I wish I didn't know the truth myself.

The minutes continue to pass like hours, and it feels like we've been waiting for ever for some kind of update. Danielle plays with her cuticles, her head shooting up whenever anyone passes by the corridor outside; Rebecca has become glassy-eyed, as though she's in Airplane Mode. Eventually she falls asleep, upright in her chair.

I fetch a blanket and place it over her gently, careful not to wake her. When I sit down again I notice Danielle staring at me.

'When I called you were together,' she says. 'Are you . . . ?'

I open my mouth to say no, because that is the answer, but the word doesn't come. I'm wondering what the answer would have been if Danielle had called five minutes later, and the weird moment Rebecca and I were caught up in had been allowed to play out.

When Rebecca told me there was nothing happening between her and Michael I felt like a complete prat for going round there, but now I'm kind of glad I did, because if there was one person in the world I would have wanted with me when I heard Jamie had collapsed it is Rebecca.

I look at Danielle, but her eyes are now set on the fuzzy grey carpet.

'The only real friend I have left is Jamie,' she says. 'And what if now . . . ?'

A solitary tear emerges from the corner of her eye.

'I think he was going to do it,' she says.

'Do what?'

'At the competition. I think he was going to get to the national finals. He hadn't even had his turn yet but there was no one there like Jamie.'

'Of course he was going to win,' I say.

I look back to Danielle just in time to see her eyes dart to the corridor window. Seconds later the door opens, causing Rebecca to jolt awake.

Something in Dr Stevens' expression fills me with dread.

Chapter Thirty-four

REBECCA

Dr Stevens' expression is serious as he looks from one face to another, before taking a deep breath.

'The craniotomy wasn't as straightforward as we would have liked,' he explains.

Danielle covers her mouth with her hands, and I hear Ben swear under his breath.

'There were complications,' continues the doctor. 'It was touch and go for a while. But . . .' He looks around the room again, his expression softening. 'We managed to get through it, and both the complex arteriovenous malformation and the blood clot have been successfully removed.'

I have to bite my tongue to stop myself yelling at him to just tell us whether our friend is going to be OK.

'He's in the recovery room now,' clarifies Dr Stevens. 'And once his pulse, blood pressure and breathing are stable and he's alert, he'll be taken to the Critical Care Unit and monitored closely from there.' The corners of his mouth turn up into something approaching a smile. 'I don't anticipate any long-term damage.'

'You should have opened with that,' I snap as everyone else breathes a sigh of relief.

Dr Stevens looks taken aback and I feel the others' eyes on me. I don't want a scene so I try to sound less aggressive as I ask when we can see him.

'It's family only for at least twenty-four hours,' he says, even though there's no sign of Jamie's family yet. Where are they? Even with the drive from Manchester they could have been here hours ago. 'You can come during visiting hours after that.'

Once the doctor has gone the three of us look at each other. We haven't been in the same room since Ben's birthday in the cable car, and in any other situation this would be all kinds of awkward, but this isn't any other situation, and simultaneously we break into smiles. No one needs to say anything because the words we're all thinking wrap themselves around us and pull us together like a force.

Thank God.

The door opens and though I recognize the couple that walk in, it's not until Ben speaks that I place them.

'Hi, Mr and Mrs Hawley,' says Ben.

'Ben,' says Jamie's dad with a nod, while his wife offers a small smile. They don't tell Ben to call them by their first names, even though they've known him for ever. Nor do they acknowledge Danielle and me, though I'm sure they know exactly who we are.

Danielle looks my way and rolls her eyes and I shake my head in return. Have she and I really not spoken for months?

Ben starts to tell the Hawleys what Dr Stevens said but Jamie's mum cuts him short, telling him they've already spoken to the doctor. She seems affronted at the suggestion they're not up to speed.

I'm suddenly swept up by an anger on a scale I've never experienced before.

Where were you when he was on the operating table? I want to shout. *And when Jamie opened his bar? And at the reception after graduation? Did you really need to jump on the first train up to Manchester after the ceremony?*

I need to get out of here before I give in to my instincts, because the last thing Jamie needs to hear when he wakes up is that I roundhoused his mum in the face.

'Just going to grab a coffee,' I tell the room.

I punch the buttons on the dispenser, wishing I'd paid more attention to Michael's calming technique earlier. It must have looked rude that I didn't offer to get anyone else a drink, but I've no intention of going back in yet. With my cup in my hand, I walk in the opposite direction to the waiting room.

On the wall at the end of the corridor there's a huge sign with arrows signalling the various wards, and on impulse I follow maternity. It feels like my best chance of finding a happy place.

Five minutes later I find myself standing in front of a glass wall, where six babies in tiny cots are spread out in two neat rows. Amazingly, five are sound asleep, but the one closest to the window must have missed the memo that it's the middle of the night, and lies on its back, blinking at the ceiling with the uncertainty of someone who's just learning how to use their eyelids.

I strain my eyes to read the name on the white tag on the bar of the cot. *Mimi.* It's a girl.

I'm suddenly overcome with a desire to go into the room and lift her up, but even if that was allowed, I know I'd be terrified. I've never held a newborn before. She looks so fragile. Her fingers twitch; she's just learning how to use them too. Look how tiny her hands are!

I can't believe I was ever that small. Actually, I don't think I was – Dad says I was *born* with long fingers and big feet.

An image of Dad sitting in a hospital waiting room pops into my mind and I can't breathe – it's like the wind has been sucked out of me.

The pain I felt waiting to hear if Jamie was going to be OK was unbearable. It doesn't feel like there could be a worse feeling. But for Dad, that was his wife. It was the mother of his young son, and his newborn daughter. And the worst happened. She didn't make it.

A salty tear reaches my lips. How did Dad ever get through something like that? And still manage to be a loving and devoted father to the person who took away the person he thought he would spend the rest of his life with?

I've never spoken to Dad about this. I've never asked how he felt, or how he got through it. I don't know if he's come to terms with it, or if he falls asleep every night feeling the emptiness of the space beside him.

Emotionally stunted, Ben called me. Does he truly believe that? Or was he trying to hurt me in the heat of the argument? I was trying to hurt him with the things I said about his lack of ambition, but I meant them too. It did always get to me.

Maybe it is odd that I waited so long to tell him about my mum. Maybe I should have let him in more – even if it made me feel exposed. Maybe that's what love is – giving your whole self, even if it sometimes hurts.

I press my forehead against the glass and gaze at

334

Mimi, her eyes closed now. *What do babies dream about?*
I wonder.

'Sweet dreams, Mimi,' I whisper. Have a good life.

I hope you have a dad like my dad.

And a friend like Jamie.

Chapter Thirty-five

BEN

Monday, 2 March

I feel nervous as I walk into the hospital, like there's a shit load of winged insects buzzing around my stomach, but they're more like moths than butterflies, because there's nothing pretty about your mate having brain surgery.

Dr Stevens said the surgery was successful, but I haven't got a clue what I'm walking into. I don't even know if he'll be awake, or able to talk. I guess I'm expecting the worst, but when I spot him in the fifth bed on the left, I almost have to double-take. He looks . . .

. . . fine.

There is a small bandage to the side of his crown, and the top of his bed is raised to elevate his head, but apart from that . . .

'They haven't even shaved all your hair off?' I say, with fake annoyance.

Jamie cranes his left arm towards the bandage. 'A little bit around where they cut,' he says, as if that was the thing he found most distressing about the whole ordeal.

I realize I've pretty much been holding my breath for the last two days, and now that I can finally let go, I can't seem to summon the words to describe the relief, and so I stand there, not saying much at all.

'You really fucking scared us there, Hawley,' I finally manage, looking him in the eye for the first time.

He holds eye contact. 'It's really good to see you, Nicholls.'

It is only when I hear the slightest quiver in his voice that I see how shaken up he is.

He shuffles across ever so slightly so I can sit on the edge of his bed, and we both sit there, looking around the ward, because somehow that seems easier than confronting what almost just happened.

'Obviously I had to keep it together for the sake of Rebecca and Danielle,' I finally say.

This amuses him greatly.

'My mum and dad send their love,' I say. 'And Frank.'

'Mate, I'd kill for one of his fry-ups right now. The food in here is worse than the bar before you came along.'

'First day you're out of here, that's where we're going.'

He smiles weakly. I'm about to tell him I called the bank and explained everything, and how they said we could rearrange our appointment when Jamie is up to it, but we're interrupted by the girls. They take turns to lean down for a kiss, then pull out the stacked chairs that I hadn't seen.

'I knew I'd get us all back in the room together one day,' Jamie says. 'I mean, I didn't think I'd have to go to these lengths, but . . .'

I look at Rebecca, and she looks at Danielle, and none of us quite knows what to say until Jamie starts

337

laughing, and it's like the first clap in a round of applause, it sets everyone off.

Our shared laughter is full of relief, and afterwards Rebecca is suddenly able to look me in the eye and Danielle no longer folds her arms like she's forgotten her coat in winter.

'I didn't know how bad you were going to look,' says Danielle. 'I've been practising my Ugly Baby Face all morning in case you were a horror show.'

Jamie looks confused.

'It's the face you do when someone's baby is ugly and you have to pretend it's the most beautiful and precious thing you ever saw in your whole life,' says Danielle.

'Show us your Ugly Baby Face,' says Rebecca.

Danielle widens her eyes and sets her mouth into a gormless smile.

'You actually look like an ugly baby,' says Jamie, taking a grape from the carton next to his leg, tossing it in the air and missing his mouth completely.

'Shame you're not going to have a visible scar when your hair grows back,' says Danielle. 'That would have got you loads of sympathy sex.'

I remember what Rebecca said while Jamie was having surgery, about him being indestructible because he was hit by a van as a kid. I didn't want to break her illusion at the time, but maybe he is indestructible after all.

'He's always got the scar from when he was six,' I say. 'What kind of van was it again, mate?'

Rebecca clocks my smirk.

'What?' she says to both of us.

I shrug in Jamie's direction, so that everyone looks to him for the answer.

'It was a toy van, OK?'

Jamie explains about Pigtail Parris, and stresses that it was still a traumatic experience, but I'm not sure the girls hear him through their laughter.

We're distracted by a brunette nurse in a cobalt-blue uniform who smiles at Jamie as she walks past with a trolley full of drip bags.

'Oh, *please*,' says Rebecca under her breath, before turning to Jamie. 'You've only been out of Critical Care two minutes and you've already got the nurses wrapped around your little finger.'

I look at Jamie, expecting him to reveal that he's already got her number or something, but he's spaced out, his forehead all taut. I follow his eyes to the window at one end of the ward. It is lunchtime, but it's one of those miserable days that never gets going, the night sky unwilling to submit completely to day.

Dr Stevens appears. 'Mind if I interrupt?'

Danielle stands up so he can get past and shine a light into each of Jamie's eyes. Satisfied, he dispatches the light into his breast pocket.

'What's your name?' he asks Jamie.

'Aeronaut Charles Hodges,' comes the reply. 'But you can call me Chas.'

'What's the date?'

'December 30, 1975.'

'Where are you?'

'On board the *Discovery II* mission to introduce authentic cockney music to the inhabitants of earth.'

Dr Stevens watches him intently for a moment and then says *Good* as if these were exactly the answers he was after.

'Remember the last time we were all in hospital together?' I say once the doctor has gone.

339

'Remember it?' Danielle squeals. 'I still have scars on my arse!'

Rebecca and I had been going out for six months and we'd all gone up to the Lake District for a long weekend. We hired a boat, but Danielle dropped one of the oars, and we learnt that if you try to row with one oar you just go round in circles, so we tried to anchor the other oar into the bed of the lake and drag ourselves towards the shore. And that was when we – Jamie – dropped the other oar. So we were literally up the creek without a paddle.

Somehow we managed to jig the boat near enough to a tree so that we could swing on to the bank using a branch. Perfect. But after levering three of us to safety, the branch snapped. With Danielle attached.

'The look on your face when you realized you'd landed in nettles,' I remind her.

'This was about as sympathetic as you were at the time, if I remember correctly,' says Rebecca.

'That's not fair,' I counter. 'We only laughed for a few seconds.'

'Yes, by which time Becs was already pulling me to safety.'

Rebecca always was good in a crisis. She was the one who thought to ring the hotel to find out the nearest Accident and Emergency, and the one who navigated us there even when the satnav lost its signal. I guess I shouldn't have been surprised she didn't lose her way when *we* had a crisis.

It is only once we're done reminiscing that I realize Jamie hasn't been saying anything. He looks tired, and I'm wondering if he wants us to leave so he can rest, but then he asks about the bar.

'Everything's under control,' I say. 'Erica's been a star.'

A few minutes later Jamie's parents arrive and stand back as though waiting for us to say our goodbyes.

'Take care of yourself, OK?' says Rebecca, reaching down for another kiss. She takes his hand loosely. 'Love you.'

Jamie brightens. 'Aw, you never use the L word. I'm touched.'

Rebecca hooks her arms into her coat while Danielle leans in to say her own goodbye to Jamie, and they exchange a smile. She steps back and I'm up, but I'm not sure I could hold it together if I told him how I really feel about him, so instead I instigate a sideways handshake, but he can barely grip my palm.

He holds up a hand woozily as we retreat, then Danielle rushes off to catch the Tube back to her office.

'How're you getting home?' I say, stopping with Rebecca in the corridor.

'Bike,' says Rebecca. 'You?'

'I might walk if the rain has let up,' I say. 'Make sure you're careful on the roads.'

'You never know when a van might come flying.'

We both smile.

'He's been a good mate to us, hasn't he?' I say. The brunette nurse passes us on her way into the ward. 'He's been the one in the middle of everything.'

'It's good that we can be in the same room together,' she says. 'For Jamie's sake.'

I open my arms to hug her, and I'm relieved when she moves into them, just for a second. I haven't had a chance to process everything that was said the other night, but one thing I'm sure of is I'm glad Rebecca is back in my life.

'Hopefully this will be a wake-up call to his parents, too,' I say.

I cannot tell if that is the moment the shouting starts, or just when I become aware of it.

A woman's voice, the brunette maybe, shouts the word *Nurse* repeatedly, the volume increasing but the tone remaining calm, level.

Rebecca and I lock eyes.

A second nurse runs towards the opening. I see his white trainers first, and then I understand it's not a nurse at all but Dr Stevens, and I should have twigged sooner because his overalls are puce, not blue.

The nurse is still shouting but I can't make out what she's saying, and there is something about her calls, their calmness, that I find disturbing, something that makes me feel like there's a lead weight in my stomach.

I hold out my hand and Rebecca's is already there to take it as we step back towards the ward.

I hear a woman shriek but it's not until we return to the ward that I realize it is Jamie's mum. The brunette nurse ushers her away from Jamie's bed as she pulls a pale green curtain around it.

Rebecca drops my hand and starts to run but a male nurse I haven't seen before stands between her and Jamie. I try to walk towards them but the lead weight is too heavy now, and it's stopping me from moving.

'I'm sorry, you can't go any further at the moment.'

Rebecca turns back to me but there is so much happening and it's as though my brain has tripped, and suddenly none of my senses are working.

I'm vaguely aware of people all around the ward staring towards Jamie's bed. The only person who isn't is Rebecca. She is still looking at me, but now she's pointing at Jamie, and shouting something. I can't make sense of it.

Another nurse appears, and she is pushing some kind of trolley towards Jamie's bed, and the male nurse is having to hold Rebecca back, physically hold her back.

There is a noise I don't recognize, like a staple gun, and I wonder if it's got something to do with the trolley. I count the staples, one, two, three, four, five, six.

I wait for the seventh staple. While I'm waiting, in amongst a blur of a thousand thoughts, I remember that I never told Jamie about the bank saying we could rearrange our meeting. It's only then it dawns on me that the seventh staple never came, and now there is nothing, no sound and no movement, until Dr Stevens appears from behind the curtain.

He stops at Jamie's parents, and what happens next is in slow motion: Rebecca looking at me, pleading with her eyes for me to do something as Dr Stevens stands rooted, no more words coming from his lips, his eyes fallen to the floor.

And I know without having to be told that everything, everything, has changed.

Chapter Thirty-six

REBECCA

Friday, 6 March

Jamie once told me that black suits me.

'Whoa,' he said when I stepped out of my room before our graduation ball. 'You look fit.'

'You only think that because it's the first time you've seen me in a dress.' I glanced at my reflection in the hall mirror and frowned. 'Wish I'd gone for something colourful. Black is a bit boring, isn't it?'

'Black suits you.'

'Because it's the colour of my soul?' I quipped.

Jamie laughed. 'Because it's classy.'

I'm looking pretty classy right now, huh, Jamie? Dirty tracksuit bottoms and misshapen vest top, hair that hasn't been washed for days, and every piece of black clothing I own sprawled across my bed.

The only funeral I've ever been to was Granny's. It was sad – of course it was – but it was happy too. It was about family coming together. It was a celebration of the fact she'd lived a full and happy life. She was eighty-nine.

How can the death of my twenty-eight-year-old best

friend be anything other than heart-wrenching?

Relentless questions I don't know the answer to cloud my brain. What shall I wear? How waterproof is waterproof mascara? What should I say to Jamie's parents? How much longer can Ben and I ignore what nearly happened the night he collapsed? How can Jamie be there one moment, then just cease to exist the next? All his personality, all his humour, his kindness, his charm – how can that just disappear? How can someone as loved as Jamie be gone and the world just carry on going?

'Rebecca?' Stefan eases open the door. 'You need to jump in the shower and start getting ready if we're going to make that train.'

'I know, but I . . .' I take a deep breath and lean against the wall with my eyes closed, trying to get my thoughts in order. 'I can't do this,' I sob, sliding to the floor and burying my face in my hands. 'I can't say goodbye to Jamie. I'm not ready.'

Stefan sinks down next to me and wraps an arm around my heaving shoulders, pulling me towards him. 'I know you're not. But you'll pull yourself together and get through it. You're a Giamboni.'

The train takes just over two hours to get to Manchester, and it's another twenty minutes on the tram to get to the church. I knew Jamie was popular but nothing prepares me for the number of people crammed inside. And there are still people arriving. Some I recognize from the bar, or from university, or his block of flats. Others I don't recognize at all.

Ben is sitting at the front, in the middle of the left pew, with his head bent forward. Is he weeping? My own eyes start to prickle.

As though he can sense me watching him, he stands and turns. Our eyes meet. He strides down the aisle towards us, folding a piece of paper into his top pocket as he goes. He must be practising his eulogy. How the hell is he going to stand in front of all these people and talk about our dead friend and hold it together?

'Hi.' He stops in front of me.

'Hi.'

'Hey, Ben.' Stefan moves forward for a handshake. 'I'm so sorry.'

'Thank you.'

Russ and Tom walk in, with Avril trailing behind them, complete with beret and huge Jackie O sunglasses.

'What a trek,' she's saying grumpily. 'And we're going to have to do that journey all over again . . .'

'Why are you even here?' I ask.

She crosses her arms and glares at me, but Tom steps forward.

'Hey, Rebecca, long time no see. I'm really sorry about Jamie.'

'Thank you, Tom.'

Danielle is next through the church door, and as the group turns to look at her, the corners of Avril's mouth make a rare journey north. Despite the dark glasses, I know her eyes are on me.

Without words, Danielle wraps her arms around my waist and I wrap mine round her shoulders.

'This is the hardest thing I've ever had to do,' I whisper.

'Me too,' she whispers back. 'And not punching Avril in her smug face is the second hardest.'

Tom and Avril take seats at the back but Russ stays at

346

Ben's side, giving him concerned looks and attempting to lighten the mood.

'I've never been in a room with so many attractive women who appear not to have dates,' he observes quietly. 'And all so vulnerable. Shame you're not allowed to pull at funerals.'

'Says who?' asks a voice behind me.

'Jemma,' I cry. 'Thank you so much for coming.'

'Don't mention it, hen.' She hugs me. 'I've missed you.'

I went back to work on Wednesday but after Jake saw the state of me he gave me the rest of the week off as compassionate leave.

Danielle's eyes flick from me to Jemma questioningly, so I introduce them, then suggest we sit down.

'I've saved a pew at the front,' says Ben, leading the way.

Jamie's parents are sitting on the other side of the aisle, his dad stony-faced, and his mum looking overwhelmed. I nod as I pass but don't wait to see if they respond.

I feel restless during the service. The words spoken by the minister say nothing about the Jamie I knew. He keeps calling him James, the name he was christened with, and the platitudes could be about any twenty-something-year-old man who died. But Jamie wasn't just anyone.

It's not the minister's fault. He would have only spoken to Mr and Mrs Hawley, who never took the time to get to know their son properly. They never knew how lucky they were to have him.

'Now James's friend, Ben, will say a few words.' The minister steps down and Ben walks up, taking out his sheet of paper. He opens it out on to the lectern.

'I always thought the only speech I'd be giving about Jamie would be a best man's speech,' he begins, his voice shaking. A few seconds pass and I wonder if he can continue, but he clears his throat and goes on: 'On the way here we passed the secondary school that Jamie and I, and many others in here, went to, and it reminded me of our very first day.

'Our form tutor, Mr Sheldon, or Shouty Sheldon as *someone* christened him . . .'

I smile, while many around the church audibly laugh.

'. . . gave us all a blank sheet of paper and asked us to write what we wanted to be when we grew up. We all handed in our sheets and the next day Mr Sheldon had put every one of them on display in our form room. I think the point was to inspire us over the next five years.

'Nobody knew who put what but there were all the usual things eleven-year-old kids would write: Premiership footballer, lead singer, ballet dancer. But on one sheet of paper someone had just written HAPPY.

'I remember thinking it was a pretty stupid answer: did this person not know the international acclaim you got as a ballet dancer?'

Danielle and I smile at each other.

'Jamie never would tell me which sheet of paper belonged to him, but when I passed the school today I realized that I'd known all along. All Jamie wanted in life was to be happy, and I reckon he's probably the only person in that class who ended up achieving their goal.' Ben takes a deep breath, and looks at his sheets. 'Here's the part where I read a meaningful quote, something old and profound, and really, it has to be Chas 'n' Dave, doesn't it?'

He looks out into the sea of faces, and stops, as if

noticing for the first time how many people are in front of him. '*Rabbit*,' a guy at the back yells.

'Hey, I didn't say I was taking requests.' Ben smiles, composing himself. 'Anyway, I looked up some lyrics and what I found was . . . Well, let's just say that between "Snooker Loopy" and "The Bollocks Song" I couldn't find anything appropriate.'

I notice Jamie's parents glance at one another. I can't see the expression on their faces, but I don't imagine they're going for this. I don't care. This isn't for them – it's for the people who really knew Jamie.

'I do have a quote for you, though, and it's actually from Jamie himself. It was a few months ago, New Year's Eve in fact, and I'm not proud to tell you we were having an argument . . .'

I close my eyes, seeing my own New Year's Eve play out in my mind again.

'It was totally my fault,' Ben continues. 'I was moaning on about not knowing what to do with my life, which Jamie had heard a million times before, and when he pointed this out I acted like a spoilt kid. So much so that I didn't really take in the words he said until . . . Well, until he died.'

Ben inhales a deep breath, his voice starting to shake again.

'What he said was this: the average person only gets three billion heartbeats in their life and you need to make sure that as many of them as possible count for something.'

Ben's shoulders slump and for a second I'm worried he's going to break down, but he pulls himself up straight again and his voice is strong. 'Jamie didn't get his three billion heartbeats . . .'

My tears fall silently, but I can hear others crying all around the church.

'. . . but I don't know anyone who made each heart-beat count as much as he did.

'One thing I saw when I went travelling was that in a lot of countries, when people die the funeral is a celebration of their life, and knowing Jamie I reckon he'd buy into that idea. Although he's probably up there now smiling at the sight of us all crying over him.'

I laugh again. Ben is right. Jamie's life is worth cele-brating.

'He was a true gent, was Jamie, and though I'm devastated that he's gone, I'm proud to have been able to say that he was my best friend.'

He looks up at the ceiling, his eyes glistening.

'I love you, mate.'

Ben's composure can only last so long, and it's as we're watching Jamie's coffin being lowered into the ground that he loses it, with big, audible sobs. I want to take his hand in mine. I want to tell him he'll get through this, and I want him to tell me that I'll get through it. But Stefan, Danielle and Russ all stand between us.

The irony isn't lost on me: all the times he tried to take my hand in public and I let it go, embarrassed. It seems so stupid now. I'll tell Ben that when we talk. Because we need to talk. Just not today, because today isn't about us.

When it's all over, I fall into step beside him as we walk along the gravelly path towards the graveyard's exit.

'Ben, your eulogy, it was really lovely.'

'Ta, Becs. That means a lot.' He stops when we reach

the gate. 'Are you going to the wake at the Hawleys'?'

'Guess so. You?'

'Guess so.' He doesn't need to say any more – I know he's thinking the same as me. It will be hard to feel Jamie's presence over salmon sandwiches, tea and polite conversation with his parents.

Stefan and Jemma catch up with us, with Danielle, Tom and Russ just behind them.

'We're going to head off,' Tom says apologetically, but without explanation. Not that we need one. Avril waits for him a few feet away, the shades not concealing her impatience.

'What now?' asks Jemma after we've said goodbye to Tom.

'There's a wake at Jamie's folks' house,' says Danielle unenthusiastically.

'Or,' says Ben, getting that look in his eye he gets when he's about to suggest something rebellious, 'we can give it a miss and go to The Old Monk?'

No one needs much convincing and when we get to the traditional boozer, we gather round a corner table and I order six whiskies off the top shelf.

We drink in silence.

'Nice,' says Russ eventually, nodding at his glass.

I attempt a smile. 'It's one Jamie recommended.'

'He was very wise, wasn't he?' Danielle says. 'Not just about drinks but about life. He just gave really good advice without ever being preachy or patronizing.'

'I know!' Jemma claps her hand together. 'Let's go round the circle and all say the most important lesson we learnt from Jamie.' We all look at each other, silently agreeing. 'We'll call it . . .' Jemma thinks for a second. 'Lessons from Jamie. Ben, you start.'

Ben sweeps both hands through his hair, then holds them at the back of his head, looking thoughtful.

'He taught me that we make our own happiness,' he says eventually. 'He never let the fact his parents didn't support him stop him chasing his dreams. He wasn't waiting around for a girl to show up and complete him. He just lived the life he wanted to live without hurting anyone to do it.'

Everyone nods.

Ben looks to his right. 'Russ?'

Russ puts his elbows on the table and his chin on his hands while he thinks. 'That nice guys don't finish last,' he says. 'Jamie was proof that it's not just the arseholes that get all the girls.'

'So true.' Ben laughs. 'Jemma?'

'To be yourself with the opposite sex,' she says decisively. 'I remember listening to him telling some girl in the bar he'd been to over twenty Chas 'n' Dave gigs. I was thinking, *Dude! Stop talking*. You dinnae admit to that kind of shit. But then the girl's knickers fell off, so I was clearly wrong.'

We all giggle.

'What about you, Stefan?' Jemma asks.

Stefan glances at me. 'That it's not just your family you can trust to take care of you.' Looking around, he continues: 'I was terrified when my little sister went off to uni. I always felt it was my duty to make sure she stayed out of harm's way, even if she didn't know I was doing it. Who'd keep her safe when she moved away? I barely slept the first few weeks she was gone. But as soon as I met Jamie, I knew she was OK. That other people cared about her like Dad and I do.'

A lump forms in my throat and I'm relieved it's

Danielle's turn to talk, because I can't.

'Mine's similar,' she says softly, wrapping her hands around her glass and frowning into it. 'Jamie taught me you can choose your own people. We don't get to choose our families – and some are luckier than others when it comes to that – but we don't have to be stuck with anyone. You can pick the people you like best, that you think you deserve and they deserve you, and make them your family.'

I'd never really thought about it like that, but she's right. Everyone wanted to be Jamie's friend – and he had loads – but for some reason he chose the three of us as his inner circle. No wonder he was always so keen for us to patch things up. To him it was like his family was falling apart. And the saddest thing is, as I sit here with Ben on one side and Danielle on the other, he'd only just got to see it happen when we lost him.

'And Shane isn't one of those people,' adds Danielle, looking at me apologetically. 'So I'm going to tell him never to contact me again.'

I glance at her and she cringes.

'I know, I know – but I mean it this time. Anyway,' she says, obviously keen to skip past it, 'what did Jamie teach you?'

Now it's my turn to look into my glass. I know the most important thing Jamie taught me but I need to pretend there aren't five pairs of eyes on me if I'm going to be able to say it out loud.

'That it's OK to need people,' I confess. 'I know I can push people away.' A tear plops into my whisky as I take a sip. 'I guess I think I'm protecting myself. Like, if I don't need them, I can't get hurt if they're ever not there any more. But I didn't realize how much I needed

Jamie. He was always there for me.' I look from Danielle to Ben. 'For all of us. But I don't regret needing him.'

Even though he's gone and it really fucking hurts, everything I got from his friendship is worth the pain.

'To Jamie,' I add, raising my glass.

'To Jamie,' everyone repeats, clinking their glasses with mine.

'That's why I like comics,' says Russ. 'Heroes don't die in comics. Or if they do, they're always resurrected at some point.'

'Yes!' Jemma exclaims, leaning over to pat Russ's arm. 'Good for you.'

'Why?' Russ looks confused.

'Admitting shit like that and not caring what we all think of you.'

We all laugh, but it doesn't last long and a silence falls across the group, everyone lost in their own thoughts.

Chapter Thirty-seven

BEN

Monday, 9 March

I still feel numb as I set off for my first day of freelancing since the funeral. I wait on the platform, eyes set on the concrete glazed with frost. I hear the train before I see it. It whistles to a stop, and in the quiet that ensues I can hear my heart beating. I lift my eyes to the open carriage door but suddenly I can't do it.

I unlock my phone and call the office. I'm not sure they'll be hiring me again but how could I? How could I spend the day filtering job applications to make sure we're being socially inclusive? How could I make small talk with people I barely know and who barely know me? Even though I've got rent to pay, and I'm back to square one with finding a permanent job now that going into business with Jamie is off the table, how could I waste another heartbeat on this shit, after everything that's happened?

I find a vacant bench on the platform and light a cigarette, holding the first intake in my lungs for as long as I can before letting go. The cold metal soon warms under my weight and I flick through the photos on my phone, wanting to feel, to not be numb. I linger on a photo of Jamie and me. It was the first night I cooked at the bar. He grabbed my phone to take it, saying it was important to capture the moment when something significant happened. When I asked what he was on about he just rolled his eyes.

Staring at the photo, I am no longer on the platform; I am there with him, hearing him ring his makeshift bell before joining me for a drink at the end of the bar, and the only way I'm aware of the present is the thick lump in my throat.

I swipe back, my finger accelerating because, just for a moment, it feels like I can turn back time. I'm seeing photos of me and Rebecca, the two of us outside the Colosseum. With fresh eyes I notice something in my smile, a stiffness, and I recall the hour or two before the photo was taken. We'd bickered because I'd forgotten to book online, so we had to queue in a line that snaked around the circumference of the ruined stadium. I realize now that my smile is forced.

When we broke up I kidded myself that Rebecca and I had a perfect relationship, but ever since our argument on the night Jamie collapsed I've begun to appreciate that we didn't.

Needing more than pixels, something real, I walk from the platform and wait for a bus, and before long I'm standing outside Jamie's apartment block. He never asked for his key back.

His parents are coming to clear the place at the weekend before the landlord puts it back up for rent. For now, though, the apartment remains as he left it.

I wander through the open-plan space, half expecting to hear his key in the door, or to see his head protrude from the bathroom to deliver some sarcastic comment.

I study the room, tears streaming down my face. The foosball table, the old liquor adverts, the Chas 'n' Dave disc, the chalkboard with the rules he never rubbed off. I wonder what his parents will do with it all.

I always wanted to do something where I'd be remembered, but it doesn't happen. Not for most of us, anyway. What happens is that our lives become recycled. Our homes, our possessions, even the way people think of us. History isn't written as things happen, but after something has finished, so people don't remember who we were but how it all ended.

Everyone kept saying the same thing at the funeral. It's such a *tragedy*. That was the word they used. But Jamie's life was not a tragedy. He squeezed more life into his twenty-eight years than most people experience in seventy. It's their lives – our lives – that are the tragedy.

Rebecca texts at about eight o'clock. We've been messaging quite a lot since the funeral. Just about Jamie, really. I've been apprehensive about mentioning anything else, but I know I can't put it off for ever. We should probably talk about what happened in those minutes before Danielle called.

I miss him so much.

The brevity of her text, the lack of explanation and kiss, the utter Rebeccaness of it, somehow brings a smile to my face.

Me too. You ok? X

A minute passes.

Come over. Got booze. Nice to talk to someone who gets it x

*

Rebecca opens the door and I can tell from her panda eyes that she hasn't been sleeping. She imitates a smile.

'I brought you Scotch,' I say, but when she leads me into the living room I see that her thirty-year-old Glenfiddich is open on the coffee table. She fetches another glass and pours me a large measure.

We sit on the couch, Rebecca at one end with hunched knees, me in the other corner with one leg lifted so that I'm half facing her.

Rebecca stares at the space between us. The radio is playing Abba.

'Bjorn wrote this about his break-up with Agnetha,' I tell Rebecca, 'then gave it to her to sing.'

'Who was the winner that took it all?'

'Both of them, probably, after the money started rolling in.'

'We should have thought of that,' says Rebecca. 'Jamie and Danielle could have been Benny and . . . what was the other one called?'

'Frida?'

'That's it,' she says. 'Danielle could have been Frida.'

'*No, no, no, no.*'

We laugh into our drinks, forgetting who we are and what brought me round here for a few seconds.

'How's your mum?' says Rebecca. 'Does she still call you every Monday night?'

I nod. 'She's taking redundancy. I helped her get what she was owed after they changed her role.'

'They're making her redundant? She's been there, like, thirty-five years or something, hasn't she?' Rebecca titters to herself. 'Which is strange when you think about it – you can't stick at anything for more than thirty-five minutes.'

'I stuck at you for longer than that.'

I regret the words as soon as they leave my mouth, but thankfully Rebecca doesn't follow up on it, concentrating instead on pouring herself another drink. Her touch is too heavy so that a splash of whisky lands on the acacia surface.

'I'd give anything to be able to share a glass of this with him.'

'I'd give anything to sit at the end of the bar with him one last time.'

Rebecca stares fondly at the bottle. 'Are we doing that thing that everyone does when someone they know dies? Romanticizing them?' She grins, to show me she doesn't believe a word of it.

I emulate her expression. 'You're right. Jamie – what a prick.'

'I mean, no matter how much we loved him,' she continues, 'we could never compare to the one true love of his life.'

'His reflection?'

We laugh again.

'He was *so* vain,' I say.

I can tell from the way Rebecca swooshes her hand in the direction of the radio that she is drunk now. 'He probably thought all these songs were about him.'

I just about manage to retain the whisky in my mouth, and by the time I've composed myself I recognize the song that is playing. It's 'Cannonball' by Damien Rice. I picture Jamie turning it off.

'What are you grinning at?' asks Rebecca.

I try to straighten my face but it's not easy. 'Nothing,' I tell her, and she inspects me for a few seconds before conceding defeat.

'How things change.' She smirks to herself. 'I've been sitting here bawling like a baby all day and you're keeping everything locked up.'

I try not to look surprised that she's been crying.

'We've come full circle,' I say.

Rebecca kinks her head thoughtfully, but doesn't say anything. I survey the room, feeling nostalgic, and when I look back at Rebecca her eyes are closed.

I sit and watch her, her feet sliding involuntarily down the couch, the rise and fall of her chest becoming slower, deepening, until I am sure she is asleep.

I carry her to bed, clearing the duvet with my foot, and placing her on to sheets I've slept in hundreds of times. She doesn't stir as I tuck her in, the light from the living room illuminating her face.

I step towards the door and when I turn my head I see her eyes jerk, but they do not open.

I take another step back, and that is when I hear her say . . .

'Don't go, Ben.'

There is no weirder feeling than everything being both exactly and nothing as it should be.

In the tiny pocket of time where the confusion of sleep and the awareness of consciousness collide, the last four and a half months never happened. The rain hammers heavily on the window, the girl I love is cocooned in my arms, and somewhere out there Jamie is alive.

If I could freeze that feeling I would, because I can't remember the last time I woke up feeling this happy.

But it's not real, I realize with a heavy heart as I stretch myself awake.

Jamie isn't alive. And I'm not in love.

I'm not in love. The realization has been fermenting ever since the night I stormed around to the flat, but only now can I see everything clearly.

It was pride that took me around there, not love, and I no longer feel angry, or hurt, or frustrated. I'm none of those things now. And I care about her so much. But I'm not in love with her any more.

It's chilly in here, so when Rebecca kicks the duvet off herself I pull it back up over the parts of me that have become exposed.

'Sorry,' she whispers. 'Too hot.'

When she wakes up properly she looks confused. She sits up and rubs the sleep out of her eyes.

'Morning,' I say, looking up at her.

'Morning, yourself,' she says gently, closing her eyes again.

I feel my shoulders tense. What if she thinks this is us getting back together? What if her asking me to stay for the night was actually her asking me to stay for good? What if that's why we didn't do anything: because she thinks we've got all the time in the world to do it.

'You OK?' she asks.

'Yeah,' I reply, feigning tiredness even though I'm wide awake. 'You?'

'Mmmm.'

We remain still for a while longer, until Rebecca's stomach rumbles.

'Hungry?' I ask.

'Starving,' she says.

'Me too. I'll get up and make us breakfast, shall I?'

'Good luck with that.'

'You'd be amazed what I can muster up with very few ingredients.'

I jump out of bed but two minutes later I'm back.

'OK, I'm good but I'm not a magician.'

Rebecca has covered herself with the duvet now, but remains on her side of the bed. I look at the empty space I've left and decide against filling it for fear of giving her the wrong impression.

'Shall we go out for breakfast?' I suggest, not adding that we need to talk. 'Frank's?'

'But that's yours and Jamie's place.'

'I don't mind if you don't?'

A few seconds later she whips off the duvet. 'Frank's it is.'

Frank does a double-take when we walk in.

'Ben!'

He opens his arms like he's going to hug me but instead just pats me on the back. Because I'm with a girl he immediately leads us to his 'best' table – the only one with a view of the street outside.

'I was so sorry to hear about young Jamie,' he says, slinging a tea towel over his shoulder and lowering his head. 'He was a special soul.'

I straighten the knife and fork wrapped in a napkin on the table, not wanting to get emotional.

'He was,' I hear Rebecca say.

I look at her gratefully and compose myself with a deep breath. 'Frank, this is Rebecca.'

He offers a hand for her to shake then folds his arms and smiles admiringly. 'Both of them used to talk about you a lot,' he tells her. 'And now I see why.'

'What did they used to say?' quizzes Rebecca.

Frank shrugs and winks at me, then pulls the menus from the rack on the table and passes them to us.

'I'll have a full English, please, Frank,' Rebecca looks up to say. 'And a black coffee.'

'I'll have the same, please, but with a pot of tea,' I add.

'Excellent choice,' Frank says.

Once he's gone I watch Rebecca stare at the salt pot.

'Penny for your thoughts,' I say.

'Jesus, Ben – you'd literally sponsor anything. Also – a penny? That's a lot of thoughts I'm going to have to share before I can afford breakfast.'

'Actually,' I say, 'that phrase has been around since the sixteenth century, when a penny was worth loads of money. I guess now it would be *A million quid for your thoughts* or something.'

'Now we're talking.'

Frank comes back with our plates, piled high. We begin eating in silence. I steal a glance at Rebecca and catch her doing the same, making us both laugh nervously.

'About last night,' I say, at the same time she says: 'Can we talk?'

'Sorry,' I tell her. 'You go first.'

'No – you go.'

I want to insist she speaks first but it wouldn't be fair. What if she's about to ask if I want to try again?

'About last night,' I repeat. 'Thank you for asking me to stay. Talking about Jamie really helped, and it was lovely falling asleep next to you, but—'

'Ben,' she stops me, taking my hands in hers – something she would never have done when we were going out. 'You don't need to do this.'

'Do what?'

'I don't want us to get back together either. I know we're not right for each other. We used to be but . . .'

363

'. . . we're not now,' I say, almost laughing with relief.

'I know it's only been four months or something, but so much has happened and so much has changed and . . . It feels like we're different people, somehow.'

'Totally.'

'I still love your company,' she says. 'And whoever you eventually end up with will be the luckiest woman in the whole world . . .'

The relief stuns me. It's because I care for her so much, and I want her to be a part of my life, and I was worried all these words would make it impossible.

'And you're still the most beautiful girl I know,' I say. 'And you will always make me laugh.'

The moment ends when Rebecca spots Frank watching us from the counter like we're a soap opera. She drops my hands and picks up her fork.

'I'll transfer your deposit and half the cost of the furniture this week,' she says, dipping her sausage into the middle of the fried egg. 'Sorry it's taken so long. It just felt a bit . . . final, you know?'

'That would be great. Ta, Becs.'

I take a slice of toast from the toast rack and begin to mop up the sauce from my beans.

'All the things we said when you came round . . .' she says, turning self-consciously as the cafe door opens, then returning her attention to me. 'I know I wasn't the easiest person to be with.'

'It was one of the best times of my life, Becs. I don't regret a single day we spent together.'

'Me neither.' She smiles as she lays her cutlery on her empty plate. 'So what's next for you?'

I accept defeat against my own breakfast and shrug.

'I'm sorry for all the times you had to listen to me moan about work,' I say.

'That's OK,' she says, twisting the salt cellar with her hand but still looking at me. 'I don't know, maybe you should go away somewhere for the day, out of London, wherever it may be, and you can't come back until you've decided.'

Frank must sense that we're in the middle of something because he says nothing as he collects the plates, though he acknowledges my leftovers with a scowl.

'Maybe,' I tell her. 'So you gonna buy somewhere, or get someone else in the flat, or . . . ?'

'I'm not sure I could live with anyone else,' she says. 'I've realized I really like living alone. Though I hated it after you left.'

'Really?' I can't hide my shock. 'I always thought you took to single life like a duck to water?'

'A duck to whisky, perhaps.'

I chuckle, deciding against asking her to elaborate.

Frank brings the bill and Rebecca and I both reach into the pockets of our coats on the backs of our chairs.

'I'll get this,' she says. 'Call it a thank-you for answering my distress call last night.'

'No, no – let me,' I insist, dropping some cash on to the saucer. 'Think of it as a fiver for your thoughts.'

Something flashes across her face.

'What?' I ask.

She surveys the room. 'Wasn't it here that Jamie gave you the napkin?'

'That table over there,' I say, pointing.

Rebecca's eyes widen like she wants to know more. It would have been unimaginable for us to talk about any of this a few months ago, but now . . .

'You should have heard him when he handed it over,' I oblige. 'He as good as threatened to break my legs if I hurt you.'

Rebecca stares into her coffee cup after finishing it off.

'Then I realized that was just Jamie – a loyal friend to the last.'

She smiles gently. 'Yep, the loyalist.'

Rebecca looks lost in her own thoughts again, and I'm about to ask her what she's thinking, press her to open up like I might have done if we were still going out, but it dawns on me that it's not the kind of question I get to ask any more.

Two Months Earlier

Chapter Thirty-eight

REBECCA

New Year's Eve

Jamie is slicing an orange and chatting to a brunette in a white jumpsuit when I arrive at just gone midnight. He spots me as I approach the bar and waves, and when the girl turns to look I realize it's Tidy Tania.

'Hey, you,' says Jamie, coming over.

'Hey, yourself.' I hop up on to the bar stool.

'Second time today – it's like you can't stay away from me.'

'Actually, it's a different day. In fact, I haven't seen you all year. Happy New Year!'

'Back atcha!' he says with a laugh, leaning across the bar to kiss me. 'What are you doing here?'

'I'm only here for the whisky.' The taxi ride sobered me up slightly – I don't feel quite as pissed as I did when I left Sally. 'Large, please.' I look around the room again then ask: 'Where's Ben?'

'You just missed him,' Jamie tells me, his back to me as he pours my drink.

Oh.

Jamie gives me my glass and looks like he's going to

say something else, but a group of lads approach the bar.

'Shut up, mate, you're 'aving one,' the first one says to one of his mates. Then he yells at Jamie: 'Eight sambucas, please.'

'Sorry,' Jamie tells me, leaving to serve them.

As soon as he's done, two girls order six cocktails and by the time they're carrying the drinks back to their friends, the boys are ready for another round of sambucas.

I can't believe I just missed Ben. And not just because I wouldn't be sat here by myself for twenty minutes while Jamie serves, but because the whole way here I've been working myself up to talking to him, to seeing if there is anything salvageable between us.

'Fancy a dance?' Jamie asks when the rush dies down.

'Nah, not in the mood.'

He's just poured us both a drink when the band announce there's one song left, then break into 'Dancing in the Street' and everybody who isn't already dancing jumps up.

'C'mon, Jamie,' yells Tidy Tania. 'Dance with me.'

How forward can you get? I turn away, embarrassed for her, until I realize Jamie has gone, and a few seconds later he's bouncing up and down in the crowd.

I think again about the things Sally and Tommy said earlier, about me being afraid to let people in. Tania doesn't let the fear of rejection or the threat of getting hurt stop her doing what she wants. Neither does Danielle, or Jemma. Why do I care so much?

Maybe I should work on that.

I mean, I haven't had sex since Ben and I split up. I'm single now – maybe I should be playing the field. Meet people like Jamie, flirt with them and get laid.

Not actually with Jamie, obviously.

Could I?

No, of course not.

Or could I?

No.

Or . . . ?

I look around at my options. I could do worse. Like the guy who was made to drink sambuca against his will, who's now dancing on a table with his shirt undone. But can two friends have meaningless sex and still be friends after?

Ben and Danielle managed it, I remind myself bitterly.

Still, it's a ridiculous thought. He'd never do that to Ben.

'Same again?' asks Jamie as he takes his place back behind the bar. As soon as the clapping for the band dies out, Chas 'n' Dave blare from the speakers.

'No, make me a cocktail,' I tell him, lowering my chin and peering at him through my lashes the way Tidy Tania was doing when I came in. 'Surprise me.'

No harm in practising on him.

He looks confused, but pulls the whisky down and grabs a lemon from the bowl. A few minutes later he hands me a pale orange drink garnished with a cherry.

'Whisky Sour for the lady.'

'I love it,' I gush, as I sip the tangy liquid. He knows me so well.

At one a.m., Jamie calls last orders and I know, even before it comes on, that the next song will be a slowy. Sure enough it's 'Stand By Me', and Jamie sings along as he starts to clear up.

'I know your game,' I tell Jamie, getting up to help him collect glasses as the crowds start to disperse, still singing along.

371

'What game's that?'

'The music. I've worked it out. It goes all slow and romantic after last orders. That's when you seduce whatever girl you've lined up for after-hours fun.'

Jamie laughs, then stops abruptly.

'Rebecca, careful – you can't . . .' I drop the glasses on the floor with a terrific smash. '. . . stack a hurricane glass in a Martini glass.'

'Sorry, sorry, sorry.' I bend down and start to pick up chunks of glass. 'Ouch.'

'Are you OK?' He rushes over and takes my hand.

'It's a tiny cut,' I reassure him, sucking my bleeding finger.

'Sit down – I'll get you a plaster.'

Just then, Tania approaches, smiling at Jamie.

'So, my friends want to grab a taxi now,' she says. 'I guess I'll see you soon?' She doesn't look like she wants to go anywhere. I feel bad. Does Jamie still like Tania? Maybe I should leave them to it.

'Yep, see you soon, Tania.'

Maybe he's over her – he just gives her a quick peck on the cheek then disappears out back, missing the devastated look on her face. Tania and her friends are the last people to leave so when Jamie returns with a plaster and a glass of water, it's just the two of us.

'The reason I always do that with the music,' he explains, as he gently wraps the plaster around my finger, 'is to chill out the remaining customers so they feel like going home. Less chance of stragglers angling for a lock-in.'

'Is that a hint for me to do one?' I enquire.

'Not at all. Like I'd ever want rid of you.' He squeezes my hand before he drops it.

372

I sip my cocktail to hide my smile, but somehow manage to spill half of it down my chin. Luckily Jamie misses it, already crouching to sweep up the glass.

Once the bar is cleared Jamie calls a taxi, and I rest my head in the crook of my elbow on the bar. I must doze off because suddenly there's a beep outside.

I'm not sure how I end up snuggled into his chest with his arm around me, but my heart starts beating faster when I become aware of how we're sitting in the back seat.

I'm wondering whether to invite him in for a drink as we pull up at mine but Jamie saves me the bother. He simply gets out, pays the driver, then holds out his hand for me.

Oh my God. He realized I was flirting and thought this is what I wanted.

Maybe it is what I want.

His arm stays round me as we walk up the stairs. He waits for me to unlock the door at the top, then leads me straight into the bedroom. This boy does not mess about.

We pause by the bed and I look up into his face, trying not to feel shy. Our eyes lock and I need to go for it before the moment is gone . . .

When my lips touch his, his face freezes.

'Rebecca,' he whispers, lifting his head back slightly to break contact, 'what are you doing?'

'I thought . . .' Oh God. GOD. My hands fly to my cheeks as mortification seeps in.

'You thought what?'

'I thought that . . . why are you here?' I say. 'Why didn't you stay in the taxi and go home? Why did you practically carry me upstairs?'

'Because,' Jamie says evenly, gripping my arms and

peering at my face, 'for want of a better phrase, you're shitfaced.'

'I'm not!'

'You are.'

'I am not.'

'OK,' he says, nodding and dropping his hands. 'You are, though. Now get into bed, and I'll get you some water.'

'God, Jamie, I'm so embarrassed.' I flop face first on to my bed and bury my face in the pillow.

'Don't be. You'll have forgotten all about this by morning,' he says, and I gather from the way the mattress sinks that he's sitting down next to me.

'You're right, I must be drunk, or I'd never have thought you would go for me.'

'What's that supposed to mean?'

'You could have had any girl in there tonight. Tidy Tania was definitely hanging back for you. If you wanted to go home with someone, as if it would have been me.'

'It's not that at all. Look, let's not have this conversation, eh?'

'It's OK, I'm not blaming you. I'm not your type – I know that. We're friends. Let's just forget this ever happened.'

'Rebecca.' He lays a hand on my back, then seems to think better of it because it's gone again. 'The way you've been acting tonight? It isn't you.'

'Well, look where being me has got me.' My words are muffled by the pillow and I don't know if he hears.

'To say I'd never go for a girl like you is bullshit. If you want the truth, I used to think I might end up with a girl like you. Well, *with* you, actually.'

What? I turn my head slightly to peer at him. He's staring up at the ceiling.

'If you must know, I had feelings for you pretty much from the day I met you. I wasn't ready for a relationship, though.' He lowers his head and looks at his hands. 'I loved being single and away from home – I'd have been a shit boyfriend. But for a while, I kind of thought that one day, after I'd had my fun, we might, well, you know . . .'

No, Jamie, I don't know. I feel my heart thumping in my chest. This isn't making sense. Me and him? I'm glad he can't see my face, because I don't know how I'm supposed to be reacting to this.

'You're the only girl I could ever see myself ending up with. I never get bored of you, the way I do other girls. I love your company. I value your opinion. And obviously, you're beautiful.'

The mattress shifts as he stands up, and I feel like I should be saying something but still I can't think straight, and he continues: 'But how I felt changed when you got with Ben. You guys were great together, and made each other so happy. So I was happy for you both. You deserved each other. And I knew that we would only ever be friends from then on. And that will never change now.'

He stops. 'Are you still awake?' he whispers.

I don't answer. I don't know what to say. His words are lovely, and they're melting my heart, but they're also scaring the shit out of me.

'Be yourself, Rebecca,' he mutters, as he pulls my duvet over me. 'When you're yourself, you're the best girl I know.'

He turns out my light and a few moments later I hear the front door click.

Chapter Thirty-nine

BEN

Thursday, 12 March

I didn't have to think long about where to come.

When Rebecca suggested I go somewhere for the day and not come back until I'd decided what to do with my life, it was the first place that came into my head.

It was only three or four months ago that I was here last, approaching the edge of the cliffs, but it seems so much longer. Remembering it now, it's almost as though I'm looking back on another life, a different person.

Jamie dying has made life seem both far more valuable and far less important all at once, if that's possible. All that stuff that happened with Rebecca, it seems trivial now.

I step closer to the edge, the lines of a map made real. Maybe it's that the air is still, and I'm more in control, but I no longer feel scared.

I walk along the cliff, and because it's a weekday I am alone with my thoughts. There is barely a cloud in the sky and the sunlight sparkles against the sea like a million camera flashes.

I feel nervous approaching the hut. There must be a

whole team of people who do his job, I realize now, so the chances are he won't be on duty today. And even if he is, he must talk to dozens of people every day; he's probably not even going to remember me. But when I knock on the door it is Brian who opens it, and he holds his arms wide in surprise before stretching one of them for me to shake.

'Ben!'

I take his hand, pleased and a little bit relieved, then give him the bottle of wine I bought to say thanks for last time. It's only what they had on offer, because, well, I'm broke. Mum has even offered to give me some of her redundancy money, but I couldn't do that. I've told her she should invest it.

'What a lovely surprise,' he says, moving aside to let me in.

Only then do I see one of his colleagues is also here, though he's in the process of putting on his luminous jacket. Brian introduces me like an old friend, and tells him how I came here before Christmas. He doesn't explain why.

'He's a Mancunian,' adds Brian. 'But City, not United, so we won't need to fumigate afterwards.'

The man laughs before making his excuses, leaving Brian to usher me towards the Paisley chair. He draws two paper cups from a stack next to the kettle but waits for me to nod my assent before unscrewing the bottle.

'So,' he says, pouring the wine, 'did things work out between you and . . . ?'

'Rebecca. They didn't. But it's fine, you know?'

He hands me a cup and eases himself on to the stool.

'We're friends now,' I say.

Brian nods happily. 'So what brings you here?'

I laugh, at the sheer scale of the question and possible answer, and then, encouraged by occasional nods and questions, I tell him what has been happening: how Jamie and I had been planning to open a business together, about seeing Rebecca with Michael, and the call from Danielle and everything that followed.

When I'm done I almost feel out of breath.

'Life is so fragile,' says Brian. 'I know that more than most, working here.'

I look around the place, still recovering from telling my story, which is Jamie's story, really. Everything is just as it was last time except for some kind of device on the table that looks like a cross between a camera and a large torch.

'Ah, you'll like the story behind this,' says Brian when he sees where I'm looking.

Apparently it's a heat-seeking device, so they can locate potential jumpers after dark.

'The ring you found at the pub,' he says. 'Nobody came to claim it, so after a few months the landlord sold it and donated the money towards this.'

'A happy ending,' I say.

I'll have to tell Rebecca. Although maybe I'll leave out the bit about the happy ending I'd *originally* hoped for.

'You seem to be in a place where you're able to cope a bit better?'

I give him a conditional smile. 'Now I just need to decide what it is I'm doing with my life.'

He takes a sip of the wine and then his mouth crooks at some inner thought.

'What?'

'I don't think many people *decide* what they want

to do. It's like supporting a football team – you don't consciously decide, it just happens.'

'For most people, maybe,' I say. 'That was another thing I dithered over. In the end Jamie scribbled down the words to Blue Moon on a piece of paper, shoved it in my pocket and told me to meet him outside Maine Road at quarter past two the following Saturday.'

Brian laughs, then downs the rest of his drink. He tells me there is somewhere he needs to be, but insists on swapping numbers before I go.

As I'm walking back I remember what he told me last time – about being able to see clearer once the rain has stopped. I hadn't foreseen exactly how hard it would come down.

But now, finally, it does feel like I can see everything more clearly, and as my feet find the chalky path that leads down to the bus stop an idea comes to me about what I might do, but straight away I dismiss it.

I'd never be able to pull it off, would I?

I keep walking, and maybe it is the brilliance of the horizon, the almost cloudless sky, but gradually in my mind the idea doesn't seem so ridiculous at all.

Chapter Forty

REBECCA

Sunday, 29 March

I wake early with the sun pouring through the window, my bed drenched with sweat. I was dreaming about Jamie again.

In the dream, I was walking past Arch 13 and there was a van outside, and someone was loading it with red booths. I walked over and sat on one that was waiting to be moved and slid my hand down the side of the booth, finding a folded piece of paper with my name on it. I unfolded it and found in Jamie's handwriting, *You're the best girl I know*. And I cried. I'd missed my chance to speak to him about New Year's Eve. I'll never be able to tell him that he was the best boy I knew. And that although what I felt for him wasn't romantic, it was love and I assumed he'd always be in my future too.

It wasn't the worst dream I've had about Jamie since he died, though. The worst are the ones when he's still alive. They're brutal. Because then I wake up and have to lose him all over again as I remember that night that changed everything. Rowing with Ben, us almost kissing, the call from Danielle.

My breathing eventually returns to normal and I sit up in bed, gulping the water on my bedside table.

Dad is taking me for lunch today and I've a few hours before he's picking me up so I have a long shower and tidy the flat. I cancelled the cleaner; it started to feel a bit extravagant, especially after I paid Ben his share of the furniture. I'm just putting my duvet cover back on – having finally got the knack of doing it by myself – when I hear a beep outside. Dad has pulled up to the kerb outside the house, right on time as always.

When I reach the front door I find Natasha from downstairs also on her way out and trying to get her pram up over the step.

'Here, let me give you a hand.' I pick it up at the front, while she takes the back and we carry it through the door.

'Thank you so much,' she says, breathing heavily once we've put it down.

'No worries,' I say, peering into the pram at the yawning baby dressed in a pink and yellow striped Babygro, before heading for the door.

I pause.

'What's her name?' I ask, turning back around.

'Amy,' says Natasha with a grin, pulling her daughter from the pram and on to her shoulder.

'She's gorgeous.' I smile back. 'See you later.'

The restaurant is busy, and the waitress who greets us at the door seems stressed, but she manages a wide smile for Dad. 'Would you like to sit inside or outside?'

'Outside, please.' He smiles back. 'It's a lovely day.'

He looks handsome in his sunglasses and his white shirt with the sleeves rolled up, and I catch the waitress looking me up and down when he pulls out a chair for me.

'Thanks, Dad,' I say pointedly.

'Can I get you some drinks?'

'Small beer for me, please,' Dad replies. 'Rebecca?'

There's a bottle of white wine in an ice bucket by the next table, condensation dripping temptingly down its sides. It was Jamie who told me that you can never go wrong with a New Zealand Sauvignon Blanc.

'I'll have a glass of the Oyster Bay, please.'

The couple drinking the wine are about Dad's age and though neither of them are speaking, it looks like a comfortable silence.

'Did you ever think you might want to meet someone else after Mum died?' I ask Dad once the waitress has left. I don't know where it comes from.

If he's taken aback, he doesn't let on. 'I've neither ruled it out nor searched for it,' he says evenly. 'Why do you ask?'

'No reason.' I shrug. 'It's just that everywhere you go women love you. And I wondered whether it's that you've never met anyone else you wanted to be with, or if you felt like it's wrong. You know, because of Mum.'

Dad laughs. 'I've not lived the life of a monk. You remember me having various friends from time to time as you were growing up? Not all of them were just . . .'

'All right, Dad,' I groan. 'I don't need to hear any more.'

Dad chuckles, then his face goes serious. 'Is this about you and Ben?'

'Nah,' I dismiss.

Well, not really anyway. It's been five months since Ben and I split up, and apart from that one date with

Michael, there's been no one else. But I know now Ben wasn't my One. Not like Mum was to Dad – something unique and magical that can't ever be replaced.

'How's Stefan?' I ask to change the subject. 'I haven't seen him since the funeral.' He's called loads of times trying to get me out, but I've thrown myself back into work to make sure that by the time I get home each night, I'm too tired to even think.

'He's moving in with his boyfriend.'

'Jeez, Dad,' I exclaim, slamming my water down. 'You picked me up an hour ago and you've only just thought to mention that? Have you met him? What's he like?'

'He's lovely. Very polite. Seemed shy at first but was very chatty once he'd relaxed. And he's incredibly fond of Stefan.' Dad sips his beer. 'But apart from that he seems normal.'

After the waitress brings our food out, Dad asks, 'How's your cinema?'

'Good,' I say. 'We're scheduled to finish in just over a month, but there's not much left to do. It's been tough, though. It scared me a bit.' I run a finger round the rim of my wine glass. 'It didn't occur to me before I started that I might not be cut out for it.'

'I remember saying that about that job I had in the Dordogne. Remember the old wine store that was converted into apartments?'

'Vaguely. That was just before we moved to Paris, right?'

'That's right. God, I messed up so many times – forgetting to get materials signed off, and getting site procedures wrong. I'd end up having to stay late, and catch up on paperwork at weekends, then I felt bad that I wasn't spending enough time with you and Stefan.'

'I can't imagine you struggling,' I admit, genuinely surprised. I always thought it came so easily to him.

'And I bet there are people who can't imagine you struggling,' he says. 'But we're all human.'

I take a sip of wine and close my eyes.

'I just hate the thought of being a disappointment to you.'

'And how could you possibly think you could be that?' Dad asks, pushing his empty plate away and taking off his sunglasses.

'Mum died having me,' I whimper, tears escaping as I resist my instinct to close the barriers back up. 'I can't imagine how you must have all felt. You lost your wife. Stefan lost his mum. And for what? Me? Was it really worth it?'

Dad goes to say something but I cut him off.

'That was a rhetorical question. As if you'd say no – you're my dad.'

The waitress shows up to clear our plates and Dad orders us both another drink. She pretends not to notice I'm crying, and I wonder what she thinks is going on. My cheeks burn beneath the tears and I wipe them with the backs of my hands.

'Your mum knew the risks, you know,' Dad says softly, meeting my eye.

'What do you mean?'

'Having you. The doctors couldn't have made the implications of having another child clearer. She'd had complications with Stefan, and was told that she wasn't strong enough to have another one.'

I try to let this sink in. She knew it was me or her?

'As far as she was concerned, there was never any doubt about whether she thought you were worth it.'

'But you must have tried to convince her not to go through with it?'

'Oh, we talked and talked about it. And I'll be honest, Rebecca, the thought of losing her terrified me. But her mind was made up. She said she knew you were too special not to bring into the world. And you know,' he adds, putting his sunglasses back on and leaning back in his chair, 'as usual, she was right.'

We sip our drinks in silence.

'You OK?' Dad asks eventually.

'Yep. Just a little shocked, that's all.'

I feel closer to my mum all of a sudden. I've always thought of us as never having had a relationship because we never knew each other. Now I realize she loved me before I was even born.

'Sorry I never told you about Mum before. I know talking about her upsets you, but I didn't realize you thought about it like that.'

'Not about that.' I grin. 'I mean Stefan moving in with a boy.'

Dad chuckles, then tilts his head at me. 'How's Ben?'

The last time I spoke to Dad I was telling him how hard Jamie's death had hit Ben. He was more lost than ever.

'Better, actually,' I tell him. 'You'll never guess what he's doing?'

The waitress appears with the menus again. 'Anything for dessert?'

'Why not?' says Dad, taking one, then looking at me.

Chapter Forty-one

BEN

Saturday, 2 May

Erica is already leaning against the shutters when I arrive.

'Afternoon, boss,' she says.

'You can pack that in straight away,' I tell her.

'Aye, aye, captain.'

I lift the shutters and insert one of the keys, but it doesn't work. The next one doesn't either. In my peripheral vision I see Erica trying not to laugh.

'I swear that was the first one I tried,' I say when the door eventually gives.

I allow Erica to slide past me into Arch 13, where tall stools and poseur tables and mood lighting have been replaced by ladderback chairs tucked into square tables with candles, but when I follow her a memory returns to me so vividly that it's like I'm back there and nothing has changed. My first night working here, after Jamie told me his chef had walked out. Him taking the selfie of us. I think I'm starting to understand why he wanted to mark the moment.

I take a deep breath and exhale the memory. Today

my mantra is to smile, and so I smile now, at the serendipity of that day, for helping me to finally work out what I should be doing with my life.

The invites said five o'clock, but Tom and Avril arrive an hour early with the pictures.

Tom and I struck a deal. Twenty of his pieces would be on display in the bistro, and I'd get fifteen per cent of any sales. It was part of the business plan I put together with Mum after I agreed to let her invest a chunk of her redundancy.

'It's hardly the Tate,' I overhear Avril say as I go to fetch the final picture from the van Tom hired.

I don't catch Tom's reply because Mum and Dad are approaching. Mum quickens her pace, leaving Dad trailing. She is dressed up, which to Mum is all about inches. An inch added to the volume of her hair, an inch subtracted from her skirt, so that it cuts at the knee rather than below it.

'Don't you look wonderful,' she says, brushing something from my lapels before we hug. 'I'm so proud of you.'

Dad waits patiently to shake my hand. 'Me too, son.' He hands me a present. 'I got it from a car boot sale.'

I unwrap it.

'A chef's hat!' I try it on for size. 'This is awesome!'

'I made sure to wash it at ninety degrees before he wrapped it.'

'Ta, Mum.'

I introduce them to Erica, and show them the kitchen, where I've fitted a chrome griddle, a six-burner oven and a commercial freezer. I'm still waiting for the new extraction system to be installed but they've promised it'll be done in plenty of time for the *real* opening next week. Dad nods his head throughout, keen to show he's impressed.

'The lighting is terrible,' says Avril from behind us as Tom hangs up his final piece.

Mum tsks loudly.

'Tom's girlfriend,' I say. 'We try to ignore her.'

It takes me a second to understand that Mum wasn't tutting at Avril at all. She is standing slack-jawed in front of a sketch of the Queen dancing in a field. Tom has dressed Her Majesty in a short skirt.

'Have you seen this, Ben?' Mum says indignantly, but mercifully she soon forgets all about the picture.

'Look who's here!' she says.

Rebecca does her best not to look too awkward as Mum waves her in for a hug, and then Dad gets a kiss on the cheek.

'The place looks fantastic,' she says, and I can tell she's not sure whether to give me a Mum hug or a Dad kiss. I pull her in for both.

'I'm glad you could make it,' I say, and when she finally withdraws she hands me a gift of her own.

I go to open it and recognize the frame as soon as it juts out of the paper.

'How did you get this?' I ask, discarding the rest of the wrapping.

'After you told me you'd been around to Jamie's flat and seen all his stuff I called his parents to see if it would be possible to have a couple of keepsakes.'

'It's signed by Chas 'n' Dave,' I say, showing the disc to Mum and Dad, who seem confused until I explain that they were Jamie's favourite band and this was his prized possession. Tom offers to find an appropriate place to hang it.

'I kept the liquor posters and Danielle and her cousin went to pick up the foosball table,' says Rebecca, and as I draw her in for another hug I have to swallow the sadness rising up my throat.

Today, I remind myself, I will smile.

I stand alone by the kitchen, watching Erica carry a tray of Rob Roys. It's even busier than I'd hoped. Frank from the cafe is here, and lots of Jamie's old regulars, and I catch sight of Russ arriving, but he pauses by the door to let Rebecca's friend Jemma in first. The only person I invited who isn't here is Danielle.

'Ben, I'd like you to meet my wife, Linda,' says Brian, appearing in front of me.

I smile broadly and lean down to kiss her cheek.

'This place is great,' she gushes.

'Well, I probably wouldn't be doing it without Brian's wise words.'

As soon as I left his hut at Beachy Head I realized Brian was right: most people don't *decide* what they want to do any more than they *decide* their football team – it just happens. But supporting City didn't *just happen* for me. I needed Jamie to make that decision. So who better to decide what I should be doing with my life? And that was the thing, he'd already decided, albeit by accident: I would cook right here.

'I'm not sure about *wise words*,' says Brian, 'but either way you've more than repaid me with the donation.'

I spent most of the day after Beachy Head on the heath, where I'd seen Rebecca and Michael, desperately scouring the turf around the pond. I didn't actually expect to find the ring, but I did, the box sodden but still intact. Because the ring was an antique I ended up

389

getting what I paid for it, and while most of the money went towards this place, I wanted to do something to let Brian know how appreciative I was.

As I stand with him and Linda, suddenly Jamie appears in my mind's eye, charming people as they enter. I imagine him doing his thing, a lump swelling in my throat until I'm struggling to breathe.

I have to excuse myself, escaping to the kitchen to finish the canapés, and the process of chopping and shaping and putting in the oven takes my mind off my apparition, off him not being here.

'He would be so proud.'

I turn.

'How long have you been standing there?'

Rebecca walks towards me, ignoring the question. 'What are those?'

'Sautéed sherry chicken livers on toast.'

She scoops one and takes a bite. She closes her eyes while chewing, not opening them until she's finished.

'God, I missed your cooking when we broke up,' she says.

I look at her but she just laughs and I let it go. It was only six months ago, but it feels like ancient history.

'You know this is all part of Jamie's plan for you, don't you?' she says.

I eye her again.

'When he told you his chef had walked out, I'm not sure that was actually true.'

'What are you on about?'

'I think Jamie sacked him. I mean, it wasn't *just* because of you – his food was diabolical.' She laughs. 'Seriously, I could have done better.' I crinkle my nose doubtfully. 'But he knew that by sacking him he could

390

get you doing something you were passionate about. I think this was the plan.'

It takes a moment for my mind to reboot. Of course. It makes total sense. It wasn't serendipity at all. Why didn't I twig at the time? And now . . . now I'll never get to say thank you.

'Rule six,' says Rebecca with a smirk. 'Cook for Jamie.'

Shit. She must have seen the chalkboard when she went round to the flat.

'They were Jamie's way of . . .' I stutter, blushing.

When I make eye contact I see that her smirk is actually a soft smile.

'Right,' says Rebecca. 'I think if Jamie was here he'd tell me to go mingle, so I better do as I'm told.'

Alone again, I have to focus on the canapés and repeat my mantra so that I don't cry all over them.

Once I'm done I find Tom and Avril talking Rebecca through a sketch of a feminized Mussolini.

'I told him it was unoriginal,' Avril chips in, and Rebecca glares at her like *she* is Mussolini.

'Have you met Avril properly, Jem?' says Russ, the two of them appearing behind us.

'Nope,' says Jemma, putting down her drink to offer her hand, but Avril either ignores or doesn't see it.

'Like Avril Lavigne,' says Jemma, and Russ snorts through sealed lips.

'That's why you're my girlfriend,' he whispers to her, but loud enough for everyone to hear.

If it was a game of musical statues then Rebecca would win, because instantly she stops dead.

'What did Russ just say?' she says to Jemma.

Jemma takes a piece of sautéed sherry chicken liver

toast when Erica sashays past. 'Oh, yeah, he calls me his girlfriend – I prefer care worker, though.'

'This is massive!' says Rebecca. 'Why didn't you tell me?'

'Oh, you know – you've had a lot going on lately. And anyway, I've never been one to tell people every little detail of my love life.'

Rebecca laughs. 'No, of course not.'

'Well, it just proves there is someone for everyone,' Avril mutters to Tom.

We ignore her.

'When, how, where?' I say.

'I think the moment I knew I was going to ask her out was in the pub after the funeral, when she made a vagina out of a napkin.'

'It's a chicken!' says Rebecca to Jemma. 'I taught her that.'

'I was, like, *This girl is special*,' continues Russ. 'So I wrote her a little note and put it in her coat pocket so she'd find it later – that way I didn't put her on the spot.'

'I taught you that!' I say.

'Why do you pair always have to make everything about you?' says Jemma, and we erupt into celebratory laughter until . . .

'What on earth is *that*?' Avril says with a scowl.

She is pointing at the signed disc that Tom has positioned in pride of place above the till.

'I just don't get why anyone would listen to Chas 'n' Dave – it's music for simpletons.'

I see Rebecca's face. She goes to say something but is beaten to it.

'Avril?' says Tom, his lips twitching.

She barely lifts her eyes. 'Yes?'

I observe Tom's body rocking back and forth ever so slightly. The words seem to take an age to form, but when they do, they spew from him without punctuation. 'If-you-haven't-got-anything-nice-to-say-then-I-think-you-should-go.'

Our eyes shift collectively from Tom to Avril, who looks utterly stunned, so that you would mistake her for a waxwork of Avril but for her face, which is becoming redder and redder. Her mouth opens but nothing comes out. Instead, she curtsies down for her bag, turns sharply and thunders out without looking back.

No one is quite sure where to look, except for Russ who is wearing an expression of unbridled joy.

'Bye, then!' chirps Rebecca.

Russ bearhugs Tom, who seems as speechless as everyone else. Once released he picks up his coke, but after inspecting it for a second or two he puts it down, takes the Rob Roy from my hand and downs it in one.

'Welcome back, buddy!' says Russ as Tom coughs through the burn of the alcohol.

'We might as well go home,' says Jemma. 'Everything else is going to be shite on toast after that.' She takes another canapé. 'This isn't shite on toast, is it?' she says, but doesn't wait for an answer before shoving it whole into her mouth.

'Sorry I'm late!' says Danielle, waving around the group. 'Hi, everyone.'

'You've just missed the big news,' I tell her. 'Russ and Jemma are *together*.'

'Aw.' She tilts her head warmly at Jemma. 'That's great news.'

'I thought so too until I found out he had an incontinent cat,' says Jemma.

I see Rebecca and Danielle turn to one another and smile. They notice me noticing them and for a second I wonder if things are going to become awkward.

'I wouldn't mind a nose in the kitchen,' says Danielle.

'I'll give you a guided tour once everyone is here,' I say.

'It's OK,' says Rebecca. 'I'll show her now.'

And off they go, just like that.

I still can't get my head around all this being mine. Frank is casting an eye over the Queen in a miniskirt, while Tom is staring blankly in the direction of the door. He doesn't look sad as such. Just a little drunk from his Rob Roy.

'You did the right thing, mate,' I say, clutching his shoulder.

'Women, eh?' says Russ. 'You can't live with them, and you can't kill them.'

'This,' says Jemma, 'from the man who told me last night that he'd never appreciated the lyrics to "Flying Without Wings" until he met me.'

'It really is a shame you can't kill them,' says Russ.

He takes another canapé and smirks at me. 'You're hoping this place is going to be a chick magnet like it was for Jamie, aren't you, buddy?'

I laugh but don't answer. For the first time in ages I feel like I'm climbing up the Snakes and Ladders board. I'm not looking for anything else right now.

I go see Mum and Dad in the corner and Mum starts along the same lines.

'It's nice to see you and Rebecca getting on,' she says.

I put her words through my Mother Google Translate and they come out as, *Should I buy a hat?*

Together we watch the crowd mingle, and soon I'm

picturing Jamie here again. The thought of what he did with this place makes me scared. How am I going to live up to that?

Not that I'm having any doubts. I owe it to him to stick at this, make a go of it, because after all, Jamie is the person who has led me to every amazing thing in my life: Man City; Rebecca; cooking for a living.

Maybe Mum can sense what I'm thinking because she takes my hand in hers and squeezes it, and I can feel the emotion getting the better of me again, so I release myself.

'Right,' I say, with a single, mildly ridiculous clap of my hands. 'I reckon it's time we got this show on the road.'

I grab my chef's hat and put it on while people gather outside.

'Hello, everyone,' I start, and for some reason I clap again. I peer at my hands and titter, and when I look up again Russ and Jemma are peering at me like I've lost the plot. 'Sorry, I was just thinking about what Jamie would say if he saw me standing here repeatedly clapping my hands.'

Everyone laughs.

'So anyway, you lot have heard me waffle on enough over these past few months so I haven't written another speech.' Jemma boos. Russ echoes it. 'But I just want to thank you all for coming – it means a lot to me. I especially want to thank my mum, who has risked quite a lot of money on this being the first career idea that I don't change my mind about within two months.'

This bit gets a bigger laugh than I expect. I see Mum looking proud.

'I want to thank Erica for putting in every hour God

has sent this past month to help me get things set up, and also Tom for kindly decorating the bistro with his amazing artwork.'

'And for telling Avril Lavigne to do one,' shouts Russ.

'That too,' I say, and Tom, after his moment in the spotlight, stands with his chin lowered but a smile on his face, returning to his usual state of coyness at the slightest hint of attention. 'So I guess all that remains is the big reveal.'

Everyone's focus turns to the sheet covering my new sign. The old one was fine for a cocktail bar, but red neon isn't really the vibe I'm going for with the bistro. So I had something more fitting made.

I grab the thick string attached to the sheet while Russ initiates a countdown from ten, and when finally they reach one I yank the string, but something must be stuck because most of the sheet remains fixed.

Only the H and the A are visible.

I see Rebecca's lips part. She covers them with a hand. I look away, not wanting to cry in front of everyone, and yank the string again. This time the sheet does come loose, falling into a heap on the pavement. I take in the remaining letters. We all do.

HAWLEY'S.

Others emulate Rebecca, hands on mouths, and for a few seconds no one says anything. And then . . .

'To Hawley's,' shouts Danielle, and the crowd of people, my friends and family, Jamie's friends, and everyone Erica invited, all erupt, and I'm not even having to think about the smile on my face now.

'To Hawley's,' I echo, under my breath.

Chapter Forty-two

REBECCA

Tuesday, 5 May

'So, this is it – the completed works.' Bobby uses his hand to shield his face from the sun as he tries to read my expression. It's cold out here on the street, but the sun is poking through the clouds. 'What do you think?'

'Nice,' I tell him.

'Nice?' he repeats. 'Oi, Ravi!' he yells. 'She thinks it's nice.'

Ravi saunters out of the entrance and pretends to throw his hat down. 'I give up.'

'All right, lads, fine.' I roll my eyes. 'This cinema is the best thing I've ever seen with my face.'

'That's better.' Bobby nods, satisfied. 'Wonder what the first film will be?'

'Apparently new releases will be on the downstairs screen and the one upstairs will show old movies,' I explain, excitedly. 'First one is *The Jazz Singer*, which was the film they showed when the cinema first opened in 1927.' I turn to smile warmly at them both. 'Anyway, thanks so much for everything. You did an amazing job.'

'Why, thanks,' says Adam, retreating from the building.

'I wasn't talking to—'

'And you're welcome,' he talks over me.

I tut playfully. It's the building team's last day on site today so I came to say goodbye, and found Adam doing the same. I'm not sure at what point I stopped finding him irritating and started to find him amusing.

'You getting the Tube?' he asks me, after we've said our farewells to the others.

'Yep.'

'I'll walk with you.'

'Cool,' I lie, as I start marching off down the street. It's not that I object to his company – I just can't stand having to wait for people.

'Finally someone that walks at a normal speed,' he says.

'Ha ha,' I say sarcastically. 'Feel free to hang back. I won't take offence.'

When I glance at him he looks confused. And actually he does seem entirely comfortable with this pace. 'I usually hate walking with other people,' I confide.

'Me too.'

The silence that follows is more comfortable, and lasts until we turn the corner.

'Think you'll ever go to East House Pictures once it opens to the public?'

'Actually, it's about to become my local cinema,' I tell him. 'I've bought a flat down the road – I pick up the keys this weekend.'

I wasn't even looking to buy in this area. All the properties I arranged to see were south-east, but I couldn't find what I was looking for: something spacious and structurally sound but that needs a lot of love to turn into a home. Then I saw the For Sale sign as I walked to the site a few weeks ago, advertising the top flat in the big Victorian house behind it. It was in my price range thanks to the deposit from Dad, and it occurred to me I could live anywhere. There was nothing and no one tying me to the area I was in. So I made an appointment to see it, and I fell in love with it right away. The floors need sanding and the crumbling fireplace will have to be repaired, and the walls are so dirty I couldn't say what colour they were originally. I can't wait to make a start.

'Well, congratulations,' Adam says. He stops looking at me and focuses on the street ahead instead. 'What are you doing on June eleventh?'

'Um, I don't know. Nothing, I think. Why?'

'The cinema opens.'

'Right . . .'

'Would you like to come and see *The Jazz Singer* with me?'

'Oh. Er . . .'

Where did that come from? I feel a flutter of excitement before drowning in panic. Adam has grown on me, sure, and yes, I sometimes find myself thinking about that night we almost kissed. I've even considered the possibility of us actually going through with it. But go on a date with him?

'Calm down with your enthusiasm, won't you, Rebecca?' he says. 'You know, I'm going to go off you if you keep acting too keen.'

'Sorry.' We stop at a crossing and I look away from him at the oncoming traffic in case I'm blushing. 'I just wasn't expecting that.'

'You weren't?' He glances at me as we stride across the road. 'That's how it works. You meet, you rub each other up the wrong way, you try to kiss them and then even if they reject you, you ask them to a movie.'

The corners of my mouth twitch. 'A few months later?'

'Sorry, I know it's fast, but I like you.'

I laugh, a little too hard, but it's because I'm stalling for time. What should I say? My initial opinion of Adam was unfair. He's direct and a perfectionist but, if I'm completely honest with myself, I kind of like those things about him now.

'Well, you have a think about it and let me know, yeah?'

I remember the night Ben asked for my number on a napkin and I stalled, making him think it was a rejection.

'OK,' I say when we get to the bottom of the escalator, where we're about to part ways and head to separate platforms.

'OK . . . ?'

'Yes, I'll see the film with you.' My train pulls into the platform. 'Oh, I have to catch that. Email me, yeah?'

I run on to the nearest carriage and as the door closes behind me, I swear I can see Adam laughing. Why am I such a dick? There would have been another one along in two minutes.

Jemma is already waiting for me inside the restaurant, with a bottle of white wine and three glasses. Things have finally calmed down at work, and I managed to swing it so she gets a long lunch to help me celebrate my promotion. She was the first person I told after Jake called me into his office last week to tell me.

'I'm starving,' she says, picking up one of the menus the waitress just placed on our table.

'I think I might have just agreed to go on a date with Adam Larsson,' I mutter, reading my own menu. 'Who, by the way, walks just as fast as me – if not faster.' I smile smugly. 'See? It's not unnatural.'

Jemma grabs my menu from my hands and slams it down. 'You *think* you agreed to go on a date with him? What happened?'

'He asked me to see the first old film that's on at the cinema and I said OK.'

'Hmmm, right – I can see where the confusion lies,' she says, holding her palms out and shrugging. 'What. A. Riddle.'

'What's a riddle?' asks Danielle, shrugging out of her coat. 'Sorry I'm late, by the way. Bloody Tubes.'

'There's no riddle,' Jemma says. 'Rebecca has agreed to go out with a structural engineer who bears a striking resemblance to Eric Northman from *True Blood*, yet she still won't admit she likes him.'

'Ooh,' squeals Danielle. 'The Sheriff of Area Five? I love that guy. This is immense, Rebecca.'

'All right, a) it's not actually him, and b) I don't know if it's going to go anywhere.'

'He's snarky, watches shit old films and walks at a billion miles an hour,' points out Jemma. 'You were made for each other. And you know what this means?'

'What?'

'You are officially over Ben.'

I laugh. 'I guess I am.'

'How long has it been now since you guys broke up?' Danielle asks.

I have a think. 'It's been about—'

'Wait,' cries Jemma. 'Tell me the exact date you broke up.'

'Why?' I ask as she pulls out her diary.

'I just want to work something out.'

'Well, it was Ben's birthday, so November first.'

'And when did you get together?'

'Twenty-sixth of October the year before.'

'Right.' She opens the diary, which clearly has nothing written in it, and turns to the year-by-year page at the back. 'You two just talk amongst yourselves.'

'I'm glad you're over him,' says Danielle, topping up the three glasses. She grins at me. 'This Adam guy could be The One.'

'I don't believe in The One any more,' I tell her. She looks at me sadly, so I add: 'Not in a bad way. I just think that you can have more than one special person in your lifetime.'

She ponders this.

'I wasn't so much looking for The One as Any One,' Jemma mutters.

'You don't mean that?' I ask.

'Course I dinnae – Russ was right, our love is the stuff of Westlife lyrics,' she says without looking up from her diary. 'But if you ever tell anyone I said that – especially him – I will kill you. Ha!' She finally looks up. 'Spot on.'

'What's spot on?'

'Well, there's a theory that—'

I give her an exaggerated groan. 'There is no theory.'

There's no equation to getting over someone: to working out how many heartbeats they'll take up after you break up. 'Listen,' she whines. 'The theory is that it takes half the time you were with someone to get over

402

them. You were with Ben three hundred and seventy-two days, and you split up one hundred and eighty-six days ago, and today you realized you're over him. You just proved it to the very day.' She slams her diary shut. 'So stick that in your pipe and smoke it.'

Danielle and I laugh until our stomachs hurt.

'Oh,' says Danielle, recovering herself as she pulls a small square wrapped in gold paper from her handbag. 'I got you a little housewarming present.'

'I've got you a housewarming present too,' Jemma adds quickly. 'I just haven't collected it yet. Or paid for it. Or decided what it's going to be.'

Danielle hands over the gift, checking her manicure as she does in a deliberate show of nonchalance, though I can tell she's nervous. Our friendship still isn't what it used to be, but we'll get there.

I unwrap it to find a small jewellery box. Inside it is a silver heart-shaped keyring.

'Oh, Danielle, it's lovely. But you didn't need to do that.' I'm matching her nervousness. 'You know, I'd have settled for a shrunken crisp bag.'

'We're too mature and sophisticated for accessories made out of rubbish now,' she says dismissively as she sips her wine. 'Besides, did you realize crisp bags have foil linings these days? I blew up my microwave.'

Then we're all cracking up again.

And I think to myself: I hope Jamie can see us.

Acknowledgements

Thanks as ever to our awesome agent Lizzy Kremer, whose guidance we'd be lost without. There are so many people behind the scenes at David Higham who we owe a huge thanks to – their tireless work on our books is genuinely appreciated.

We also owe an awful lot to our editor Harriet Bourton, who saved this book with a hand-drawn squiggly story chart. Thanks also to Francesca Best, Alice Murphy-Pyle, Rebecca Hunter, September Withers, Tash Barsby and everyone at Transworld for their work and support – we couldn't wish for a better team of people to publish our books. And a special shout out to Becky Glibbery for designing our lovely cover and Telegramme for the illustration.

Laura . . .

You can't choose your family, but if you could, I'd choose mine: Mummy, Daddy, Susanna, David, Robyn, Heidi and Archie – they're the best.

You *can* choose your mates, and I've made some bloody good choices: this book (well, my half of it) is inspired by the humour and general excellence of the people I'm lucky enough to call my closest friends.

Shout-outs to Lizzie Goode for her valuable insight into architecture and construction (and for being

405

co-founder – and only other member of – scary film club); to Gemma and Graham Woods for providing the kitchen where I did all my editing (and Susanna for keeping my wine topped up throughout); and to everyone at Shortlist Media for being supportive and lovely.

Jimmy . . .

Thank you to the best person I know, Sunita Jaswal. I couldn't have got through a mad summer of edits without her patience and encouragement. Thanks also to my former cat Mildred, who is an unforgivable Judas but, credit where it's due, did provide a funny story that made it into these pages. Cheers also to Dr Paul Eldridge for answering my questions, and to Carl Anders and Benjamin Raine for their superhero knowhow. And thanks as always to all my family and any friends whose wit I've noted down and used as my own.

Our two brilliant authors have interviewed each other about writing as a double act, what they'd do in their characters' shoes, and what they really think of rom coms . . .

Warning: contains spoilers!

Jimmy interviews Laura . . .

Jimmy: How would the book differ if you'd written it on your own?

Laura: It would be cleverer and funnier. Joke! I think it would follow the same journey and reach the same outcome, though my Ben chapters would be less convincing. If I was writing the story entirely in Rebecca's voice I would try to do more to warm Ben up from her perspective, as that's the only side of the story readers would see. But because you do such a good job of making Ben likeable, and his actions understandable, my character can get away with focusing on her own emotions and reactions without the responsibility of having to accurately portray Ben to the reader.

Jimmy: What would you have done in Rebecca's situation?

Laura: Cut Ben's willy off and stabbed Danielle in the eye with one of her stilettos. That's a lie. I would probably be very similar to Rebecca, to be honest. I wanted her reaction to be as authentic as possible, so I asked myself what I would do and tried to translate that to the page, and I think I'd know, deep down, that

Ben and Danielle hadn't really done that much wrong, but I would still struggle to carry on as normal. I'm a very forgiving person but I forget nothing – ultimately, I think Rebecca is the same.

Jimmy: Ben, Jamie, Russ – snog, marry, throw off a cliff at Beachy Head. Go . . .

Laura: Marry Jamie, snog Ben and throw Russ off a cliff at Beachy Head. I feel bad – Russ seems like a nice dude, but Jamie is a no-brainer (handsome, kind, wise, has constant access to a lot of booze) and I just suspect Ben would be a better kisser than Russ.

Jimmy: What's your favourite bit of my chapters and why?

Laura: Probably the second Beachy Head trip – where Ben meets Brian. I just really enjoyed reading it – the writing is lovely, and made the whole scene really easy to visualize, and I got such a good sense of how Ben was feeling at this point. I also love all the conversations between Ben and Jamie, whether they're talking about the rules at the flat or making cocktails at the bar. I love a good bromance, and I think you got their chemistry spot on.

Jimmy: Be honest: did you bring Jemma from _The Best Thing That Never Happened to Me_ back because you were too lazy to think of a new character and will you ever make a solo book out of Jemma?

Laura: My reasons for bringing back Jemma were threefold. 1) Readers seemed to really like her, and I felt like she still had more to give. 2) I liked the idea of Rebecca forming an unlikely friendship with someone who is her total opposite as a result of her fallout with Ben and Danielle. Rebecca is reserved and has problems expressing her emotions, so Jemma's openness and lack of filter makes her the perfect extreme. And 3) Yeah, I was too lazy to think of a new character.

There were no plans to make a solo book out of her, but now that I've pushed her boyfriend off a cliff, there's potential for drama there . . .

Jimmy: After *The Best Thing* . . . you revealed that Holly's habit of singing songs from musicals while she runs was autobiographical. Is there anything that Rebecca does that falls into the same category?

Laura: I do recoil at overt public displays of affection, and recently I've started to really appreciate good whisky. Oh, and I did once stop for fried chicken when drunk and when the man asked me how many pieces I wanted, I told him to see how many he could get in the bucket.

Jimmy: Both Rebecca and Holly in *The Best Thing* . . . change and become better versions of themselves because of love. Do you believe in the transformative power of love that is often portrayed in rom coms?

Laura: You could also say they become the worst versions of themselves because of love. I don't believe love has transformational powers – and the danger of anyone thinking it has is that they spend years sitting around waiting for The One, believing that's when their life will truly begin, when actually they should be trying to transform things for themselves if they're not happy. But I do believe love can bring a unique, warm, beautiful quality to a person, and ultimately enrich their life. You just have a better chance of knowing good love from bad love if you're happy with yourself. Do I sound like a w***er?

Jimmy: Yes.

Laura: Shall I change that answer?

Jimmy: No.

Laura interviews Jimmy . . .

Laura: Who's more like you – Alex from *The Best Thing That Never Happened to Me* or Ben from *The Night That Changed Everything*?

Jimmy: Do you know what my mum said to me after reading *The Best Thing . . .*? That she wished Alex was her son. That's why I made Ben directionless and terrible with money. And actually, *Mum*, I think I am a bit like Alex: I'm OCD, I'm quite focused and I listen to Radiohead. But if I'm being honest, if you were to extract and find a way to analyse my mind, you'd find lots of Russ and Kev secretly lurking in there too. I suspect most blokes are the same.

Laura: If you were Ben, is there anything you would have done differently?

Jimmy: This question is going to get me in trouble with my girlfriend, who is firmly on Rebecca's side and actually questioned me, with her sternest eyes, about whether I thought his actions were acceptable. What I'd say is that it's easy with hindsight to say he shouldn't have done what he did with Danielle, but Rebecca gave him absolutely no signals that night, and then Danielle – who is very attractive, let's not forget – basically jumps on him. The secret Russ and Kev in any man is probably going to prevail. The thing Ben should have done is be straight up about the timing from the moment Rebecca found out.

Laura: What advice would you give someone trying to get over a break-up?

Jimmy: Listen to Jamie. He told Ben to stay off Facebook, spend time doing things he loved, and to not write passively emotional statuses that say one thing but actually mean another. Also, I love Damien Rice, but the point of that rule is that music accentuates how you already feel. If you're happy it can make you elated, if you're miserable . . . Well, Damien Rice might just have sent Ben over the edge at Beachy Head.

Laura: You took a trip to Beachy Head while we were writing the book – how did that impact the way you wrote that scene?

Jimmy: I was up there on my own, looking over the cliffs and thinking, 'There really should be a yellow line like they have at train platforms'. And that's when I met a real-life Brian, though his name was changed in the book. He came over to check I wasn't suicidal! When Brian says to Ben, 'I was pretty sure you weren't a jumper' – that's what the real-life Brian said to me. Because I wasn't on my phone saying goodbye and I looked pretty scared at the cliff edge.

Laura: I've played pool, and Connect 4, and Just Dance with you, and I know you're pretty competitive – how much does writing a two-hander book bring out that side of you?

Jimmy: You have no idea how much I treat this as a competition. The other day I went through the book comparing each of my chapters with each of your corresponding ones to see which was best, and then tallied them up.

Laura: Who won?

Jimmy: Annoyingly, you just edged it with your pretty-damn-awesome final chapters.

Laura: How do you describe our books to other blokes who ask what kind of books you write?

Jimmy: I used to really struggle with this. Because I didn't read women's fiction or watch rom coms, I was slightly embarrassed talking to lads about it. Then I watched *When Harry Met Sally* and I realized: rom coms can be pretty cool. Now at home it's me who suggests watching them. I've also realized that women's fiction, when it's really done well, is just Nick Hornby for women. I love Nick Hornby, so that's often how I describe it.

Laura: Both Ben and Alex in *The Best Thing* . . . were desperate to 'make a difference' or 'make their mark'. Are you secretly having an existential crisis?

Jimmy: I worry about time a lot. That's where Jamie's line about 'You only get three billion heartbeats' comes from. Sometimes I get a bit mad in the car if the lights are green and no one is moving. I'm thinking: you've just wasted six of my heartbeats because you weren't paying attention. Actually, I'm thinking the same thing while I'm waiting for *you* to reply to my emails! For me, the book is about that line. You've got to make as many of your heartbeats count for something as possible.

Have you read Jimmy and Laura's fresh,
funny and romantic first novel?

Everyone remembers their first love.

Holly certainly remembers Alex. But she decided
ten years ago that love wasn't about mix tapes and
seizing the moment – though she's not exactly sure
it's about secret dates with your boss, either.

But what if the feelings never really went away?

Alex wants to make every moment of his new job
count. It's a fresh start in a big city, and he's almost
certain that moving to London has nothing
to do with Holly. Almost.

How do you know if it was meant to be . . . or
never meant to happen at all?